TOGETHER AGAIN

The stars glittered wildly overhead as Tammi and Daniel studied each other, gazing deeply. Daniel's eyes burned like dark blue flames. He touched her soft, quivering mouth, realizing that the dam was about to burst on her rigidly held control.

Her sobs reached his heart, and he moved to take her gently into his arms. "Hush, Tamara . . . hush, darling," he whispered, stroking her silver-honey hair and pressing her to him as if protecting her from the world.

Finally, at long last, he could feel her crying subside. He took her lovely wet face in his dark hands to turn it up. "Tamara, Tammi, my moonlit maiden. How I love you, have always loved you!" He kissed her lips, and to his intense pleasure he found her mouth responding to his.

Daniel's kiss sang through her veins and sent currents of desire raging through her. This was Daniel, truly Daniel . . . her love. "Oh, it is good with us," she murmured. "Just like before. So good it hurts."

"Yes, angel eyes," he replied, kissing her again. "And much better yet to come." His arms tightened around her. "Now," he said, his breath hot against her ear, "now the loving really begins."

SONYA T. PELTON

CAPTIVE DOVE

ZEBRA BOOKS
KENSINGTON PUBLISHING CORP.

For
Suzanne and Lisa,
because they loved the first one.
Mom

ZEBRA BOOKS

are published by

Kensington Publishing Corp.
475 Park Avenue South
New York, NY 10016

First printing: March, 1991

Printed in the United States of America

Minnesota Legend

1873

Looking up and seeing Tamara leaning against the door frame, Daniel began a new story. *"Many springs ago upon an island in the middle of White Bear Lake a young warrior loved and wooed the daughter of his chief. He had loved her since they were small children, and it is said that the pretty maiden loved the warrior. But Wolf had again and again been refused the maiden's hand. The old chief alleged that Wolf was no brave—and his old consort called Wolf a woman!"*

Danny chuckled, patting his father's arm. "Woman." He pointed to his mother. "Mom!"

"Yes, Danny, Mommy is a woman. Now, let me go on."

"O-kay."

". . . The bright moon had risen high in the night-blue heavens, when the young warrior Wolf took down his flute and set out alone. Once more he

would sing the story of his love. The mild breeze gently moved the two feathers in his headband, and as he mounted the trunk of a leaning tree, damp snow fell heavily from his feet."

"No," Danny said, trying to say snow.

"Yes. *As Wolf raised his flute to his lips,*" Daniel went on, *"his blanket slipped from his well-formed shoulders and trailed on the snow beneath the tree. He began his hauntingly wild love song. Soon he felt cold and, as he reached back for his blanket, some unseen hand laid it gently across his shoulders."*

Danny blinked up at his father. "Who?"

Daniel smiled across to Tamara who still listened. *"It was the hand of his love. She took her place beside him, and for the time being they were happy. The Indian has a loving heart. . . ."* Daniel smoothed back wisps of hair from Danny's forehead, and the child leaned back, blinking, listening.

"As the legend goes, *a large white bear . . . approached the northern shore of the lake . . . and noiselessly made his way through the deep heavy snow toward the island. It was the same spring that the lovers met, and they . . . were now seated among the branches of a large elm which hung far over the lake.*

"*Afraid they would be found out, the warrior Wolf and the maiden talked almost in whispers. . . . They were just rising to return . . . when the maiden uttered a shriek which was heard at the camp. Running toward the warrior, she caught his blanket, but missed her footing and fell, bearing the blanket with her into the great arms of the ferocious monster.*

Danny called out, "Monner . . . Mon-ner!"

6

"That's right, Danny. Monster." He looked up at Tamara and they both laughed and laughed until she wiped the happy tears away with the dish towel.

Holding her aching sides, Tamara pleaded, "Then what happened, Daniel?"

"And then . . ."

Part One

The melancholy days are come,
the saddest of the year.
            —William Cullen Bryant

Prologue

1869

As fast as her feet could fly, the pale slim beauty
was running toward the autumnal trail in the woods
and the arms she knew would be waiting to enfold
her. To Daniel! Her man! Her love! He would be
there this time, to ask her to become his bride, and she
would shiver in his embrace and give her immediate
answer: *Oh yes, Daniel, yes, yes, yes!*

Though she had not actually spotted his tall, lithe
frame, she had heard him call to her from the woods
in his special way . . . like an Indian beckoning his
mate. Deep. Wonderful.

Tamara was quite certain she was carrying
Daniel's child. Since she had been queasy and a bit
green around the gills two mornings in a row, she
had decided she must be in the family way, and there
was no shame in this. She and Daniel had always
been meant for each other . . . all that was required
now were the marriage vows and God's blessing. To

bind them into one.

Tamara smiled sweetly, poignantly, as a white-tailed doe paused and then darted through the blueberry thickets and between the tall, stately pines. In a graceful turn, a wistful sigh escaping her, she scanned the wooded glade in search of Daniel Tarrant. From here, at about this exact spot, she was sure he had called her to him. Tamara walked several paces to the left. Maybe it was from there. . . . Several paces to the right. Or there . . . No Daniel.

So, he must be playing tricks on me, she decided, since Kristel, the orphaned child she had taken under her wing, had also heard Daniel calling Tamara.

"Daniel!" Tamara Andersen shouted. "Ohhh, Daniellll!" When she received no answer, she sat down on an old log, flipping the waterfall of silver-honey hair over her shoulder. She had undone her braids in anticipation that Daniel would come back to her—and this time ask her to become his wife. Daniel preferred her hair down. He liked to brush it sometimes and to run his long bronze fingers through it. Silkily and slowly.

She heard the booming call of the horned owl from the deep timber, the incessant crying of the killdeer. "Please," she said aloud, "I wish you would not play tricks on me, Daniel. *Where are you?"*

Still no answer.

Hugging knees covered by her yellow muslin dress, Tamara told herself she could wait all night if need be. This was not so new, since it seemed she was always waiting for Daniel. "Where do you suppose he ran off to this time?" she asked the gray squirrel gathering nuts for winter, trying to sound cheerful in case Daniel was nearby and playing a game with her. A fat frog croaked on a log nearby, seemingly serenading her with its hoarse song, its big buggy eyes watching. She smiled. The frog is waiting too, she told herself.

As she sat there hoping for Daniel to come to her, her mind threaded back into the year that had gone by faster than greased lightning. . . .

She had been driving through a forest that was like a winter wonderland, the runners of her sleigh murmuring along the white carpet of snow, when the Minnesota Lumber Camp had loomed before her . . . and so had a tall man wearing a red-and-black lumberjack's shirt. She had almost run him over! In her high-collared beaver coat with the Eskimo hood pulled down to cover her silvery blond hair, she had looked like a boy to the stranger. Before that day, Tammi had never seen Daniel Tarrant, though she knew most of the lumberjacks. With his coloring, the man could be half-Indian, she had guessed, not realizing how exact her presumption had been. But his eyes were a startling shade of blue with large pupils, obsidian as an Indian's. His cheekbones slanted from jawline to temple and his face looked as if it had been carved from wood—dark, smooth, polished wood.

That day in the loggers' camp, Tammi had freed one hand from her oversized, furry mitten and had tucked a tendril of blond hair back into her hood. Mikki, her brother, had watched the two of them with burning curiosity. Astonished, Daniel had turned to her brother, saying he never knew Mikki had a sister. "You never asked," Mikki had responded. Her brother had not liked the attraction he had sensed between the pair, since he had set his sights on his sister's wedding Ole Larson, the blond giant from Norway, sister country to Finland where their parents had come from. No doubt about it, Daniel Tarrant had been amused to discover a female beneath the heavy winter clothing. His dark blue eyes had been pleasantly mocking before he'd returned to his timber-built house in the loggers' camp. Tammi had felt so terribly alone then . . . and in the weeks and months that followed, she found Daniel Tarrant had become a fire in her soul—one that was not easily extinguished.

Now Tamara stood, brushing from her hands the tiny pieces of bark that stuck to them. Her heart took a plunge when she saw the sun going down between the tall trees and evergreens. Shadows of leaves and branches mottled her face, making her appear even more dejected than she was already. "Daniel . . ." She knew her lips moved even though they felt numb, numb as her heart.

Daniel. Gone again, she thought. Like the moon in early morning, when she gazed out the window upon its pale cherubic face. There one moment, gone the next.

Slowly, Tamara walked back to the little house where she knew Kristel would be readying for bed. She turned around to look back at the moldered log she had vacated only moments before, then stood very still, remembering . . . reflecting back to two weeks before. . . .

Daniel. He had been standing there, absolutely silent as a cat hunting prey. Stoically proud, like his

Indian ancestors. Why does he not come to me? she had wondered. Why does he just stand there watching? So silent. So alone. He had moved then, off to the side and had allowed someone to step before him. *Kristel!* He had brought Kristel back to her. The beloved lost child was not her own but the younger sister of the man she had married—a marriage that had been faked by Ole Larson and his devious friend, Lou LaCroix, who had posed as a minister. Ole had wanted a housekeeper and a woman; he had not wanted the ties that bind. She had discovered that too late. Well, it was all water under the bridge . . . and Ole was long gone.

Tamara shook her blond head, freeing her mind of the remembrance of Daniel in the woods. That had been two weeks ago. Would he come back to her when she least suspected? He was like that. But why was he always so mysterious? When would she know the heart and mind of the man she loved more than life?

She desperately wished to tell Daniel of the child she carried. He had said he loved her, believed in her, and Reverend Brown had told her that Daniel had come a long way in understanding himself. He had even confessed his love of her to the reverend. But does he really love me? Tamara wondered. Does he really care about *anyone* for that matter?

She had revealed her dream about Daniel to only one person—the reverend. Daniel had been abandoned as a child, but in the dream Tammi had learned that he lived only because his mother had spared him and brought him into safekeeping. A babe left on the steps of a stranger, carefully, lovingly, wrapped in an Indian blanket, Daniel was living proof of the love of his mother, a woman who had been fleeing in the night from an angry man.

But where is he now? Tammi wondered, fearing he had come to some harm. Then she decided that Daniel was a grown man and could take care of himself. Sometimes she suspected he was a ghost who went about tormenting those who loved him, but she knew he was flesh and blood. He had made love to her, tender and aching love. He had taken her to heights of ecstasy.

As Tamara reached the little house she began to wonder if God were punishing her for having lain with Daniel whom she had not married. Still, if anyone knew how faithfully she loved Daniel, it was God.

Suddenly she was angry with herself for having been so foolish. Daniel did not want her! He had only used her body to relieve the screaming frustration in his own soul! Had she not heard him inadvertently confess that he had been with other women? "You are special, Tammi. I want you, more than I have ever wanted any woman." *Lies! Lies!*

What about Helen Mattson? Had she not seen with her own eyes as Daniel made love to Helly in the Olskys' barn? As before, Tamara thought: He plays with my emotions, he has always done this. Daniel Tarrant has made me no better than a whore. Of my own free will I went to him. Then he shunned me at every turn as if I were a dirty plaything he could toss away. A discard.

Deeply troubled now, she thought of Ole Larson, who had gotten Lou LaCroix to perform the phony marriage ceremony. Why had she agreed to marry Ole? Mikki, her now-deceased brother, had said that she would come to love the big Norwegian, and he had repeated this so often that Tammi had begun to believe it was true. But, oh, the horrors she had gone through in that fake marriage. She had lived in constant dread that Ole would someday harm her, for he had not been gentle with her. He'd been a drunken monster.

Closing her eyes, she remembered with pain her brother Mikki's accidental death. Drunk, he'd been showing off for Ole and the other loggers. Mikki . . . golden-haired Mikki . . . her big brother whose beautiful eyes she would never look into again. Not on this earth.

The Minnesota pines surrounding the cabin wistfully murmured a twilight song. Fragrant and lovely, they enlivened her senses, and Tamara's shoulders straightened. She had warned herself months ago that she would lose what self-respect remained if ever again she yielded to Daniel Tarrant.

"I want to go to him as he wishes—yet I do not. Will he make me his bride if I yield to him just one more time?" She had groaned in the misery of indecision. Then, like a silly little fool, she had tossed caution to the winds and had gone downstairs in the Olskys' house, knowing Daniel was waiting for her. She had met him in the hall, into which moonbeams spilled gloriously. They were all alone that night. She had faltered, her legs trembling. . . .

"There is danger in loving," she had told him when he stood suddenly before her, Indian-dark and masculine. And hard.

17

Daniel's voice was deep and thrilling. "I am a Fox . . . I am supposed to die. . . . If there is anything difficult, if there is anything dangerous, that is mine to do."

Softly he had spoken, as if singing the words to her. A song of the Sioux Kit Fox warriors. Dangerous. Yes. Their loving had been that . . . and more.

"Come with me," he had said in a throat-deep whisper. "I will not hurt you in any way. I only wish to make love to you . . . long and slow. You want me, love—your pale body quivers with anticipation."

"No. I will not let you get to me again, Daniel." She had been determined to return to her room, intending to withhold herself from him that night. But he had eased her down, kissing, caressing, and driving her wild. And when she'd been ready, he had filled her, deep, and deeper. Awed by the cauldron of lava that fired her, stupefied her, and drained her will, after his powerful release she made to scurry from the bed, but his arm shot about her small waist, trapping her close. "I'll make you pregnant. If I haven't done so already."

"You will have to catch me first!" she cried and squealed as he dragged her back, and he laughed deeply.

"I have you," he murmured against her cheek. "Can you not feel my body next to yours?"

"Yes." She thought for a moment, wishing she could read the truth in his chiseled face. "I will leave here then and go where you will not find me."

"I'll find you," he said, and planted a kiss at her throat, tickling it with his hot tongue.

She gazed up into unreadable dark blue eyes. "I

will run away. Far away."

"Again, I will catch you, Tammi. You will be mine. . . ."

"I will never marry you!"

"Aha, I never mentioned marriage. I said you would be mine—my woman, my fragile, yearning heart, always within reach."

"No!" Tammi turned her face away when he would have kissed her lips. But he caught her, held her, made her captive.

"Then, my little love, I will ravish you again and again."

"You will never have me again, Daniel Tarrant!"

"Oh?" He moved intimately between her naked thighs. "Let me show you how serious I really am."

She could not resist Daniel's hands as they stroked her hips and loins. She grew utterly faint, helpless beneath his renewed passion. "Open your legs, Tammi. Yield to me this time."

Fires stirred, then licked between her thighs. "Ah," he said. "That is better. So very much better."

"Daniel, how can you do this?"

"Easy. You belong to me, you know. You always have, even before you became a twinkle in your mother's eye and were born."

She denied him nothing then. They spun and wavered, were sucked away in a whirling pool of ecstasy, following each other into the violent sweetness of mutual passion. He had roused her to new heights, murmuring endearments. Then they slept, dreaming together, bodies touching. When she awoke and reached for his pillow she found him gone! Gone like spring snow. Illusory.

Now Tamara looked around the darkening area surrounding the little house, the house she had shared with Daniel for only a short time. Sitting peacefully, she watched one of God's wonders, the sunset-colored forest, trees tinted red flame, then brownish mauve, then shades of twilight gray. Nightfall.

He was not coming.

The moon rose and spread its golden dust across the land. A deep, cold silence pierced her heart as she stepped into the little house. The wide wooden planks of the floor creaked softly, in loneliness, as she glanced toward the curtain behind which stood the beds. She was fading into lonely and shadowy wastes again, the desolate, uninhabited places in her heart.

Never again, Daniel. You have hurt me for the last time.

With swift, resolute strides Tamara went to light a fire, never realizing that her eyes shimmered with unshed tears as she hugged herself while waiting for the flames to rise.

The time-honored phrase flooded her mind: Rain falls on the just and the unjust.

Waiting for the flames . . .

But nothing would warm her—ever again.

Smooth, and lavender'd . . .
—John Keats

Chapter One

1872

They saw at once that she was lovely.

When Tamara Andersen rushed into the lobby of
Nicollet House at the same moment the train into
Minneapolis, Minnesota, sounded its whistle, all
eyes swept her way, newspapers rustled to a halt, and
those just checking in looked up from the register.
The men strolling about tripped on edges of carpets
and got icy glares from their female companions.

Tamara turned upon the "gentlemen" a cool
regard that deflated male vanity. Indeed, those who
frequented the establishment called her ice queen,
since she was unwilling to consider their attentions,
but there was still a feminine warmth about Tamara.

Her hair was like milk and honey, so light it was
almost silver in places, and she was beautiful even in
her inexpensive walking suit, which proved a stark
contrast to the rich trappings of the hotel lobby. The
youth who carried the guests' trunks to their rooms

hurried across the foyer, and the assistant manager watched. As his eyes lit on Tamara Andersen, he wished once again that he was not a married man.

When Tamara had first come to Minneapolis two years before, the owner had been reluctant to employ her as a chambermaid. Upon discovering that she had a baby with her, he would have turned her away had not Arleen, the manager's wife, stepped in, promising she would help find a place for the destitute mother and her young son to stay until Tamara saved up enough money to pay her back.

Tamara had been quiet, almost childlike then, whereas now the owner of the Nicollet House perceived an air of maturity and seriousness about her. Still, a sadness lurked about her lovely, large green eyes that were reminiscent of sun-ripened sage. Soft and velvety.

Tamara's movements were all fluid grace, and she was kind and soft-spoken. Everyone noticed that. But she was cool and aloof, keeping to herself mostly, and also there was a purposefulness about her. Arleen, her only close friend at the hotel, would not reveal what her purpose might be. Nonetheless, Tamara allowed no man to court her. Every afternoon she returned to the boardinghouse to be with her little son, Danny.

Once at the boardinghouse, she worked until midnight at cleaning the rooms of the boarders. When she awoke she set about her tasks at the Nicollet House. Her life was all work and no play.

Now Tamara slipped into the maids' room, where she put on her white apron and then set a cap over the pale knot pinned atop her head. She did not pause before the cracked mirror as the other chambermaids did before going out into the hall but went right to her work. As usual.

She halted before a door, unlocked it, and pushed it wide open, pulling the tools of her trade within the suite. She moved briskly, the glossy black uniform hiding none of her shapely curves. To the other workers in the hotel, Tamara looked fragile and delicate, but they knew that her appearance was deceptive. She worked harder than any of them, but if one looked closely enough, in her clear green eyes was a cloud of uncertainty and vulnerability that belied her cool air of control.

Dorothea, one of the chambermaids, shyly approached Tamara when she was just finishing making the bed in the most luxurious suite. The girl paused in the doorway, twisting the feather duster in her hands. Tamara's lavender scent wafted to her.

"I . . . Tamara, I hate to ask this of you again . . . but I . . ." Dorothea faltered, then hurried on. "You see, my boyfriend has only this afternoon in town, and he mentioned a picnic by the river and I . . ."

Tamara smoothed the counterpane over the pillows, then straightened to tuck a blond strand up into the neat bun she always wore. "Yes, Dorothea."

Dorothea blinked, looking at the young woman only a few years older than she was. Nineteen. Yet Dorothea knew Tamara never went out with men. Still, she envied the blonde's impeccable politeness and regal air. Yes, she was regal, even in the drab gray

23

or blue dress she always wore home when she was through with her work. It was rumored that Tamara never bought new clothes because she spent every cent on her son and on the two rooms and bath they had taken at Smith's Boardinghouse. It was said that she even did her own cooking instead of eating with the other boarders.

Tamara seemed much older than she really was. She never wasted working time mooning over a man, nor did she gossip like the other chambermaids. She was secretive about her past life and about what she planned for the future. Gleaming floors and perfectly made beds at the hotel and boardinghouse were all Tamara seemed concerned about. The girls were beginning to think she was strange, rather spinsterish.

"Of course, Dorothea," Tamara said. "I will take over your work again." She did not even display a frown of annoyance.

It was Dorothea who looked flustered and embarrassed. "I promise that this time I will give you a part of my earnings, Tamara." First she had to pay off that new outfit. Then, she promised herself, she would pay Tamara.

"Think nothing of it, Dorothea," Tamara took up the polishing rag to run it over the mahogany surface of the bedside table. "You deserve to be out with your new young man."

"Oh, do you think so? You should see him, Tamara. He is so handsome, blond and with lots of muscle. Would you like to meet him? He is waiting for me downstairs." Dorothea blushed then, hoping

Tamara did not realize how sure she had been that she would get the afternoon off. "You *are s-o-o-o* kind," Dorothea gushed. Then she rushed off, pulling her apron and cap off and leaving them for Tamara to retrieve from the bed.

Tamara sighed. Picking up Dorothea's things, she finished her work in the suite, then pushed her mop and heavy pail into the hall, gathering up all the tidying tools to be used in the next room, where she would take up Dorothea's task.

Arleen approached Tamara just as she was about to unlock the door with the key Dorothea had left her. "May I have a word with you?" The older woman glanced at the scatter rugs on the floor, piled neatly outside the storeroom door. Tamara, always the well-organized, systematic one. A real gem.

"I am awfully busy, Arleen. Can't it wait until tomorrow? I'd like to clean the rest of the rooms so I can get home to my son."

"I know you want to get home to Danny as fast as you can, Tamara. But this is important. Like it or not, dear, I must speak to you. Come in here."

Tamara carefully placed her buckets and mops and brooms against the wall where no one would trip on them; then she followed Arleen into the little office reserved for the managers of the establishment. She took a seat when her friend offered one.

"I know what you have done, Tamara. First it was Greta's work, now it is Dorothea's. You can't keep up with this, my dear." She paused, then drew a slow breath. "I am giving you the rest of the afternoon off—because you deserve it. You have been working

25

too hard." She sighed. "Please, Tamara, you are not a workhorse. It will not hurt you to take some time for yourself. We will not suffer if you are gone for the afternoon. I have other girls."

Tamara sighed. "I am rather weary. But really, Arleen, I can finish Dorothea's work and get off in time to be home for my son before my landlady—"

"Before your landlady wants some of your time?" Arleen took a deep breath before going on. "Mrs. Smith is very kind, but I am sure she charges you for the time she watches Danny."

"It all works out to Emily's and my advantage, Arleen, because I also clean rooms at the boarding-house."

"Do you happen to know any of the men there?" Arleen asked, a hopeful gleam in her eye.

For a moment Tamara was startled by the question, then she recovered. "It is a respectable boardinghouse, and it suits Daniel's and my needs very nicely."

"How old are you now, Tamara . . . twenty?"

"Just twenty-one. But I do not see what—"

Arleen pressed her lips together. "If you do not leave here within the hour, Tamara, I will fire you. Do you understand?"

Dark gold lashes fluttered. "I understand. But—"

"No buts!" Arleen snapped, not meaning to be cross. "If you work yourself to death, we will lose the best chambermaid we have ever had in this place." She leaned forward. "Tamara, for God's sake, can we talk? I have been your friend for over two years now and you have never once confided in me. Sure, you

26

tell me about your wonderful son and how well everything is going. But is it?"

"Of course." Tamara blinked, wishing she were not having this conversation. Arleen had never before pried into her private life. "I have everything I could ever wish for."

Arleen eyed her closely. "Do you?" She looked aside, then back to the young woman who sat stiffly in the chair, not answering her question. "Dear God, Tamara, you are beautiful and young. Have you looked outside?" When she received no response, Arleen went on. "It is a day meant for lovers."

Tamara looked out the window and saw that it was indeed a gorgeous day, the sun shining brightly, the air full of fragrant summer blooms. "It is a nice day, but I have so much to do that I never stop—"

"To smell the flowers or walk in the moonlight," Arleen interjected. When Tamara hung her lovely blond head and smoothed the glossy black skirt she wore, Arleen said softly, "You are very special to me, Tamara, and I am concerned about you. Will you not let anyone close to you?"

Tamara closed her beautiful eyes, then pulled back her shoulders. When she opened her eyes, they were full of pain.

"I happen to know you are not as frigid and remote as the gossips say. You are no different from any other woman. You need appreciation and closeness. Tell me, what is hurting you so?" The older woman's eyes were full of compassion. "I want to know so I can help in any way that I can. Please believe me, I am your friend."

Caught off guard, Tamara swallowed hard. The tears came fast. She wondered if Arleen really did want to know what had happened to her in the past? But what good would telling her do? Arleen could not find Daniel for her. He did not wish to be found, especially now that she had his child.

"Who is the father to your son?" Arleen asked, as if she had penetrated Tamara's thoughts. "Where is he? Don't you ever hear from him?"

Tamara stared away from her friend's concerned gaze. "Please, Arleen, may I return to my work? Daniel is not . . ."

She let the sentence dangle and fastened her gaze upon a stack of papers on the desk. The despair that filled her was evident.

"Daniel, hmm? The same name as your son." Arleen spread her hands, then stood. "All right, Tamara. You may return to your work since you persist in doing so, but if you ever need someone to talk to, please come to me. I am willing to listen to anything you might have to say. I am a friend. Always remember that."

Rising to her feet, Tamara turned, and when she was about to walk out the door, Arleen called out.

"Remember, some of us have only one chance at happiness, and when that chance comes, we must grab it."

"I am not sure—"

"Tut, tut. Grab it for yourself and your son, Tamara. Don't forget, things are not always what they seem."

"I will remember that," Tamara softly said. Then

she hurriedly went out into the hall, where she had left her cleaning equipment, never lifting her eyes when a gentleman in elegant attire cast an appreciative gaze her way.

Busying herself once again, Tamara tried not to think of anything but her work. However, her soft green eyes were full of visions of the past.

The time and my intents are savage-wild;
More fierce and more inexorable far
Than empty tigers or the roaring sea.
                              —William Shakespeare,
                              Romeo and Juliet

Chapter Two

Framed by long black lashes, the soot-blue eyes remained unflinching and cold as Daniel Tarrant stared out the barred window of the prison while pressing dark hands flat against the stone walls on either side of the window. He tried to see the sun. To him, each day he spent behind bars seemed longer, darker than the last.

Daniel's arms bulged with long, ropelike muscles. Everything about him, his every movement, spoke of pantherish grace, of power. But the only exercise he got was when darkness came and he ran in place, making certain that no excess fat would accumulate on his taut, bronze body.

Cringing inwardly, he tried not to listen to an unceasing stream of vile language. But he was compelled to hear it, day and night. That and the other crude sounds made by these wretches.

Daniel pushed away from the wall and ran his fingers through shoulder-length black hair, crisp and shining and straight. Sometimes he braided it in one long length that hung down his back, wearing a blue headband around his forehead.

For two lonely years he had been incarcerated in this stinking hellhole, a prison he would love to see the last of.

He was a man of decent habits, one who had been thrust into a narrow, foul-smelling cubbyhole much like the cage of a wild beast in a menagerie. It was too dark in the cell to read with comfort, and since there was not a chair he could pull over to the tiny window high in the wall, he had long ago given up one of his favorite pastimes, studying law and the logging industry. Besides, the jail had a limited supply of reading material.

There was not even clean bed linen, and the clothes he had slept in on chilly nights were foul smelling. They would not come clean in the brackish water, nor could he do much with the sliver of soap provided him on washdays.

Daniel sat on the narrow cot, his long legs bent at the knees, his outer calves resting on the floor of the bug-infested cell. He wrinkled his nose when a cockroach the size of a cigar butt hurried across the floor. At least he had not found one in his food that morning.

Almost entirely alone for two years, with only bugs for company, he was lucky to be sane. The blue headband he wore accented lighter flashes of color when he lifted his eyes heavenward, but all he saw was the damp, crumbling ceiling. Not a sky full of sunshine. No stars and moon. Just the same depressing ceiling staring back down at him.

He thought of the sheriff. On the one hand the

man felt that detained prisoners should be treated humanely, and to do that he was compelled to relax discipline somewhat. On the other hand, however, the sheriff's common sense ruled out providing soft beds and luxuries for a tramp or petty thief. As a result, the detained prisoner suffered.

Two years. And he should not be in jail at all since he had committed no crime!

"Crime" used to be a word Daniel knew little or nothing about. But he'd now seen young men arrested for the first time lose their scruples and begin to hate society, resist authority; to desire only revenge for imagined wrongs against themselves. Most youths came in as novices, Daniel had learned, but departed fully tutored in the ways of crime. To keep a clear mind, he had prayed to the Great Creator to keep him sane and as pure in heart as the day he had entered this hellhole.

Well . . . somewhat pure in heart, he thought, with an almost pleasant curving of his crisp, shapely mouth. He could not rule out thoughts of sex. Not when he dreamed about Tamara.

The buttocks of Daniel's snug black denims pulled even tighter as he leaned forward to brush a cockroach from his pantleg. "Get lost." Daniel flicked the ancient creature with his middle finger. "And don't show up in my *dinner*—such as it is."

Impatiently, Daniel stood and paced the confines of his lonely cell. He would soon be released, his time served for the robbery charge, a crime he had never committed. But who had set him up? he wondered, a hardened gleam in his jet-blue eyes.

How many times had he lain in bed at night and

wondered what it would be like to hold Tammi again?

That last day he had walked free under a blue sky, sunset tinting the clouds pink, in the North Woods, was when he had called to her and was waiting for her to join him. But he had been struck on the head and taken to a lonely stretch of road, then dumped there. What had happened after that was a nightmare he would always remember, one he had relived over and over, every day and every night for the last two years.

What had hurt most was that he had been just about to ask Tammi to become his bride. About to make the sun shine in her sage green eyes. About to walk forever with her at his side. He had planned that no shadow would fall on her path from that day forward.

Tammi. His heartbeats picked up, becoming stronger, faster at just thinking about her. He was anxious to see her again.

Daniel's jaw hardened in his lean dark face. She would have forgotten him by now. *Maybe.*

He cupped his chin in his hands, thinking he could not blame Tammi for not loving him anymore. It did not matter, since he had enough love for both of them. In time, if she had not already married some other man, she might grow to love and trust him again.

Daniel knew as certainly as the sun rose outside these ugly prison walls, he would never be content with another woman. He knew his life would be meaningless without the delicate blonde beside him.

Lowering himself down on the cot, he clasped his

hands behind his neck and stared up at the hated ceiling. Closing his eyes, he reflected back to three years ago when he had first met the enchanting little blonde who had stolen his heart. When she had almost run him down in her sleigh in Moses's logging camp.

And the second time. With little Kristel, Tammi had come down to Tibbet's Brook, the landing where they could watch thousands of logs float by on the way downstream to the mill at Minneapolis. He had been at work, a logger, and they had come from the river while Cookie spread his table on the shore. He remembered the sunny day well, only because she had been there. . . .

His long strides had slowed, for he had caught sight of the one who caused his heart to thunder. Beautifully delicate, like a pale, straight China doll she was. Then on that awful night Kristel had disappeared into the woods. Tammi had been searching for the child, her stepchild, and exhausted, she had fallen into his arms. "Why did you ever have to come around? Why did you step in front of my sleigh that day?" she had asked him.

He remembered posing a question of his own then. "Why am I even alive?"

She had looked tormented and weary, driven. "I never asked you to come into my life." For long moments she had studied him, he recalled, and the pain in her question had twisted his gut. "Why did you come into my life?"

Had she been dreaming of him when the child disappeared? Was that why she had been so riddled with guilt? He thought so, even now.

Sadness had moved through him then. For her. For himself. "No one ever asks that, Tammi. It just happens. I came into your life, that's all," he had told her.

What he had really wanted to do was bury himself in the dark of her, to make her weak with joy instead of sadness. But she had been married then, had *thought* she was married in that phony ceremony performed by the dark-hearted friend of Ole Larson. She had never really been Mrs. Larson, had never rightfully become the burly Norwegian's wife. If only he had known that at that time . . . Then, after Ole disappeared, he had had plenty of chances to make Tammi his own, but he had been wrapped in his own pain, the pain of having been abandoned on a stranger's doorstep as a baby.

Now he wanted to make everything right with Tammi, if only . . . Daniel gritted his teeth. First he had to be released before he could find the man whose crimes he had been paying for. Then, maybe then, he might be able to live again. He dearly hoped so.

Daniel groaned, an animal sound in his throat. Only if Tammi was going to be beside him. He lay down in misery, wanting her badly. Deep down.

Only Tammi—the young woman who governed his every thought . . . his heart.

He dreamed of the lovely blonde that night and woke with a dark curse on his lips. In his vision, she had been with another man, and she had laughed tauntingly when he'd approached her to take her away from the dark stranger.

And she had run away from him, with the faceless phantom in his dream.

Now Daniel reached deep into his pocket for the fine gold chain from which a beautiful cross dangled. It caught the light of the encroaching moon, sparkling like moondust on a meadow at midnight. It mocked him, taunted him as it turned in the pale light like something alive. It was Tamara's. Tammi . . . Tammi . . .

Daniel moaned and crushed the tiny cross in his palm, then drew his legs up, curling himself into a ball and resting his forehead against his knees.

He prayed harder than ever before.

Merciful God . . . Tammi, why didn't you wait . . . why?

It hurts. Oh hell it hurts.

In the darkness of the tiny cell his tears blended with the shadows on his deeply chiseled features. He never looked more savage than in that moment of dangerous speculation and agony.

There would be troubled waters ahead. Deep waters. For him. For Tammi. And for whoever had dared become involved with the woman who was his. Forever his. In three months' time he would know for certain who had tried to steal his woman from him. Three months. He could hardly wait, but he prayed the time would pass quickly.

A tall, dark man unfolded himself from the confines of a rented carriage as it pulled under the shade of some elm trees at the side of the road. He was charged with a strong, exultant emotion. James Strong Eagle stood quietly, however, staring at the homely walls of the county prison, imagining his twin brother suffering and condemned to years of unjust captivity.

His smile was evil.

What James Strong Eagle did not know, not yet, was that Daniel would be released in three months. James thought he had plenty of time to introduce himself to the lovely Tamara Andersen, to get her to fall in love with him. She had been in love with his twin, so it would not be hard for her to love him, he thought. It had taken years to discover her whereabouts after she had disappeared from the cabin in the North Woods. But now he had found her again.

From the moment he had seen her with his brother, Tall Thunder, Strong Eagle had been enchanted and had known he had to make this woman his. At that time, as he had stared at his likeness, he'd had no idea that Daniel Tarrant was his own flesh and blood, his brother. How could he, since he had been taken away to the Cheyenne shortly after he and Daniel were born. It was only lately that he had learned he and his twin had been separated immediately following birth and their mother had run away with her lover, the French trapper.

James Strong Eagle's mouth became a cruel curve. There was more, but Daniel Tarrant would never hear the whole story of the terrible quarrel that drove their parents apart, he and Daniel as well.

He had no love for Tall Thunder, this Daniel Tarrant, who was his twin. James loved no one, never had, save for the delicate blonde who had captured his heart the moment he had cast his eyes upon her.

James clenched his fist. "She will be mine, this

Tamara Andersen. The White Dove is destined to become my woman."

He had learned that she worked at the Nicollet House and that she had borne a son two years ago. All those first months he had been searching for her, she had been carrying Daniel's child in her belly. James knew the torture of acute jealousy, the fiercest emotion he had experienced since learning he had a twin brother!

His hand squeezed into a fist meant to kill. Tamara Andersen was seductively pictured in his mind, a sweet dove he meant to teach all that he knew of lustful love. They would not always share a tepee; he would build her the finest house money could buy. She would never want for anything.

He meant to steal plenty of money to keep her and himself in luxury. No more living in poverty as he had when growing up on the Cheyenne reservation. It was Flying Horse who had taken him back to the Sioux camp, back to the land of their father, the majestic and wild Dakotas. Then he had learned the shattering truth that he still had family, a brother he cared nothing about, since he had not grown up with Daniel Tarrant and did not know the man.

James chuckled and his slate blue eyes narrowed into nasty slits. When Daniel was released, James was again going to make sure he was caught for "crimes" James had committed. James's friends, all outlaws, would make certain that no one found out the truth. After all, James was their leader.

"James . . ." the deep voice from within the carriage, purred. "You have stared at that ugly place long enough. I would like to get something to eat. I am very hungry."

James climbed back into the carriage, sitting beside the raven-tressed woman. "You are always hungry, Pink Cloud, and I always have to feed you." He flicked the ribbons over the back of the sleek black horse. "I will drive this time."   •

Pink Cloud snuggled next to her lover, the skirts of her lavender and red lace-trimmed dress brushing his ankles. The beautiful half-breed Indian girl did not realize James flinched when she rubbed her ample breasts against his arm and pressed her chin into his shoulder.

Her dark eyes lifted. "Will you always steal from the white man and give to Pink Cloud and her people?"

"Always."

"Even when you are married to the white woman you mean to seduce and betray?"

James snarled, "What are you talking about, woman? When I marry Tamara Andersen, she will come first and you will only be my kept woman."

Pink Cloud screwed up her pretty face. "Mistress, in the white man's tongue. I do not want to be your mistress, Strong Eagle, I want to be the woman who is first in your thoughts and your life."

James twisted Pink Cloud's wrist, almost snapping it in two. "You will be what I say . . . if only my kept woman."

"You are hurting me, Strong Eagle." When he loosened his grip, Pink Cloud pouted. "I will make you love only me, you will see."

"I am the leader of my men," he said proudly. "I am Strong Eagle, first in everything. No other will be above me and take what is meant to be mine."

"You talk mysteriously. I do not know what you mean when you speak like this. It frightens me."

"It is not for you to know, Pink Cloud. You only need pleasure me, that is all."

But Pink Cloud did not think that was all, no. She needed all of Strong Eagle, and one day, when she discovered what it was that the woman named Tamara had that she did not, she was going to get it.

When Pink Cloud continued to chatter, this time in the Cheyenne tongue, James ignored her and submerged himself in his own dark thoughts. Tamara, yes, she would be his, and when they were safely wed, he would dispose of the child who carried the same name as his brother. Daniel . . . Danny—they would both perish beneath his hand, and if that was not possible with Tarrant, he would then make certain the man spent the rest of his days behind bars. Away from Tamara. Forever.

A grin that would make Satan envious spread James's lips, revealing straight white teeth. "Prison. This is where I should have been instead of Daniel." He chuckled. "Too bad."

In the land of the Decotah,
Where the falls of Minnehaha
flash and gleam among the oak trees,
laugh and leap into the valley.
—*Hampshire Gazette*, 1870,
St. Anthony, Minnesota

Chapter Three

While the gauzy white curtains fluttered at the window, Tamara stared into the swirling, soapy water and lifted out a shiny dish which she dipped into the rinse bucket; then she set the dish aside in the drainer to dry. Scrubbing the cast-iron skillet next, she leaned forward to glance out the window, for a moment watching the tall heads of the golden asters nodding in the morning sun. Among the grapes, there were wildflowers growing alongside the fence, decked in a hundred different shades—wild indigo, golden alexander, white-fringed orchid, and a handful of shooting stars with rose, white, and purple flowers, their petals turned back to catch the golden kiss of the sun. Butterflies flitted all about.

Daniel, oh Daniel, why have you stayed away so long? her lonely heart cried as she bit back a sob on a soapy knuckle.

"Mommy, Aunty Kristy comin'!"

Danny toddled into Emily Smith's sun-washed kitchen, reminding his busy mother that they were

43

expecting company that morning.

Wiping her hands on a kitchen towel and closing a drawer with the thrust of her hip, Tamara turned to smile mistily at her little son. She saw that his pudgy fist was closed around something.

"I know Kristel's coming, darling. What do you have there in your hand?"

Danny thrust out his fist and opened it when his mother lowered herself down to his height and hunkered on her heels. "Pretty marbo!" Danny exclaimed, excitement in his beautiful dark turquoise eyes. For a moment, worries struck Tamara like piercing Indian arrows. Then she pushed them aside, telling herself she had no time for such nonsense.

Brilliant sunlight spilled through the kitchen as she thought of how much she loved her son. "Yes, I see it now, a marble. You can play with it as long as you keep it out of your mouth. All right?" She kissed his forehead, a strand of silky dark brown hair pleasantly tickling her chin.

"Uh-huh." Danny shook his dark head, his eyes wide and innocent. "I won't swaller marbo."

She hugged him to her. "You mean you will not put marbo in your mouth to begin with or—"

"Or else Mama will take pretty marbo away and you will never see it again!" said a cheerful, girlish voice from the doorway.

Tamara whirled. "Kristel!"

"Kristy! Aunty! Aunty!"

Danny sped across the room as fast as his little legs could carry him, to propel himself into waiting arms that had flown wide when Kristel had seen the

44

energetic boy launch himself from his mother's side.

Tamara smoothed her heather muslin dress and stood back to look her friend over, noticing that Kristel's hair definitely had turned a darker shade of gold. In her bottle green frock, however, she looked very healthy and happy. Still, something else was different about her. Tamara had yet to discover what it was.

Kristel hugged Tamara while Danny hugged Kristel's legs. "It has only been four months since we last saw you, Kristel," Tamara said happily. "But you have grown. Have you put on a little weight, sweetheart?"

"Yes, Tammi-Mama." Kristel blushed from ear to ear then. "Gosh, I am still calling you that after all these years."

A gentle smile lightened Tamara's face. "I never stop loving to hear it, Kristel." For a moment, a remembrance of happier days took precedence over the current times. "Now, fill me in on what has been happening in Saint Cloud since last we saw you."

Tamara set about to prepare a hearty breakfast while Kristel's gay chatter filled the kitchen. When the eggs had been scrambled, the bacon fried to crisp perfection, the toast removed from the oven—all with Kristel's help, Danny getting in the way—it was time to sit down and ask the Lord's blessing. When that was done, Emily Smith came into the room, bending to chuck Danny beneath the chin as he sat perched in his highchair at the long table between his mother and his aunty.

Tamara looked up and smiled while Emily placed her portion of breakfast onto a sparklingly clean plate. "I cleaned Aldwin Thomson's room this morning but did not get to Henry Dade's, Emily." She missed the respectful look directed at her when she gracefully bent her head over her coffee cup. "I will get to it as soon as I return from the hotel."

"No hurry, dear, you know that," Emily chirped. "We have all the time in the world for cleaning rooms. Besides, you always work too hard. Don't know how you can rise at 4 A.M. every morning."

Reminded of the time, Tamara glanced at the tall clock standing just outside the kitchen door. Hurriedly, she sipped her hot coffee. "I have to be at work in half an hour." She looked at Kristel who was happily munching her bacon, realizing that the girl had put on several pounds.

"Are you happy staying with the Olskys, Kristel?" Tamara wanted to know.

Before Kristel could swallow the food in her mouth and answer, Emily said, "Slow down, Tammi honey, it won't hurt if you're a little late for work." She blew a kiss as Danny waved his fork in the air as if he wielded a weapon. "I told you, honey, there's no hurry for you to clean Mr. Thomson's room this morning. Lordy, that room's so spic 'n' span you could eat soup off the floor."

"She is *so* nice," Kristel said, meaning Emily. Then she grinned back at the impish Danny who was now tilting his dark head sideways and pushing himself up and down in the highchair.

Emily had walked away, humming a gospel tune as she scooped some more eggs and bacon onto her plate, then went out the screen door to sit on the back porch swing and rock to and fro, her breakfast perched on the lap of her flowered housedress. She did not notice the dark man concealed by the abandoned house across the street, watching all that went on, noting every movement behind the kitchen window. Emily was engrossed in thoughts of selling her boardinghouse to the first prospective buyer who could assure her of a cash profit. She had tacked up a notice in the general store just that morning.

The landlady looked up only once in partaking of her breakfast, to watch as a bluejay landed in the one lonely pine among several elms in the side yard. She resumed her meal, making a mental note to inform Tamara of her plans to sell the big white house, then shrugged, knowing that Tamara would stay on with Danny. Emily would miss them when she went to stay with her ailing sister in Boston. Tamara and Danny were special. She would make certain that the buyer was a kind person who did not plan to use the place for anything other than boarding.

Inside the house, Kristel was saying, "Mrs. Smith is nice, and I like her very much." She cut up some of the softer portions of bacon for Danny, then looked up at Tamara. "You asked me if I like being with Jenny and Harold Olsky. . . ." Her blue eyes twinkled as Tamara looked a million miles away for a second. "Yes," she said when she had Tamara's attention, "I like their new neighbor especially."

Tamara tilted her blond head. "Oh?"

"Mmm-hmm, he's eighteen and his name is Bruce, and he brings me chocolates all the time."

Tamara's laughter was pleasant. "So that is why you have filled out so nicely and have cherries in your cheeks."

Kristel laughed. "I am getting fat!" she declared, unaware her new plumpness would soon pare down to womanly curves.

"Fat!" Danny echoed, tilting his shiny dark head to peek up at Kristel.

Rising from the table, Tamara carried dishes over to the sink. "Just be careful you do not get too pudgy, dear, or else Bruce might look the other way, even though he volunteered the tasty nourishment in the first place." Tamara lifted her eyes heavenward. "Chocolates, mmmm . . ." Then she shook her head, resisting the temptation to stop for some of the delicious morsels on the way home as she pressed a hand to a still slender hip. Creamy, cherry-filled chocolates, melting in the mouth . . . no, *no!* "Ah, oh yes, we were discussing, umm . . ."

"Yes, I know, boys *are* funny. Bruce already warned me that I had put on a few pounds. Men! Are they all alike?" Kristel asked, grinning at Danny who was poking his fork into the air like an Indian lance, as if in protest of Kristel's innocent remark.

With a heartfelt sigh, Tamara gazed out the window, unaware that someone was looking back at her. She had no ready answer for Kristel because she herself did not know any men personally. As acquaintances, yes, but that was as far as it went, though several had sought a more intimate relationship with her.

While continuing to gaze out the window, Tamara felt her face grow hot, then hotter, until she wrenched herself away. She stood for a moment fighting to catch her breath. Was it a premonition she had experienced a moment ago? Moving away from the sink, Tamara composed herself since fainthearted emotions were something she could not afford. She could not walk around afraid of her own shadow, she had to keep busy and get on with her life, such as it was.

When Tamara began to turn into the hall, she sensed someone right beside her and she jumped, catching a vase her sudden movement had almost caused to topple to the floor. She tried to set it aright and nearly dropped it. Kristel stared at her with a worried expression.

"Are you all right, Tamara?"

"Yes, I am fine, dear." Tamara looked down and saw that Danny had joined them, and she smiled at both him and Kristel. "I am all butterfingers today, that's all."

"Oh, Tamara, I love you so much!"

"And I love you, sweetheart."

Kristel wrapped an arm about Tamara's slim waist, envying for only a moment the woman's slenderness. Here was someone who had stuck by her after she had lost both her parents, had even married Ole in order to care for her and her two sisters. Valda was sixteen now and seeing boys; Sigrid fourteen and seeing nothing but her love of horses. Greta would have been the youngest. Despite Tamara's devoted nursing and visits from the local doctor, frail little Greta had gone to be with God after a bout with pneumonia.

Tamara, too, was steeped in the past in that moment. She recalled the first day she had gone to Greta's bedside, that same day in the loggers' camp when she had almost run down a tall man, a mysterious man with sooty blue eyes. Now he was gone from her life, and she did not wish to discuss him, though she knew for certain that Kristel would soon bring up the name of Daniel Tarrant . . . in fact she felt it coming at any moment.

Clutching the hand of a squirming Danny, Kristel gazed up at Tamara and inquired, "You have not heard from Daniel?"

"No, I have not."

That was that. Kristel knew when silence was golden.

Tamara hugged her once more, for good measure. "I have to go, sweetheart, or else I will be late for work. Today I must be on time because there is a lumberman's convention in town. The rooms will all be filled, and we will be swamped with work."

Placing her apron on a hook in the hall, Tamara bent to hug Danny and he hugged her in return, strong as a little bear cub. "You be good for Aunty Kristy and My Emily."

Danny hopped on one foot, then crashed to the floor in his antics. Seated on his plump behind, he rolled onto his back. "My Emily too!" he shouted as if angry, and then a giggle followed his childish frown. From the time he had learned to say the name Emily, he had used My to precede it.

With Danny at her side, his little hand in hers, Kristel watched from the porch as Tamara shut the white gate behind her. She waved, then raised her head to stare at the boarded-up Spanger house.

"I will most likely be home late," Tamara called before moving down the dusty road. She turned around to wave once more before disappearing behind the houses dotting the streets of Minneapolis.

With the youngster playing at her feet, Kristel looked around the yard, meticulously kept, even the grape vines. She had a good idea that Tamara had something to do with that. There was a sizable garden off to one side, and that, too, was neat and orderly. Weeding it, Kristel was certain, would give one a sore back! A proud smile broke out on her young face. There was not a weed in the garden, though, thanks to Tamara.

Scooping the child up, Kristel held him close to her face. She wrinkled her pert nose. "Well, Danny, what should we do?"

"Play!" Danny gently placed a hand on each side of Kristel's pretty face. "Walk first."

She kissed his brown button nose. "All right."

She walked with Danny along the porch that ran around the back side of the huge, white frame house. As she walked she breathed in the clean air.

Though a young city, Minneapolis was surprisingly orderly and respectable. A stranger alighting at the railroad station, as she had many times, was impressed with its cleanliness and its general appearance. Kristel lifted her head, hearing the 8:15 train just huffing into the station, not too far away.

From that station one could walk onto the main business thoroughfare, but even in the evening when the sidewalks were full of people, the crowd was well behaved. Kristel avoided looking at the spooky house across the way.

"Come on, Danny, let's sit on the swing."

"My Emily?"

"Oh, she went in." She held the little boy close, wishing one day to have a child as handsome and healthy as he was. Of course she'd have to fall in love and get married first.

Like a hawk watching its prey, that was how the eyes peering from behind the elms watched the young girl with her armful of energetic child. First, James thought, he would go in and introduce himself to Emily Smith, and then, if there was time, he would take himself over to the Nicollet House and come face to face with the woman of his dreams. How she would react was yet to be seen.

Tamara hurried on to work. The streets of Minneapolis were laid out in lines as straight and regular as those on a checkerboard. The business part of town was not far from the river, great flour mills and other factories positioned close beside it. Back from the river and extending out onto the grasslands were the dwellings of the town's prosperous. Here, it seemed, each man competed with his neighbor to make his home more attractive.

As she walked, Tamara thought of Emily's boardinghouse. Her place was not so showy, but it was neat, comfortable, and tasteful. Of course, there was a little clutter here and there, otherwise a house was not a home. Emily strove to make hers as unpretentious and pleasant as possible for her boarders.

The prevailing style was the white frame house,

each surrounded by its own green yard, with bright beds of flowers here and there, graceful vines trailing over doorways and windows to heighten the pleasing effect. There were brick mansions, too, handsome and wide, belonging to the wealthier and more prominent manufacturers, and a few wooden Victorian-style structures, like Emily's place.

Tamara was nearing the Nicollet House where she worked. She could see it now.

The fine hotel was made of stone, a sort of gray granite, five stories high. In the winter months, this edifice was heated by steam, and the inside was splendidly furnished, the rooms fit for royalty. When she had first come to the hotel, Tamara and Danny had stayed there for one night, and she had felt like a queen. Arleen said she could come and stay at any time, for a weekend, but Tamara had not done so in the two years she had worked at Nicollet House. She preferred the boardinghouse, which she thought was more respectable for her and Danny.

As Tamara passed between the stone lions guarding the entrance, she recalled Dorothea telling her about the chatty wife of a New York merchant who was gossiping to one of her companions while staying at the hotel for an extended weekend: *I have visited the bridal apartments of our New York hotels and saw none where so much money was wasted as upon those of this hotel. Still, I feel like a queen when I am here.*

Tamara did suppose that in hard times the hotel would look like a great extravagance, and there had been many such times following the Civil War. Better days were coming, though, and the hotel was looking better and better, Tamara reflected, feeling that the Nicollet House had given her and Danny their first break, thanks to Arleen.

As Tamara stepped into the lobby, she knew what the Minnehaha Falls must feel like after it came rushing down to perform its *ha-ha* leap, seeming to say *I've done it.* She had. Tamara was making a living for her son and herself. In that moment she recalled the words Daniel had once spoken to her: *Someday you will be like a strong, enduring oak.*

I know, she had thought back then, but only if you love me, Daniel. My heart is in your hands . . . forever.

On the boardinghouse porch, Kristel looked down at the boy just opening his eyes. "That was a short nap," she said, for they had been closed for just five minutes. She gave him a hug and a playful tickle in the ribs.

"*Kristee!*" He squirmed out of her lap. "Play now!"

"Soon. But first we have to help My Emily straighten the kitchen." She quit staring at the abandoned Spanger house across the way.

Danny followed her inside, the screen door slamming after them. All the while a dark man had stood just across the street, concealed by the grouping of elms, even when Tamara Andersen had stepped outside on her way to Nicollet House. From his vantage point behind the trees, he had watched her progress down the street to the business section of town. She had not taken the horse and buggy from the carriage house. But never mind, he told himself, thinking she preferred to walk.

Now he moved to the side of the house, looking in the direction Tamara had gone, telling himself he would catch up with her later. First he had some business with Emily Smith.

Straightening his buff jacket, James Strong Eagle looked over his shoulder, always watching his back, never realizing that the girl Tamara had been conversing with on the porch was going to receive the shock of her life.

Emily Smith was conducting business with a man in the stuffy little office situated at the back of her house when Danny burst in and crawled right up onto her ample lap, unaware that she had company. He had not seen the man yet.

"Danny, you little imp," Emily said, deep laughter rumbling in her chest. She wiped the sweat from her brow because it had suddenly turned hot, pushing back fine gray strands of hair from her forehead, and rose with a jolly chuckle to dump the child from her lap in a playful heap.

"Lord, it's close in here," Emily said, going to stand by the window, preparing to open it. Then she spotted Kristel in the doorway. The girl's mouth sagged open, and her eyes were as wide as Emily's parlor window.

Kristel gaped and mouthed softly, "Daniel."

The dark man seated in the horsehair chair did not bother to stand as the girl in the bottle green dress took a tentative step toward him.

55

Emily stood still, asking, "Kristel, what is it?"

James Strong Eagle decided that this girl had mistakenly recognized him as Daniel Tarrant. Ah, he thought, this is working out better than I had first planned. He would just let this Kristel believe he was Daniel and watch his step in case she might spot some significant difference in him and become suspicious.

Amnesia! Ah! . . . that is it. James's wise friend Flying Horse had told him about this strange illness that afflicted some people following a terrible experience or injury.

Emily finally got the window open, while Kristel held Danny's hand and stared at the man as if in a trace, until Danny began to stare too. The boy looked puzzled and began to whine, having felt the anxiety and tension in the room.

Sensing something was amiss, Emily sat down beside her cluttered desk, the light summer breeze cooling her neck. "What did you say your name was?" she asked, looking from Kristel and Danny back to the strange dark man who had answered the advertisement she had posted at the general store.

James did not look at the girl and the child as he answered Emily. "Mrs. Smith, my name is Mr. Tarrant."

Kristel made a ragged sound, then came further into the room. She halted, however, when she noticed the cold look in the man's slate blue eyes.

"Daniel," Kristel began cautiously. "Are you Daniel Tarrant?" She smiled and knew he had to be, but why was he staring as if uncomfortable and unfamiliar with her?

James turned a little to peer down at the child who resembled him, the boy's coloring and features so much like his own . . . why, this could have been his own son. It hit James then: This is my nephew . . . my own flesh and blood! He might just be able to like this child with the huge, inquisitive eyes of deep blue-green, the soft, tan skin like that of an Indian angel.

"Man!" Danny exclaimed, looking up at Kristel, then over to My Emily for approval of his outburst. He hugged Kristel's skirts and stuck two fingers in his mouth, sucking them while fingering the bottle green material with his other hand.

"I am Daniel Tarrant," James said, then quickly added, "but I do not know you, miss. I have never seen you, and I do not know how it is you seem to know me."

Kristel blinked away the mistiness of years gone by. "How is it that you do not remember me, Daniel?"

"I am sorry," James said. "I am afraid that since my accident I do not remember anyone." He kept his eyes trained on her pretty face, not on her budding breasts. "You I would have remembered"—he slyly halted—"if I could. But, you see, I had an accident . . . I think it was . . . yes, two years ago." He saw that the older woman felt sorry for him. This was good. "Since then I do not remember anything of my past."

"Nothing?"

Wondering what she was up to, James answered tersely, "Nothing."

Kristel frowned. "How is it you know your name then?" She looked him over carefully.

James Strong Eagle looked surprised and for a second, angry. Then he recovered. "A man on the street in Saint Cloud."

The blond's delicate brow furrowed again. "What? Saint Cloud?"

"He called out my name, and that is how I learned who I am," James said with a shrug. Kristel seemed to buy that, but . . .

"Who was it that called out your name?"

James clenched his teeth, not liking the manner in which this foolish girl was questioning him. He did not care either for the suspiciousness that had dawned in her bright blue eyes moments ago. He would have turned back to Emily Smith in order to ignore the inquisitive girl, but he had no wish to get on the bad side of Tamara Andersen.

James shifted uneasily beneath Kristel's hard blue stare. "I do not remember, miss," he said as kindly and humbly as possible. He forced his eyes to mist with tears. "I wish that I could recall more." He sighed sadly.

Compassionate now, Kristel walked over to the man she believed to be Daniel and took his long-fingered hand in hers. "Oh, it must be terrible not to remember your friends!" She turned to Emily, so that the man could not see the tears starting in her eyes. Tamara was going to be so happy! At least, Kristel believed she would be.

Once again Kristel faced James Strong Eagle. "I will help to remember, Daniel, before Tamara comes back home. Later, in the parlor when you have finished your business."

"Good." James patted her soft hand before he

58

withdrew his own. *This is very good.* "Now, Mrs. Smith, about the sale of this boardinghouse . . ."

Silently, Kristel took Danny's hand so they might leave the stuffy little office where Emily Smith conducted all her business.

Closing the door, she heard Daniel declare: "I believe I will be able to afford this place. How much are you asking, Mrs. Smith?"

As Kristel walked back toward the sunny kitchen and out onto the porch with Danny, she found herself frowning again, however. She gazed downward, to the wooden tub filled with the aromatic herb mint, and then up to see what Danny was trying so hard to reach. She contemplated the hanging basket of tiny red tomatoes aflame in the late morning sun. Picking out one of the perfect fruits, she handed it to Danny who soon had red juice and seeds all over his chin. Leaning to one side, Kristel peered back into the darkness of the long hallway running to the office. She squinted and blinked, brightness surrounding her like a halo of white and gold. Then she looked away.

From the steps of the porch, Kristel looked up at the house, with its deftly turned millwork and pink gingerbread, airy detailing that could easily be the product of a playful giant's cookie cutter. The house, like Tamara herself and her rooms upstairs, was soft and feminine . . . it was as if My Emily's house had been waiting for one whose tastes were completely feminine and pastel. It suited My Emily too, with her gentleness and goodness.

That man . . . Kristel frowned again.

Frowns will give you wrinkles, dear. She remembered Jenny Olsky's kindly advice and smoothed the worry lines from her forehead. Try though she might, however, Kristel was soon frowning again, wondering what it was about Daniel Tarrant that did not sit right with her. There was something different about him, and she had yet to discover just what it could be.

She might be young, but she was not stupid or blind. It would come to her, sooner or later.

Here, impossible romances,
Indefinable sweet fancies,
Cluster 'round . . .
—E. Pauline Johnson
Tekahionwake

Chapter Four

"You have to remember that when a man touches your breasts, he considers that you belong to him."

"Touches . . . my . . . breasts?"

"Indian ritual . . . for lovers."

"Yes," she whispered, echoing, "lovers." She clasped and led his bronze hand to cup one of her perfect little breasts. . . .

Tamara stood before the mirror she had been cleaning, blinked, and came out of her trance. She had been daydreaming for several minutes and now told herself that she would have to make certain it did not happen again, since she had been doing too much of it these last few days. Daydreaming was foolishness.

But as she continued with her work, cleaning the many mirrors in the hotel suite on the fifth floor, she found that she was staring back in time again, gazing into her own bewildered eyes, at her reflection that became blurred in the mirror.

She had been remembering her first time with

61

Daniel, that memorable night when he had first made love to her. He had calmed her fears there in the moonlit glade where she had met him, while Ole Larson was back at the little house drinking himself into a stupor.

Tamara closed her eyes and sighed. Daniel had talked to her in a low voice, almost crooning, making her breath leave her body in a long trembling sigh. She had felt her tension dissipate as he put her at ease. A shiver went through her as she felt his lips touch her hair, heard her name whispered ever so softly.

Tamara's polishing rag circled one corner of the mirror, over and over, in the same exact spot. Her eyes were dream-filled. Her lips were parted. She could see nothing but the past, naught but Daniel and herself moving together in the forest and moonlight. His fingers working their magic, tenderly, with gentleness, as he loosened her hair until it fell free around her shoulders. His lips lowering to take hers for the first deep kiss they would share.

As before, Tamara felt the hot, licking flames begin. Her pulses raced at the earthy smell of him. He lowered her to the leaf-cushioned floor while he continued to hold her in his powerful arms. They hugged and kissed hungrily, with savage desire. Tongues meeting, lips melting.

Halting her rubbing of the mirror, Tamara did not feel her lips move, did not know she was speaking out loud. *"Daniel . . . please."* She had begged him to at last free the flame. She had had an ache in her loins she had never known before. He had been aware of this, of her innocence, her never having experienced total fulfillment before. He'd told her as much.

Tamara moaned and swayed before the mirror. Her bodice had been torn in his haste to cup a naked, freed breast, the cotton parting easily with weakened threads and many washings. Her flesh had filled his hand perfectly, and his lips had swooped down to cover the rosy peak while he'd molded the white flesh as if his hand had captured a little dove. When at last they had lain down together, they'd been ready to receive and give satisfaction. The moon had bathed them in a wash of silvery light as Daniel had positioned himself above her, his muscled leg sliding between hers to make ready for his entrance. . . .

Tamara's eyes opened wide. . . .

"Yes, Mr. Tarrant," Arleen was saying to a customer out in the hallway. "This is one of our finest suites. It is also the largest. You will find . . . ah, Tamara is just cleaning the rooms. She is so efficient in her work, there is hardly a speck of dust to be found when she is finished."

For a moment Tamara stood very still, wondering if she had heard Arleen correctly. *Tarrant?* Her heart was hammering against her breastbone when she lifted her eyes ever so slowly to the mirror, her back to the two who had just entered the room she was cleaning.

James Strong Eagle slowly turned his head and stared at Tamara Andersen. He could see her reflected from the waist up in the mirror, but she could not see him from her angle, not unless she moved to the right.

As he had been years ago, James was again blinded by her pale beauty, and he instantly became aware of the haunting scent of lavender. She was even more

63

desirable than he'd remembered. More a woman now, since she had filled out nicely in all the proper places, he thought, his dark brows drawing together. He stepped farther onto the varnished floor.

By a sheer effort of will, Tamara made herself turn from the gilt mirror to face the man she had only glimpsed when lifting her head. He had his back to her when she completed the turn, and she at once noted that his hair was black and he was tall. Wide shoulders stretched the white linen shirt, crisp and without wrinkles, taut across hard flesh. It was tucked into dark gray trousers. Lean hips. Long legs. Just like . . . Tamara's heart ached, and she almost cried out. *Oh Daniel, is it you, Daniel?*

Arleen crossed the room to pause before a Chippendale chair. "The view of Minneapolis is quite stunning from up here, Mr. Tarrant."

James found a quick reply. "It is not for myself, ma'am, but for a relative." Quickly, Pink Cloud had come to mind. He couldn't tell the manager he wasn't interested, that he had only come to look the chambermaid over.

Arleen's eyes lifted from his string tie. "I had the impression you were taking this for yourself."

Not giving a name, he said, "For my sister."

"Ah. In that case, maybe you would prefer something more feminine?"

"Not at the moment. I will be staying here at the Nicollet House for a few days until my business is completed, and this will do nicely."

Arleen frowned, wondering why the handsome man seemed to be so confused and nervous. Was he ill? Or merely a flustered businessman? She decided on the last possibility.

James had turned around by this time and was looking Tamara right in the face. As if a hawk had swooped down to snatch life from him, he felt breath leave him, was certain it flew to the open window where a breeze was playing with the curtains. Several moments passed before he was able to speak. But his pulses were beating like ceremonial drums.

Soft as summer wind, Tamara said, "Daniel?"

James shook his head as if to clear it. "She is the second person who has recognized me today," he said for Arleen's benefit, for the woman was staring at him, a puzzled expression on her face.

"I am afraid you have lost me," Arleen said. "Maybe you can explain yourself better— Oh, Tamara! What is it?"

Arleen rushed to the blonde who swayed backward, one hand positioned limply across her forehead, the other behind her to break her fall onto the edge of the bed.

James reached Tamara before Arleen, having brushed the woman aside in his haste. Before Tamara's back could strike the bed, he caught her around the waist—such a tiny waist—and lowered her gently, fully onto the soft feather mattress.

With concern written in his dark eyes, James looked up at the woman wringing her hands. "Has she been ill lately?" he rapped the question out as Arleen hurried across the room to pour fresh water into the washbowl.

She returned with a moistened cloth and handed it to the stranger. "N-no, not that I am aware of. But Tamara does work much too hard, putting in long

65

hours here and at the boardinghouse where she lives."

James pressed the cloth to Tamara's forehead, gazing with longing into the fairest, most flawless face he had ever seen. His hand shook a little as his fingertips contacted the fine, silvery blond hairs growing at her temples. If she opened her eyes, he knew he would become lost in them, as he had moments ago. They were a most unusual green, like some of the beautiful hills in the Dakotas.

He spoke to the woman beside him. "She must know me. This is the reason for the shock she is going through, I believe."

Arleen looked confused. "I still do not understand what is happening, Mr. Tarrant. You are talking in circles."

James was gazing down at the pale angel who had caused his heart to beat violently upon awakening from a dream of her, as it was beating now. "I was injured, ma'am, and it caused me to lose my memory. Tamara Andersen must have recognized me, but I do not remember this angel. I should. She is lovely to look at, and it bothers me not to know what part I have played in her past."

"It must have been *some* part, judging by the shock Tamara has received." Arleen frowned lightly. "How did you happen to know her last name, Mr. Tarrant? I do not recall telling you what it is, and you have stated that you do not remember."

James cleared his throat, again thinking fast. "Mrs. Smith at the boardinghouse told me her name," he lied, hoping he would not have to explain at a later date. "I am in the process of buying the place Emily Smith has for sale."

Arleen looked disappointed for a moment. "Oh . . . I had no idea that Emily was selling."

Suddenly Arleen realized what it was that had been bothering her. *Daniel.* Before Tamara had fainted she had uttered the name Daniel, and her son's name was Danny. This was no coincidence. Arleen's eyes moved over the man, ascertaining for herself that he was truly the boy's father. Had to be, for their coloring was so alike, as were their features. This was the one Tamara had been pining for.

Arleen looked the man over again, inch by inch. No wonder. She would do the same in Tamara's shoes, since Mr. Tarrant would turn any woman's head. He was gorgeous—tall, dark, and unmistakably part Indian.

Tamara groaned and came to full consciousness, only to stare up at the man who seemed more a stranger to her than her lost love. While he was possessively looking her over, she detected a dark force moving behind the slate blue eyes. What was it about him that she could not define? Something different . . . frighteningly so.

She shivered when he smiled down at her. "Daniel?" she asked again.

"I am Daniel Tarrant."

This was all he offered. He just stared as if he could not get enough of looking at her face. Then he slowly moved away from the bed and went to stand at the window, staring down into the dusty street, the billowy curtains almost shrouding him from the female occupants of the room.

With a frown between her tawny eyebrows,

Tamara shifted her gaze to her friendly employer. "Arleen, it is Daniel, but something is dreadfully wrong. I can see it in his eyes." And in the smoky aura about him that she could not define.

Arleen patted the younger woman's hand. "He is suffering from the loss of memory, dear." A smile lifted the corners of her red mouth. "You are happy he has come back to you, are you not, Tamara?"

With a troubled look on her sweet face, Tamara turned her head so she might stare at the tall, broad-shouldered form at the window. "I am not so sure, Arleen. This Daniel is not the same man I used to know, and it frightens me."

"All that will change, dear, when his memory returns."

Tamara propped herself up on her elbows and looked up at Arleen. "What if his memory does not return and all that we shared is lost, never to be remembered?" Her voice was hushed, husky sweet, and she tried not to stare at *his* back.

Arleen gently squeezed Tamara's shoulder. "You can make new memories, Tamara, brand-new ones that might be better than the old ones."

The manager stared at the young chambermaid who, lounging upon the bed, looked more beautiful and dainty than ever. Tamara watched the sunshine spill across the varnished boards bordering the huge, bright Turkish rug covering most of the floor's surface, brilliant rays slanting into her eyes.

"He might not wish to, Arleen, he might not even have come back to me at all, but to someone else."

Arleen laughed, automatically thrusting out her generous bust. "After the way he was looking at you?

68

I seriously doubt that. This man has a hungry look when his eyes fall on you."

Tamara's long feathery lashes flew upward, and her voice was faintly husky. "That is what I am afraid of, Arleen. That look. It is not like Daniel."

Not like Daniel at all. This man seemed to be a ghost of the man Tamara had known and loved. . . .

Neither woman could see the white edge to James's lips as he envisioned Tamara, seeing her pale beauty set off by the black taffeta uniform with the white lace apron pinned to the front. He did not have to turn and look at this white dove to know he loved her.

His heart wrenching tightly in his chest, James Strong Eagle silently vowed, She is going to be mine. *Soon.*

Dreams are but interludes that fancy makes ... when monarch reason sleeps, this mimic wakes; Compounds a medley of disjointed things.

—John Dryden

Chapter Five

The night was dark save for a splattering of moonlight here and there outside Tamara's bedroom window. She stood with the curtains circulating soft night air about her, her silvery cornsilk hair flowing over her gently rounded breasts and on down to her waist.

Softest moonlight kissed her form and cast her natural beauty into high relief. Her lovely face was sad and winsome.

Danny was asleep in the adjoining room that had at one time been a huge closet. She had preserved this hour before bedtime for herself and her thoughts at day's end. But this night she was troubled more than ever because Daniel Tarrant had suddenly stepped back into her orderly life and she had no idea how to cope with that, even though she had long dreamed of it.

She had fled the hotel after work, afraid and yet anticipating that Daniel would follow. To face him again after so recently experiencing the shock of her life would be hard on her nerves, to say the least. Had he turned from the window as she went out? She had no idea. Was he looking for her even now? Where was he and what was he doing at this moment? He had checked in at the hotel, Arleen had informed her before she went home for the day.

Tamara gazed up at the misty moon. She would have to face him in the morning at Nicollet House, and once the shock of seeing each other again faded, they would have to talk. She was still angry and bitter that he had abandoned her several years ago, yet something had happened to Daniel after he had called to her from the woods. Memory loss, Arleen had stated. Today, Daniel had not spoken to her again, had just turned his back to her as if afraid to look at her. This, too, was not like the Daniel she knew; her Daniel had not a timid bone in his body.

Tamara finally lay down to get some rest, and though she tried hard to close her eyes and slip into peaceful slumber, the memories returned, those that would be engraved upon her heart and mind forever. Long-to-be-cherished memories, painted upon the beamed ceiling of her room as she fixed her concentrated stare upward. She remembered the moon, the glorious starlight, and the man. . . .

Like a golden-centered rose, blushing and new-born to the kiss of the sun, the pale blonde flowered in the arms of her Indian lover at midnight. There was no burning shame in this moonlit tryst, only a longing to be one with him forever in a love that purified and overshadowed all the hatred in the world. She held fast to the undying truth: Only one man would ever know the fire that was in her blood.

She had become aware of this while still innocent.

And now, in her frustrated dream, Daniel pressed her into the forest floor for one last kiss, then the moon bathed the lovers in a wash of silvery light as he moved back to position himself above her. A muscled leg slid between hers to ready her body for joining.

Tamara stirred in her dream, and then the memory of their first time together continued. His bronze warrior hands reached behind to lift her slowly, carefully taking possession of her parted softness . . . then the whole surging as he penetrated swiftly. Even as he promised there would be no pain, she felt the burning, swordlike pressure of his fullness. She did not cry out as his thrust went deep, the veins in his brow pulsing beneath the glisten of sweat that bathed his triumphant face. The strength of his probing staff came and went, probing depths of ecstasy she had never dreamed it possible to reach. His jet hair fell over his forehead, then back as he lifted himself away, but not completely, before straining forward again to press himself against the mound of her womanhood. The forest caught fire around them and became a deep purple swirl of passion. Shivers of sweetest delight began to pour through her.

When Tamara felt a tingling sensation begin at the base of her spine and crawl around to her middle, her eyes flew wide and she came fully awake before the tremors could start. Only a wispy chain of the dream swirled in her consciousness, leaving her body shaking with unfulfillment. Pungent smells of deepening night, summer flowers, and dew reached her, wafting on the air stealing in her window.

Tamara's head rolled on the pillow, her hair a

silver spray cascading over the bed. The sweetness and splendor of that first time with Daniel could never be repeated. She knew this and was sad in her heart. To try to capture Daniel's heart would be like chasing a wild wind that was raw and dangerous and fleet as it whipped elusively before her, hurtling her behind like leaves in its wake. Their night of love in the forest had faded to an almost forgotten memory. But now it was back as was the man, haunting her in full force and giving her no peace.

Certainly they would never love again, she had thought back then as she did now. Yet they had, and he had given her the most beautiful gift a man could bestow upon a woman: their child.

Daniel awoke with a start, his eyes jet black in the deep cold shadows. It was dark in his jail cell. Restless from longing—in his dream he had held the silver angel in his embrace once again—Daniel folded his arms behind his dark head to stare up at the empty ceiling. The moonlight stole into his lonely cell and bathed his bleak surroundings in a blur of silver.

In his dream he had beheld gold hair dusted with a sheen of silver, quivering like a live jeweled creature. Soft, dovelike eyes. Sweet, gentle curves that were a visual delight. Aroused, he had wanted only to bury himself in her. In Tammi. To be sent to heights that he could reach only with this woman.

Daniel stirred. He had almost known release in his sleep and was burning still with unsatisfied desire. He had never experienced such a grinding ache in his loins, not since they'd first met and he'd desired her so. He stirred again, restless and full of longing.

Again, strong emotions.

The way she had tossed her long silken hair after washing it, coyly spreading its glory about her shoulders. What was he thinking? There was no coyness about Tammi Andersen. Teasing, yes, she had been teasing him while drawing a wide-toothed comb through the sparkling strands. He wondered now as he had back then how her dainty neck could support a tumbling mass of the thickest hair he had ever seen on a woman. Not even Indian women possessed such an abundance of hair.

He had plenty of time to dwell on the past and its moments of glory and sadness. When would he see her again? *Would* he see her again?

Daniel rolled over on the hard bed and groaned, hugging himself as if chilled. He had thought Tammi too tempting and a danger to his heart, since he had not desired serious commitment. He felt sick as Helen Mattson came to mind, the pretty woman in the red dress. Her well rounded breasts had swayed with a sensuous beat as she had walked over to stand before him. She had been attending the party at the Olskys. He had not realized that Tammi was there too; in fact, she had been staying at the Olskys. He had been solely out for pleasure that night, like a hungry wolf on the prowl for a bitch in heat, and Helen had been just the one he had been seeking.

Trying to erase Tammi from his mind, he would dally with another for a while, usually a very short while, and then toss her aside. Exactly as he had when a younger man. Repeating the same mistakes.

Helen came to mind again. He recalled never having seen such sinfully juicy red lips, lips that seemed to be waiting for a tongue to be thrust between them. At the party, he had known desire for Helen . . . until a flash of yellow muslin had come into his range of vision. What he had beheld then had struck him hard, mesmerized him. Out the window, he could still see the afternoon sky, the pink clouds, feel the freedom, the strength of his manhood. Why could he now recall the way the sky had looked and what color Tammi had worn? he wondered. She, too, had looked as if she had just been struck by lightning.

Tammi, Tammi. He could still see the longing in her eyes turn to anger, a woman's anger; the narrowing into gray-green slits. Cat's eyes had looked Helen over as she had stuffed herself with sweet confections, everything going into that red mouth. With a flick of her yellow skirt, Tammi had whirled away, an admirer following close behind as she drifted into the kitchen. Daniel's gaze had fallen onto Helen's fine-boned profile, his interest in her dwindling as rapidly as his desire. For a while.

His breath now rose and fell sharply. In spite of everything, even the little flashes of feminine coquetry that Tammi had displayed, he had gone with Helly into the barn. The thought of marriage had frightened him. He had wanted to marry Tammi, but he couldn't bring himself to become a husband because of his painful past. The hurt of being rejected by his parents. A mother and father he had never known because he had been abandoned . . . and so he had abandoned Tammi when she'd needed him most.

When he'd fought for the North in the Civil War he had had his share of women, an orgy of beds one after the other, those of the ragged Southern belles that had needed comforting. He had been begged to lie with more women than he liked to think of now. Not one had stirred anything inside him. Helen had meant nothing to him but a means to satisfy a lustful craving; all he could think of was Tammi while making love to her. He had been left with the feeling that he had somehow been unfaithful to Tammi, and he had not liked having her possess him like that. But all the beds had only confirmed his passion for Tammi. His attempts to erase her image in a swirl of careless lust had failed dismally.

Tammi had been a part of him for so long, Daniel now believed that their souls had been united when he was born. He could live with himself now, prison had taught him this, but could he have Tammi? Would she forgive him for all the times he had hurt her and abandoned her?

In the morning, with pale light filtering in, Daniel reached into the pallet for his hidden knife. He could have used it many times on one of the guards—slit a throat—but he'd never killed senselessly and would not begin now. He had come by a chunk of wood when his parolee friend brought it from the "outside," and he was whittling a fawn, one of the creatures of the wild that Tammi loved so much. His old friend Gus had called him a man of many talents when it came to working with wood. He had chuckled, calling Daniel "a carpenter woodsman." And Daniel had built his own house of fragrant logs deep in the Minnesota woods. There, the pines stood thick on the banks of the nearby stream, to which he had gone ofttimes to bathe or to cool his body of desire for Tammi when she had been in that farce of a marriage to Ole Larson.

Daniel sat back, letting his hands, still holding the tiny wooden creature and the knife fall limply to his lap. Woman of Thunder had once said to him: "You are a very troubled man, Daniel Tarrant, Tall Thunder. . . . Ah, your heart is with the morning hair, the one I have learned is called Little Oak. It is good you talk of your pain to me." She had nearly begged him to pour out his feelings. "It is *hinziwin*, yellow-haired woman. I knew this when you could not love me well when she was in the camp."

"Damn it!" Daniel pounded his fist on his thigh. He had not been able to make love to Woman of Thunder.

She had lowered her head, shiny black hair brushing her shoulders. "You should not be ashamed. This happens to a man when his heart and body cry for another. You do not eat. You stare at nothing outside. You work like a crazy man. Your body does not sleep when weary. It is she who pulls so strongly at your heart."

Hunhunhe, he had said to Woman in the language of the Dakota, the word for sorrow. She had answered with *mitawicu*, meaning he should take the blonde woman to wife. But Tammi had been married, so he had thought, and Woman had shrugged, saying only *winu*, the word for captive.

"I am not a savage! That is out of the question!" he had retorted.

Now, in his prison cell, he realized he could not

78

force Tammi to part with the one she was with—if she was in fact married as his dreams had revealed. To win her heart, once and for all, would take total commitment. The time for taking and hurting was past. Fantasy and romantic notions had ceased. Now reality must take over. He had only to find it and hold it fast.

Two weeks more. Then he would know.

In the dark shadow of the moon, in the yard below Tamara's bedroom window, a tall man moved restlessly while looking up at the house. He was like a huge cat on the prowl, ever on the alert, watching and waiting for a glimpse of the pretty feline at the window. Yet nothing moved behind the dark square in the house, and he soon gave up his midnight vigil to go and seek his pleasure elsewhere.

But James Strong Eagle knew as he walked away, keeping to the darkest shadows, that he would not go in search of Pink Cloud this night. He had to make plans for tomorrow, for his and Tamara's future. Before Daniel Tarrant was released from prison. In fact, he thought he might be able to make sure Daniel did not see the light of day for at least two more years.

James entered by the cellar doors, going into the shadowy depths of the old, abandoned Spanger house.

Of all the tyrants the world affords,
Our own affections are the fiercest lords.
—Earl of Sterling

Chapter Six

Sun streamed through the little kitchen window, the big trees outside creating swimming patterns across the white cupboards and waxed floor. Tamara was boiling coffee, scrambling eggs with bits of ham, while Kristel played with Danny at the table. She wore her hair drawn softly back from a center part and caught up on either side of her face, a mass of pale blonde waves in back tumbling and spiraling all the way to her waist. Her eyes appeared more luminous than ever because of the soft lettuce green, muslin dress she was wearing, which had become faded from many washings. She would put her hair up in a knot later, at work, she decided.

All of a sudden Kristel asked the one question Tamara had been dreading. "Have you seen Daniel?"

"Yes." Tamara worked the indoor pump by the sink. "At the hotel."

Kristel blinked, staring at the whooshing water. "He was there?" She stared at Tamara's lifting shoulders.

Tamara's voice was faintly husky, "Yes."

The answer was unsatisfying, but that was all Tamara offered. Kristel would not reveal that Daniel had visited Emily in her office. She would have spoken but knew Tamara was closemouthed on the subject since too many conflicting emotions were raging inside her. Harold Olsky was picking her up early in the afternoon, and since Tamara soon had to go to work, she would not be able to greet her old friend as she had wished. Harold and his wife, Jenny, often came to Minneapolis for he had business at the sawmill, a bookkeeping position that took him from his Saint Cloud office four times a year.

Already Danny was cranky, so Kristel settled him down for a nap. Returning to the kitchen just as a dark cloud gathered above the house, she saw the cheery sunlight suddenly fade. "I looked out the upstairs window, and it's pretty stormy in the west," Kristel said. "I think it's going to rain in an hour or so." She nibbled on a piece of bacon, then looked up as a rumble sounded in the distance. "So . . . maybe sooner."

Tamara was just passing the coat rack and decided to take her slicker in case Kristel's predictions proved correct. "That came on quite suddenly," she declared, while she slung the oilskin coat over her arm.

She smiled at the girl who was like her own daughter. After Kristel departed she would not see her for several months, but Kristel had come to love the Olskys and they returned her affection. Besides, Kristel had made many friends her own age in Saint Cloud.

Glumly Kristel stared at a framed photograph of

My Emily's sister, then became tearful and went into Tamara's outstretched arms. "I will not see you for a while, Tammi. I mean Tamara. I should get used to calling you that, because that's the name you go by now . . . since you became a full-grown woman."

Tamara laughed. "Am I really?"

Kristel snuggled against Tamara's shoulder, loving the fresh violet scent of the woman. "Oh, yes. You are so much more grown up since you have come here to the boardinghouse. But you will always be my Tammi-Mama."

Emily Smith came out onto the porch to stand by Kristel and wave as Tamara stepped outside, but a strange feeling came over Tamara as she looked at the old Spanger house, an eerie chill. A cold wind scuttled down the street as the clouds gathered strength, gray, and moving low and swiftly.

Emily cupped her hands and called, "Be sure to wear your slicker!"

"Be seeing you," Kristel shouted, and then, "Love you!"

"Love you too!" Tamara called back, hurrying against the wind. "See you in a few months, Kristel!"

Tamara hastened down the street, hoping to make it to work before the rain began in earnest. Just as the first drops started to fall, she stepped inside the hotel and was instantly greeted by Dorothea who trailed her all the way to the dressing room. The girl chatted constantly and Tamara found it markedly annoying when Dorothea began passing on the latest gossip of the hotel maids.

She was just tying on her apron when Dorothea

burst out anew. "Well, have you met the newest occupant of the fifth floor suite? He won't be staying long, you know."

Tamara was silent for several moments while gathering her items for cleaning. She felt a stab of irritation at realizing that all the other maids had noticed how handsome Daniel Tarrant was. Dorothea could not keep her mouth shut on the subject.

"Yes," Tamara finally said, pushing her cart out into the hall while the chatty maid trailed behind, in no hurry to get to her own floor. She felt sorely tempted to tell the girl to go about her business.

"Well," Dorothea went on tauntingly, "I heard that *you* fainted when you saw him—I overheard Arleen talking to one of the clerks."

Maybe now Tamara will get herself a man, Dorothea was thinking, that is if I do not get to him first!

Dorothea chatted on, her pert nose in the air. "I almost fainted too, when *I* laid eyes on that gorgeous creature. Lordy! Midnight blue eyes. And what a deep masculine voice . . . he really set me on my heels!"

Tamara walked away, leaving Dorothea blinking as fast as a shutter in the wind. "What did I say to make her act so uppity?" she asked herself. "Well, well. Do you suppose the ice queen is jealous? Hmm. He must really be some man to catch *her* eye."

Gathering her own cleaning things, Dorothea walked along the hall, deciding she would get to Mr. Tarrant first and do some flirting. Tamara wouldn't have a chance once she got her claws in him. And she would be the talk of the hotel, snatching a man from under the nose of the ice queen!

Tamara cleaned rooms like one obsessed. The gentlemen who patronized the hotel wondered why this pale beauty was working her fingers to the bone when she could be leading an easy life if she would only consent to becoming someone's mistress. Some of these men had begged her to do so, saying they would even leave their wives if only she would come around. To Tamara, however, her job was a way to work out her frustration, plus it was supporting her and Danny.

She felt "Daniel" behind her before he even spoke. He had been watching her for some time, the gentle swaying motions of her sweet body, her intentness on her work making him feel the intruder. But he could take it no longer. James had to make his presence known.

"You work too hard," he said abruptly, coming up behind her as she laid her dust rag down. "You should not. You do not have to."

Tamara became still. Why was his voice pitched so differently? She had not noticed this yesterday. Chills of apprehension coursed through her, while excitement brazenly insinuated itself.

"It is my job, Mr. Tarrant, and I believe there is nothing wrong with hard work. In the Bible, Paul tells the Thessalonians, 'that if any would not work, neither should he eat.'" *Besides, hard work has kept my mind off things.*

If he could have done so, James would have knelt before her, begged her to become his bride. But he was not a beggar. He could always take her captive if things proved difficult, he told himself. He was able to provide for her even now; she would not have to work. He and his friends had put on masks and robbed some wealthy individuals late last night, so he had plenty of cash.

"You will share the evening meal with me?"

"Have dinner with you? I am sorry, Mr. Tarrant, but I have to get home to my child."

James moved fast, pulling her into his arms, breathing in the soft violet scent that threaded through her hair. "I have missed you very much, Tamara. Even as my mind forgot everything else, your image was there, haunting me day and night."

Tamara? Daniel had always called her Tammi . . . but somehow the shortened version sounded immature to her now. Then again, Daniel could not be expected to remember everything, not with his memory loss.

Tingles of delight—or apprehension—were racing through Tamara, and she was suddenly assailed by nostalgic remembrances of days gone by. Days of sunlight. Nights of moonlight. Tender touches and forbidden embraces.

"You could come to the boardinghouse for dinner, Mr.—"

"Hush." He placed a long bronze finger across her lips. "Do not call me that. Call me Daniel."

Being so close to Tamara was affecting James quite strongly. All he wanted to do at the moment was take her in his arms and make love to her. He knew he was a good lover. Pink Cloud had boasted that no man could equal his prowess in the act of love.

"Release me, Daniel. I do not wish to stand here in the hall like this."

James's body shook with desire. "In my arms? Tamara, this is where you belong and where I want you always to be. You are my woman, you are mine. It is true no other maiden has suited my eyes. I have been in the Land of Lost Souls without you. I now shiver like one with marsh fever."

Tamara's head spun. This was happening too fast . . . it was too confusing! She looked up at him again. It seemed to Tamara, carefully studying him, that his harshly planed face, the high, slanting cheekbones, the midnight blue eyes, everything about him, even his speech, struck her as strange. *This is Daniel . . . ? What has so altered him?*

"Do you want to come to the house and have dinner or not?"

"Yes, Tamara." He stepped away from her as another maid came along the hall, eyeing them curiously. "I will come to eat at the boardinghouse of Mrs. Smith."

Tamara wavered. *He is coming to dinner tonight!*

As she watched him walk toward the stairs she again sensed that something was out of place. The voice. The walk. The way he acted. Could it just be the amnesia? Or was it that they had grown apart? They had never been together long enough to become truly close. And their relationship had been stormy from the beginning. Yet, she recalled one of the last times they had met. . . .

Marry me, Tammi, become my bride. Daniel had fallen asleep after murmuring those words to her. They had just made love and she had been fighting to surface from the whirlpool of blissful passion. What was it . . . ?

Her eyes flew upward.

How had Daniel learned she was staying at Smith's Boardinghouse? Arleen? Yes, she must be the source, she decided. Later when Arleen came down the hall to oversee the maids, Tamara being the one exception for she was always on her toes, Tamara called the older woman over after she had finished speaking to the new maid who appeared to be part Indian, with her long shining black hair. The girl seemed none too happy to be working at Nicollet House, but Tamara had no time to puzzle over this, since she had to question Arleen.

"Did you let Mr. Tarrant know that I am staying at Smith's Boardinghouse?" she asked.

"Well, now . . ." Arleen thought for a moment. "I'm not sure, Tamara. I might have, since that man befuddles my senses. He's so handsome and strong."

Not you too!

Tamara resumed her work, while Arleen stared at the beautiful blonde's back. What did I say? Tamara in a huff? This cannot be possible, Arleen thought. Then again, Why not? Since the man of Tamara's heart had stepped back into her boring life. Lost love found. Hopefully, Arleen prayed, it was here to stay. For Tamara's sake. And Danny's.

Arleen went on to find the new maid, Pamela Clayton. Strange girl, but strong enough for the tasks

88

of hotel maid. She had a feeling that Mr. Tarrant had told Pamela Nicollet House needed a replacement for a girl who had become pregnant and had had to leave. That did not bother Arleen . . . except for one thing—the way Daniel Tarrant went out of his way to avoid bumping into the dark-eyed maid. Now that troubled Arleen. The evasion was as plain as the nose on one's face.

The feather atop Emily Smith's pert hat trembled delicately as she stepped down the long polished hall in her boardinghouse. "Good day, Mr. Englebritson. Did you have a nice dinner?"

Mr. Englebritson's shoes came to a squeaking halt. One and all knew when the old man was coming, and Danny even had a name for him, KeeKing Man. Englebritson had cackled loudly and coughed at length the first time he'd heard the child announce it.

"Oh, it was quite delicious, My Emily."

Emily smiled at that. "Did you have enough of the cherry tarts"—she giggled—"KeeKing Man?"

"What's *that?*"

"The cherry tarts."

KeeKing Man angled his head closer to Emily. "What about them?"

"Did you— Oh, dear, never mind."

"I consumed *three* of them!" he all but shouted, then resumed his squeaking walk to the staircase that wound upstairs to the second floor.

Emily shook her head, muttering as she entered the kitchen, "The dear old man. Someday I shall be like him, I suppose, and I will want others to have patience with me. 'Do unto others' is the adage."

Tamara did not look up as she reset the dining-room table for her special guest. "Did you say something to me, Emily?"

"I said KeeKing Man *consumed* three of your cherry tarts." She ruffled Danny's head. "He is sleepy. No, no. You keep setting the table, and I'll put the lad down for the night."

Tamara looked up after placing down some silverware. "Are you sure?" she asked, watching Danny tiredly screw a pudgy fist into his eye. "Here . . ."

"Never mind, dear." Emily held the precious child out of Tamara's reach. "You worked hard enough today."

"So did you, My Emily, preparing that enormous roast, the vegetables, gravy, the homemade noodles—"

Emily nodded, breaking in. "And you came home from work and busied yourself with preparing cherry tarts right away, even before you changed out of your clothes. Now, be an angel and do go up and change your dress."

"I am not going to change for dinner, Emily. This is the dress I am going to wear."

"But you have nicer ones, dear, the ones you wear to church. How about the strawberry muslin with the snowflake bodice . . . ?"

Tamara smiled at Danny who had fallen asleep against Emily's ample bosom. "I am not out to impress anyone, My Emily. This dress will do as well as one of the others. I will just freshen up before Mr. Tarrant arrives." She smoothed out the snowy white tablecloth Emily had insisted she use after the boarders had partaken of an extended meal and the table had been cleared.

When Emily returned after having put Danny to bed for the night, she found Tamara standing near the stove and staring out the window, a cup of steaming jasmine tea in her hand. A twilight glow filled the room. The clean fragrance of lavender . . .

"Don't burn yourself on the stove, dear. You look like you're in another world. What is it, Tamara?" She paused. "I am sorry, I should not pry into your private thoughts, however troubled they might be."

"It is all right, My Emily. I was thinking how slowly the days used to drag by, and now, now they seem to go by fast as lightning over the hill."

"Mr. Tarrant was here, you know."

"He was?" Tamara took her cup with both hands. "When, My Emily, when was Daniel here?"

"Well . . . it was just a few days ago, I believe."

Sudden tears came to Emily's eyes at knowing someday soon she would have to leave. She still could not bring herself to reveal her plan to sell the house and move away to Boston. It was going to be hard enough to leave Tamara, and little Kristel had been a delight too, but Danny, ah, he was the one she was finding it most difficult to walk away from. She had never had children of her own, and Tamara and Danny had become like family. God willing, she would be able to visit them once a year to see Danny grow up.

"Mr. Tarrant will be here soon," Tamara said, standing back to survey the table. "I cannot remember if he likes coffee or tea." She stared a hole through the fine tablecloth. "I—"

"See you later, dear." Emily looked flustered, but Tamara seemed not to notice. "I am going to put flowers on Ernest's grave. He was such a good husband, you know, always so loving and kind." Emily chuckled. "He even attended church services now and then, unlike so many husbands who never go with their wives, not even on Christmas."

"You have told me that, My Emily, but I would love to hear more about your husband."

I think Mr. Tarrant is going to buy my boarding-house, Tamara. You will be very happy . . . but I shall not be here, my dear.

"Did you say something?" Tamara asked over her shoulder.

I shall always love you both . . . and Kristel. I will tell you, Tamara . . . soon.

Emily did not turn back to voice these thoughts, but just kept walking out the door, heading toward the windy cemetery on the little hill overlooking the river. Afterward she was going to visit a friend and would return home late.

"My Emily . . . what do you think? How does everything look?"

Silence.

"Is the roast heating?" When Tamara turned she found herself alone in the room. My Emily had already gone out.

*   *   *

Covertly James watched from the hall as Tamara and Emily conversed softly while the child in the older woman's arms fell asleep. As before, he was delighted with little Danny. Now there were two he wanted for his own: the child and the woman. He would have both, or his name was not James Strong Eagle!

James waited in the shadows beneath the staircase while Emily Smith put the child to bed and then left the house herself. He smiled widely, knowing what would be awaiting her when the evening grew dark— Raymond and the others. His friends would be wearing the garb of lumberjacks, just one of the many disguises he and his outlaw friends employed for their dirty work. He himself often dressed as an affluent gentleman. All he'd had to learn to do was ape the fancy white man's talk, and by now he thought he was good at it. He was unaware of how many times he lapsed into the mannerisms and speech of his Dakota kinsmen, sounding like an Indian who had just learned to speak English.

"You move about as if this is your own home, Tamara."

She laughed softly, placing another helping of roast beef on his plate. He pushed it away, telling her, "You must eat more."

"I have had plenty." With a red-and-white napkin she covered the long loaf of bread she had cut into several pieces . . . it seemed neither of them were very hungry.

James sat back in his chair, satisfied with the

dinner and the polite conversation they had shared. "Tell me. Why is it?"

"Like my own home?" She waited for him to nod, then she went on. "Emily made us feel right at home the first day Danny and I moved in. When I would sit in my rooms with Danny for hours, she would come up and make me join her downstairs. She was so kind and charitable, at once taking me into her kitchen and telling me to prepare anything I wished. When I told her I did not wish to impose, this was her house, she would just look at me, and say, 'Please, be my friend, child,' and then I knew that Danny and I had found a good Christian friend, one we would have for a lifetime."

The man stood and followed as Tamara placed dirty dishes on the sideboard, not facing him as she continued. "We have become like family. My Emily means a great deal to Danny and me."

As she stood working the pump at the sink, a stab of jealousy attacked James, but he hid it well. "My Emily," he said, wondering.

"Danny calls her My Emily. He is very jealous of the time she spends with people other than myself and Kristel. I believe it would be hard to live without her now, for she is very special to us."

James's eyes burned with a strange glow. "That is nice, Tamara. I am happy to hear that you have had people to love while I have been away."

Tamara felt her back stiffen at the remark. "Yes."

He stepped closer. "You are cold in your manner all of a sudden. What is it that troubles you?"

Whirling to face the man, Tamara was surprised to find him standing so near, but she could not hold back her outburst. "Where have you been, Daniel? Why have you stayed away for so long?" She looked down and away, her unseeing eyes resting on the blackened coffee kettle that squatted on the stove like a great-bellied buddha.

Moaning deep in his throat, James reached out to pull the shivering woman into his warm embrace. Undeniably, Tamara found his body, his muscle, his hands, everything, to be familiarly hard and manly. Still . . .

"Do you not know, Tamara, that for two years my mind was in the Land of Lost Souls? You do know that I have found my way back to you, *hinziwan*, and I will never leave you. You are my woman."

A reminiscent pang shot through Tamara. He had called her *hinziwan*, the Dakota word for Yellow Hair, and it was spoken like an endearment.

She smiled softly, and to James Strong Eagle it was the smile of an angel. He dug deep into his mind and then began, "Do you know how beautiful you are, how the sunshine puts yellow fire and stars in your hair, how the night makes your eyes like the wild Dakota plains in twilight?"

Thinking his poetry odd, Tamara stammered, "St-Stars in my hair?"

James told himself he should quit staring at her as if to devour her whole, but he could not help it. He remembered the first time he had seen her, she had appeared so much younger than the womanly creature before him now. Every detail was engraved upon his mind, even down to her small, high breasts. They were larger and more rounded now. She was the most beautiful creature in the world, and he wanted

95

to make certain the real Daniel did not look upon her again before he had captured her heart.

It was too late by the time Tamara realized that Daniel was bending toward her. He was going to kiss her!

Really, Daniel, stars in my hair? was all she could think of as the man's lips came down on hers like rock crushing ice.

Ice. Yes . . . That was what her lips felt like. *Passionless.*

Every path has its puddle.
—English Proverb

Chapter Seven

It was not like being swept away on a glittering star to a secret paradise. Not like it had been with Daniel in the past. She was shaken, but in a strange way that left her feeling guarded instead of wonderfully aroused. But this was Daniel . . . *Daniel.* And different though he was, she found herself thrilled in the moments they clung together in a long embrace. When his lips finally lifted from hers, he was breathing heavily and she knew his body had become aroused, even if hers had not. She was not lightsome and jubilant as in past times.

His voice was laced with strong emotion. "Marry me, Tamara." He again drew her closer, but she pushed away and he looked down at her angrily. "Why do you not wish me to hold you any longer? You wanted me before."

"Things have changed, Daniel. You have changed and I have, too." Turning, she busied herself with the dirty dishes.

James knew the cold bite of jealous anger,

suspecting she had felt much more in the arms of Daniel Tarrant, for he had seen them together, laughing and happy, her eyes full of worship for his twin. He stared at her back and knew this woman must be his.

"I will go now, Tamara, but I will return tomorrow and then I would like an answer as to whether you will become my bride or not." Moving away from her, he bowed slightly from the waist. He had earlier witnessed a gentleman at the hotel make this gallant gesture to a woman in the lobby. "Thank you for the food, it was excellent." He had overheard similar things said in the hotel dining room. "You are a wonderful cook, Tamara."

After Daniel had left the house, she stood shaking her head, trying to clear it of the confusion she had felt in his presence. Her whispered plea trembled on the air. "Oh Daniel, Daniel."

That night while she lay in bed, soft moonlight illuminating her bedroom, her pillowslip rustling, she found she could not shy away from examining her own emotions. She could not allow herself to fall in love with Daniel again . . . but had she ever stopped loving him? In her heart of hearts, she knew she had not.

Deep in slumber, Tamara again relived the night she had spent in Daniel's cabin, after the fire had left her alone and with no place to call home. . . . A thrill shot through her. Across the crude table, Daniel held her gaze, his blue eyes probing. Already he had taught her the beauty and ecstasy of loving, and she shivered warmly to think of the next time he would hold her in his virile embrace. Would she have to wait long? she wondered, feeling a sting of anticipation.

Night wind danced through the forest, and darkness enveloped the little cabin Daniel had fashioned with his own hands. "Be a good girl, Tammi." There had been quiet laughter in his voice, almost mocking. "You might be in danger alone with me here tonight."

She had giggled after sipping the homemade wine he poured for her. "What will you do to me, Daniel, that you have not already done?"

"You really do not know, do you?" Suddenly he switched the topic. "Enjoy yourself Tammi, I love to see you so happy. You, fair lady, deserve it."

They shared a long, intimate conversation then, discussing her past, their mutual friends. But when it came time to speak of his past, he clammed up, looking almost angry. Tammi was suddenly afraid of something she could not put a name to. She wanted to warm his body and his soul. She wanted to make him forget his pain in never having belonged anywhere or to anyone, this man with a child's sadness buried somewhere deep in his heart. They stood together, his look unfathomable as he came to stand before her, and she closed her eyes, shivering in anticipation. Daniel's grasp grew tighter, he drew her savagely toward him, flipped back the crimson sash of the Yankee officer's uniform he had worn that night, and crushed her against his chest.

Her face glistening with sweat in the moonlight, Tamara remembered Daniel shaking her a little as she swooned into him, her arms wrapped around his shoulders.

"Oh, Daniel, how wanton I was with you . . . and innocent of men and their ways." She remembered freeing a hand that had sought the male part that had hardened between them. He had taken up the hand and pressed it against her breast in a gesture of refusal, hurting her more than anything he could have said. But his next words had served only to sting her anew.

"There is only pain in tender loving, danger in giving one's heart. Never will I do this, Tammi. I have said this before. You might be in danger. I mean it."

She had shot back: "You seduce me with gifts and hot looks and sly caresses. Now you leave me cold as stone!"

He had uttered a swear word. "You are a married woman!" He had stood apart from her then. "You tempt me until I can't even see straight, much less think clearly. Keep away from me, Tammi Larson. I warn you now, next time you tease me, silvery girl, I will take your seduction into consideration—for more than one night."

"Your heart is too precious to be given to another?" she had hissed over her shoulder.

"I know how women are," he had retorted.

It wasn't long after that Tamara had heard hoofbeats as FireScar took Daniel deep into the forest. He had ridden away from her, into the night, and whatever solace it could give a tormented man.

Tamara could not sleep now, for his words came back to haunt her. *You tempt me . . . I will take your seduction into consideration—for more than one night.*

Staring at the curtains billowing in the warm night wind, the deepening eve so peaceful, Tamara asked herself who had seduced whom that night. Whose arms had ached more to embrace the other?

Take your seduction into consideration—for more than one night.

That could only mean that even back then he had wanted to marry her!

Now he was back, and his desire was to have her for *more than one night.* Tamara rolled over and groaned into her tear-damp pillow. He was back! He wanted her for his wife! Dear God, why wasn't she more pleased at the prospect? Why?

She needed time, she told herself. So much had changed . . . and things were just not the same between them. When he had kissed her it had almost repulsed her. Something was missing . . . a thing that was vital. Love. A love which is deep, strong, and enduring. She did not want a love anchored in a world of make-believe—charming princesses, white horses, glass slippers. Daniel now seemed to believe that their life together would be perpetual romance, hugs and kisses. He had spoken much of money during their meal, and she had begun to think he lived in a world of fantasy, where nothing was real but the moment. Conversing with him had been like walking on a precipice, with no firm hold available.

She had to have a man who could hold on along with her, one who would not let her dangle when the going got tough.

What if he were to discover that their lives would also include day-to-day chores, running noses, an occasional catastrophe, doctor bills, fevered brows, sleepless nights, and perhaps little time to spend together. Romance by itself could not sustain a marriage. To her, love had to come from the respect a couple had for each other, their awareness. That type of love springs from character and unselfishness.

Tamara chewed on her lower lip. Their renewed relationship seemed to have become one-sided, fragile, on his part based more on receiving than giving. He wanted her, and that was that. A bride, strong and willing, capable of loving *him*. This was not the Daniel she had known. He had spent time with her, sharing her joys and her sorrows, her hopes and her dreams. Save for marriage.

Why was Daniel suddenly in such an all-fired hurry to marry her? In the past he had never wanted her so badly he'd almost gone down on his knees to beg. Daniel was not a begging man, thus her respect for him.

Tamara sat up in bed. "No, I will not become his bride just now, even though Danny needs a father and . . . I need . . . I do not know anymore. Dear God, I just do not know."

Sliding her legs over the edge of the bed, she went to check on Danny, holding the wide, embroidered hem of her nightgown off the floor while stepping into her slippers. She walked directly to his bedside, not making a sound, and, like a slim ghost in the dark, bent over him, her long hair moving across her shoulder in a silken motion.

Seeing her baby peacefully asleep, one chubby arm bent so that it looked as if he were hammering his nose with his fist, Tamara felt an overwhelming protectiveness come over her. This was her child, and she was not going to make the mistake of marrying a man who might some day recover from his loss of memory to wonder what he was doing married to her.

She had a son now, and she would do everything in her power to see that no harm or suffering came to him. Not even love and romance could come between her and Danny. No, nothing could tempt her, not even Daniel himself.

In the shadows of the Smith Boardinghouse, James Strong Eagle stared up at the darkened window behind which Tamara slept. Then he cursed his luck, and his stupid friends, when he saw Emily Smith come walking down the dusty moonlit street, the feather in her hat twitching, her step light and easy as a young woman's. He pulled himself from the deepest shadows.

She is alive! His friends had failed him. He cursed in the white man's tongue. He should not have sent them to do the job.

About to step into Emily Smith's path and attack her, James pulled himself back into the shadows when a screeching cat, a gray- and black-striped one, pounced between them. When the woman was safely inside the house, James cursed his own stupidity. What had he been thinking? To have killed the woman outside her own home would have been the craziest thing he had ever done. Yet he wished to squeeze the life from Emily Smith with his own big hands. He hated her for sharing love and laughter with his woman, and because Tamara had given some of herself to another.

James decided he would allow Emily Smith to keep her life, but he would take her for every cent he could.

He would make sure she was on a train to Boston as soon as possible, and get her out of Tamara's life!

Tamara was his. She would give him much pleasure in the weeks and months and years to come, or his name was not James Strong Eagle. He moved quickly toward the abandoned house.

It was Saturday, a gorgeous summer afternoon with yellow-white sunshine that dazzled the eyes. The grasshoppers were hopping about in the grass, frantically fleeing from the squealing lad chasing after them.

Softly Tamara laughed, watching Danny as she paused to straighten her spine and press her palm against the small of her back, the elegant curve of her neck and shoulder reminiscent of a cameo.

His blue britches already grass-stained, Danny ran, then dropped to creep swiftly on all fours, smacking a palm down but never catching one of the springing bugs that flew from the wee lad's reach.

"Atta boy!" Joshua, Danny's KeeKing Man called from the porch, the sun gracing the top of his silver head. "You get 'em, but remember those sly critters got springs in their hoppers. You gotta be faster'n that, boy!"

The sweet-faced child puffed his cheeks at KeeKing Man and showed off, making quite a performance of his antics and momentarily scaring the old man when he tried to stand on his head, then rolled from his shoulder in a sideways somersault.

"Roly-poly li'l bugger, isn't he?" Aldwin Thomson poked Joshua in the ribs, "Eh? What'd you say?"

"Shut up, Al, I didn't say anything."

Aldwin snorted. "You couldn't hear yourself if'n you did, old fool."

"No. You didn't hear this time, 'cause I didn't say anything when you was talking about Danny."

"She sure is a fine-looking woman." Joshua shook his hoarfrost head dreamily as he gazed at Tamara who was hunkered in the garden, wearing a floppy hat and dusty rose cotton frock. "Wish't I was younger; she wouldn't be alone. No, I'd take good care of her."

"'Youth like summer morn, age like winter weather'" Aldwin remembered far back enough to quote. "Me too."

"You too?"

"That's what I said. Say, did you hear there's a handsome dude gonna buy My Emily's boarding-house?"

"This one?"

"Of course, this one, dummy! Wait till he gets a

good look at our silver girl, eh? He just better be nice to her and Danny, else we'll gang up on him, right?"

"Right!" KeeKing Man almost shouted. "I'll take the stud right by the bullets and shake him till his—"

"Hey! Tamara's goin' to hear you, dummy, keep your voice down! You want her to think we're boisterous? Yup. I thought you wouldn't like it if she thought we were just like some fellers who smoke, drink, carry on, and cuss blue streaks." Aldwin sighed, "Just look at her . . . pretty as a portrait of a fairyland princess."

"Yeah."

"Ah. To be young and in the pink again."

The young woman at work in the garden did not feel like the vision of loveliness the old fellows painted. She did not hear them sigh, only caught snatches of their conversation as she pulled weeds, worked the rows with a hoe. Pushing back a straying yellow strand, she got dirt on her forehead and cheeks. She was bending, stooping, pulling, yanking, calling to the child running through the rows of carrots and bush beans.

"Mommy, look!"

Tamara straightened as Danny held up a small carrot for her to see. "My, that sure came out easy." She smiled. "Oh, you are strong, my love, just like Sampson. Here, I have a bucket of water over here. I'll wash that off for you."

Danny sucked on the carrot his mother had washed, the long green top, bigger than the orange root itself, waving in the air. Tamara stopped, a bunch of fragrant herbs in her hands. She knew

Danny could not eat the carrot yet, but he liked to pretend.

Danny played with the vegetables his mother had gathered in a bushel basket and, tiring of that, toddled over to the back porch, calling in a loud voice that ended on a weary note, "My Emily . . . !"

"Yes, yes, little one," Emily crooned, coming swiftly along the hallway after she had heard his summons.

"Danny's calling," KeeKing Man announced when she came out the screen door. "Yup, here he comes."

"I heard him, dear." She brushed by the older man, reaching for the child crawling up the stairs to meet her. Over the tot's dark head, Emily smiled at Tamara who was lugging a bushel of brightly colored vegetables. "My, we *are* going to have a feast, aren't we! Oooh, baby's tired."

"Me too," said KeeKing Man, smacking his lips as he trailed behind Emily. And then came Tamara, Aldwin Thomson after her, wishing he were strong enough to carry the hefty basket for silver girl.

My Emily's big gray tomcat barely made it in as the screen door slammed shut with a bang.

Tamara was cleaning vegetables in the kitchen when Emily's heels clacked along the hall. The older woman had a hat perched saucily atop her head, a purse swinging from her arm. "I have to go downtown to take care of some business," she called in her cheerful voice. "Tamara . . . Oh, she must be in the kitchen . . . that child loves to cook as much as I love to eat."

"Yes, My Emily, I am in here," Tamara called over her shoulder as she mixed a bean salad. "I have some lunch ready for you, would you like to eat in the kitchen or out on the porch?"

"Oh my goodness, child!" Emily cut across the kitchen, laughing girlishly. "Not in my hat and best downtown dress. Wouldn't I look rather silly partaking of lunch on my porch swing decked out like this?"

"No." Tamara smiled at the kindly woman who had befriended her when she was in need of support and love. "You would never appear silly to me, and not to the neighbors either, My Emily. You could wear a beaded Indian dress and still look beautiful anywhere, at anytime."

"Oh, my dear, you are *too* kind." Emily studied Tamara closely. "A beaded Indian dress, hmm? I just bet that fellow who's been coming over here every day—Mr. Tarrant, it is—has seen an Indian squaw or two up close in *his* day, although he couldn't be a day over thirty. By the looks of him, he must be part Indian himself . . . or Italian?" She sighed, pretending she gazed up at the moon instead of her whitewashed ceiling. "Ah, *bella luna.*"

Tamara dropped the pan of fried chicken back onto the stove with a loud clatter. She turned slowly, spatula in hand. "Mr. Tarrant . . . has been here to visit every day?"

"Yes, dear."

Emily helped herself to the fluffy, buttered biscuits, then slipped an apron over her head to protect her best dress, a cool one with a garden of colorful flowers printed on a white background . . . she had made Tamara one exactly like it but of a smaller size. My Emily's shoes were a serviceable black leather with string ties, not as high in the heels as Tamara's good pair were. Her hat picked out the blush-rose in her dress, matching it perfectly. Tamara had helped her to select it in a town store.

Danny was whining again, and Tamara bent to scoop him from the floor. He wasn't feeling well, and had already taken three naps that day, short ones that left him feeling crankier than ever.

Tamara looked at Emily again. "What did Mr. Tarrant want? You did not say." She felt strange calling him that when he used to be Daniel to her—just Daniel.

"Oh." It is time to stop being elusive about the matter, Emily thought. "He, Mr. Tarrant, is planning to, ah, to buy the boardinghouse."

Tamara was not surprised. "Kristel said something to that effect, but I did not wish to discuss the matter when she brought it up—or Daniel Tarrant."

Daniel? Emily blinked. "You know him?" She shook her head. *Of course, am I becoming senile?*

The older woman received the shock of her life when she looked at Danny who was falling asleep against his mother's shoulder. Why had she not realized the truth the first time she had laid eyes upon Mr. Tarrant? The boy was the spitting image of the man who could be none other than his father.

"Yes, Emily, I knew Daniel Tarrant before I came

here." Tamara felt a pang in her breast at recalling the passion that had once stirred her.

But he is not what he used to be, she wanted to tell My Emily. There is some mystery about him. *And when had Daniel gotten that half-moon scar on his chin?* It did not look like a fresh one but one acquired years ago.

Tamara waved her spatula at a fly. "Rather . . . I *used* to know him."

"He is Danny's father." My Emily's statement hovered between them.

The younger woman could not deny the evidence any longer. "Yes." Tamara squared her slim shoulders, placing a crusty piece of chicken on Emily's plate.

My Emily only stared at the delicious piece of white meat surrounded by lettuce, baby carrots, radishes, and homemade noodles. "Well then, it is so much better, my dear, that *he* is the one to purchase the boardinghouse."

"Have you made up your mind"—Tamara pressed her lips together—"to sell it to Daniel Tarrant?"

"I have." My Emily stood firm. She had no idea what had happened between the man and the woman, but the child needed his father and his parents ought to be together. "Put Danny to bed, Tamara dear. He's asleep."

Later in the day Tamara was enjoying part of the peaceful afternoon on the porch swing. One of the elderly boarders had taken Danny in for a glass of water. The boy was so cranky Tamara wondered if he was coming down with something like a summer cold. His nose did seem to be stuffy.

Still, she was alone for a few moments and relished the time to herself. Resting her head against the padded back, her eyes half closed, she idly watched the robins that hopped about in the yard, hearing the low hum of the bees hovering over Emily's herbs and flowers. These grew in huge pots that sat on the gray-and-white porch. The swing creaked lazily in the summer afternoon.

"Hello, Tamara."

The swing groaned to a sudden halt as Tamara's slim fingers grasped the suspended chain and she whirled about, her silver-gold hair, fastened with a huge clasp at the back of her head, falling over her shoulder in one hank.

He had come through the house and was now standing behind the screen. Tamara's eyes flickered as she tried to see him. A dark figure of man. In shadow, the man was even more mysterious and compelling than when standing face to face with her, as if a part of him was now put together and he was as he should be.

Tamara's heart suddenly went wild. "Hello, Daniel." She felt giddy, as if this was their first reunion after a two-year absence.

She rose to walk over and wind her arm about the tall, white post supporting the porch roof. Suddenly the garden came alive with the chirping of insects and bird calls, and there was a white glow to the summer afternoon. Everything was alive and seemed beautiful. Daniel had returned. *What was missing?*

He was here. Still, there was a sense of the unknown, a thing that seemed just beyond her reach, like a distant star.

At the moment she was not tense, just bewildered when Daniel stepped out onto the porch . . . in the flesh . . . and came near.

"Tamara." His voice was deep, husky, all male as he cupped her fine chin and gently forced her to face him. "Marry me, I beg you. Today. Now."

Tamara's heart was pounding, she had waited an eternity for Daniel to ask her to become his wife—and now he had asked her twice, almost demanded it of her.

James gritted his teeth. "What is wrong, Tamara?"

Her deep gold lashes were down, covering her lovely gray-green eyes. "I cannot, Daniel . . . not . . . at least, not yet."

"Why?"

Her lashes fluttered up, showing him the sadness deep in her soul, a sadness he could not fathom. "I need time to think on this, Daniel."

Stop calling me Daniel! he wanted to shout. Instead he clutched her shoulders and Tamara was shocked at the violence she could read in his eyes, in every hard plane of his face.

"Danny needs his father" was James's argument. "You should not deny him this."

Tamara moved away from the man, who now clenched his hands at his sides. "Danny and I have survived without his father this long and . . . I am not so sure I want to get married at this time."

"You are afraid."

James came around to face her, taking up a hand that was smooth despite her heavy workload. "You must not be afraid, woman, I am able to care for you—and the child. I have money enough, I have already said. Will you not believe this?"

He had said nothing about love.

She laughed lightly, but not joyously. "Daniel, you sound like an Indian sometimes. I know you have the blood of the Sioux—"

"Oglala."

Glancing up at him Tamara saw that he was proud, fierce now.

A corner of her mouth lifted. "Are you on the warpath?"

"You are making fun of me."

"No. You are like a different person to me."

"I am"—he gritted his teeth—"Daniel." He thought for a moment, then added, "Tall Thunder."

"There. You are so Indianlike again. The next thing I know you will be wanting Danny and me to move into a tepee with you."

"You are having fun with me. But yes!" He stroked her arm in a distracted way, though he really wanted to lift her pretty skirts and bury himself in her soft womanly warmth, so deep she would cry out at his fullness.

"Yes?" She looked into those deep, dark eyes.

"Why not? You would like to live in a tepee, wear your yellow hair in braids, and cook the meat I would provide for us. I would show you how to sew twenty hides together to make our tepee. And you would

113

gather wood and water, dig and prepare vegetables."

"Oh . . . I do not think so."

"Yes, you would," he insisted, visualizing them under the stars, their bodies wrapped together. To James, it was immaterial that Tamara did not share his view, and he stubbornly refused even to consider her opposing arguments.

Tamara shivered at the primitive scene he unwittingly invoked . . . living as a slave in a primitive shelter. She frowned, looking over the railing onto the neatly laid-out garden. "Daniel, you must have gone back to your people and found out something about your past. As I said, you seem more Indianlike than ever."

James had known this moment would come sooner or later, that she would begin questioning him in depth. "I have found out some things, Tamara, but not all there is to know about my parents—that part remains a mystery."

Reaching up, Tamara brushed a finger against his chin. "When did you get this scar? I did not see it before, and it appears to have been made long ago."

James's brow became hooded, for he would not reveal to her that one of his cousins had struck him with a bear-claw necklace wound about his hand. Two years and a little more time had passed since Jeremy White Horse had defended Tall Thunder when James had spoken against the man he had recently discovered to be his brother, his twin.

"How can you speak with hate in your heart?" Jeremy had asked James. "You do not even know your brother, this man you have only discovered

114

shares the same blood with you."

Yes, it had been like looking into a mirror the very first time James had seen Tall Thunder, and had hated him for being with the woman of his dreams, the yellowhair whose vision had come to him often while he slept before he had ever looked upon her in the light of day.

James had clenched his bow. "He has stolen something that belongs to me, a thing I treasure more than my own life." James would not add that the "thing" was a "woman."

"Pah!" Jeremy had scoffed. "You have just learned of your brother. That means you have white blood too—that of the burly Frenchman who sired you and Tall Thunder."

The hands of James Strong Eagle knotted into dangerous fists. "Do not speak of that one who spirited my mother away! His name is forever banished from our People, and from my mind. I wish never to see him or my mother again."

"How can Daniel, Tall Thunder, have something you covet? You have said yourself that Daniel and you have not had words to this day. How can this be that he has stolen a thing from you?"

Dark clouds gathered on James's brow, as if a storm were brewing in his dark soul. "I say this to you, White Horse, this man of my blood has something I covet and someday it will be mine!"

"Ah. You say it yourself, cousin. You *covet* what he has. This must be a woman you speak of—a very special woman."

At that moment James had lifted his huge fist,

intending to strike the older and much larger man. But Jeremy had proved that, despite the few years he had on Strong Eagle, he was the swifter. He yanked at his bear-claw ornament, and before James knew what had struck him, blood was trickling down his chin. The warrior White Horse had walked away, leaving James staring after him, hatred of the darkest imaginable kind stirring in his savage soul.

Suddenly yanked back to the present, James found sage green eyes looking up at him in bewilderment, for he had not yet answered her.

Tamara repeated, "When did it happen, Daniel?"

"Long ago . . . more than thirty moons."

"That is over two years ago," she calculated, watching him closely. "You must heal very well, very quickly."

"Yes." He recalled the first time he had seen her. "That was when it happened."

Now Tamara was confused, and rightly so.

"But I would have known about it, Daniel."

Argghhh, he hated that name more each time she said it!

"Do you not remember that we were together two years—and more—ago?"

James feigned confusion all of a sudden. "You speak true, Tamara. This must have happened when they . . . they hit me."

"Someone struck you? When was this?" *If only he could remember what happened that night, then I might begin to get some facts straight and we could begin anew.*

She looked at him. "Daniel—someone struck you

116

on the head? You were knocked unconscious?"

"Yes, this is so. When I came to my senses . . ."

"Oh, Daniel, try to remember! This could mean so much to us." Maybe he would begin acting normal, she thought. Like his old self, instead of like a stranger.

Now James groaned for effect. "I believe . . . yes . . . I believe I came to in . . . prison."

"Prison!" Tamara choked back a gasp. "You were locked behind bars when you regained consciousness?"

"I . . ." James shook his head as if to clear it of the snare of cobwebs his brain had been in. "I cannot seem to remember, Tamara." He took her small suntanned hand to press it against his taut cheek. "Please forgive me, my love."

"Oh yes, Daniel! I will forgive you, darling."

Pressing her hands together prayerfully, he kissed them. Then his lips slid up to brush a kiss on hers. He stood back, looked at her for a lingering moment, then was off the porch and away down the street, the reason for his haste being a sudden premonition that he must get away from that house—and fast!

Tamara was still frowning when Danny, water sloshing from the cup he carried, toddled over to her and handed it up. "Thank you, sweetheart," she said, staring off while her little boy gazed up at her, his mouth hanging slack, his Indian-blue eyes wide and wondering. *"Mum!"* He tugged at her skirts. "Wa'er! *Mum!"*

"Oh yes, love!" Tamara scooped up her child while staring down the street, the boy following her line of vision, then shouting, "Man!"

With a weary sigh, Tamara said, "Yes, darling. Man." Unconsciously she sipped the water while Danny pressed his cheek to hers and clung to her in a monkey hold.

Long after the gaslights had been doused in the boardinghouse and Danny had been put to bed, Tamara was still awake, unable to escape from the conflicting emotions battling within her.

At suppertime she had eaten little food, had drunk a good deal of coffee, and had then returned to her vigil by the window. Her mouth softened as she thought of Daniel; she rested her head against the black stove wall, drawing her lids down until they shuttered her soft green eyes. Then, opening them, she looked at the moon-scarred earth outside before turning and climbing the stairs to try to sleep. How she needed sleep.

Crickets chirped. Glowworms emitted greenish lights. Birds ceased their twittering. A quarter moon climbed high and trees gently swayed in silhouette against its pale glow; an owl hooted in a nearby tree.

Tamara tossed, then turned. Her pillowslip often rustled, providing the only sound in the room.

"Daniel," she murmured in the dark. "What is it about you that troubles me so? Why has our passion seemed to cool? When you kiss me, embrace me, it's as though you are a ghost of your old self."

Amnesia?

She bolted upright in bed, shaking her head, and her silver-honey hair slid over the shoulder left bare

118

by her scoop-necked nightgown. Loose wisps rimmed her face, and she brushed them back. She ruminated, studying the yard shrouded in mysterious haze, then lay back down to stare and stare at the eerie glow upon the ceiling. All was not right in her world. Daniel was back, everything should be perfect, she should be laughing and dancing instead of frowning over dark premonitions.

Something, dear God, was still missing.

What was it?

He who reigns within himself, and rules passions, desires and fears, is more than a king.

—John Milton

Chapter Eight

On July eighth the stage into Minneapolis was running late as it came rumbling along Territorial Road, through Saint Anthony, across the Mississippi River. If they did not run into a big deposit of sand blown in by strong winds, they should reach Hennepin Avenue by two P.M.

The road they had traveled had heavy and frequent use, but it was not surfaced. This new one was better, being shorter and free from marsh. Still, its sandy stretches, fine sand at that, were all but impassable for very heavy loads. At the famous waterfall of Minnehaha and along the bluffs of the Mississippi the Saint Peter sandstone was found, from its formations blocks used for building purposes were obtained.

One of the occupants of the stage piped up proudly. "Yup, the Lower Magnesian furnishes two especially handsome building stones—the pink limestone known as Kasota, and the cream-colored stone of Red Wing." The thin-lipped man looked around. "I hope you are all listening, 'cause you might take a lesson and use this latter stone if you're thinking of building. Both these stones are easily worked, and they harden under exposure to atmospheric changes." As he went on Daniel listened with half an ear.

Overlying deposits of sand, gravel, boulders, and clay could be found in most portions of Minnesota— a sandy loam, very finely divided, rich in organic matter, deep brown or black in color. "And of the greatest fertility!" the talkative man went on. "It is this soil which has given this state its reputation for productiveness."

That year the change from winter to summer had been rapid, vegetation seeming to leap into full and active growth within the space of a few weeks. Now the summer months brought days of intense heat, but, with comparatively rare exceptions, the nights had been deliciously cool.

The passengers looked out from the stage windows, one man a lawyer who had spent several years at Harvard, blond, tall, with gray eyes, and the other dark with midnight-blue eyes. They had conversed pleasantly most of the way and now fell silent for a time, looking out at the emerald draperies of trees that trailed the river paths on which trapper and trader, priest and Indian alike had walked when conveyances were not available. Forests skirted the shores of the picturesque lakes of Minnesota, and their waters, abounding in various kinds of fish, were clear and blue and cool.

The female passenger sighed often. Having left the sparse Dakota prairies for the first time, she found the greener, hillier country of Minnesota lovely, saw the beauty of the scene near Fawn's Leap and Silver Cascade brooks, and when passing under the river bluff to Main Street in Minneapolis.

The chatty fellow with the round, red face took up his talk again. He smelled of strong cologne, his blue eyes were small, clear, and lines of weariness rimmed them. His words were clipped and precise. "Did you know that Minneapolis, 'Laughing Water City' or 'Village of Falling Waters,' as Saint Anthony was named, derived its name from *Minne*, a Sioux word meaning water and the Greek *polis* meaning city, of course. But Louis Hennepin, a Recollect monk, who visited the Falls of Saint Anthony in 1680, gave them their name, that of his patron saint." Becoming exasperated when no one listened, the talker shook his head—it was covered with strands of baby-fine hair—and sat back, smacking his thin lips.

The tall, dark-haired Mr. Tarrant exchanged a look with the man nearer his own age; they both silently agreed the other man must be a little loco to demand the attention of weary travelers right to the last. The stage slowed and came to a halt. The lawyer, James Lamb, had scribbled some addresses on a piece of paper for him before they alighted. Smart man, Daniel thought, since he had asked no personal questions, unlike the pest. Daniel stepped down and bid his fellow passengers good-bye; then he swung down the street with a light step, keeping his eyes straight ahead.

Carrying only a small piece of luggage, Daniel Tarrant, finally free of the walls that had kept him in a living nightmare for two long years, headed straight for the Main Street stables. Writing a promissory note to the man there, he chose a fine black mount with powerful limbs, thick mane and tail, and then made his way to the lumber mill to look up a friend of Harold Olsky's.

Daniel entered the office and sat down to wait, stretching his long, lean legs out before him like a big, lazy cat. The secretary looked him up and down, a pink flush rising prettily from her throat to her cheeks. Daniel only smiled. Then, embarrassed at being caught staring, the woman looked away.

The deep blue in Daniel's eyes did not waver—not for this woman. Seeking out women for lustful pleasure suddenly held no allure for him. It was Tammi he wanted, Tammi alone.

A man wearing industrial overalls emerged momentarily from the inner office and nodded briefly to Daniel. The secretary then said in a husky voice, "Shouldn't be long now, Mr. Tarrant." She smiled and blushed again before turning back to her work.

Since Daniel knew this business like the back of his hand, he was confident he would be given a job—plus he had friends, like Harold Olsky and Bernie, the lumberjack. Bernie's last name escaped him. . . . Hill, that was it! Bernie Hill.

He smiled again as he opened his eyes to catch the redhead's blue eyes sweeping over him.

Long ago he had read up on the lumbering-and-mill business; if he didn't know the extent of it by now, he could learn. Having been a lumberjack was a grand beginning. With Olsky as a partner, Daniel knew he would never be in need of funds, and the industry was really making progress. If he still wanted to be a logger he could do that, too, for wages were still on the increase.

The most important industries in Minnesota at this time were flour and timber. Railroad construction was being energetically carried forward. A road to Lake Superior, in northern Minnesota, was already completed, while the Northern Pacific was fairly under way. His lawyer acquaintance from the stage had filled him in on the details.

Daniel's sensitive ears picked up the sounds of production. Sawmills buzzed on both sides of the river, some of the timber being shipped from Saint Anthony, the rest being marketed locally. Among the small, older towns were Stillwater on the Saint Croix, where lumber manufacture began years ago in 1844, and Anoka, north of Minneapolis, also an early lumber town. Daniel already owned two hundred acres up north, but now he wanted to purchase huge tracts of land and make other investments along the expanding frontier. In Minnesota, there was an almost limitless opportunity for growth, development, and profit. As soon as possible, he would transfer his funds from Saint Cloud to a Minneapolis banking house.

Alert and aware of his surroundings, Daniel stood up when the balding man stepped from his office. With a friendly grin splitting his florid face, the man walked over to pump Daniel's hand. "Daniel Tarrant, eh? Wait till Harold gets wind that you are back!" A huge paw of a hand rested on Daniel's back as he was led into the inner office. "Where the heck have you been, lad?" the older man blustered, unaware of the impostor who had employed Daniel's name while his twin had been incarcerated for two long years. "Where?"

"Away."

"Well, you're back, and that's all that counts."

Daniel was mildly surprised but made no reply.

Tamara left the hotel early. She had gotten all her work completed and was on her way home when the stage came jogging down the street . . . at the precise moment she turned as a neighbor called to her from a storefront, waving and bidding Tamara good day.

"Come for tea one afternoon, dear," Mrs. Williamson said warmly, now climbing into a carriage. "We ladies always love to have you—we might even begin a quilting bee with that lovely group from church." Laurine Williamson waved one last time. "Come if you can, dear . . . and don't forget to bring that delightful child of yours!" The woman stuck her head back inside, exclaiming to her neighbor, "My Lord, the way the sunlight picks up the colors in that girl's countenance, and that hair, like the purest wild honey, so thick, so . . ." Laurine paused, patting fine strands of hair back into her own coil which sat like a gray-brown nesting egg atop her head.

Ethel Dempsey agreed. "She is a very beautiful and sweet young woman."

Laurine said nothing to that but, with a pat to her tweedy brown skirt and a jerk of her head, went on to gossip in her friend's ear. "Have you heard? Some of our religious friends are having serious trouble on the question of dancing among our youthful population. It is hard to differ with good, earnest folk. Of course, there are those who regard this matter as unimportant or look upon dancing as a lesser evil than something it might replace. I believe we should condemn it at once."

"But Laurine," Ethel began. "The amusements of young people are just as important to them as their religion. All animated beings require joyful relaxation, and these young folk have to have it, and will. It is a necessary of life, as much as food and water. Linnea Filbert says dancing is one of the most universal of all the heaven-appointed means of happiness."

Mrs. Williamson sat against the back of the seat stiffly. "Oh . . . hogwash!"

"Laurine, think of it. All nature dances, the waves in the sunlight, the leaves on the trees—even the goats dance upon the mountains, the lambs upon the hillsides."

"I, for one, condemn it," Laurine said archly.

Ethel had only one thing more to add. "My dear friend, there is no good reason why any man should be buried until after he is dead."

"Humph! If we all believed as you and Linnea, we might as well dance and cavort at the taverns all night long—and bring the young ones along too." Laurine's eyes shone overbrightly. "Well then, what do you think about the practice that is still prevalent among young ladies, has been ever since the daguerreotypes started up? We *are* old-fashioned enough to consider that practice *very* improper."

"You are alluding to the young women giving daguerreotypes of themselves to young men who are merely acquaintances. I know of it."

The other woman's nose was elevated several inches. "We, the ladies of the club, consider it indelicate in the highest degree, and we are astonished that any young girl should hold herself so cheap as this." Laurine squirmed in her seat a little. "With an accepted suitor it is of course all right, but even in this case the likeness should be returned if the engagement should by any misunderstanding cease." The authoritarian woman went on. "We should warn any young girl about to give her daguerreotype to a gentleman acquaintance, let her realize that the remarks made by young men when together—concerning what is perhaps on her part but a piece of imprudence or impudence . . . maybe even stupidity—would, if she heard them, cause her cheeks to crimson as she burned with anger. Not to mention *shame!*"

Laurine Williamson stared out the window and wondered if Tamara Andersen would ever consider such an improper practice. She thought not. One thing she would never tell the young woman— Laurine had promised herself that when Tamara had first moved into the boardinghouse—was the rumor about the former owner having had a scandalous affair with the Spanger woman who'd lived across the way, in the weathered gray house that had been boarded up and abandoned for years. Laurine pursed her lips. The shame of it all! Yes, she would spare the sweet Tamara from hearing *that* sordid tale!

Glad to have escaped the chattering Laurine, Tamara let her hand drop back to her side after waving at her. She did not head down the street for several more minutes, just stared in the direction the stage had taken, and saw the gray dust cloud dissipating after its passing.

There was that tingling sensation again. She whirled expectantly, certain to find someone standing nearby and watching her. But there was no one.

Who, Tamara now wondered, had she hoped to find. Shakily she thought, Daniel?

The fragment of hope was shattered, and she continued down the street, while the air, anointed with a midsummer fragrance, subtle but heady, seemed to trail after her, permeating her mind and her senses until her head began to swim.

A stored memory, submerged, now suddenly came alive, and she was shockingly aware of herself as a full-grown woman. She shivered. It was as if her beloved was very close by. That could only mean one thing . . . Daniel was at the boardinghouse and she was going to . . . Yes, she had made up her mind. She would give him her answer when he came to call that evening. But would he come? All day long, as she'd worked, she had not seen him. He was giving her time to mull over her answer, she told herself. Yes, that was it!

Night birds twittered their gentle bedtime lullabyes. A misty moon invaded the downstairs windows, and the smell of roses in bloom stole into the room. Tamara waited—and waited some more. But Daniel never presented himself. She had put Danny to bed for the night, kissed his velvety black head, his bronze baby's cheek, and had stood back to watch as he fell asleep, his jet silken lashes fluttering closed.

All afternoon Tamara had anticipated having Daniel stand at the crib with her this night, his arms encircling her waist, while together for the first time they watched their son fall asleep.

With a loud sniff, she dabbed her nose with her handkerchief and then curled up in the huge armchair to continue to wait. The minutes ticked maddeningly by. Half an hour. Then an hour. She heard Emily go into the kitchen for her usual bedtime snack . . . slippers padding back to her bedroom . . . the door closing softly in the night.

Tamara sighed again, and yet again. Turning up the wick and lighting it, she set the lamp on the table next to her. Reaching down into a bookrack, she pulled out some newspaper clippings, in an album that My Emily was fond of poring over. The one that caught her eye read: *"17th December.* Steamboat Excursion! The Ladies of the Home for the Friendless invite the Citizens of St. Paul to a Steamboat Excursion on . . . Saturday, December 17, 1870, at 12 o'clock, noon. The Steamer *Nellie Kent* has been tendered for the occasion. A Hot Lunch will be served on the boat to all holding tickets. GOOD MUSIC to enliven the entertainment. COME ONE! COME ALL! For further particulars read all the papers."

She sat back against the cushions, hugging a lace-edged pillow, in the shape of a heart, against her chest. And she wondered, and dreamed. What would it have been like attending that excursion with someone she cared for, dancing, if there had been dancing, and being held close under the stars while the steamboat skimmed over the moonlit waters? Uhmmm, romantic, that's what.

Leaning a little to one side, Tamara turned down the lamp until darkness was once more her companion.

She then rose to fetch her soft white robe, pausing only long enough to braid her long blond hair. After checking on Danny, she returned to the chair and snuggled deeper under her robe, trying to block out the cold bite of loneliness. Alone again, with only the creaking of the house in the night and the occasional cry of a bird to its mate coming tentatively from the garden hedge.

She felt a twinge of disappointment. She had not seen Daniel for two days, not since the last time he had proposed to her on the back porch. He had been in a big hurry, and she had wondered why. Arleen had informed her that he had checked out of the hotel early that morning, thinking he might be moving into the boardinghouse. Yet Emily had not seen Daniel either.

Just when Tamara was prepared to give their relationship another try, he had up and disappeared. That was not unusual, just Daniel up to old tricks. Possibly another woman waited somewhere in the night—with open arms!

In bed, with the threadbare robe still on, Tamara gazed at the moon, its fine light filtering in. She was more lonesome now than if Daniel had not stepped back into her life. Occupying her hands until sleep beckoned, she unbraided her hair and brushed it back from her face, allowing the hank to coil in a loop down her back. She set her brush aside and sighed, then again checked on Danny before padding barefoot back to her lonely bed—a bed that seemed larger than before.

For two more long, dragging hours, Tamara lay listlessly on her bed and brooded over what tomorrow would bring, whether Daniel would reappear or not. With heavy heart, she fell asleep at last, just as the clock in the hall softly chimed the hour eleven.

In a dimly lit room on the other side of town, Daniel Tarrant reclined atop his bed at the Winslow Hotel, his lanky form stretched out on the deep blue bedspread, one arm tucked behind his dark head. Buck-naked and cool, he stared at his brown toes. He was deliberating future plans.

That afternoon he had sent a telegram to Saint Cloud, asking that Harold Olsky get in touch with Gus, the old-timer who lived in the North Woods where Daniel's cabin was located, who no doubt had looked after his interests when he had so mysteriously disappeared. Also, he should have amassed some capital from his business venture with Olsky. No doubt that had flourished since Harold was a shrewd businessman who had always been successful. Harold left no stone unturned, and Daniel liked that in a man.

All of a sudden Daniel sprang up from the bed and walked, barefoot and tall and naked, to the other side of the room where he snatched up black trousers and a clean gray shirt, and began to get dressed. Damn! He was going to discover Tamara's whereabouts this night! He would question and search and question some more. He just could not believe that she had been seen, as the boss man at the lumber mill had said, with a dark-haired man that resembled him so much he could be his twin. He snatched the porcelain pitcher from the washstand, then . . .

Twin! Daniel helped himself to hot water from the hall tin.

His body coiled, like that of a panther about to spring. So, this man, someone very like him, must have been using his name. This very day, two people had stopped him on the street to say hello. Both had called him Daniel, and one of them had been a lady whose eyes had solicitously scanned his male anatomy. Make no mistake, she had greeted him as if they'd been together just yesterday—but *he had not been here yesterday!*

His face was stone hard. The impostor must be his man, the same one who had been responsible for his being sent to prison.

Dressed and downstairs in five minutes flat, Daniel strode to the desk, causing a sleepy clerk to glance up and come suddenly awake as he stared up into dark fathomless eyes.

"Ah . . . can I be of some help to you . . . ah"—he glanced down at the register then swiftly up again— "Mr. Tarrant?" Gulping loudly, the clerk sent his Adam's apple to bouncing.

Daniel rolled off some borrowed money and held it up before the astonished man's now wide-open eyes. "Who is the biggest gossip in town? Give me a name, and there's more of this for you by the time I check out."

"A name? At this time of night?"

"Right." Daniel pushed the money in front of the man who stared around the empty lobby, then leaned forward. "Make it good, or don't bother," Daniel warned, slapping his hand over the money the clerk was reaching for.

"Well . . . there's Lil, who owns a, uhmm, respectable boardinghouse over on the bluff."

"How respectable?"

"She . . . ah . . . well, she has been known to have a midnight caller or two and . . . and she indulges in careless gossip."

Scooping up the money, Daniel placed it into the shaking man's fist, squeezing that with his own hand. "An address, and tell me how to get there."

"S-sure."

The clerk leaned forward and whispered, even though there was no one else up at that hour to hear. When Daniel had what he needed, he strode from the lobby and out the doors between the twin lions guarding the entrance to the Winslow Hotel.

It was midnight.

Day glimmered in the east, and the white moon
Hung like a vapour in the cloudless sky.
                                    —Rogers' *Italy*

Chapter Nine

Silent and catlike, the man moved into the slant-roofed room to approach the bed. He moved not a muscle, only his eyes, as the lacy curtains fluttered at the window and he felt the hot night embrace him, along with the exciting and elusive scent of lavender that delicately assailed his nostrils, acting like an aphrodisiac.

As he stared, his eyes glowed a phosphorescent blue; his expression was warm and caressing. How long he stood there staring down at her, he could not say.

Like a star-sprinkled princess she lay, unconsciously seductive. The old-fashioned robe, a white one, had come away, leaving the golden grace of her sleeping form open to his warming gaze. Her thick hair was spread across the pillow in a tangled mass of platinum. Her downswept lashes were sooty yet silken; her neck long, shapely. The thin nightgown showed him her other glorious assets: graceful arms and legs, curving hips and thighs, delicate feet, and rounded, uplifted breasts.

A fierce, compelling desire surged through him and set his loins afire. He lingered but made no move to awaken her, each rhythmic breath she drew making him struggle for his own.

Endowed with womanhood, she was a child no more. No girl, but at an age where her body would know how to respond to and pleasure a man. He stared at the perfectly formed mouth with the sensuously full lower lip, and he was abruptly aware of how long it had been since he had made love to her. There was something else, a newness he would have to view in the light of day. Soon he would enjoy her sweet charms—he smiled—if she was willing. Oh God, she had to be!

Words Daniel had spoken to her on the moonlit porch at the Olsky home came back to haunt him: *I like to touch you. Like silk, that's what your skin feels like. So warm, inviting a man to kiss this spot.* He remembered how she had whirled away from him when he would have planted a kiss at her throat. "I asked you not to do that!" she had snapped. She had been angry, and justifiably so, for he had been caught earlier that week tousling Helly in the barn. *Oh, if only I could turn back time!*

Her hand twitched suddenly in sleep, and Daniel's breath caught in his lungs. He finally released it, letting it out slowly. His heart hammered like thunder in his wide chest, and a sense of melancholy twisted within him. He made a move to awaken her, but amended his actions. This was midnight madness, invading the privacy of her slumber. He would see her in the light of day . . . not like this, scaring the hell out of her should she awaken to see him standing over her like a ghost from her past!

Slowly, cautiously, reluctantly, he stepped back. Tomorrow would be soon enough to be with her, to talk, to let her know how he had missed her, to love her . . . maybe . . . if she allowed him this pleasure. He would not press her or frighten her. He would take things slowly, as they came. She was yet unwed, he had found that much out from Lil, who'd been more than generous with her gossip but he had promised the woman nothing and she'd realized from the onset that he was not there for a night's pleasure. She had told him to return, they could be friends, but he'd told her he thought not.

Now Daniel slipped out the way he had come, never hearing a child sigh in his sleep in the adjoining room.

While Tamara was working at the hotel the next day, little did she know what was happening around her. Under the same roof, a tall, dark-haired man sat quietly conversing with Arleen. She called him Daniel, and he listened to what she had to say. He learned very much in the short time he visited her. Then he returned to the boardinghouse where Emily Smith was prepared to conduct business with him. And he intended to take advantage of whatever hospitality she had to offer. He had to know.

Daniel had found the day quite interesting and enlightening. He had even purchased some new clothes, but he had not liked having to deceive the delightful lady at the boardinghouse when he spoke to her of what he had worn just the week before. In order to purchase the clothing he desired, it was essential that he ferret out all he could about his emulator.

Emily Smith had filled him in on behind-the-scenes information, unburdening herself of the heartache of having to leave Tamara to fend for herself when she took leave of the boardinghouse and her friends.

"Oh, but Tamara is strong, I shouldn't really worry. Still . . . I wish there was someone who could be counted on to take care of her. She needs a friend and—and she needs love so very desperately." Slyly, Emily had peeked up at him from beneath the hand cupped over her forehead. "I . . . I have knowledge that you are the child's father and I only wish that—"

Daniel shot up from the chair he had been occupying and leaned across the cluttered desk. "Child? *What* child?" He caught the ink bottle before it could spill, but his eyes were wild as they stared into hers.

"Why"—Emily blinked in confusion—"you *know very well* which child I refer to, Mr. Tarrant!" Now her feathers were ruffled, and she faced the towering man squarely. "You saw him yourself just two weeks ago. Don't tell me you are going to deny having fathered him!"

With a sinking feeling in his gut, Daniel sat back down in the chair he had recently occupied. "This impostor must look more like me than myself," he muttered under his breath.

"What did you say?" Emily puffed up like a nesting hen. "Impossible? No, it's certainly not impossible, sir! You should have married Tamara long ago—*that's* what!"

"Tamara?" Daniel asked. "Why do you keep calling her that? She is Tammi."

My Emily blinked. "Tammi? I have never heard Tamara called by that name." All of a sudden she turned to him and assumed a gentler tone. "Oh Lord, please forgive me, Mr. Tarrant, I plumb forgot you've been suffering from the loss of memory. How remiss of me."

"Oh, so I have lost my memory, have I?"

"Of course, you poor dear. See, you can't even remember that you are ill or that Danny is your precious son."

All of a sudden Daniel was up and out of the chair, walking—no, stalking like a panther—to the window. He looked out . . . at nothing, and his taut expression softened a little.

"My son—where is he now?"

"Sleeping as usual, this time of day. I thought you knew all— Oh, I am sorry, you have not gotten used to the lad yet. Why, I believe you saw him only that one time when you first came here inquiring about the boardinghouse . . . let me see, a little more than two weeks ago. Well now, let's get the sale of this boardinghouse over and done! The sooner I'm out of your hair, the sooner you can move in and get comfortable with your . . . You *are* going to make Tamara your wife this time, aren't you, Mr. Tarrant?"

The sooty blue eyes remained unmoving, as did the curved lips on the deeply tanned face.

Emily went through her desk, searching for the

papers the lawyer had given her to sign. "Mr. Tarrant? Oh, I do so pray you will fully recover your memory soon, so that you can get on with your life, for Tamara, for Danny."

Daniel still had not turned away from the window. Softly, so softly, he said, "Oh, Danny . . ." He swallowed hard. "Danny . . . my son."

Three days later. Under the advisement of lawyers—James Lamb representing the buyer Mr. Tarrant—the sale of the boardinghouse was completed. My Emily said nothing about the finality of the sale to Tamara, as Daniel Tarrant had instructed. He had informed her that she was doing the wisest thing by not telling Tamara yet, for he wanted to surprise Tamara when Emily pulled up stakes and withdrew to Boston.

How very clever of the man, Emily thought to herself.

While Tamara was at work one day, Daniel slipped into the boardinghouse and quietly walked past Emily Smith, who was busily packing in her bedroom. He almost collided with a bespectacled man on his way to the privy, but pulled back just in time and waited for the old fellow to slam the door at the end of the hall.

Daniel entered Tamara's bedroom and quickly closed the door behind him. Without giving her quarters a second glance, he went straight to the nursery, but found that the crib was empty of the

140

child he had wished to see. Then he recalled that Emily Smith had said a neighbor lady often watched the child during the day when Tamara was working and Emily was busy.

Returning to Tamara's room, Daniel slowly walked around. He ran his hands over her things. An English pine box, probably for letters—empty. On the dressing table was a silver spray bottle, and he lifted it to smell the delicate fragrance, then continued to run his fingertips lightly over her things, feeling them as she no doubt had just that morning. Decorative boxes adorned with ribbon rosettes; a feminine array of satin lingerie bags; delicate laces, ribbons, pearls, and silk roses; a hand-painted lap desk with carved heart atop.

Inhaling her sweet-spice fragrance, a jolt of emotion slammed through him. "Ah, my love," he said, breathing her in, breathing her out like a scent one wore.

When he sat in the lady's boudoir chair, a lavender one crowned with a white lace antimacassar, his eyes snagged on a trumpet-bearing angel floating above a gold cup of dried baby's breath. Then he stood to wander about, pausing to flip open a ledger-type book and read the feminine scrawl within. A schedule, for her work as chambermaid at the hotel. She must have written it out when she'd first started work.

MONDAY. The carpets and floors to be swept. The heavy curtains dusted, and the mirrors and doors—with a long feather duster. These are the early morning duties.

TUESDAY. And every day. Make the beds, empty the slops, wash the basins, dust the furniture, hang up the clothes, and neaten the rooms. (Touch nothing if the occupant asks for privacy.)

WEDNESDAY. Floors scrubbed and polished, all furniture cleaned and polished, wash stand well cleaned. All drawer handles cleaned and painted walls washed free of fingermarks.

THURSDAY. (more schedule) . . .

FRIDAY. (yet more) . . .

SATURDAY. My Emily goes shopping. My day to bake breads, cakes, and pies. Take rugs out to the back yard to shake. Make vegetable stew with barley and tomatoes and beefsteak. Wash Danny's hair and take him for a walk. Clean and polish his shoes.

AND SUNDAY. Go to church and come home to make dinner, then relax for the rest of the afternoon!

Oh. Remember to put on a clean apron and cap every day at hotel! Wash black dress every other day to make certain of its freshness.

The book still held in one hand, the fingers of his other hand pressing the pages flat, he stood next to a vase filled with violets and pinks, and he leaned over it, smelling the sweet fragrance of the flowers, so like that of the woman herself. An expression of longing tugged at his features, and his heart slammed hard inside his chest. His fingers rose to caress a petal of violet-blue. He knew that Tammi had picked the flowers just that morning, that she had smelled them as he was doing, but while the dew was still on the bloom. He could picture her face, a pale cameo against the backdrop of green yard and garden, spring butterflies flitting about her head. There would be gorgeous monarchs at the end of summer, those orange-brown butterflies with black and white markings, many of them, sailing against an August sky. He stared around the room, hoping he would occupy it with her before then . . . before the monarchs came.

Now Daniel closed the schedule book and quit the room. Tammi was more alive in his mind and heart with each passing day. He had only to come face to face with her—and let her know who the real Daniel was.

Pausing at the door, he looked back over his shoulder. They were going to share this room. Soon.

Blue, darkly, deeply and beautifully blue.
—Robert Southey

Chapter Ten

The thunderstorm released its damp fury upon the boardinghouse while the wind rattled and knocked at the windows. Then, when the sun came out, clouds—brushed fine like angel hair—swept across a pale blue Minnesota sky. The day, now into early afternoon, was graced with dazzling sunlight and warming breezes that tousled the hair and rustled lazily down the street as Tamara and My Emily scurried for the twelve P.M. train.

"You do not want to miss it, Emily!" Tamara called as the engine steamed and puffed in the railway station. "Oh, God! I'm going to miss you," she cried out achingly.

Hurriedly, plastering her silly hat down with one hand, Emily turned one last tearful time to give Tamara and Danny—balanced on the young woman's hip—a great big hug. "Don't forget to write to me!" she said to Tamara, and to the boy, "Take care of KeeKing man, precious!" With her overloaded bag in one hand, the handkerchief she would wave in the other, Emily sniffled and backed toward the train, almost colliding with a stranger assigned to her car. The man's Western hat was pulled low over his forehead, and when he bumped into the woman, he growled a hasty, low-voiced apology. Then he jerked away and tipped his chin lower than before, grasping the handrail.

Hopping aboard the train, James Strong Eagle cursed his luck and headed straight to the back of the car, where he slumped into the shadows after yanking the shade down over the window. When he thought of Daniel Tarrant, a cold, powerful emotion called hate stole over him. He peeked along the edges of the sun-faded shade, his heart pounding strongly as he looked out at Tamara, his heart's desire.

Curse my fool's luck again! James thought. Daniel Tarrant had come along to spoil everything for him. But that was the least of his worries at the moment. He was again being pursued by the authorities for swindling money, and he had to hightail it out of town as fast as he could go. They had learned his real name.

But he was not finished with Mr. Tarrant yet. The day was coming when he would get it all—and Tamara and the kid.

His journey on the train would be a short one. He planned to board the riverboat to New Orleans in the morning, start a fire aboard, and fake his own death while the bodies floated downriver. What did he care if there were no survivors—not even James Strong Eagle, the name he'd use when boarding. Just to make damn certain his plan would succeed, he intended to change his appearance. He'd already had his hair cut short, a thing he'd hated to do, since his Indian-straight hair looked best long and blowing in the wind. At that moment James tossed his head arrogantly, forgetting that his hair was no longer shoulder length, but for only a moment. Soon he was frowning as darkly as ever.

He had decided to take a new name for a time, something like . . . He glanced down at the *Pioneer Press*, a newspaper printed in Saint Paul, that was lying on the seat across the aisle, noting this phrase: "at the mouth of Rice Creek and Elk River." James Creek. Why not? It was as good a name as any for an Indian half-breed.

Frowning with wonder, Tamara watched the tall man with the broad-brimmed, high-crowned hat board the train, tipping the brim even lower over his dark, lean face. That was all she could make out, a dark, lean face that could belong to any tall, virile stranger with cropped jet hair. Yet, he appeared somewhat familiar to her. He looked something like Daniel.

Just then, as two women dressed in traveling clothes, wearing white gloves and carrying leather bags, walked by, their loud burst of laughter jarred Tamara from her preoccupation with the mysterious stranger.

My Emily caressed Danny's silky black head one last time, then turned to mouth the words "I love you" as she stood on the iron stairs waving before hurrying inside to wave again from a window as the train shrieked its departure.

Danny giggled and shook his chubby fist as the engine chugged, puffed, and clattered out of the station, great plumes of steam momentarily blotting out the sunny blue sky as the black, serpentine chain of railroad cars wound its way out of Minneapolis.

Tamara stood looking after the train for what seemed an eternity, long after it had huffed away into the dreamy sunshine. She swallowed hard, closed her eyes, and then glanced back at the smaller gray puffs the train was now leaving in its steamy wake.

"Oh, My Emily, we are going to miss you so very much!"

Danny blinked at seeing his mother display such strong emotion. Then he, too, looked in the direction the train had taken and shook his dark head like a playful puppy with a bit of rag between its jaws. "My Emily! Go *choo-choo!*"

"Yes, my darling. My Emily has gone on the choo-choo."

Danny dipped his dark head, almost bumping his mother's nose. "My Emily come t' home?"

"No, love, she is not coming back home for a while." Tamara coughed to hide the tears in her voice, but Danny detected his mother's forlorn mood and lovingly caressed her cheeks with gentle pats and little nose rubs.

"Mom!"

Hugging her child closer, lifting him higher in her arms, Tamara gave Danny a view over her shoulder, of the depot behind them, unaware that someone had been watching her—and Danny.

In the flickering shadows of the train depot, Daniel Tarrant stared with smoky eyes at the young woman balancing the child on her hip, first one hip and then the other. Now she hoisted the lad upward, and, against her shoulder, the child turned to stare at the exact spot where Daniel stood. The boy's sooty blue eyes glowed clearly and intelligently. His rosy mouth was a perfect cupid's bow in his smooth, creamy tan face. He was smiling as if he had just learned a secret, and Daniel did not know what to make of this. All he could do was stare at the beautiful child.

And the woman. Oh yes, the woman. He could not remember when he had seen anything so lovely.

Daniel noticed that the train was long gone, yet she stood there, possibly wishing her beloved Emily back even before the train had rolled out of the city. It was not hard to understand why Emily Smith was so cherished—and already dearly missed.

An oblique shaft of sunlight descended upon the young woman's bright head and the boy's dark one. Their colors were as different as night and day, yet beautiful to behold, like those of a fine museum painting. Daniel studied the pair hard, his expression revealing emotions so deep and strong he appeared almost formidable, when in truth his thoughts were fanciful, hopeful. He felt as soft and furry inside as a Sioux kit fox.

Inhaling deeply to steady himself, as he stood there

in a mote-filled shaft of sunshine, watching the woman and child, he moved slightly, to shift his weight since one of his legs had fallen asleep and there were pins and needles in his foot.

Then the picture of youth and loveliness began to move.

Daniel moved a little more. A natural caution took over his senses. *Whoa boy, go at it easy. You've got all day.*

"What? Stupid, after you've waited this long to see her and talk to her, you're going to wait all day?"

A pimply faced lad stopped, pointed at his own chest and asked the tall dark man, "You talkin' to me, mister? You callin' me stupid?"

"So?" Daniel drawled, shaking out his awakening leg. "What if I am?" He straightened to his full height—six feet, three inches—and peered down at the boy who was in his teens, by the look of him.

"Well, just don't do it again, huh?"

"Sure," Daniel calmly called after him. "Just don't eavesdrop on my conversation again."

The boy looked around and, seeing no one in the area that the man could have been conversing with, shrugged his shoulders and walked away, dragging his feet.

Not long after, Daniel vacated the place where he had been standing for over an hour. He was now impatient to get on with his life.

On the way home, Tamara parked the horse and buggy a few times so she might pick up some needed

150

items at stores along the way. She was fresh out of peppermint tea, good for stomach ailments or headaches, and she felt one of the latter coming on. She took Danny inside with her each time, and this slowed her down considerably since he was curious about what the barrels contained, knowing some held cookies. By the time she left the second shop, where the woman had smiled patiently at Danny, Tamara wondered if she was coming or going.

Entering the cool, dark interior of the boarding-house from the bright sunlight left Tamara blinded, and it was a moment before her eyes adjusted. *What's this?* All the shades had been pulled down and were casting flickering lemony shadows across the pink-and-green flowered wallpaper. "Joshua? Is that you I hear in the parlor?" It must be, since he was the only one who spent leisurely Saturdays there, but surely not with the shades pulled so low! KeeKing Man loved fresh air and sunshine, not this shut-in gloominess of a sick room.

When Tamara entered, she was just in time to see the newspaper lowering to the lap of a tall man who sat not where KeeKing Man usually did but at the end of the sofa, one elbow resting on the puffy, taupe brocade arm, his dark fingers loosely holding one edge of the newspaper.

"Hello, Tammi."

Her breath catching at the old nickname, Tamara licked her lips and stepped further into the room. Danny followed and stood unblinkingly at her side, a fold of her skirt clutched in one hand. Two fingers of his other hand, he poked into his mouth.

151

Tamara finally found her voice. "Daniel?"

The fingers popped out from Danny's mouth and the grin he'd displayed at the train station came back to his cherubic face. Saying nothing, he only stared as if mesmerized.

At last Daniel stood. Tamara's heart slammed into her throat.

This time it was as if she had no breath to draw in. She found herself staring at a long dark-trousered leg. Quickly her eyes flew upward and, for a moment, she was totally, inescapably aware of the man. It was as if she could sense him with every part of her woman's body, though her eyes were trained on the half-smile curving his mobile mouth.

How different this time, she thought. And yet so very familiar. She was tossed back in time as she stared at the corners of his chiseled mouth, dizzying sensations puzzling her, an unreasonable awe assailing her.

Tamara could not explain this new reaction to him . . . the tremor of excitement that had raced through her when she'd first seen him seated in the shadows of the dimly lighted parlor.

"It . . . it is dark in here," she said, then swallowed with difficulty.

"Yes. But you are like a ray of sunshine in a dark room, Tammi. You light up everything . . . my soul."

She stared at him, unable to utter a single word. The darkness of his lean bronze face, with its slanted cheekbones and full dark eyebrows . . . Her mind went back to an evening of starlight and gray moonbeams, of making love, of reaching those unreachable stars in a magic place far removed from the world. She recalled, as she stood there in a trance, another moonlit night when he had asked her: *What are you trying to do, Little Oak—plant your sweet little tendrils right in my heart? You are dangerous, fair lady.*

Daniel, too, was remembering that night, and many others. He had stared down at the blond head, the hair that reminded him of spun silver threaded with finest wisps of gold. Though he had allowed the blood to warm in his loins, he had told himself— warned himself—over and over that he would not allow the warmth to reach his heart. It had, oh yes. How his heart had warmed to her. Back then he'd said to himself countless times: *You are in love with her—so why not marry her and have done with it? Tammi is everything you want in this world. What more, dear God, could you ask for in a woman?* All the savage, yet gentle emotions of love had pounded fiercely in his heart—feelings he had scorned all his life.

Will she want me now? Is it too late? he asked himself for the thousandth time, as he stared at the gentle curves that now proclaimed Tammi a woman. "You do not speak. Why?" he asked.

Unable to cope with her pent-up emotions, Tamara whirled and ran into the kitchen where she pressed her palms against the drainboard and drew in great gulps of air. Her senses whirled.

A deep voice came from behind her. "If you keep breathing like that you are going to find yourself flat

153

on the floor, with me trying to revive you." He found a cloth, hung on the flour bin.

After busying himself at the sink, pumping up water, he squeezed out the cloth, then began to move closer to her as Danny toddled into the room and stood watching the pair with unblinking dark eyes. Daniel desired more than anything else to scoop that beautiful child into his arms. Later, he told himself. Hold him later. First Tammi needed his attention . . . Tamara. He had to try to remember that, for Mrs. Smith had called her Tamara, not Tammi.

"Daniel!"

Tamara pressed her back to the drainboard, looking up at him as if she'd seen a ghost. He stared into the eyes that had grown large and luminous, noting that her mouth had opened in gentle surprise.

"What is it?" He hoped she had not already noticed that he was not the same man she had been seeing the week before. "Have I grown two heads?"

"Please, do not be funny. Your scar . . . where is it? The one we spoke of? You had it the last time I saw you."

Oh, great, Daniel thought, now I have a scar. What next?

He held onto the rag as he felt his face, pretending. *Oh Lord, it is time he put an end to this game.*

"What scar, Tamara? I have no scar. Can't you remember?"

"Oh, Daniel, please do not play games with me," she begged softly.

"Yoo-hoo!"

Daniel shuddered. "What is that?"

"I believe it's Mrs. Williamson . . . our neighbor. You do not remember Mrs. Williamson? She was here the last time you visited. You were very nice to her, My Emily said, and I pray that you will be this time also."

Daniel licked his sensuous lips, his ash blue eyes straying to her heaving bosom. "Only if she's not staying long. We have a lot to catch up on. Before answering the door, Tamara, I think you might try taking a few deep breaths."

"Is anyone home? *Yoo-hoo!* I know you're in there."

"Oh-oh," Daniel said with a smirk.

Just then Danny toddled up to the tall man, tugged on his dark trousers and shouted for all the world to hear.

"Dah!"

The boy looked up at the tall man, an angelic smile plastered across his face. With his heart in his eyes, Daniel scooped up the child, gently and lovingly.

Casting a look at Tamara as she paused in the doorway, he asked, "Dah? Where did he get that?"

Tamara frowned, placing a hand to her forehead. "I do believe My Emily and I have discussed you somewhat in Danny's presence . . . and I am sure he has heard at least one of us call you Daniel."

"Oh . . ." Daniel nodded. "Of course." *The bastard! Just who is this man who has been going around using my name! Damn, I can't wait to get my hands on him!*

Grinning happily toward the rattling door handle, Danny called, "Aunty Kristy!"

155

"No darling, it is not Kristel," Tamara said as she went to answer the door.

Smiling as if he held a bit of paradise in his arms, Daniel smoothed back the child's black hair and kissed his forehead. "Aunty Kristy, huh? Has she been here to see you?" Daniel remembered the blond girl Tammi had taken care of years ago, the very same one he had brought back when she had been given up on, considered lost or dead. He had discovered that Kristel was in the hands of some of his Indian friends, safe and unharmed.

Danny answered the man with two words combined: "Yuhumm." He fiddled with the collar of the brushed cotton shirt, then pressed a wee finger into a buttonhole. "Kristy comin' t' home."

A strange mistiness in his eyes, Daniel put his chin gently on the boy's silken forehead, then blew dark strands aside to kiss it, his lips lingering there, his eyes closed. And when he reopened them, he found Tamara standing before him, her eyes searching, misted. Her chest was rising and falling, and she seemed to have difficulty swallowing.

"Th-this is Mrs. Williamson," she began, then started all over again. "I mean, Mrs. Williamson is here." She groaned inwardly. "Look who is here, Danny."

Tamara shook her head as if trying to clear it. Turning her back on everyone while she fished in her pocket for something, she came up with a hanky and dabbed at her eyes.

"Ah, Mrs. Williamson," Daniel blurted out. "How are you?"

156

"Mr. Daniel Tarrant, I believe. What a *pleasant* surprise to find you here." She eyed the trio speculatively. "At this time of day," she added as if in afterthought. "Why, Mrs. Gordon was just telling me the other day about your daily visits, and I told her, 'Oh, it just cannot be true. Tamara is such a little lady, how could anyone question her sweet, old-fashioned virtue.'"

Mrs. Williamson clucked her tongue before going on, shooting Tamara a look of careless camaraderie though the dark man's studied calm nettled her. She had hardly given the child a second look, but that was coming, and Daniel was prepared to observe the woman's shocked reaction. He wondered if his "twin" had ever held the child in Mrs. Williamson's presence. He thought not. From what he'd garnered, the man seemed to be the type who would balk at domesticity.

This thought made Daniel hug his beloved child even closer, and Danny ate up the affection as if he had been starved for this kind of manly attention. He was happily excited, that was plain, and Tamara noticed this more than anyone else in the room, though KeeKing Man had popped in to see who these visitors could be.

Unconsciously Tamara had moved closer to the man and child. While Mrs. Williamson kept up her chatter, she observed that they seemed to be a happy threesome. KeeKing Man had stuffed his hands into the pockets of his baggy trousers. He felt the tension building, and he was awaiting the fireworks.

He didn't have to wait long, for Mrs. Williamson

157

was growing more vexed by the moment at seeing that the half-breed had eyes only for Tamara and the cute little lad. "Oh, and I was telling Mrs. Gordon that Tamara Andersen is the picture of gentle woman-folk," she said. "Yet there is suddenly a fly in the pudding."

KeeKing Man could not contain himself. "What kind? Vanilla or raspberry?"

Mrs. Williamson's graying head jerked. "Oh, hello, Mr. Englebritson." She turned away from the boring old man to livelier company. "Now . . . Oh my, you are put together rather well today, Mr. Tarrant."

"Nasty-minded biddy," KeeKing Man muttered under his breath.

Daniel's features suddenly seemed unyielding and harsh, not handsome as when he was smiling, the high cheekbones more prominent. The tall dark devil, Mrs. Williamson was thinking to herself.

Now Daniel's mouth curved in a mocking twist. "You are right about one thing, Mrs. Williamson. Tamara is all that a woman *should* be, if you understand my meaning, and let that be a lesson to yourself and your *ladylike* friends."

Danny clapped his hands together, as if in applause of his father's clipped speech. KeeKing Man licked his lips, then braced his old body for more action, his neck stuck out like that of a perched eagle about to swoop on an unsuspecting mouse.

"Well!" Mrs. Williamson was certainly flustered. She took a long hard look at the boy in the man's arms, and a sour expression came to her birdlike face.

"Why . . . the boy, he . . . he looks . . . Could it be? Huh!" She tossed her chin higher. "Tamara never *did* say who the father was but now it is quite apparent. It seems the *devil* is back to swing his staff her way!"

"Huh!" KeeKing Man gaped at the virtuous Mrs. Williamson. Lordy, such vulgar language coming from the mouth of this high-minded woman.

Just then a shriek rent the air.

"Bitch!"

Mrs. Williamson winced as if hit with a wet rag.

She whirled to see who'd shrieked at her, "Aldwin Thomson, *how dare you!*" she hissed, her proper bun coming loose, her cheeks blossoming crimson. It seemed the overwrought woman had suddenly lost all her composure.

Tamara began to apologize for the aged man's rude outburst. "Oh, Mrs. Williamson, I am so sorry."

Facing Aldwin Thomson, Mrs. Williamson went on as if she'd not heard Tamara. "Bitch, you say? Well, I shall tell you, Aldwin, you are going to suffer in hell for that one little word." Pointedly, she glared at Tamara. "You may call me a bitch, but I certainly could not be called a whore!" Her thin shoulder shot up imperiously and she lunged for the door as if she had been bucked from a wild horse. "Heathen . . . child of lust . . . whore," she muttered as she went. "All . . . all sent up from the bottomless pit!"

Tamara was taken aback. *"Mrs. Williamson!* That will be quite enough!"

"Don't you touch me, y-you harlot!" the woman screeched as Tamara approached her.

159

Tamara's jaw dropped. "How dare *you* come into my home and insult my child and—"

"And your Indian lover, you were about to say, you daughter of Satan?"

Setting Danny on the floor, Daniel slowly approached the two women. "Now, now. Is that any way for a woman of your virtues to speak? You, a leading figure in society, befriending lost souls . . ." Daniel went on and on, extolling all of her proud and lofty accomplishments.

After each word of praise, Laurine Meredith Williamson nodded and preened her ruffled feathers. Finally she broke in. "Yes, *ohhhh* yes, I am all that you say and then some. I have done more than anyone in this community to see that our children grow up with a sense of right and wrong. . . ." She went on and on, boasting that she was a woman with her own mind who did her own thinking.

Daniel's sudden smile was without humor. "I have only two words left for you, Mrs. Williamson."

Her chin rising to a lofty position, she instructed, "Laurine Meredith, you may say. Well?" She waited. "What are the two words?"

"*Get out!*"

"Oh! I'll see you run out of town on a rail, Mr. Tarrant. You are the devil himself!" Before closing the door, she shot Tamara a smug look. "Think he's yours, eh?"

"You are getting carried away," Tamara said, though she was worried over what the woman would say next.

"Regrettably I must inform you, Miss Prim-and-

160

Proper, I've seen your lover sneaking around with that half-breed Indian girl Pamela Clayton who works at Nicollet House. Heard tell from an eavesdropper—fresh drunk from the saloon—that he saw 'em doing it in back of the hotel, rutting like the dirty redskins they are."

With that, Daniel stepped forward to slam the door in the woman's face. A high-pitched wail was heard before the crone took herself down the street. Hands on lean hips, Daniel then directed his attention to Tamara, but before he could speak, KeeKing Man exclaimed, "I say, what a bi—" He looked at Danny. "What an old bat!"

"I agree," Aldwin said to his compeer. "Spring, summer, autumn, or winter, don't matter, that woman's always got her yapper flappin' in the breeze. Atta boy, Dan, you sure gave 'er what for!"

Joshua added, "Yeah, Dan, did you hear the latest about Mrs. Williamson? Her husband said to her t'other day: 'I'll just be the front part of the horse. Laurine Meredith, you be the back.' Ain't that rich, heh!"

Daniel could only shake his head, both amused and confused, wondering who else he would meet who would call him by his name. Strange, not knowing if the next person you met would be friend or foe.

With his hands stuffed in deep trouser pockets, he walked toward Tamara, a thoughtful expression on his lean face. "Sorry, Tammi . . . Tamara."

"For what? The cussing or your womanizing?"

Silence reigned for only a moment as Daniel's

shoulder pressed against the doorframe.

"I'm gone," said KeeKing Man.

"Me too!" Thomson quickly declared.

With that, Daniel and Tamara found themselves alone, for Danny trailed the two old men out onto the porch. The screen door slammed—three times in succession. *Bang! Bang! Bang!*

"So . . ." Daniel peeled himself from the doorframe. "That's a new word, 'womanizing.' Didn't even hear that one while I was in jail all those long and lonely months, holed up with the nastiest fellows this side of the Dakotas. Every day you were in my thoughts and dreams, come rain or shine, Tammi, and not one hour went by that I did not think of this day when we'd be together again."

Tamara's anger rose to new heights. "Oh, you were in jail, were you? Please, Daniel, don't give me that line again: The reason you could not come to me was because you were locked up for a crime you did not commit."

With a narrowing of midnight blue eyes, Daniel said, "I told you that, did I?" He made a sound that indicated his disgust. "Just who the devil is this person, this man who . . . who has been telling you all these things? Tammi, we have to talk. Seriously."

She shook her head. "Stay away from me Daniel. I do believe you are ill. You need a doctor. Badly."

Hands planted firmly on his hips, Daniel swayed toward Tamara, little by little, inch by inch, then his head was closing in on hers. "Who the hell is he, Tammi? Damn it, I mean Tamara. Give me a name and I'll murder the bastard!"

162

Tamara's hand shot out, and she slapped him so hard his dark head jerked to the side. Her stomach trembling, she stared into brittle, sapphire black eyes. "Do not ever use that word in my presence or my son's. I will not tolerate such language in my home!"

With a twist of his neck, Daniel cocked his head and stared back at her. "This house is mine now, Tamara, lest you forget. As is everything in it."

"I don't know what you are driving at, or why you have become such a madman, but I want you to leave—immediately!" She picked up and brandished a long-handled cooking utensil, the gesture accenting her words.

"Sure." Daniel nodded, eyeing the harmless spatula. "If not sooner."

With that, he strode to the door, all but ripped it from its hinges, and was gone.

Tamara bit down on her knuckles to keep from screaming. But there was no help for it.

Racing up the stairs to her bedroom, flushed, her breath emerging in small gasps, she flung herself face down on her bed, pulled a pillow over her head, and stifled a shuddering, bloodcurdling cry.

The early morning has gold in its mouth.
—Franklin

Chapter Eleven

Midnight passed and still Tamara tossed in her bed. Stars hung low and the summer night was cool, the moon a huge silver ball. The dew had formed. Every blade of grass shone, every tree leaf was lustrous with night mystery, and the garden earth smelled damp and cool where the rabbits hopped in what was now their domain.

Tamara had at last fallen into deep sleep. It seemed to have just embraced her before she was startled awake. The room was bathed in darkness as the moon hid behind the clouds and stars blinked wearily.

Meanwhile, on the other side of town, Daniel lay naked on his hotel bed. He had fallen asleep after having nursed the bottle of whiskey that stood half-empty on his bedside table. The headache he had gone to bed with still throbbed inside his skull. He stared now at the blue overstuffed chair. After leaving Tamara he'd entertained thoughts of seeking comfort in a woman's arms. He ached, for he had not been with a woman in a long time. Instead he had found some comfort in the whiskey, which he had drunk until he had reached a state of tipsiness.

Reaching over, still slightly woozy and intoxicated, he corked the bottle and tossed the remains into a nearby wastebasket. Drinking had never been one of his favorite pastimes, and he was not about to get into the habit of doing it. What he needed to soothe the grinding ache in his loins and the loneliness of his soul was a woman. But he needed the right woman!

She needs me, too, he thought with an arrogant smile as he pulled his trousers on, slightly tipsy yet. She sure does, but she doesn't know it yet!

Tamara couldn't get back to sleep; she tossed and turned. Restless, lonely, and plagued by a throbbing headache, she finally lay staring up at the ceiling, at the wall, the ceiling again, the other wall. Finally she turned onto her stomach and squeezed her eyes tightly shut.

She groaned.

She punched her pillow.

She lay on her side. Her back. The other side. Returned to her stomach not much later.

"Oh, my goodness, this will never do," she said in exasperation.

Frustrated and ready to scream, she wrenched her body upright and tossed the pillow onto the floor. It landed at the feet of the tall man watching her with some amusement, since he had felt this same way not long ago but had doused his frustrations in the worst way possible—drink.

Tamara saw him then, as the moon made a reappearance, its flickering rays revealing him. What she did not see was the lonely man inside Daniel Tarrant. He had been lonely as a child and as a young man growing to manhood, ever since his parents had abandoned him as a wee babe. Now he was a full-grown man, still lonely, but aware of just what it was he wanted from life, what he wanted to give the woman of his dreams.

"You are not a ghost," Tamara murmured, still not sure whether she was asleep or awake. She looked at him groggily. "You are really here, aren't you? This time it is really you, Daniel."

In the moonlit bedroom, Daniel nodded, still without speaking.

To Tamara he was like an approaching gale, a tempest, as he advanced on the bed. Her heartbeat accelerated, for his shadowy presence was wreaking havoc on her, awakening and inflaming her languid senses.

With one hand outstretched, only desiring her welcome, Daniel moved closer, shocking Tamara out of her passionate mood. While moonlight stained the man azure and gray, she shook her head and scuttled to the farthest corner of the bed, clutching the patchwork quilt around her.

"Please go, Daniel. I have been hurt enough to last a lifetime." She started to tremble and quake. "I do not want to be with you. I once loved you, but not anymore." An aching note in her voice, she added, "Y-you are too late."

The silence spun out, and Tamara swallowed

hard. If only he would say something! Instead he moved toward her, silent, catlike, menacing. Oh, Lord, the walk she remembered too well. Again she wondered. Are there two sides to Daniel or was the difference only caused by loss of memory? Why does he seem so different after a week's absence?

The flush in Tamara's cheeks darkened as the moon, peeking through the lace curtains, made a honeycomb of her sweet lovely face. By an act of will, she tore her eyes from Daniel's unwavering stare. When she spoke her voice seemed to come from far away—a distant place where she wished she could be at that moment! Her voice quavered. "Why do you just stand there and say nothing?"

If only she knew the effort it took for him to stand there without wavering to and fro! Damn the liquor! Damn himself for being foolish enough to have walked out on her so abruptly, to have cruelly left her more bewildered than ever. He had always done this to her. He had hurt *her* more than anyone else in his life.

Tamara's eyes flew to the closed door. "How did . . . you get in?"

Now he moved his shoulders in a shrug. "I rode in on my flying horse, Pegasus."

She shook her head. Pegasus? The winged horse that sprang from the blood of Medusa at her death. She knew that Daniel once read everything, including her Bible . . . but Greek mythology?

"Not funny," she said, still afraid she would reveal her excitement.

Her eyes grew round and luminous as Daniel reached across the bed to caress her bare shoulder, and she wrenched violently away from his scorching touch, pressing herself against the headboard, avoiding all contact with him. But she had already felt him, knew his caress. His hand was warm, not cold and clammy as his touch had been just the week before. Why is that? she wondered. Now his mere presence was endowed with enchantment.

"I want to lie with you, touch you, go to paradise with you, Tamara."

The smoldering flame she saw in his dark eyes jolted her. "I . . . I prefer that you do not sit here, Daniel," she said, her hand on her palpitating breast.

What is happening to me? I have never before felt this desperate kind of emotion! Maybe my memory has failed me and I have just forgotten. But why now, dear God, and not two weeks ago? Why is he affecting me so strongly?

Anxiety, like a swollen river, surged through her as the bed creaked when Daniel settled his weight on its edge. He then moved slightly, shifting his long lean body. Tamara's eyes closed, and she drew a single, sharp and almost painful breath. He was a twisting, beckoning flame, touching her heart as no other man ever had.

"How did you get in?" she asked again.

The warmth of his smile was repeated in his voice. "This is my place, Tammi. I own this boarding-house now . . . remember, I told you that. No, I suppose you do not, you were too angry as I recall."

Her mouth suddenly dry, Tamara looked at him as if she'd not heard him correctly. "You own it," she said, as if in a daze. Where would she go with Danny now? She had lived too long on her own, been the breadwinner for her little family. Now he was here to change all that. Why was she afraid to accept it?

Daniel went on as if she had not spoken. "Do you know how very lovely you are, huddled under that blanket like a scared little girl, all big green eyes and bare shoulders and long, luminous, buttercup yellow braids?" He wanted to free her hair, to see it flowing wildly about her shoulders, to rake his fingers through the wild silk of it and— "Tangle our bodies together until we are wrapped forever in paradise, in a satin cocoon," he said aloud, his voice like velvet smoke.

"Daniel . . . please."

"Please?" Drawing a finger across her chin, he only smiled sadly when she jumped at the contact. "Unusually squeamish and bursting with prim-and-proper nervousness, aren't you, love? I can take care with you, Tamara, and make you as peaceful as a balmy summer afternoon. You go about in a never-ending rush, don't you, lovely lady?"

Every line of Daniel's Indian-lithe body proclaimed his intention. He had not seen her or been with her in a long time. He, too, was bursting. But not with anything one could call prim and proper! He meant to take her this night, with or without her permission. A night of love was just the ticket for Tamara . . . Ice princess—or queen—something like that they'd called her at the Nicollet House. She was his. Always had been his woman. She would never escape that fact.

Daniel knew his skilled hands and lips, the pressure of his body, would wrest permission from Tamara even though her maidenlike heart remained

170

reluctant. Unwilling she might be for a time, but not when he was through bringing her body alive. Not after that.

Tamara stared at the man looming over her, on her bed, a bed no man had been in before. Not ever. She would be helpless, not because of Daniel's superior strength, but because of the treachery of her own body where he was concerned.

Even now she was aching for his caresses. His body arched boldly over her like the curve of a hunter's bow, pliant, trusty, carefully adjusted to fit her. But it was her resolve that he not know her that way until he made her his wife, for never would she live in sin again, and be hurt after he had his way with her and then walked away. He had done it before, but he was in for a surprise if he meant to use her again.

Seeing her clasp her hands protectively over her breasts, he caught her wrists, breaking them apart before she could close herself to him. His was an unbreakable grip, and he forced her arms down above her head on the pillow, pinioning them there.

"You cannot force me, Daniel," she hissed, defiantly, knowing there was no one to stop him.

"I thought there would be no need for force, Tammi." He freed her hands and turned his back to her, sitting on the edge of the bed. "What happened? You don't care for me anymore? How could that be after what we shared?"

Tamara thought he sounded genuinely bewildered, but so was she. "Care? You dare to speak about that to me? You who left me"—she was about to say with child but thought better of it—"you ask me to trust and believe in you? How many times did you come from your Indian mistress's bed to mine? From Helen's? *Care for you?* You no doubt have come fresh from one of your women this night, and with liquor on your breath to boot!"

She stopped at realizing what she had just said. She had not been kind, but had sounded like a jealous shrew! Still, she could not help herself; he seemed to be bringing out the worst in her.

Still frowning, Daniel turned and caught her hands. "That last charge, at least, I can prove to be false."

This time he showed no mercy, but with one hand held her wrists pinioned above her head while she pleaded to be set loose. With his free hand, he unbuckled his heavy belt with the huge hunting knife in it and unfastened his tight, black denim trousers.

Tamara squeezed her eyes shut and turned her face into the pillow in order to escape the reality of what was about to happen. She could not believe he would do this to her. No, she would not let him, even if she must claw his face to ribbons, this face that was a mask concealing so many personalities she did not know which was really Daniel's—the one from last week or the one presented her now.

"Tamara, look!"

Daniel's voice was rough with passion. When she would not comply, his fingers clamped on her trembling chin and he demanded, "Look, you little fool! Does a man come fresh from a whore in such a state?"

He swore in the Dakota language, but his voice crackled and broke with huskiness, with loneliness, with the need for her to believe him just this one time.

She blinked, forcing her eyes upon his body. A pulse rapped erratically in her throat as she yanked the covers back over her enflamed face. What was he doing? Was he truly insane, forcing such an indignity upon her?

Daniel drew a ragged breath. He was lost, he knew he would not have her this night, but he must prove to her that she was the only woman to cause this loving lust to stampede in his blood.

"Oh, Tamara, you must think me more animal than man, if you believe I could satisfy some grasping slut and still be ready to be a man to you."

From beneath the pillow came a whimper which sounded like "Leave me alone." But she had heard his words.

"Tamara, Tamara, if you will not look, then *feel!*"

She spoke in a broken whisper, *"N-no!"*

"My patience is worn thin, Tamara."

Reaching out, he forced one of her small, work-worn hands down the length of his torso, to the smoothness of a bronzed bare hip, to the nest of black curling hair from which his passion sprung erect and hard. Mewling sounds were coming from her throat. Daring much, she cast her eyes downward and blanched; but still she was enthralled and a little afraid of what she beheld. So much man!

Her heart skipped a few beats as she felt his quivering manhood beneath her fingertips. The look in her eyes stole Daniel's breath away. She was looking at him, and he loved to have her eyes on him. In that instant he knew he would make her his bride, soon, very soon. But he had to make it right this time. He had to leave her old-fashioned virtue intact this night.

"Oh my," Tamara breathed.

Daniel's laughter sent strong vibrations down into his loins. "Do you really think I have been pleasuring others this night, angel eyes?"

She made no move to answer. He was well aware that the question of his absence was still unresolved and weighed heavily on her mind. If only he could know the nature of the conversations she had had with the man who was so like him he could be a twin. It was apparent that the other had confused her just as much as he himself had.

Now Tamara opened her hand, though she had been desiring to stroke the silken manliness of him with the tips of her aching fingers. For shame! Mrs. Williamson would have clucked, had she read Tamara's evil thoughts. She was again overwhelmed by the sheer beauty of his tall, dark, male body. She closed her hand over him and wondered again how it was possible he had not hurt her more when they had made love. A quiver raced through her loins at the thought.

Daniel pulled away and Tamara was instantly embarrassed that she had held on for so long. "Oh! I . . . I should not have. What must you think?"

He broke across her sentence with a short laugh. "I thought we were discussing my sinful ways, Tamara, not yours. As if you had any to speak of. You are still an innocent at heart."

Remembering and already missing the feel of her cool hands on him, Daniel had to catch his breath. Then he fastened the front of his trousers.

174

His look was deep and hard, under control. "You did flatter me for a while, Tamara, but I am not that industrious that you could mistake me for a jackrabbit. I am a flesh-and-blood man." When she looked at him as if puzzled, he smiled poignantly. "I am happy you have remained the same, still the little lady. Unaware of all the joys ahead of you, those shared by a man and a woman." He was going to show her, stick with her this time, even if domesticity killed him. "What time would you like breakfast?"

Had she heard right?

Her eyes felt sandy from lack of sleep and she stammered. "Br-breakfast?"

"Of course. You know, the stuff you crack into the cast-iron skillet, the smoked crispy things from the back and sides of a hog, and the flat white squares you put butter and jam on, the black liquid we scald our insides with but love the smell of on the morning air?"

With a shy laugh, Tamara bit her lip. She just had to give him an answer or appear stuffy like Mrs. Williamson. She stared at the patterns of moonlight across his face. "Tomorrow is Sunday. I would like breakfast before going to church—seven A.M. But I will fix it. I always do, for the boarders, Danny, and myself."

"I want to." He glanced at her earnest green, moonlit eyes and for a moment envisioned the two of them walking the land together, pictured her constant awe at the wonder of love he could show her.

When he would have closed the door before going out, Tamara informed him in a whisper, "I like the scaldy stuff with milk, or with cream, when I have

175

time to take it from the steps and separate it from the new bottle.'' She stared at him briefly.

"I'll meet the milkman at the door by the crack of dawn and''—he winked—''I just happen to have brought my cream skimmer with me. Good night, Tamara. I love that name. All grown up. It suits you now.''

Then he was gone, not a sound in the hallway to tell of his passage. Hushed, Indianlike.

"Good night, Daniel.''

Tamara closed her eyes, wishing she could have but a glimpse into the future. Tomorrow, the morning, what would it bring on its dawn-white wings?

Confusion now hath made his masterpiece!
　　　　　　　—William Shakespeare

Chapter Twelve

Sometimes we can't see what we stand too close to.
Tamara was recalling My Emily's words as she went
straight to the cool icebox following church. After
giving Danny his drink of milk, she poured herself a
chilled glass of lemonade, then leaned back against
the white-painted cupboard, remembering the wonderful feeling that morning when she had come
down to find breakfast waiting for her, just as Daniel
had promised it would be.

Walking out onto the porch, Tamara paused to
smell the wild honeysuckle growing over the picket
fence. It sent forth such sweetness she felt she could
gather it to her in handfuls. Honeybees and hornets
and hummingbirds made themselves welcome here
in its blossoms. The honeysuckle vines flowed over
into the grapes, and the wire fence for the Concords
was beginning to fall over with the added weight,
tendrils of the vines having wrapped around every bit
of wire in it. Tamara had learned that it was wise—in
the woods, in the country, or in a city garden—to

understand the growing habits of everything, not only the wildlings but everything she planted herself.

Turning around and leaning far back, Tamara filled her lungs with the summer air. This was the season for roses, when ramblers burst into splendor: deep crimson, creamy ivory, and peppermint pink. The Silver Moon roses were such a pure, lovely white. Wild, they grew on stone fences, on picket fences, on trellises, and on the tumbledown sheds just outside town. What a glorious day! Sunday. The Lord's day. Clouds tinged with color seemed to have settled over the city. Heady. What was it William Shakespeare said? "A rose by any other name would smell as sweet." Tamara smiled playfully. If roses were called stinkweeds, she did not think they would seem to smell as sweet!

KeeKing Man poked his silver-frost head out the kitchen door, told Tamara that Daniel had left a message. "Said he had to go pick up some things at the Winslow Hotel, but he'll be back before you can miss him!" Sleepily, he turned to go upstairs. "Oh, Danny fell sound asleep on the sofa."

Tamara gave KeeKing Man a smile of breathtaking sweetness. "Thank you, Joshua."

The old man beamed from ear to ear, then mumbled as he climbed the stairs to go take his afternoon nap. "Ain't no one called me that in a long time." He shook his grizzled head, smiling. "Almost forgot that I had a first name, with that bonny lad callin' me KeeKing Man all the time. Joshua. Yep, the name fits all right . . . me, at the battle of Jericho." Smacking his lips, he closed the door to his room, hoping that Aldwin next to him would not

178

snore so loudly that afternoon.

With Danny asleep on the sofa in the living room, Tamara slipped inside and stayed where she was, enjoying the coolness of the house after riding in the surrey on this hot summer day. She recalled the conversation they had picked up when, following a delicious breakfast, Danny had gone out to sit with Aldwin and KeeKing Man on the porch. . . .

"Now, hopefully we can talk without any interruptions, especially from that dragon of a lady Mrs. Williamson."

Mixing a batch of oatmeal and bran cookies to be enjoyed later, Tamara smiled. "Laurine means well, really she does. She is just a little straitlaced, that is all."

"A *busybody*, straitlaced woman, that would more adequately express what she is." Tugging on her apron strings, loving the apple green dress she wore, one that displayed all her luscious womanly curves, Daniel went on. "I asked you before we were interrupted, who is it that has been telling you all these things about me?"

"And I must repeat: I believe your loss of memory has taken a turn for the worse, Daniel. You should really seek medical attention and advice, since you have become like a chameleon, changing from one week to the next. I suppose you do not realize this yourself but others do, believe me."

Pulling her away from the table where she had been whipping up the batter for cookies, Daniel placed his hands on her shoulders. "Look at me,

Tammi, forget the cooking for just a minute, will you?"

"Tamara," she corrected.

"All right, Tamara then." His voice was commanding and cool. "Tell me, do you see any scars? You said that I had one a week ago. Well, where is it?"

Tamara pressed her lips together before answering. In confusion she stared at him. "No. There is none that I can see; I told you that already." She gazed into the sapphire-black eyes impaling her.

"Well?"

She pushed at his arm. "I have to churn the butter and awaken Danny from his nap."

"You are avoiding the issue, Tamara. Where do you suppose the scar went? The place where all good little scars go? Look at me, Tamara, and look at me well. Am I the same man you talked with two weeks ago, ate with, walked with, possibly even made love with?"

She slapped his hands away from her waist. "You know this past month we have not made love!"

"Ah. Good," he said with mock severity. "That's something off my chest anyway. Well then, what *did* you and I do? Play cards? Kiss? Stroll about in the moonlight and hold hands? Tamara, love, what did we do a few weeks ago and why, tell me, did I disappear, with my little scar, and then reappear without that flaw? Can you explain that to me, little lady?"

"Oh"—Tamara sounded shaky—"you are regaining your memory, aren't you? Oh please, Daniel, say it is true, that it is not something of a more serious nature. Please."

"It's serious, all right, but not in the way you think."

A look of cold determination came to his face. "Tamara, sit down. We have to talk about something, very seriously, and I want you to open your mind to the events of this past month. You must think hard—and clearly!"

"Daniel?"

His eyes darkened with emotion; he loved hearing her speak his name. "Yes."

Her eyes were like gray-green marbles as she stared up at him. "You are frightening me."

"Ohhh," he said at length. "That's just a start."

"What do you mean?"

She tried to look away, but he held her gaze. "Never mind. I don't want you passing out on me before the morning is out. Go back to your work and then perhaps . . ."

Tamara loosened her apron and tossed it onto the counter. Then she smoothed the skirt of her Sunday dress. "I am finished for now." Placing the batter into the icebox, she gathered Danny from the porch where he'd been playing with a red rubber ball beside a dozing KeeKing Man. Having sent one more look at Daniel, she set off to church looking remarkably prim and proper.

"Don't you want me to join you?" Daniel called impishly from the porch, one hip resting indolently against the porch railing. "We could be wed, if you feel up to it, while we're there."

She gave him no answer, just marched to the surrey she had gotten ready forty-five minutes before.

181

Securing Danny beside her, she set off at a neat clip, the shining rump of the horse baking under the sun like a ripe chestnut.

Daniel grinned at the old man who'd come up beside him and called again to her, "Didn't know you could drive such a fancy rig!"

Over her shoulder, she called back, "It does not take much doing, Mr. Tarrant," she emphasized the name. "All you need is a little muscle and some brains."

"Gettin' feisty, ain't she?" KeeKing Man said, clicking his tongue. "Never seen Tamara so uppity to a person."

Daniel was still grinning. "I guess I bring out the worst in her, old man." Turning to face Englebritson, he asked, "Would you say I have changed very much during the last couple of weeks?"

"Well . . . I guess you could say so." As his eyes roved over the tall frame, he blinked repeatedly. "For one, you never hardly gave me a second look—that was when you first come here, let's see, about a month ago, I'd guess. The last couple days, though, you been really different. Think Tamara notices it, too. Yep, you are a changed man."

The old man's grin seemed to say he held a secret. Curiously, Daniel stared into the faded blue eyes. "Why do you say that? Is there something significant in this change?"

"Yeah . . . yeah," KeeKing Man slowly responded. "Know what it is for sure now. Your speech is different. You used to sound kinda like an Indian when I come up on the porch and heared you talkin' to Tamara. You sound more learned now." Tilting his head back, he peered along his nose at Daniel Tarrant. "Yep, and your hair is blacker than t'other's."

"What do you mean? Hey, wise old man, you are saying that we are not the same?"

"Nope. But you got a twin, young feller. You be the good; t'other's dark as a fallen angel. His soul is empty, and I could tell he was tryin' to get Tamara to fill it up for him. She could never do it, though. No one could, see, 'cause he closed the doors a long time ago. Better be careful, Dan, your twin is out to get you, but mostly he's after Tamara and the kid." He gave a tap to Daniel's arm. "Always knew a shining knight would come and rescue her someday." Nervously he coughed. "I mean . . . a fierce and dauntless warrior, a noble hero. She deserves it, the little lady does."

Daniel was embarrassed and a little shocked by what the old man had just revealed and predicted. He tried to hide a smile. "I will take your warning to heart, Joshua Englebritson." He watched the old man puff up with importance. "You are very much like a friend of mine we call Grandfather. He lives on a reservation near the Minnesota–South Dakota border. He foresees many things, and I'm going to visit him in the near future to discover more of my past."

"Good." Joshua winked. "You're a wise lad."

With that, the old man with the squeaking shoes walked tiredly into the house to go and rest in the shade of Emily's parlor. He still thought of it as such. But now this house had a man in it, a real hero. It was about time. Tamara had been too long without the warrior of her heart, he thought, easing himself down into the coziest chair in the room and immediately nodding off beneath the colored print of an old white house with yellow roses climbing the trellises by the door, a girl in Colonial costume on the front steps. On the wall across the room was an oil painting of Rebecca at the Well, and another of cud-chewing cows knee-deep in pink- and white-blossomed clover.

Now Tamara waited for Daniel to return. She had just put Danny to bed for the night after she had spent hours playing with him, and she went quietly through the house, missing My Emily dreadfully. An early twilight gray was creeping down the stairs of the boardinghouse, creating eerie shadows and distortions. Or is it, she wondered, going downstairs, all in my mind?

Might it be that she was asleep and would awaken soon to discover Daniel Tarrant only a dream again, to realize he had never truly returned? Why did history seem to be repeating itself? When would Daniel become reality? When could she welcome him home to her heart to stay?

After putting away the last of the washed and dried dishes, the remaining food already having been placed in the icebox, Tamara stood still at last to remove her apron and look over to the door to find Daniel lounging casually against the frame. Her faint smile carried a touch of sadness.

She was keenly aware of his dark eyes, and she at once forced her confused emotions into order. "How long have you been standing there watching me?" she asked.

He had been delighted to observe her, slipping into the house as he had done before. From outside he had seen the gaslight go on, sending a yellow glow through the lace curtains to where he lingered outside, feeling warm, as if he had come home at last after the lonely days and nights in prison.

"Tammi. You are lovely, like a white blossom kissed by the moon and the falling dew."

Tamara blushed. "You are waxing poetic, Daniel Tarrant." Yet, if she remembered right, and she did, he used to be something of the versemaker on those lovely summer nights when they had sat outside his rough-hewn cabin in the woods.

"I love being here with you," he said softly, tenderness welling inside him and wanting to burst out and enfold her. As if he'd read her thoughts, he went on, "One day soon I would like to take you back to the cabin—as my bride this time."

Now he is going to ask me to marry him, she thought.

She sighed. "I know you want me to marry you, Daniel, you said so over a week ago, but I still haven't decided what is best."

Oh no, he thought, not that too. The man must work fast, asking her to marry him, but not fast enough, for she is still an unwed mother. The thought wrenched his heart, what she must have gone through without a man by her side to protect her and Danny from harm, and to make sure they had enough to eat, clothes on their backs, a nice place to live. He groaned inwardly at the thought of her

185

having had to bear so much all by herself, even the birth of their son.

Daniel was determined to see her happy once again, maybe for forever, if she would let him. "Tamara, come out onto the porch with me, we'll watch the fireflies flicker and sit in the swing where the moon can't find us."

Laughing and suddenly gay, she brought out a pitcher of lemonade, which she placed on the porch table along with two tall glasses.

June bugs bumbled against the parlor window and moths blindly sought the light. Crickets sang a song of a white summer night, warm and still and hauntingly lovely—like Tamara, Daniel thought to himself as he sat at a proper distance from her on the swing. Proper, that was the name of the game now, for he realized that to get close to Tamara, as before, he would have to tread slowly, carefully, so as not to frighten her away. She was not a frantic child in search of someone to cling to as she'd once been. Now she wanted and needed someone solid, unmovable as rock, a shelter from life's storms. He prayed he could become her rock, her fortress, her mainstay.

Taking her hand in his, he slid a little closer and began. "Someone has been assuming my identity, Tamara." That was all he said, meaning to let her reflect on those words a few minutes.

She stared at him, unblinking, and pondered this strange bit of news. "I do not think I follow you, Daniel. What are you trying to say to me?" Even as she spoke, Tamara felt a sinking feeling not unlike dread.

"I have been trying to tell you that . . . I am not the

186

same Daniel of two weeks ago. That was someone else," he stated simply, a grave look settling on his dark face.

"What!" she responded in surprise.

"Yes." He nodded. "I'm afraid it's true."

Panic rose within her when he looked at her so seriously, but she fought it down.

His fierce sapphire-dark eyes seemed to bore into her for a moment. Then he gazed at her face, his eyes settling on her mouth when her breath caught in shock. "Think back, Tamara. Recall the first time we met. Then place us in the moonlit woods together, under the stars, and in the bedroom of the Olsky house." He believed those were the only two places they had made love, once in the woods and twice—or was it three times—in their friends' house. While Jenny and Harold had been away visiting, of course, otherwise he doubted it would have happened.

Her mind traveled back two years.

Choose me, Daniel. Not her . . . not Helly. She is a slut . . . take me, please! She had been dreaming, afraid Daniel would take Helly over her. For days following that dream she had walked about in a trance, Daniel's deep voice touching her heartstrings and drawing her closer to him. As she washed dishes, her gaze had encountered the deep blue one coming across to her in the Olskys' kitchen, eyes like feelers wrapping her in a silver cocoon fashioned of gossamer threads, making her a prisoner all over again.

The time she had fainted, when a cool hand had brushed her forehead . . . The dark form above her had hovered—a man, his creamy shirt intensify-

187

ing the darkness of his bronze skin. She had responded acutely to each sight, sound, and movement the tall, dark male made. She remembered her thoughts: You are mine, Daniel Tarrant, and soon you will know this.

Until that time she had told herself she would conceal her love from him. He had been confused by her iciness, and this was just what she had wanted, to have him wondering what she was up to, what she would do next. She had stared at the black hair the lantern light turned blue.

Daniel's hair, she thought now, blue-black like it used to be.

Daniel's eyes, the eyes I loved to drown in, to lose myself in their liquid depths.

Daniel's smoky voice.

Daniel, the man . . . How lovely his name is.

The darkness of his face deep in thought, with its slanted cheekbones and eyebrows. Eyes, deep, almost blue-black. Sometimes troubled . . . as they are now. . . .

Tamara was growing warm as memories stirred in her. Daniel was watching her closely to determine her mood, to see if she had come any closer to the truth in the minutes she'd sat looking dreamy and spellbound while her mind had sped back in time.

His voice broke into her reflections. "Think of all the times we spent together, the good and the bad, in the cabin." As he looked at her, she nodded. "Now, look at me real hard, Tamara. Am I the same man you had conversations, perhaps even more, with?" Suddenly he yanked her to his chest, his lips lowering to move over hers languidly, earth-shatteringly. He pulled away, looking at her flushed face, the shock of the kiss in her eyes. "Am I the same man of two weeks ago, the one you were with under this same roof?"

Tamara could only stare at him, her mouth still tingling, her heart a wild tom-tom in her breast. "You *are* different. Your kiss is not the same. Your hair is blacker. Your eyes . . . My God, Daniel, please tell me what is taking place. I do not understand all this." She spread her hands on her lap, almost knocking over her lemonade glass. She did not say so, but this kiss was his *old* kiss, one that enraptured, not the sterile kiss he had pressed upon her weeks ago!

Not the same . . . not the same. Not—

Tamara's face was pale and drawn in the white moonlight as she rose from the swing to lean against the porch railing.

Standing behind her now, Daniel went on ruthlessly. "And you'll not want to forget the scar, Tamara. Remember, I had that scar last week, and it's gone now." He moved to look into her eyes. Moonlit, they were like freshwater pearls. "How can this be, Tamara? How can I have a half-moon scar one week and not the next? Where is the flaw now, Little Oak?" He used the name his friends had called her.

Desperately she tried to think, to no avail. All thought seemed to have fled. She felt Daniel's hand clench her shoulder more tightly. He let go of her then. "I am truly sorry," he said quietly and sadly shook his head. "I did not mean to hurt you."

Her shoulders lifted slightly. "This is so crazy," she whispered, half-afraid to look at him.

But she did glance up at him, her eyes wide with an

unearthly fear, and despite himself Daniel felt a chill prickle the back of his neck. It was frightening to have someone running around who looked so much like him he could be his twin.

Out loud Daniel said, "You have heard that everyone has a twin somewhere in the world, someone who looks so much like the other person it's frightening. In my dreams lately I feel as if this horrible phantom follows me and at every turn I will run into my twin. It is like looking into a room whose mirrored walls reflect the same familiar face. I only wish the man would stand up before me. But he never does."

"Daniel . . ."

Softly, so softly she murmured his name, he thought first he had been hearing things, possibly even dreaming on this moonlit night. But she said it again.

"Daniel . . . Oh, Daniel . . . I . . ."

She looked up and found him staring into her moonlit eyes. The words died on her lips, and she seemed unable to pull away from his gaze. It seemed chains bound them together, fast and hard. His hand reached up to touch her cheek, and his fingers ran, lightly as a butterfly's wings, across her face, her eyes, her forehead.

"Is there anything else different about me, Tamara?"

"Yes, many things in fact. You are more *you* now that we have spoken together like this. But last week—the past two weeks—you were a total stranger, and I could not understand why."

"Exactly so!"

"You mean . . . there are two of you? How can that be possible? You would have to be identical twins!"

"Right again. I have a twin somewhere out there, but I don't even know if he is of my flesh and blood."

The stars glittered wildly overhead as they studied each other, seeking understanding. Daniel's eyes burned like dark blue flames as he gazed at her soft, quivering mouth, realizing that the dam was about to burst on her rigidly held control.

Her sobs reached his heart, and he moved to take her gently into his arms. "Hush, Tamara . . . hush, darling," he whispered, stroking her silver-honey hair and pressing her to him as if protecting her from the world.

Finally, at long last, he could feel her crying subside. He took her small, lovely, wet face in his dark hands to turn it up to look at him. "Tamara, Tammi, my moonlit maiden. How I love you, have always loved you."

"Oh, Daniel!"

Slowly he leaned down before she could say more and kissed her lips; and to his intense pleasure he found them responding through her fear and confusion. Parting her lips, she raised herself to meet the kiss. He kissed her again and again, his kisses becoming more prolonged until he gently opened her mouth with his.

Daniel's kiss sang through her veins this time, and the gentle friction of flesh on searing flesh sent currents of desire through Tamara. His tongue thrust deep in a half-gentle assault. His hand moved under her dress to flatten against her hips and thighs. Then he pulled her to his chest, exploring the hollows of her back with his other hand.

"Ah, Tammi, oh Lord, I want you!" he said in happy desperation.

A fire was growing wildly within him, raging out of control. Easy! he reminded himself. Go easy! Don't scare her away now that she has come this far with you.

"Do not be frightened of our passion," he whispered against her ear. "I promise to be very gentle with you, because I realize it has been a long time since we bedded. And I haven't been with anyone either," he murmured as an afterthought. "I mean it, Tammi. There has been no one. Give to us what we both need now, my sweet."

Tamara knew she should stop him, but she did not want to. She felt only that their hearts and bodies were made for each other, as if they were already bound by the holy rites of matrimony. Still, if only they were now man and wife!

Her head rolled backward, her eyes closed, and when his fingers found the roundness of her breast an involuntary shudder racked her slim frame.

Daniel kissed Tamara's lips, her creamy throat, her flushed face, her closed eyes, as his eager hand slid down along the soft curve of her hip, found the bottom of her apple green dress, and slowly, slowly crept upward, his fingers leaving a scorching trail against her bare skin, seeking out the core of her being.

He was desperate now. To feel Tammi, all of her, naked flesh against naked flesh, this was his most fervent desire. "Tammi," he whispered hoarsely, tugging upward on the hem of her dress. "Take this off."

A dreamy look in her eyes, Tamara roused and studied him. This was Daniel, truly Daniel, her love!

"Oh . . . it is good with us, Daniel. Just like before. So good it hurts."

"Yes, angel eyes," he replied, kissing her again, "and better yet to come."

Quickly Daniel pulled his shirt off, and she gazed at his wide chest, the skin as dark as that of his bronze face. He smiled and reached for the tiny buttons of her bodice; her hands stilled him.

"Wait."

His eyes were glittering midnight blue, like ice on a pond. "What, my love?"

"Not here. Over there, in the grass, by the trees, like the first time . . . outside under the moon."

"Oh, God!" he ground out, closing his eyes, his breath coming in short, quick gasps. "Come on then!"

On the other side of the garden, where the misty purple Concords grew in wild profusion, Tamara and Daniel paused like breathless children playing a nighttime game.

Again he reached for her dress and she pulled it up over her head, tossed it aside, and knelt, naked in the cushiony grass, then looked up, waiting for him to come join her.

Lowering himself to the grass, Daniel groaned. *How white she is, how pure and perfect and white, like a pearl-colored angel, silken-tressed, glittering, marble-limbed . . . and mine, all mine for the taking!*

Watching her every movement, her shy smiles, her expectant gaze, he rose to his knees, quickly

193

unfastened his trousers, pulled them off with near-violent tugs, and kicked them away.

Soft grasses cushioned their love nest. Reaching for her, he held her full against his hard body, soaking in the feel, the warmth that was Tamara, the woman. Her hands crept slowly around his back and lingered on the corded muscles there.

The smell, the warmth, the strength of him felt so good, so comforting to her. This was love in its purest form. She shivered as his hands ran expertly down her back and slowly caressed her buttocks, pressing her tighter against him.

Now he was kissing her again, with ardent feeling, his mouth more insistent, exploring the slim column of her arching neck, going lower and lower until she gasped aloud when his seeking lips found her swelling breast and lingered there.

A raging torrent filled Tamara's head when his fingers lightly stroked her breasts, then held them like precious captured doves while his grazing and lapping tongue came and went, his emboldened mouth returning after feeding on the honey at her lips and spreading their nectar until she was slick all around.

He was breathing heavily against her skin in his eagerness to mount the glorious creature that was his this night, and she thought surely the roaring in her head would deafen her.

Now he was embracing her feverishly, bearing her down onto the dew-kissed grass, the winking fireflies lighting their special nest while the starry firmament encircled it in nighttime beauty.

Tamara thought in that instant she would explode

before he took her. When he moved between her legs, carefully entered her, and she felt him begin to move against her, she shattered into a thousand fragments, as a tree explodes when struck by lightning.

"You are supposed to"—he sucked in his breath—"wait for me. . . ."

Daniel clenched her tight with his knees, and her name was torn from his throat in that moment of ecstasy. A moonlit haze surrounded them as they surrendered to the contentment that settled in their souls. Then he was still, his thrusting past, his arms holding her in a fiercely possessive grasp, his cheek resting in her dew-damp hair.

Tamara did not want the moment ever to end, the aftermath of their mutual need. She wanted to stay that way forever.

They lay there spent, midnight moonlight filtering through treetops that stirred softly in the summer night. In the near distance they could hear an owl hoot, detect the damp smell of rich soil in the garden not ten feet away. The garden, Tamara thought, where just a few days ago I gathered new peas, lettuce, and strawberries. A bothersome buzzing came closer and closer. . . .

Daniel slapped at a pesky mosquito. "Ah." He laughed huskily, with all the sensuousness of a virile male who's just been deeply satisfied and is pleased and happy to be alive. "I got the little sucker."

Feeling happier than ever, Tamara playfully returned, "Oh look, now they are coming after us with lanterns!"

"Those are fireflies, my love"—he squeezed her hip—"not mosquitoes."

She looked at him in mock seriousness. "If you insist."

"Oh, I do. And I also insist that you make love to me again."

An involuntary moan escaped her lips when she tried to turn her head, to rise and run, and in a breath's span he had captured her and had her beneath him once again.

"Now," he said, his breath hot against her ear, "now the loving really begins!"

For thy sweet love rememb'red
such wealth brings . . .
　　　　　—William Shakespeare

Chapter Thirteen

The white summer night stretched on, as if
endlessly, for the lovers who lingered there in the
downy grass, hands clasped and fingers entwined.
Like happy children, Tamara and Daniel had crept
upstairs in the house to check on their child, then
back down to the kitchen for a snack of cheese, crusty
bread with leftover fried chicken, and lemonade,
which they took outside and ate on the moonlit grass,
sharing a midnight picnic. Playfully they had
applied to each other a strong potion of rubbing
alcohol to ward off the invasions of pesky mosquitoes. Now they had returned to the porch swing,
in order to be closer to their child in case he should
awaken in the wee hours, his window being directly
above the moon-washed porch roof. Daniel's eyes
had grown soft as blue silk. He was content; he knew
what he wanted out of life now.

Tamara sighed, happier than she could remember
ever being. "You have never talked of these things we
are sharing this night, Daniel. At least, not this

deeply ... Tell me of your past, what you can remember of it. I realize it has always been a thorn in your side, not knowing who your parents were and where you really came from. All you remember is the village you stayed in when you were a little boy ... and before that, the man who named you Tall Thunder."

"I've no remembrance of when I learned I was alone in the world," he said into her hair. "As far back as I can see into the pale mist of my childhood I have been Daniel and I have been alone. No mother or father to remember. All I did was accept the state of being alive." Almost unconsciously, his hand squeezed her knee, then moved slowly to the inside of her thigh to caress her.

Tamara's eyes closed in quiet ecstasy. They had made love for hours, and yet she would say yes if he asked for more of the same.

"Who knows how far into the past memory reaches?" she murmured, gazing at the moon, loving the feel of his hand possessing her tenderly, languidly, slowly as if they had all the time in the world. "Are the familiar faces and incidents of our known past—far back—all tucked into memory, never to be pulled out and examined?"

Daniel wondered too: Does memory have its ghosts ... wistful phantoms of reality that once existed? Something that the heart has known and touched and loved, but is unable to grasp in the light of day?

He kissed the curve of her neck and shoulder, loving to hear the wispy sigh that escaped her lips. Then his voice came to her out of the empurpled night shadows.

"When I was a child such flashes often came to me—as to most children I would suppose—maybe as I lay in my small buffalo robe hazy with drowsiness, or on my back on the friendly and familiar earth. Fact and fantasy flowed in and out of my mind like clouds offering up pretty scenes and pictures."

"Yes, I remember such moments too," Tamara said, hoping Daniel would continue to open up and speak of his past. "I was a fairy-tale queen or princess, yes . . . a princess in a gossamer gown dancing in a magic circle"—she laughed—"ringed by splendid and gallant courtiers pursuing me with careful and devoted attentions. Or I became a snow white dove flying against the blue sky, looking down from the heavens above. Oh, I believe these fantasies are felt by every child, and have come to us all."

"You would have made a beautiful princess . . . but were you a bird, a dove, I would have been sad and would have tried my best to turn you back into a lovely princess." While his fingertips skimmed down the length of her arm, then back up, he went on speaking of his past. "There were other pictures, some that had no connection with anything I ever remembered happening to me. Two of these came more often than others. One was a room, if you could call it that—a small place with one window. In those early dreams it floated across my mind's eye. But, for some reason, this picture left me feeling alone and desolate, small and lost. Even when I shut the picture out, the sense of desolation remained."

"How sad, Daniel. I do not think I have ever felt that way, and I suppose it is because I always knew

199

who my parents were, and that I had a brother—though he is gone to the angels and I will never again see him in this life.''

They were silent for a time, enjoying each other and the night.

Tamara let Daniel ease her up so that she lay back against him in the swing, his body supporting hers. ''Daniel? What was the other picture that came often to your mind?'' she wanted to know.

''That was the one I never shut out because it made me happy. It was of a couple . . . the woman with black hair, but never really clear. But I knew them better than anyone I had ever really known. The man's eyes were somehow sad and lost-looking . . . or they might have been the woman's, I'm not certain. I knew her smile and the touch of her soft hand when it held mine. One thing was clear, she brought me a sense that I was loved and cherished.

''That memory of her—and of the man—came to me mostly in the night, when a child's hungry heart is eager for that which it has been denied . . . the feeling of being loved.''

''Your parents?''

''Maybe. But how? I was only a wee babe, I think. I don't know how old I was when I was set on the church doorstep. . . . Or was I left at an old man's house? I can't even remember all the stories now.''

''They must have loved you, Daniel, dearly, those that placed you on that doorstep. I had a dream of you once—actually more than once—and in the one I recall most an Indian woman appears after I have fallen into a bottomless pit.''

''That sounds like a nightmare,'' he said, caressing

the top of her head with his chin.

Staring out at the forget-me-nots that were a pale, almost white-blue in the moonlight, Tamara recounted the dream, seeing it in her own mind's eye. "There loomed a flame-lighted wall before me and a long, deep passage with eerie drafts blowing between its high sides. Who can say what that deep, dark way meant?" She shrugged against him. "Just a passage into my dream, I would guess. The cold wind—I could actually feel its icy fingers in my dream—was blowing upward over my body and under my skirts.

"When the deep passage came to an abrupt halt, I walked out onto flat moonlit acres. Then I stood, bathed in the beams of moon, but not alone as I had first thought. There was music, strong and quick—drums, they must have been—and I seemed to float forward on the primitive beats. I entered a level space, with oddly shaped tepees surrounding me. Suddenly, a woman of proud bearing stood before me. Her hair glistened like soft black velvet under the moonwashed skies."

"My mother, this must be she." Daniel's voice was soft and low. He tensed, waiting for Tamara to reveal the rest of her dream. Somehow he had to hear it, *he must*, for it suddenly seemed very important to his happiness and Tamara's.

Tamara thoughtfully went on. "She was young, but not as dark-skinned as most Indian women—"

"Go on, Tamara. Forget the color of her skin."

"I . . . I am trying to remember, Daniel." She pressed her fingertips to her temples. "She was taller than most Indian women, with two shining black braids hanging down over shoulders covered with soft tan doeskin."

Daniel sighed impatiently as Tamara continued to describe the woman. "Hush, Daniel. This might be important," she chided. "Just listen. In my dream she could have been entirely white except that her forehead was very high, her dark brows were too straight, and the bones of her cheeks were too prominent to be a white woman's. She stared at me through the dream's whirling mist . . . and her eyes were not like an Indian's eyes at all, yet they had their own kind of darkness and fire. Blue fire, Daniel, the kind I often see in your own eyes."

"Was there anything else you can remember?"

"Yes. Her blanket was hunched up in back as if she carried a papoose."

Curiously Daniel asked, "Only one papoose?"

"I believe so. Yes, I could see no other, and no one else was holding a babe of the same age."

"Tamara, is there more to this night vision that could help me see into my past?"

"You must let me finish before you interrupt, otherwise I could forget it all of a sudden. That has happened in the past when I have tried to recall the scene. In the far corner of the mist stood an Indian . . . talking to a burly white man who stood next to a tall tepee decorated with many snarling wolves. Something passed between them . . . words . . . a look. The Indian was now threatening the woman with raised fist, and her body seemed to sag, as if he'd already struck her before the blow fell. . . . Actually I never did see him hit her."

Eagerly Daniel urged her to go on, to reveal more before her glimpses of the vision departed. "What

202

happened next?" His warm arm came around her, the flat of his hand resting on her belly.

She cleared her throat softly. "The Indian man reached for his knife, but the white man was quicker and the blade floated to the earth . . . yes, ever so slowly in my dream . . . harming no one. Two names were muttered in anger, and in my dream I thought they sounded foolish. . . ."

"What were they? Try to recall, Tamara. This is very important to me." His long, lean fingers pressed against her pulsating softness, inside her under-things, and he smiled at her gasp of pleasure. "Think—*hard*."

"Oh! Tall Thunder was one!"

"The other?" he breathed out the question against her ear, his fingers beginning their tender coaxing. "I must hear the other, Tamara!"

"Ohhh . . . it was Strong Eagle!"

Daniel said the name over and over, repeating it under his breath. "Can you tell me any more?" he said, knowing she was stirring eagerly to his touch.

"Yes." She stretched languorously, enjoying the luxurious pleasure his touch was producing, re-laxing. "The white man . . . he gave the Indian a push, and the woman saw her chance to flee. . . . She rose on wobbly legs, taking care not to lose the precious papoose—"

He found her silky wetness, asking, "There is still only one papoose?"

"Yes . . . only one that I remember from the dream. . . . Then they doubled themselves low and ran. They walked a dark road, finally going through an equally d-dark village. . . . *Oh!*"

"Who, Tamara? The Indian woman and the *white* man?"

"I . . . I believe it was the white man . . . *yes!* of course. He gave the Indian a push so she could find the moment to escape. . . . After passing through the village, they c-climbed high wooded h-hillls . . . and finally turned in at a g-gate! They were afraid of something. Maybe it was what they were about . . . about to do!"

Daniel's voice was deep, sensuous, pure black velvet. "And . . . that was?"

"With no thought but for the safety of the wee child, they left him in his blanket on steps that led to a garden. The moon poured its color on the river"— she hurried on, eager to fully enjoy what he had started—"as the two fled . . . and a wolf howled. . . . That was the end of the dream."

"Wolf," Daniel murmured thoughtfully. "The wolf howling at the end of your vision means something . . . so do the wolves painted on the tepee you saw. They could have to do with the name of the Indian, the one who threatened the woman with raised fist."

"The Indian . . . your father?" Tamara ventured.

"Perhaps. I know I am half-white, anyone can see that. But perhaps the burly white man is my father."

"I had another dream, shortly after the first one, but not on the same night."

"Tell me about it, Tamara. I hope to discover something significant about my past from your visions. I must learn if I truly have a twin brother, one who is hiding from me now."

Tamara snuggled back against his chest, hoping

for more of his indulgent caresses. "The child in my first dream returned in the next one, bigger and older than before. A boy this time, no older than ten or eleven. He wore long hair as black as a raven's wing, a scarlet headband tied around its unruliness at his forehead. His skin—your skin—was as brown as a hickory nut, a copperish hue brushing your slanted cheekbones." She smiled ecstatically as he entered that first tiny bit, his brown fingers moving in a slow circle that tormented and made her beg for more with swirling thrusts of her hips. "Your brows were sc-scowling, ahhh, giving you the fierce look of a . . . of a . . . young hawk . . ."

Daniel drew his head back and laughed at her pleasure. "Can you remember how I was dressed at this later time, my love, hmmm?" His head lowered, and his moist tongue pressed into her ear. "What kind of clothes was I wearing?"

"Your leggings were quilled doeskin . . . uhmmm, oh yesss. But the eyes—oh, Lord, the eyes—ah! ah! ah!—they were blue with flint-gray clouds that moved—oh blessed Mary!—moved mysteriously, sadly in them. . . . So sad and alone!"

He hugged her fiercely as she cried out, shocked at what was happening to her out on the porch swing. *My Emily's porch* . . . swiiiinnnggg!

"Not alone now, love, not ever again," he murmured as she joined him in a wonderful ecstasy and, finally, blissfully tired, was carried upstairs to her bed.

Tamara rested her shoulder against the door

frame, listening to Daniel tell their son a story. Becoming involved in the picturesque legend, she left off drying the dish with kitchen linen and became still. The look in Danny's large dusky eyes was dream shrouded and full of delight. As Daniel got to the ending, the boy's pudgy fingers lazily picked at the black hairs on his daddy's arm.

Looking up and seeing Tamara listening, Daniel began a new tale. "Many springs ago upon an island in the middle of White Bear Lake a young warrior loved and wooed the daughter of his chief. He had loved her since they were small children, and it is said that the pretty maiden loved the warrior. But Wolf had again and again been refused the maiden's hand. The old chief alleged that Wolf was no brave—and his old consort called Wolf a woman!"

Danny chuckled, patting his father's arm. "Woman." He pointed to his mother. "Mom!"

"Yes, Danny, Mommy is a woman. Now, let me go on."

"O-kay."

"This island was visited by the Indian band for the purpose of making maple sugar. The sun had again set upon the "sugar-bush," and the bright moon had risen high in the night-blue heavens when the young warrior Wolf took down his flute and set out alone. Once more he would sing the story of his love. The mild breeze gently moved the two feathers in his headband, and as he mounted the trunk of a leaning tree, damp snow fell heavily from his feet.

"No," Danny said trying to say snow.

"Yes. As Wolf raised his flute to his lips," Daniel went on, "his blanket slipped from his well-formed shoulders and trailed on the snow beneath the tree. He began his hauntingly wild love song. Soon he felt cold and, as he reached back for his blanket, some unseen hand laid it gently across his shoulders.

Danny blinked up at his father. "Who?"

Daniel smiled across to Tamara who still listened. "It was the hand of his love, his guardian angel. She took her place beside him, and for the time being they were happy. The Indian has a loving heart, and his pride is as noble as his freedom, which makes him the child of the forest." Daniel smoothed back the wisps of hair from Danny's forehead, and the child leaned back, blinking, listening.

"As the legend goes, a large white bear, thinking, perhaps, that polar snows and dismal winter weather extended everywhere, took up his journey southward. He at length approached the northern shore of the lake, walked down the bank, and noiselessly made his way through the deep heavy snow toward the island. It was the same spring that the lovers met, and they had left their first retreat and were now seated among the branches of a large elm which hung far over the lake.

"Afraid they would be found out, the warrior Wolf and the maiden talked almost in whispers. To avoid suspicion they were just rising to return before they were missed, when the maiden uttered a shriek which was heard at the camp. Running toward the warrior, she caught his blanket, but missed her footing and fell, bearing the blanket with her into the great arms of the ferocious monster.

Danny called out, "Monner . . . *Mon-ner!*"

"That's right, Danny. Monster." He looked up at

207

Tamara and they both laughed and laughed until she wiped her happy tears away with the dish towel.

Holding her aching sides, Tamara pleaded, "Then what happened, Daniel?"

"And then . . ." Daniel paused. Putting on a serious face as Tamara moved into the room, setting dish and towel onto a table, he went on. She tried not to break out into another round of laughter and sat gingerly on the edge of the rocking chair, waiting to hear the rest.

"Now, we left the maiden in the arms of the monster. Shhh, Danny. Instantly every man, woman, and child of the village was upon the bank, but none brought weapons. Cries and wailings arose from every mouth. 'What should be done?' In the meantime this white savage beast held the breathless maiden in his huge grasp. The deafening yell of her lover, the warrior, was heard above the cries of his tribe. Dashing away to his wigwam, Wolf grasped his trusty knife, returned quickly to the scene and rushed out along the leaning tree to the spot where his treasure had fallen. He sprang, with the fury of a panther, upon his prey.

"The beast turned, and with one stroke of his paw brought the lovers heart to heart, but in the next moment the warrior plunged his blade into the beast's heart, and the dying bear relaxed its hold."

"There must be more?" Tamara said.

"Yup. That night there was no more sleep for the band or the lovers, for young and old danced about the carcass of the dead monster. The gallant warrior was presented with another plume, and before one more moon had set he had a living treasure to add to his heart."

"Did they marry?" Tamara asked. "Did they have children?"

"Yes." Daniel's eyes twinkled as they ran over her from head to foot. "Their children for many years played upon the skin of the white bear, and the maiden and the brave remembered long the fearful scene and rescue that made them one, for Kis-se-me-pa and Ka-go-ka could never forget their fearful encounter with the huge monster that came so near sending them to the Happy Hunting Grounds."

"So, Daniel, what is the moral of the story?"

"Store*eee!*"

"Well, Danny." The man turned back to the child picking at a button on his shirt. "You should never go anywhere without permission. And when you do go, be sure to take along some protection so you'll not have to run back home to get some."

Tamara shook her head, saying with a smile, "But, Daniel, children cannot go around carrying knives with them. They might hurt themselves or some other child."

"Not if they learn how to use them. Knives are useful, even in our day and age. For cutting down a twig, whittling, and for making a fire if one should get lost and be far from home."

"Making a fire, in Minneapolis?" Tamara laughed. "That would surely cause Mrs. Williamson's tongue to wag. The whittling part is fine, but I really don't think Danny is going to come across any bears or monsters, and he really won't be needing a knife for some time."

"Monners!" Danny said, rolling his eyes. "Wanna

get down." He squirmed off Daniel's lap, racing toward the kitchen. "Gonna get t'knife and get a monner!" Like a flash, he disappeared into the hall.

Daniel and Tamara exchanged wild glances, then rushed off after Danny, just in time to hear the kitchen-utensil drawer grind open.

Before suppertime arrived, a new knife rack was installed high above the reach of any adventuresome, *monner*-slaying children.

Part Two

I love thee to the level of everyday's
Most quiet need, by sun and candlelight.
                    —Elizabeth Barrett Browning

Chapter Fourteen

There was a sudden explosion on the riverboat plying the Mississippi to Louisiana! *Boom! Boom!* And *boom* again!

As the flames shot into the air and sparks showered down along the shoreline folks came out of their shanties, black faces shining, eyes bulging. Even some poor whites came out to see what was going on after hearing the tremendous blasts.

A loud hiss and a cloud of steam came from the mammoth boilers, and the paddlewheeler creaked and groaned like a sea monster in demise. Arching and twisting, she sank into the water, the burning wood hissing as soon as it touched the Mississippi.

Stealthfully, he moved with graceful and powerful strokes to the mossy, willow-tufted bank, his head hardly noticed above the undulating gray waves. He could have been a part of those waves, so cleanly and unflaggingly did he swim. Upon reaching his destination, he paused to glance around from the concealment of the overhanging bank, then slipped,

213

clean as a water snake, up into the cover of the slender weeping willows.

An evil look came into James Strong Eagle's eyes as he looked into the canvas bag he tore from the string around his waist. He smiled then, a smile that matched the dark force moving in his eyes. Jewels, many of them, winked up at him. They rested amid the soggy currency he'd also lifted before he'd eradicated the riverboat.

"All mine." He chuckled deeply. "All mine . . ."

"The *Lindsey Jo* went down!"

"She exploded and sunk!"

"There any survivors?"

"Not on the *Lindsey Jo*. They be all goners!"

"How'd it happen? She was such a well-built riverboat, the *Lindsey Jo*."

"Waaal, like a bright star, that floating palace had her heyday, and now she's sunk like a waterlogged hunk of driftwood and can't shine from where *she's* at!" The riverboat captain who now spoke had been in competition with the *Lindsey Jo* and its owner. "Heh-heh . . . all gone. Too bad, I'd say, too bad."

"All dead . . . There ain't no one alive to tell just what did happen."

"Someone set off a dynamite charge, maybe a jealous husband whose wife was on board with her lover?"

"Wonder what did happen. . . ."

Along with the men who worked on the riverboat, another man was patronizing Gray's Riverfront Tavern this dusky afternoon. Deeply shadowed,

James Strong Eagle lounged at the rear, nursing a tall glass of foam-topped beer. He still felt the chill of the river's swirling waters in his bones . . . and he was fortunate to be alive after the long icy swim. He was an excellent swimmer, but the current had almost taken him, the undertow trying to draw him to the watery grave of the others on the *Lindsey Jo.* Bad spirits in that river, he thought. And they had tried to take him under, to steal the life from him. But that would never happen, not to James Strong Eagle.

He had slipped into his room behind the tavern, being careful that the proprietor did not catch his soggy entrance. Days beforehand, he had stowed his dry clothes in the dark, musty riverfront room he'd taken and paid for, a week in advance.

His plans had gone well. He felt no remorse for the dead of the *Lindsey Jo,* no pity for those that survived them, friends and family. Not even the children who would be left without parents troubled his heart. For him, the dead might never have existed . . . especially one by the name of James Strong Eagle. He had a brand new identity. He was Creek now—James Creek. He was sure his real name would be among those listed in the newspapers come tomorrow.

All the papers up and down the Mississippi carried the story. One account read:

A TERRIBLE DISASTER!

*All passengers killed by an explosion
on the steamer* Lindsey Jo!

The boilers of the steamer *Lindsey Jo* exploded at 7 P.M. today, just after she left St. Louis, or, as some have deduced, there was foul play. To create an explosion such as this one would have taken a very large load of dynamite. Sixty-five persons are presumed dead, as no survivors have come forth. . . .

A list of names followed, whereby it appeared that among the sixty-five dead were the captain, first mate, second mate, and second and third clerks; also the pilot and several members of the crew. The names of passengers on the ill-fated *Lindsey Jo* followed.

It was a gray, gloomy morning. Inside the boardinghouse, oatmeal cooked on the stove and aromatic coffee boiled in counterpoint to the rain spilling outdoors.

"Look at this, Daniel."

Tamara placed a copy of the Minneapolis newspaper on the breakfast table, then sat down to sip her coffee and watch as he read the page spread before him. Soon, she knew, he would look up, an astonished expression on his face, as she had when she'd scanned the article on the way in from the porch.

A few minutes later, Daniel was frowning when thunder cracked at almost the same moment he exclaimed: "What the devil!"

Tamara nodded, saying, "I knew you would react this way."

She watched him pace the kitchen floor, unaware that his young son raced a toy wooden gig with painted red wheels between his moving feet, exclaiming gleefully as it came out on the other side.

"Be careful . . . ! Danny's playing at your feet!"

Daniel's eyes contacted Tamara's for a split second, and they were both thinking the same thing about James Strong Eagle.

He then looked down at the boy playing with his toy gig. "Oh, I'm sorry, Danny."

Reaching down to scoop the boy into his arms, Daniel shifted him up and around until Danny was riding atop his strong shoulders. The two-wheeled carriage was forgotten now.

Danny squealed at this fun, spreading his hands flat on the crown of his father's dark head. "Dahh! I wanna go higher, Dahh! Pwease!"

"I don't think so, Danny, you are high enough."

Daniel's eyes caressed Tamara's and hers caressed his right back. How she wanted him!

Tamara sat back, smiling and so very happy these days since Daniel—the real Daniel—had come back into her life. He made every day glorious and fulfilling, and in the evenings . . . well, they had not made love since the wonderfully romantic star-studded night out in the garden. This time she was going to make sure he married her, the honorable thing to do!

She stared at him, helplessly aware of his masculinity. On this rainy day that kept them all indoors, he was wearing faded jeans that molded to every muscled inch of his long, lean legs; his turquoise shirt was unfastened four buttons down, to reveal part of his smooth coppery chest. A silver buckle, beautifully worked like an Indian charm, was set with a huge round of polished turquoise that glinted when it caught the glow of the gaslights set in sconces about the kitchen. A small silver pendant hung from a leather thong around his neck, below the shadowed curve of his jaw. He was man, all man.

Daniel swung his boy down into the high chair and set buttered toast down on his tray. Then he turned to Tamara. She was still waiting for him to say something about the terrible disaster of the *Lindsey Jo,* even more so about the name appearing at the bottom of the list.

He sat down and shook his dark head. "James Strong Eagle. It had to be the very same man, perhaps my twin, who came here posing as . . . me! Now . . . dead?" He clenched the hand resting on his knee. "But I wanted to—oh, how I wanted to—do something to him for causing you such confusion! What, I can't say. I would have enjoyed watching him die slowly, but it would be like . . . like— oh Lord I know this sounds crazy—like killing a part of myself . . . if he truly is my twin. Going by that dream you had, he would have been of my flesh and blood. I can't understand it, Tamara, how you had this night vision of me and my parents . . . maybe even of my own brother."

Tamara smiled, gave him her hand as he reached for it. "It is because I have always loved you, Daniel, you are a part of me for ever and ever." Her voice was soft and low and gentle. Womanly now. "You and I can never truly be parted, not by prison, not by others, not by death even."

Daniel stared at the woman he loved. She was beautiful, as always. Today she was dressed in a

218

white dress, pristine, airy. Eyelet embroidery decorated its scooped neckline. It was a ladylike little dress, making him wonder what she had on underneath it. Shaking his head, his equilibrium restored, he looked at her again, with love in his eyes, and knew that she had been saving this dress for a special day, for he could tell that it had never been worn before; it was so new, so fresh, so right for their reunion.

Lifting her hand, Daniel kissed her gathered fingertips, the back of her hand, her wrist; smiling a crooked smile when Danny shook a piece of toast at him. "You'll get your kisses later, kid. Right now your mama and I want to make eyes at each other and . . . uhmmm, kiss . . . and kiss, and kiss some more. Then we might even indulge in a more exciting form of entertainment."

"Enough of that, Daniel!"

Tamara shot up from the table, scooting around the edge as he threatened to rise and come after her. Danny's fawn brown eyebrows rose and fell at his father's antics, while he slammed his toast up and down on the little tray. Pieces of it flew here and there until he sat holding only a tiny crumb in his buttery fingers.

"Da . . . fun-eee!" he cried, ending on a high-pitched screech. Then he rubbed tiredly at his eyes and sighed loudly, slumping down in his high chair, down, down, until Daniel came around to carefully lift him out.

"Time for your nap, Little Bow," he said softly, pressing the child's head into his dark neck and inhaling the mingled smells of baby sweetness and

219

honeyed butter. As he carried Danny, he trembled at the thought that he might have died before he'd ever seen and held his son. He could have married Tamara and saved her so much in the way of loneliness. He could have been there for her, to share the joy of learning she was pregnant, to share in the child's birth, to watch Danny grow from baby to toddler. He never wanted to miss this experience again, that is, if she got pregnant again, and if he had anything to say about it, she would in due time!

"Little Bow?" Tamara questioned softly as she came up behind them in the nursery. "I have never heard you call Danny that before." She smiled. "I like it; it fits him, Daniel."

"I know," he said, tucking Danny into the big blue crib. "Now"—he took her hand—"let's go downstairs and have our talk, but first . . . hmmm, come here."

His hands enveloped her waist, tightening as he pulled her toward him, and she laughed, sliding her own hands up his arms to his shoulders. She gloried in the feel of the smooth copper skin that rippled under her palms.

"Eh, Dan?" It was Henry Dade calling from the top of the stairs. He had no idea they were in an upstairs bedroom.

Daniel sighed, letting Tamara loose while she smiled with a playfulness he'd never seen in her. From the bedroom, Daniel responded quietly. "Yes, Henry, what is it?" *No doubt hungry again . . . These older folks seem to have two stomachs.*

"What time's supper?" Henry asked, louder than necessary. He was still unaware that they were in the bedroom.

Daniel looked at Tamara. "What time's supper?"

She lifted her elegant shoulders in a helpless little shrug. "Same time as usual."

The younger man's voice went out to the older. "Same time, Henry."

Dade smacked his lips. "That's all I wanted to know." Then he shuffled back to his roomy apartment. Never looking right, left.

"Now that Joshua, Henry, Aldwin, and Danny are tucked away, how about our talk?"

Tamara's soft amber brows lifted. "What talk?"

"You'll see."

The fabric of his jeans pinched him as he walked, and he passed a hand over the front, pulling at the tight denim to ease the restriction. Her eyes flew upward, and he grinned helplessly into her face. He knew she had noticed his state of arousal. He was just glad the others could not see so well; then again, one never knew about those crafty old folks!

Feeling the rush of heat that gathered between her legs, Tamara went with him down to the living room, then joined him when he settled his tall, lean frame into a corner of the sofa, beckoning her to come snuggle there. "Daniel . . . what did you want to talk about?" she asked again, resting her palm on his trouser leg, feeling the hardness of muscle and bone there, but mostly muscle and tendon.

She felt a hot redness creep up her neck when he cupped one of her firm young breasts. "You blush like a red currant berry," he said in a deep voice filled with love and emotion.

Her legs turned to butter when she heard his

221

words, and she felt him stiffen uncomfortably when she accidentally ground her elbow against his groin. "Oh . . . ! I am sorry, Daniel, but when you put your hand on me I reacted in surprise." A little imp inside made her smile. "Are you all right? I did not hurt anything important, did I?"

Daniel growled against her throat, nipping her skin. "I don't think so, my love," he said in a high-pitched voice that sounded much like a woman's. His tone then became deeper. "Mmmm, I love the smell of you, the feel of you, everything—even down to your bright little toes. Oh, how are *they*, by the way? I remember you burned the soles of your feet in the fire at the Larson place. Do they bother you anymore?"

"Yes, at times. If I walk too much or work too hard." She toyed with a buttom on his dark blue shirt. "But I can take it; I am used to it by now."

"Ahh, Tammi, Tammi." He had lapsed into calling her by the old nickname. "You should not have had to work so hard! It angers me that that bastard Strong Eagle, if that was he, had me sent to prison for crimes he committed."

"Why would you think that, Daniel, that he sent you there?"

"It's plain for anyone to see, Tamara. He looks so much like me we could pass as identical twins. I was sent to prison for a crime I knew nothing about. Maybe this Strong Eagle is a thief. Did you never believe that could be possible? I mean, just think, he shows up after I am in prison for a crime I didn't commit."

"Almost two years later, Daniel?"

"Well . . ." Daniel shrugged. "Maybe it took him that long to find you." He toyed with a glass-domed compote filled with nuts.

"I hardly think so. Then again, I did leave the cabin and come to Minneapolis shortly after I thought you deserted me once again."

He hugged her to his chest. "Did I desert you that many times, love?" Forlornly he gazed into her sage green eyes.

"Yes." She thought for a moment. "Really, when I think of it, what claim did I really have on your heart? It was yours to do with as you pleased."

"No, never that, Tamara. My heart has always belonged to one woman: you. It just took me a long time to realize you were the love of my life. I was a fool, Tamara. Can you ever forgive me?"

"Of course, Daniel. You never have to say you are sorry when you love."

He chuckled, and his lips bussed the crown of her bright head. "I'll bet there were many times you were not so forgiving and you wanted to strangle me. I could not fault you for that, Tamara."

She brushed her forehead against his shoulder. "No. I'll admit I was filled with anger at times, but I never wanted harm to come to you, Daniel. I just . . . just wanted you to come find me. My heart was broken to think that you had finally deserted me for good. I thought it best to release my hold on you and go elsewhere to find a life for myself and my . . . our son."

Daniel gazed down on Tamara's hands. They were resting in her lap, primly, but were still close enough to his thigh to send warm currents through him. She was truly a full-grown woman, a complete, self-reliant person in every respect. She had proved herself a shrewd breadwinner and a homemaker. So, what did you expect? he asked himself. She had been forced to turn her domestic talents to making money and had not sat idly waiting for some man to come along and provide for her and the child.

If only I had wed her long ago, Daniel reflected, I would be established as a lumberman, with wife, child, and a loving home graced by the most beautiful woman alive. But now . . . ?

He studied her glorious assets: lovely alabaster skin, tumbling masses of silver-honey hair, and many more. For all her delicate beauty, Tamara displayed little interest in the usual feminine concerns, otherwise she would have been bombarded with gentlemen callers. She seemed bored with the things women of her age were in the habit of getting caught up in, and that was because she was a woman of single-minded determination. She did not need all sorts of friends to amuse her, either. She was a pure jewel. A rare one. He was not about to let go of her.

But, Daniel thought, something in those clear, sage green, direct eyes has remained unchangeable as the sun and the moon. Love. Love for him. Love he had almost lost.

"Tamara," he said now. "It is time we married, don't you think so? We have a son, you know."

Her voice was soft and low. "I . . . I know that well enough, since I have taken care of him since he was born."

"Born of my loins and your heart, Tamara. He should be with his father, with us, all together. Do not be bitter now, love. There is no more time for that. We must plan to be a family."

"Yes, I know that, Daniel. I am just afraid sometimes."

"You have nothing to fear. I own this place now so we will have a steady income. I also own the cabin up north; we can make that bigger someday. I have a job at the mill any time I want to work there. And the two people I love most in the world are here—right here."

"You do love me, Daniel?"

He turned her face up to his. "Of course, sweetheart. I love you and I always have; it just took me a long time to realize it. Remember, the time in prison gave me a second chance, a look at what was missing in my life."

"Prison. The other you, your twin, mentioned that he had been in prison, but he lied about so many things. Oh, Daniel, all this time I had really believed you had lost your memory. Strong Eagle really had me fooled, and I shiver at times to think of what he could have done to us."

"Dangerous he might be. But, really, Tamara, did he have you all that fooled? Think of it."

She pressed her pink lips together, then released them. "Yes, more like confused."

He groaned as she unconsciously placed her hand upon his leg again. "Let's make love and then get married in the morning." He kissed her cheek, nibbled at the corner of her sweet rosebud mouth, wanting to tumble her onto the soft Wilton carpet.

"No, Daniel. Let's get married and *then* make love

again. We have lived too long without God's blessing. I want it to be right for us this time, so that nothing will go wrong."

"Aha. You are more wise now than in your youth, I see."

She twisted to look up at his serious face. "Was I really all that young to you, Daniel?"

"Yes, and I was afraid to make love to you, so tiny you were." His smile was devastating. "But I knew what you wanted me to do, sweetheart."

"Daniel!"

She put her head on his shoulder. "Is this time for real, Daniel?"

"It is real, sweetheart."

"I am happy then."

He studied her peaceful face, as he had in his mind's eye before drifting off to sleep in his prison cell. There he had often found himself dreaming of being home once again, under warm and sunny skies, and of strolling arm in arm with a fair-haired girl in white. His Tammi . . . Tamara now.

"Well"—he stood up—"I think we should get the ball rolling, don't you?"

"G-get married? Now? Today?"

"Why not?" he shouted, sweeping her into his arms in a joyous hug that took them spinning into the parlor.

She laughed delightedly. "Oh, Daniel. At last!"

"Yes!" he shouted right back. "At last!"

"Daniel!" she sang out. "Daniel!"

He swung her around and around, her knees trussed up against his. Things were looking infinitely brighter. He impulsively squeezed and kissed her again. "Well then, let's go into town for a marriage license." He laughed aloud. "Today is the beginning of our new life. Let's begin it right. We'll wake our son immediately. He should be the first to know that his mother and father will be married today!"

There is no believing a liar, even when he speaks the truth.
—Aesop

Chapter Fifteen

Traveling along the prairie outside St. Cloud, Jay Creek had decided it would be less dangerous to go by that name instead of James. At the moment he sat in the shabby kitchen of a tumbledown house. The dwelling was boxlike, filthy, and ill furnished. A slatternly half-breed woman moved about the small room, serving the three men around the table, indifferent to the conversation they were having. With a huge wooden spoon Wadena plopped beans and greasy tortillas onto their dishes, then moved away with a shuffling, slow gait.

Horse Face, who went by the name Raymond Horse in the white world he so despised, tipped back his chair to pat his huge stomach and belch loudly. His hair, unkempt and dirty, hung in tangled black strands about his long, ugly face, which resembled that of a rawboned horse. His body and his face seemed ill matched, as if he'd been given a head that belonged to another person entirely.

The third man was of medium build, pimple-faced

and mean-looking. His name was Rufus, just Rufus, and his eyes narrowed to nasty slits as he passed some news on to James Strong Eagle, news that his friend in crime would relish hearing.

"Overheard some talk in town the other day, Creek." Rufus did not make the mistake of calling him James. "A bit of dirt about Daniel Tarrant. Seems your twin was almost found guilty of the murder of a paleface a few years back."

Strong Eagle's face darkened as he watched Rufus's dark fingers toy with a water-spotted glass of tequila. "Who was this man?" he snapped curtly.

"Man by the name of Ole Larson."

Wadena chortled, wiping the back of a meaty hand across her mouth. "Hah," she said again, hating any name with "son" on the end of it.

Horse Face spat off to the side and swore. "Larson. Very much paleface, white hair, that one. It is better he is dead."

"Shut up, Horse." Strong Eagle gritted his teeth. "Tell me more, Rufus. I wish to know everything that happened between Daniel Tarrant and this Ole Larson. Is this paleface Larson not the one Tamara Andersen was living with—him and his family?"

"It is so," Rufus answered, while Wadena sloshed more tequila into his glass. "Daniel was never cleared. Not really. Never saw the sheriff about the matter like he was supposed to. Don't even know if the sheriff has gathered all the facts yet about that case."

"Not gathered the facts . . . after two years!" Strong Eagle thundered. "He never went after Tarrant?"

"Well," Rufus drawled, sneering, "you should know, James—Creek, I mean. You were going about as Tarrant for a while, sniffing around his woman's pretty skirts. Hell, you might've got yourself tossed into prison right beside—"

"No!" Strong Eagle pressed his fingers into his temple to ease the ache there. "They knew Tarrant was already in prison. Maybe this is why he stayed there so long."

"I do not think so." Rufus peered over the rim of his dirty glass. "These men said Tarrant was never caught and proved guilty because he disappeared. Get my meaning?"

"You mean I did the bastard a favor?"

"Sort of," Rufus answered; then he added, "But not really."

James's eyes glittered. "This is so. Now I must make sure my twin gets sent back to prison for the murder of this Ole Larson."

"How you gonna do that?" asked Horse Face, half-inebriated by now and sick to his stomach from mixing the greasy fare with strong liquor.

Strong Eagle abruptly stood. "I will think of something."

It has to be soon, he thought, because the longer Tamara is with Daniel Tarrant the harder it is going to be for me to pry her away from that man. Once Daniel was out of the picture, he would have to work fast to get her to hate and distrust him all over again, and that would not be easy since she had once been very much in love with Daniel. But will she see through my new appearance? James wondered.

"Watch out you don't get yourself tossed into the

coop!" Rufus called out the door.

"Well, Rufe, if I go, you go with me." Strong Eagle glanced over his shoulder through the moth-eaten screen door. Lower now, he said, "But I do not think I will be caught. I have a new name."

"And a new look," said the sneering Rufus as he moved away from the door frame he'd been leaning on. "Looks ten years older, he does."

Strong Eagle's black hair was shorter, and he wore a western-style hat. He had been forced to buy new clothes since he had put on a great deal of weight, which puffed out his face, made it shiny, and distorted his usually handsome features. He even sported a potbelly and wider—padded—shoulders.

All in all, James Strong Eagle was not the same man. He was now Jay Creek, dangerously over-weight and paunchy, which made his heart pound at the least bit of exercise. Still, he told himself, no one would recognize him in the folds of fat.

One man would have known how very dangerous indeed Strong Eagle's foolish game was, and he was Chief Wolf Pass, Eagle's stepfather. At the moment, miles away to the west in a hidden Indian village, the chief was waiting for his shaman to return with the vision he had gone off by himself to seek. It should tell Wolf Pass what he must do with the secret he had lived with so long, the old bitterness that was killing him. That would kill Strong Eagle also, for the younger man's hatred was more powerful even than his own. . . .

. . . a power that would kill those he loved most.

After experiencing his vision, the shaman returned to the leader of the Dakota to tell him what the Great Spirit had revealed. "Learn to forgive," the holy man advised Wolf Pass. "For with bitterness in your soul, you can never be happy. Thus spoke the Great Spirit."

"What must I do?" asked Wolf Pass.

"You must seek out the husband of your late wife, Lady Slipper."

Wolf Pass's eyes were blacker than midnight. "Gallagher. Father of the twins. My dead wife's lover. I hate him. You know this."

"I have seen this vision, my chief. Your other son is called Tall Thunder, Daniel Tarrant. He lives with a woman so fair she is like a white dove."

"They are not my sons," Wolf Pass growled angrily. "I care not for him and his woman."

"How do you know the sons are not truly your own?"

"What is this?" Wolf Pass blinked in the sunlight glancing off the stream running near his village. "Strong Eagle has blue eyes, and so his brother's must be that same color. Long ago I sent Strong Eagle away when he came to me in the hope of forever staying among our people in this village. I told him then he is not my son. How can this other one be my flesh and blood when Strong Eagle is not of my loins?"

"You loved your wife, true?"

"This is so," Wolf Pass said, beginning to see the shaman's meaning. "You are saying I must love them as I loved her while she was living?"

Wisely the shaman responded, "Strong Eagle is the

evil one who seeks to destroy Tall Thunder. He has already done much to hurt his twin. Strong Eagle is a thief and a murderer. He would have Thunder's woman for his own and has already sought to achieve this."

Wolf Pass sadly shook his head. *Why should I care what happens to either of them?* he seemed to ask himself.

"You might wish to see Lady Slipper's grandson?" the shaman said, then fell silent.

The old chief looked up. "Grandson? Whose son is this?"

"Thunder's own, born of the white woman the People call Little Oak. Cat-Face says she is very beautiful and kind."

Shaking his gray head, all Wolf Pass said was, "I cannot love this evil one."

The shaman shrugged. "You will do what you must. Thunder is in torment because he knows not who is parents are."

"Where does Tall Thunder, this Daniel Tarrant, dwell?" Wolf Pass wanted to know.

"He lives in a place called Laughing Water City, 'Minnehapolis' and I have learned in my vision that he calls his son Little Bow."

Wolf Pass's eyebrows shot up. "My own name in childhood?"

"It is so."

Wearily Wolf Pass sat down upon a log, his leathery face wrinkled around his eyes as he squinted into the sun. "Strong Eagle must be kept from destroying his brother. Are there others involved in Strong Eagle's evil scheme?"

"There are. One is called Horse Face." He waited for Wolf Pass to grunt his dislike before he went on. "The other man is known as Rufus, a very bad man who will do anything for coins in his palm. They are all thieves of the worst kind. My vision says they plan this evil even as we speak. They seek to steal all from Thunder, and Strong Eagle wishes to have the white woman called Little Oak. Then there is the grandson of Lady Slipper to think about. What will be his fate if Strong Eagle's plan is to succeed?"

With a wave of his hand, Wolf Pass dismissed the shaman with the words, "As you say, I will do what I must."

"It must be soon."

Wolf Pass did not reply. *I believe Tall Thunder to be a strong man*, he thought. *He will come here to congress. With me.*

I know a bank . . . where ox-lips and the nodding violets
grow. . . .

—William Shakespeare,
A Midsummer Night's Dream

Chapter Sixteen

The wedding day had arrived. It was to be a private
affair. A neighbor by the name of Mrs. Grant, Mary
Louise, had come to stay at the boardinghouse, to
take care of Danny and the elderly folks while
Tamara and Daniel raced hurriedly off to be wed at
the most romantic spot in Minnesota: the Falls of
Minnehaha which had achieved worldwide fame.

They stood, arm in arm, gazing often into each
other's eyes while the water tumbled and roared,
pitching and foaming against the rocks, spraying
upward like silvery ghosts, and the minister had to
speak loud to be heard above the awesome din. The
roar of this immense volume of falling water was
often distinctly heard at St. Paul eight miles away.

As they said the vows that would make them man
and wife, the waterfall glistened in the wonderfully
scenic background, spray shooting up in the sunshine, the thundering cataract a sullen roar in their
ears, the beauty and sublimity of the scene impres-
sive. Arleen stood by as witness and smiled while she

dabbed at her moist eyes with a lace hanky.

Earlier that morning, Daniel's gaze had immediately fallen on Tamara's gown that was almost floor length. Made of a soft green material, silky to the touch, it accentuated her narrow waist and lovely, fuller breasts. After being helped into her beautiful gown by Mary Grant, she had piled her shining blond hair on top of her head, and now several spun-silk tendrils curled about her face framing it so enchantingly Tamara's beauty rivaled that of the Falls.

As she smiled radiantly while speaking the vows, Daniel felt very proud of the lovely woman beside him, and he assured himself that he was doing the right thing, the desired thing, by marrying her. "Part your lips, love," he murmured close to her ear. And she did. Oh, God, he desperately wanted to make love to her.

At last the happy couple had given themselves into the state of holy matrimony when the minister concluded the nuptials. The bride was now Mrs. Daniel Tarrant, the fulfilled woman she had sought to become ever since that wintry day she had first encountered Daniel during that sleigh ride through the northern woods.

The newly married pair said their goodbyes to the minister and a dewy-eyed Arleen, then hurried off to the St. Charles Hotel where Daniel had earlier gotten them rooms for their two-day stay.

Their honeymoon had begun.

He carried her upstairs while onlookers smiled

from the foyer of the St. Charles. Kicking open the door after he had managed to unlock it with the hand supporting her back, he found his other hand had become all thumbs. She buried her flushed face in his neck after he set her down and secured the door for the remainder of the afternoon. Then he turned with her in his arms, so that they faced their room. It was nicely decorated, with velvet-draped windows facing the street, and at that moment the whistle of a steamboat could be heard coming off the river below.

"Mmm-mm, something smells wonderful," Tamara said, looking across the room to the big bouquet of roses, white mostly with a few pink ones here and there, and baby's breath.

He whirled his wife around in a dizzy circle, and she panted, not entirely from dizziness. "You are beautiful," he said with adoration.

"I am happy you think so, Daniel," she said and her breath quickened.

Daniel lowered his head to brush his hot cheek against hers, then nipped an earlobe playfully. "I want to kiss every gorgeous inch of your velvet flesh." He smiled provocatively. "Every inch."

She moved her hips closer and gasped at the hard feel of his arousal, and when he took her lips she breathed a stream of pure pleasure into his mouth. Whisperlike kisses, pure and golden, fell against her face and throat while he stood there moving slowly, grinding, driving her mad with his teasing hips and thighs. He gently stroked and caressed until her eyes became heavy lidded. Her dusky pink peaks were already taut beneath the silky bodice of her gown, standing to attention against the hardness of his chest.

Tamara moved back a little, tilting her head up. "I am hungry, Daniel." She smiled. "Famished."

He chuckled deep in his throat. "And so am I."

"For food," she said, and laughed.

His tongue outlined the sweet bow of her lips, and he stopped to gaze into her soft green eyes. "For honey," he said, "and meat. Love food."

"Honey?" She moved away from him in a lovely feminine motion. "Meat?" she asked coyly, as if she did not understand his loveplay fully.

"Come here and I will show you." A wave of his long-fingered hand indicated the good-sized bed awaiting their pleasure. "Of course, love, our table has been set for us to share. Why don't we go and sit— I mean lie—down and begin our meal. I can't wait to eat." He paused, his face flushed with desire.

Tamara whirled away in a gauzy green cloud, letting her hair down as she spun in an enchanting circle, feeling as if a fairy godmother had touched her with a magic wand. One arm was flung wide, and her head was tipped to one side, making her hair a golden spill all around her delicate shoulders and down to the middle of her back.

Daniel's eyes watched. Enraptured and aflame, he was like the hummingbird who comes on flashing wings to feed upon a flower in the garden . . . on one special white flower. A waxen lily, pale, wholesome, lacelike, and sweetly womanly.

Her perfect globes of flesh swayed in a gentle motion as she bent to brush out her long blond hair. "Sweetheart," he murmured, still watching her, "you are much more than my dreams led me to believe." His tan fingers rested on the brass bedpost.

How he wanted her.

And at that same moment Tamara turned and ran into his arms, tossing the brush aside. They fell onto the bed, as one. Undressing her quickly, as quickly as so much clothing would allow, he lowered his thick lashes and stared. Now, clad in only a camisole and simple lace drawers, she was a long-legged princess with high, firm breasts and hips that were snow white.

When the last bit of cloth was on the floor, Daniel lowered his head while her legs were still bent in a compromising position. He laid his palm flat on her chest for mere seconds and felt her heart pounding, then kissed her, and feeling near to desperation, she arched up to press into that moist contact. He took her into his mouth to taste her and she cried out, lurching upward. He felt her arms tighten around his back and gave her what she wanted, his tongue thrusting into her in darts of intense pleasure.

"I want you," he said, lifting away.

"And I want you," she panted.

"Now?"

"Now, Daniel, now."

"At once?"

"At once!"

Not bothering to remove his own clothes, he undid his fly and entered her warmth, tenderly, fully. Thick lashes lowering, he closed his eyes, telling himself he was home, finally home, where it felt so good to be. He was with the woman of his heart, his soul, his very being.

Where his fingers had been warm, then hot, they

now seared into that part of her that became pliant under their tips, his palms, his knuckles even, as he lifted away and then returned, his eyes locking on the thatch of darker blond hair. . . . And now he felt himself begin to quake.

His finger gently probed and found the warm womanly swell. Then the throbbing began inside her, like a fully unleashed storm, and when his fingers slid further she cried out in that first promise of fulfillment.

When her breath became ragged and labored, and she gave a deep shudder and cried out while convulsive movements wracked her, Daniel let go.

They rested for a time, breathing endearments between them, touching, brushing lightly, nibbling, licking. She was rising again, moaning softly for him to join her in her desire. After he had guided her hand to close it about his hard shaft, he shivered as though in a red-hot heat. She was like a white flame wrapped about him. Quickly he reared over her like a ready stallion and, with one bladelike plunge, came into her, filling her. She was still very small, and her muscles tautly clutched his manhood.

"Daniel, Daniel, I love the feel of you inside me," she whispered.

That was his undoing. One last surge brought them to the ultimate in bliss. She saw him gazing down at her, his white teeth a flash of brightness in the softly illuminated bedroom. He was smiling like a triumphant warrior who has just claimed his prize and is exulting.

Daniel's dark head fell back, and he rolled onto his side to rest, still joined as he drew her with him. He caressed the gently sloped valley between her achingly lovely breasts, mentally likening them to twin doves perched on a soft hill.

"God is smiling down on us at last," she told him, seeing where his sooty blue gaze rested.

"And," Daniel said, his palm cupping her rib cage, "I am smiling at my woman—my own at last."

Soft moonlight spilled into the room, bathing the milky paleness of her body in the silver rays of nighttime's lover's lamp. Her face and throat were brushed with a sprinkling of silverdust as she looked up, loving what she saw—Daniel. This man . . . now her beloved forever. Her wonderful mate. Her husband.

Nothing would ever go wrong again.

Taking a basket filled with cold chicken, two loaves of crusty bread, chilled butter, slices of swiss cheese, and a chilled bottle of sarsaparilla, they set out on their honeymoon picnic. When they sat down near the river's edge, Tamara found she was starving after their activities of the night before. Daniel grinned as he watched her butter three slices of the bread, one after the other, then devour two chicken legs to his one breast.

Their appetites satisfied, they strolled along the river, talking about the "good old days" while the sun poked in and out of lacy clouds curtaining a pure blue sky.

"The good old days were actually not all that long ago." He chuckled. "Considering how young you still are."

243

"Still, they are the olden days to us, Daniel, the times we remember from our youth. Life was difficult, to say the least. The first home my father built was a sod hut dug into the ground. Then came a cabin with clay chinking between the logs. Sometimes the chinking fell out, the unsealed cracks letting in rain, snow, or even winter winds. And the Larson house was not much better. More than once, Kristel and I sat with our backs to the fire while winter winds howled outside, holding hands with Valda and Sigrid to keep warm, wrapped in shawls or blankets."

Daniel nodded in response to her chilly tale, reminiscing with her. "While the coffee froze in front of your nose," he added. "I remember the floors were just hard-packed earth, but it was home, such as it was."

"How did you build the floor in your cabin, Daniel?"

"With split logs. I tarred the round sides and set those in the ground." Blue-black eyes met misty green ones. "They formed the flooring."

Her mind wandered back in time again. "You made your own furniture, if I recall right."

Tamara's words seemed to amuse him. "A one-legged bed with two sides built into the corner of the room. The mattresses were sacks filled with corn husks or marsh hay, resting on cords and wooden slats. I fashioned the fireplace of wood and stone, lined it with clay."

"We did all our writing, knitting, and sewing by the light of the hearth fire," Tamara recalled.

"Kerosene did not come into use until the Civil War."

Daniel chuckled low. "Some people hesitated to use the kerosene then because it was very explosive; then it was discovered that adding salt to it made it less so."

"I know. I also recall my mother Meri and I stitching our own dresses, and the boy's and men's shirts and pants, all the underwear and towels and bed linens. The housekeeping never seemed to end."

"True. Housekeeping was difficult," Daniel agreed. "And so, my love, was outdoor work. The roots of the prairie grass were so tough and so deep it sometimes took ten yoke of oxen to a single plow to break the sod. I used to help Gus and some of his farmer friends hitch up the oxen."

"Dear old Gus, I would love to see him again. He used to come over with his fiddle, and the girls and I would dance while he scratched out a tune. I hope he is well."

"He's one of the first settlers in the northern area that I got to know. Some of them were from Stillwater. They were a hardy lot. He told me about the times they were starving, walking all the way to Fort Snelling to get pork that had been condemned by the Army. And they made it home on foot, with hundred-pound sacks of flour over their shoulders. But the flour often became hard caked and had to be scraped and ground all over again before it could be used."

Tamara looked down at a flower that was a dusty pink shade, very tall, the plant displaying whorled leaves on its stem. "What is that called?" she asked him, pointing down.

"That is the joe-pye weed, my love. It is said to have medicine in it—Indian medicine. It has been used to treat fevers, including malaria."

"I know what the red flower is." Tamara pointed to the reddest flower that grew on the banks of the river. "It is called the cardinal flower."

He looked her over seductively. "Colorful, bright, just like my new bride."

Daniel's voice was mesmerizing, his breath caressing her cheeks and fanning the ringlets that framed her lovely face.

Tamara looked up into his lean dark-skinned face and, in one forward motion, found herself in his arms. He held her so tightly that she lost her breath. Letting her go, he caught her face between his hands, the soft, wispy curls slipping through the tips of his fingers. He lowered his mouth and claimed her waiting lips, his tongue's rhythmical stroking sending shivers of desire coursing through her. Within moments it plunged in deeply, mercilessly, the full force of his desire behind its penetration. His skin tightened over his cheekbones as if drawn taut, and between her small, jutting pelvic bones, Tamara could feel his deep arousal.

She looked up, into dark blue, velvety eyes that were as potent as his embrace had been. They fell to her creamy neck, then rose, studying, waiting, intense.

Yes, the look in her eyes told him, *oh yes right here, right now.*

They moved away, walking together in silent

agreement toward a secluded spot, both utterly quiet.

Against the backdrop of brown and green, a river blue-gray, the shifting glint of the sun above their heads, they moved into the shade and into each other's arms.

Inch by intimate inch, he moved into her, where they lay upon the mossy grass bed. It was bliss, pure and white-hot as he began to quench the fire. They were man and wife now. It was what she needed . . . to be completely his, possessed by him. The whispering wind and the swooshing sound of the river filled her ears, adding their rhythmic sounds to the ones they made together. And the excitement of making love quickly, before anyone could come along, her skirts hiked up to her thighs, his trousers flapped open, heightened their breathtaking feelings.

Like a thundering stud, Daniel slipped through her narrow forest trail, and Tamara's admiration for her mount increased as she felt her own stamina stretch to the limits when she rolled with him and took the initiative on top, riding him now, feeling the roughness of his pants chafe her thighs. The sweet throbbing that followed was all the more ecstatic because he came with her.

Purple wildflowers peeked up at them through the grass when he brought her to climax, then followed right behind, flipping her onto her back and spilling his love fluid into her, crushing the pretty flowers beneath their combined weights.

While she lay dazed from the vigor of her release, he paid homage to her with his mouth and hands, seemingly unable to stop loving her even for a second. She smiled, experiencing the power and warmth of the gentle fingers brushing across her skin with tenderness, fondling and cuddling. He was the caretaker of her heart, and in that moment Tamara knew she would love him forever.

After a time, they got to their feet and adjusted their clothing, unaware of the crushed flower petals tangled in Tamara's hair.

While the low afternoon sun filtered through the leafy, swaying branches along the river's edge, the newly married pair stopped to stretch out upon a flat rock to enjoy the late summer day that was fast fading.

Eyelids fluttered as the peacefulness of late afternoon surrounded them in a marigold halo, hazy, wispy, and dreamy. Languidly they reclined next to each other.

Daniel reminisced about his cabin, moments spent on a misty blue battlefield during the Civil War, and riding through the Minnesota woods astride Fire-Scar, times when he had enjoyed nothing more than to be alone for long stretches. He might even have been proud to be called a loner. Then he had felt a need for companionship during the long stretches he used to revel in, after Tamara had come along. And soon he'd noticed a shift in his outlook. While incarcerated the loneliness had become overwhelming, and it had occurred to him that he *wanted* to be married to one certain woman.

Daniel smiled down on the bright head beside him. Her eyes were closed, not even a flutter of her tawny-dark lashes. The idea of giving up his privacy and freedom no longer felt like a deprivation. Indeed, he found he rather liked being a father. Hell, he loved it. He chuckled to himself, thinking that love with the right woman felt like water finding its way home.

As if she had heard his thoughts, Tamara snuggled against Daniel. He was her husband at last, no longer as elusive as the whistling of wind through the trees. Now he had become like the trunk of a tree, never shifting but always growing and right there whenever she looked for him.

Tamara believed this would always be the way of it from now on, that Daniel would give to her and she, in return, would give to him. She recalled one of old Gus's sayings. *You only keep what you give away.*

After the sun went down, night fell swiftly and the half-moon cast a romantic light that made the river look silvery, the soft moonlit and starlit background making Tamara seem a fairy-tale princess walking beside her handsome warrior—the man holding the white wicker picnic basket with green calico tuckings.

Slowly they walked back to the hotel under the Minnesota moon. Yes, Tamara thought, everything is going to work out just fine from now on . . . *if* . . . if only I didn't have this feeling that something, one tiny thing, is *not right*.

> Evil companions bring more hurt than profit.
> —Aesop

Chapter Seventeen

During the dark night hours Pink Cloud, going by the name Pamela Clayton, paced the carpet runner in the Nicollet House, then returned to her room on the lower floor to slam the door shut. She didn't care if she awoke the whole place! She was angry with Strong Eagle for deserting her at a time when she needed him most.

For a solid two weeks she had seen nothing of Strong Eagle—James . . . how he made her angry sometimes!—and she was beginning to wonder if he had left her for good this time when she heard a knock on the door and flew across the carpet.

She knew it could only be one person at this late hour. "Strong Eagle!" The words were out before the door completed its swing.

"Hush, Pink . . . er, Pamela."

Strong Eagle came into the room, closing the door behind him. He waited for Pink Cloud's reaction to his new image, not caring if she liked him or not. Tamara was the one who really mattered to him, no one else.

Pink Cloud blinked wide eyes. "Strong Eagle?" She backed to the edge of the gray and blue carpet, then tripped and fell against the foot of the bed. "It is you?" She looked up, her black hair a silken fall against the side of her face. "No! It cannot be. Wh-Who are you?"

"Have I changed that much, woman, that you do not know me for sure?" Inwardly he smiled, rejoicing in his deception.

The voice was the same, maybe a little deeper. She swallowed hard, then scooted over to the bed to sit upon it with her coltish legs tucked beneath her while watching him remove the huge-brimmed hat.

Pink Cloud's currant black eyes roved up and down. "Strong Eagle, it is you . . . but why have you become so . . . *fat?*"

It is time to really test my new look, he thought. "I am Strong Eagle's cousin—Jay Creek."

He had moved beyond the circle of pale light coming from the single bedside lamp. Pink Cloud stared at his shadow-chequered face, the straight dark hair that was shorter, falling just below his ears. Her gaze dropped further, to his paunchy middle. Strong Eagle had always been lean, handsome, commanding, and in perfect physical condition. Like a warrior, he had held his head high, and walked with nonchalant grace. Now this dark figure of a man presented himself, telling her he was Jay Creek. What was she to believe?

Who was this man . . . really?

"I think you should leave my room now," Pink Cloud said, apprehension in her dark eyes. "I do not like what you have said to me, that you are Jay Creek. If you are not James Strong Eagle, then you must go at once and never return."

Strong Eagle almost laughed aloud at her look of fear, his fat face melting in a buttery grin.

"Why?"

"Leave now!" she insisted, cautiously sidling to the edge of the bed. "I do not wish to know you, even if you are this man called Jay Creek, Strong Eagle's cousin. You must not play these games with me, whoever you are."

James threw back his head and gave a roar of laughter. "This is very good!"

"What is?"

Pink Cloud's brow furrowed. This man is crazy, she thought, darting glimpses at the door in the hope of escaping. Her heart began to hammer in her chest, her palms moistening.

He drew closer, then, when she made a move to run toward the door, lunged across the bed to grab hold of Pink Cloud just as she would have made good her escape. She was puzzled and more than a little nervous.

"Evil man—let me go!"

Clamping a hand over her mouth, a leg across her lower extremities, James whispered against her throat as he made seductive moves meant to tame her. They had always worked in the past when she had become unmanageable and pouty, or just plain defiant.

"Pink Cloud." His voice was deep, masculine, and he spoke the remembered words of passion in the Dakota language. "I know what you like when we make love." He touched her, brushing her intimately, knowing just how to please her best. "This is what you like, woman. Is it not so?"

"Strong Eagle . . . it has to be you!"

Pink Cloud wrapped her arms about him, more in relief than happiness, kissing his chubby face all over. She halted all movement then, her eyes opened wide. "You have frightened me, Strong Eagle."

He laughed, tugging at her black hair. "It was in my mind to do so."

"Why? Do you like to torment me?"

"You ask many questions, woman. Are you not happy to see Strong Eagle?"

"Yes," she lied. "But why have you become so fat, Strong Eagle? I liked you much better before, when you were a lean warrior."

"I will be again. For now, I must be this new man to fit into my plan." He laughed, his large stomach quivering. "'Fit into,' that's a laugh, do you not think so, Pink Cloud . . . Pamela?"

"I do not like it." Pink Cloud pouted and flung back her long fall of black hair. Angry with him, she thought of getting back at him for all the worry and loneliness he'd caused her. "You will become ill because of your—"

James stilled her abruptly. "Because of what, Pink Cloud? What is it you would have said?"

"Your heart. The one that pumps your blood."

"My heart?" James frowned in perplexity. "I am strong, as is my heart. I am named so."

Pink Cloud was frightened when he looked at her fiercely as he was doing right then, as if his eyes were poison-tipped arrows that pierced one's soul. "It is nothing, Strong Eagle. Someone once said you had been born with a weak heart—but I do not believe this."

"Who said so? I would know the truth, Pink Cloud?"

She was shivering now, wondering why she had begun the lie that might get her into big trouble. Her thoughts flew about, like wild birds with no place to roost, in those fleeting moments he stared at her, waiting.

James was irritated. He looked at Pink Cloud with a passionless stare and thought back to his times with her, which, truth be known, could not equal the passion he had known just kissing, caressing, and holding the white dove—the lovely Tamara. Pink Cloud had always been too willing to do his bidding. Even now he could feel her yielding against him. Though she was frightened of him, she would give him all he wanted in bed, he was certain.

The truth was, Pink Cloud was revolted by Strong Eagle's new look, for he was much too fat and there was now a fierceness in him that made her think twice about again making love with him. Still, she was happy to see him, because she had been so lonely working at the hotel, with whites surrounding her and giving her strange over-the-shoulder stares. Only the chambermaids befriended her.

"Will you answer me?" Strong Eagle ground out, pinching the soft flesh of her upper arm. "Who has said that I have a weak heart?"

"Your stepfather, Wolf Pass. He said you almost died when first beginning to walk, your heart was so weak." Part of this was true, but not all. Wolf Pass

255

had only said that someday the puny Little Eagle would be strong . . . perhaps.

Strong Eagle gritted his teeth. "What about my brother, has he also a weak and wasting heart such as my stepfather claims I possess?"

"I would not know about your brother. But your mother, Lady Slipper, was said to have a weak heart such as yours." The truth now. "This was the reason she died at a young age, Strong Eagle."

Pink Cloud had a humorous thought: It would be great fun to call him *Fat* Eagle! Or Plump Eagle! She almost laughed aloud at the names that suited his new look.

James punched the mattress beside Pink Cloud's head, startling her. She was afraid of him, but he did not see her fear at that moment, he was too intent on his own thoughts.

"What about my twin, Tall Thunder? Does he also suffer from this heart affliction?"

Pink Cloud's eyes went wide. "You have just repeated that question, Strong Eagle. Again, I know nothing about your twin . . . I have never met him."

"Someday you will," he said, an evil look in his eyes. "I promise this to you."

"What do you mean?"

"You will see, when the time comes." He did not know how he would arrange it, to cause Tamara's heart to turn from Tall Thunder when she saw Pink Cloud embracing his twin, but it would be set up, somehow. "Now we must speak of how we will begin to destroy Daniel Tarrant."

"Daniel Tarrant?"

"Tall Thunder. Do not pretend to be stupid, Pink

Cloud. I will need you to use your brains when we rob a bank—"

The young woman sat up in bed, jolted upright, her movement causing James to halt in midsentence. "We? I do not know anything about being a thief, Strong Eagle." She saw the evil lurking in his eyes. "You must not ask me to do this thing! Jail is not a kind place for a woman who is a breed!"

Gripping her shoulders, he snarled, "I do not ask you, Pink Cloud, I tell you. You will also help me prove that Daniel Tarrant is guilty of the murder of the paleface who used to be called Ole Larson. You can say you saw the killing. Back to the robbery. You will "case the place" as Rufus calls it. Dress real pretty, like a white woman. If you do not agree to look these places over before we rob them, and to call Thunder a murderer, it will go hard on you, much harder than if you were sent to prison. My friends would not mind sampling your charms once I gave you over to them.

"And they would be less kind than I. There is one who would take pleasure in slitting your pretty throat when finished with you." His mind was on a paleface who got pleasure from being cruel to women. "One more thing: You must call me Jay Creek. Now, come here and show Strong Eagle"—he laughed—"I mean Jay Creek, how much you still love to please him."

"Your heart, Strong—Creek!" she squawked. She pushed at his chest, feeling soft places that had never been there before. "In your condition . . . I mean"— she was thinking of his excess weight—"you will weaken your heart if you do too much in the bed.

Please . . . no!" *Ugh!*

Pink Cloud had thought the story about his heart would keep him from taking her. But it would not prevent it, she could already see that.

Ignoring her pleas to leave her be, Strong Eagle took hold of her blouse, ripped it all the way to her waist, and flipped her onto her back. Since she used to like this kind of loveplay, James was not about to worry about gentleness at this late stage in the game.

Eyes, dark as the black night hours stretching before them, stared down at her dispassionately. "Do not worry, Pink Cloud, I have no heart to speak of. Only this . . ."

As it turned out, Strong Eagle didn't have to physically force her to yield. She had missed him, his body, his vigor, his virility, what it could do to her. He was so big, so much bigger than any man she had ever been with.

At last, it was she who fell into wanton abandon, she who eagerly introduced him into her sheath. In their coupling was all the savagery of their Indian blood, all the aching frustration of a man denied the woman he most wants. . . .

. . . Tamara.

O, my beloved . . . my morning and my evening star of love!

—Henry Wadsworth Longfellow

Chapter Eighteen

The hues of dawn's bright trailing hems—rose and gold, pale lavender and saffron—tinted the sky as Tamara and Daniel stood together at their bedroom window, watching the day awake, With a sudden flutter of wings, birds rose to the trees' sundrenched crowns. Still, the newly wedded couple did not stir. They lingered, his arm about her waist, her head tilted to rest upon his shoulder. Theirs was a love that bound them gently, like a delicate golden chain.

Night, the brilliance of stars and moon flung against the evening sky, unframed and vast, had been theirs to gaze upon. The ecstasy that had claimed them then lingered in their hearts. Yet, the hours crowded in too fast to drink life's nectar to the brim.

A sudden memory of their entwined bodies filled Tamara's mind, and heat coiled through her.

Daniel breathed against her neck, his dark head bent over her. "Mmm, your perfume smells of night-blooming flowers," he murmured, kissing the sen-

259

sitive place where her pulse had beat erratically the night before.

"Perfume?" Tamara said. "I have no perfume on, Daniel."

"Then I guess it is your own special scent, my angel, my love." Lashes of a coal black shade dropped over his glistening dark blue eyes as he bent to nibble yet another tender spot. "Should we forget the old folks and the baby, breakfast and hot coffee, and get back under the covers for another go at it?"

Tamara laughed softly. "Hardly, my love. This is a respectable boardinghouse, lest you forget."

Daniel groaned. "Now you sound like that dragon of a woman Mrs. Williamson."

She looked up, smiling. "That lovely strait-laced neighbor of ours?"

"That woman would make cream and milk curdle in the icebox."

Escaping from her husband's light embrace, Tamara whirled away. "Shame on you, Daniel Tarrant."

"Can I say the same for you, Mrs. Tarrant?" His winged, black eyebrows rose. "Remember your lusty embraces of this past night? Or did you already forget how wanton your behavior was when you—"

"Hush, someone might hear and believe the worst of me. Then I will have to tell how you behaved when you were beneath the covers and you—"

"Hush, lady, or else we'll both get tossed out of this respectable boardinghouse."

"Oh?" Tamara picked up her hairbrush and drew it through her long blond hair. "And who is going to do the tossing? Henry? Aldwin? Joshua?"

Daniel thought for a moment, then said, "Mrs. Williamson?"

Tamara brandished the hairbrush in the air. "Just let her try!"

Now Daniel became serious. "We will make a trip to the North Woods soon. Remember, I promised to take you."

"Yes?" Tamara was waiting, aware that more was coming.

"First, I must visit the land of my forefathers, go back and speak to those who first informed me of my Indian blood."

Hiding a delicate frown, Tamara said, "Like Woman-of-Thunder?"

Daniel assumed a high-pitched voice, sounding very much like Tamara herself. "Oh, I am not jealous of Woman anymore, Daniel. I promise you this, I will never have to battle that emotion again, not where you are concerned." His voice deepened once again, "Last night, recall?"

"No," she softly answered.

As the sun rose higher, the activity in the bedroom increased. Danny awoke, and his parents fussed over him, dressing and grooming him for the day as if the President were coming for a visit. Daniel was very aware that Tamara's soft breasts now and then brushed against his arms. He was having difficulty resisting the temptation to put his hands to those soft mounds, to feel again the way they had filled his palms so perfectly the night before. But Danny's curious eyes were trained on them. Still, he could not keep images from coming to mind: soft lips parting in deep cries of pleasure, thrusting hips. Lord, heat was pulsing in his loins!

They had been evading the issue foremost in both their minds. Now Tamara voiced it. "Daniel, what if James Strong Eagle is not really dead? If he returns while you are absent, then what will I do?"

"You don't have to worry, love. You have a houseful of men to look after you."

"Be serious, Daniel. Old men and a child?" She thought for a moment while he was dressing for the day. "Strong Eagle spoke of an Indian village where he would like to take me someday, to live in a tepee like an Indian squaw."

Daniel fitted long, muscular legs into his trousers and buttoned up the fly. "He said that?"

"Yes. He was in such haste to wed me. Then right before you appeared, he disappeared."

"Naturally. I believe James Strong Eagle is a crafty one . . . or to be more exact, the devil himself."

Tamara shuddered. "He is not as learned as you are, Daniel, because he spoke in stilted English. At times, in fact, he lapsed into speaking just like an Indian who struggles to conform to the white man's world."

"Ah. He is more Indian in his heart than I, then." A melancholy frown flitted across his face. "He must have grown up in an Indian village."

After dressing in a pale green housedress, Tamara put on her high-buttoned shoes and stood. "Daniel?"

"Yes?"

"Do you think, just maybe, he could be your real brother?"

"We've been through this before, Tamara. Perhaps

you can answer that better than I, my lovely bride."

"I . . . Yes, our twin could be your flesh and blood brother, or perhaps a cousin. He really had me fooled, Daniel. But there is something about him. . . ." She let it hang.

"Yes. What is it?"

"It is my impression that he can be dangerous."

"How dangerous?"

"Very."

Danny's head was going back and forth, first to his mother when she spoke and then his father. It was all very confusing to the child who wondered what they could be talking about so furiously. He grinned. "Yak-yak-yak," he said, repeating the noise Henry Dade had made the other day when Mrs. Williamson's name came up. He clapped his hands, but his parents were not noticing him. "Eat! Wanna eat! *Hungery!*" he bellowed.

No response.

"Well then, I'll not leave you alone when I head for the Minnesota-Dakota border. I am not sure you'll like who I have in mind."

Tamara was startled, but only for a moment. "Who?"

"Cat-Face."

"Oh, you need not bother getting him to watch over us." She heard Daniel chuckle, but went on. "I can really take care of myself and Danny. I have done it all these years"—she smiled—"and I have a pretty big broom in the closet. I know how to wield it quite well should anyone come after us."

"Even James Strong Eagle?"

"Especially him . . . that is, if he really is alive and

did not perish in that steamboat disaster."

Walking over to her, Daniel pressed his fingers over her lips to seal any further protests. "Cat-Face. I mean it, Tamara."

She nibbled her lower lip. "What if you are unable to contact him? It could take an awfully long time to set all this up, Daniel, and then it would be autumn before you get started."

"Autumn will be fine. Then I will return before the snow flies."

"Oh, Daniel, I am afraid to have you leave us again. We've been together for such a short time, and Danny is just getting to know you. Do you suppose it can wait until the spring? Wouldn't that be preferable to risking trudging home in the snow?"

Daniel smiled tenderly. "I would trudge home through mountains of cow-pies to reach you, my darling."

Tamara was not aware that her lower lip had begun to tremble. "Will Cat-Face not frighten the neighbors . . . he is so fearsome to look at. I mean, he resembles a slinking panther, even his eyes."

"Really?" Daniel had to smile at that as he scooped a whining Danny from the floor. "A general misconception shared by most folks. Truth to tell, dearest heart, Cat-Face has a whole passel of Indian girls and palefaces chasing after him. When he takes a woman, she becomes the envy of every other woman in the Dakotas. Last time I saw him, I thought he had filled out nicely. He had lots of muscle and brawn, and had grown a head taller."

As father and son followed Tamara out the door, she said over her shoulder, "But Daniel, you didn't answer me, what about the neighbors?"

Going down the stairs to the sunny kitchen, he decided to end the conversation for the moment. "They'll never even see him. He was not named after the cat for nothing."

"*Cat!*"

"Yes, Danny—cat."

Daniel lay beside Tamara, lazily and slowly caressing her. He wanted to take his time with her since it would be the last night they spent together until he returned from his mission to the Indian village. He bent and kissed her eyes shut, ran his fingers through her loosened hair.

Tamara felt more urgency than he did, and was almost in despair, thinking of the weeks upon weeks before she would see him again. She rolled over to lean against him, her dovelike breasts pressed to his tanned chest. "Oh, I wish you were not leaving in the morning. . . ." She rested her head against his shoulder, hiding her face, her voice husky and sweet.

His lean strong hand caressed her spine, and he drew her closer to him. "The days will be long, dearest heart, the nights even longer until I see you again. I will remember your green eyes, soft and happy as they are now."

He rolled her over lazily, to half lie on her, winding a leg about hers, and she responded instinctively, her legs curling about his. Their lips met, clung, and experimented with open-mouthed kisses, tongue caressing tongue. "Umm," he murmured. She pressed her tongue into his warm mouth, ran it along his teeth, tasted the insides of his cheeks. As his hand moved up and down her spine, emotions welled in her—love, desire, passion.

He settled more of his weight on her, and his breathing sharpened, quickened. But still he lingered, not hurrying. They indulged in love play for a long time, drawing it out deliciously, tormentingly. They knew the movements of this ancient love dance, for they had done it countless times. Still each coming together was different, more revealing, closer.

She stifled the sound in her throat, but he heard it and whispered, "Ah, the kitten in you is purring, love."

She laughed. "It is not a kitten . . . but a tigress!"

"Agreed!"

Then she sobered. She could not play or laugh or pretend to purr. Tears were imminent. She felt the pain of his parting too deeply.

Daniel was aware of her fears. "Tamara, dear, don't do this. Love me, don't turn away. Make this night one to be remembered forever. Make it good, not bad. Come now, let us love and be happy."

She moved her head in protest, unable to speak. Then she said, "You are right, Daniel. Always you are right. Always."

"Remember the pearls I gave you this day?"

"Yes."

"Put them on."

She reached over to the bedside table where she had placed the pearls that afternoon. He had returned from the lumber mill and the bank, wearing a mysterious smile, saying he had only gone those two

266

places, and then he had held out his hand and the beautiful pearls had spilled from his fingers. He had gone to get a gift for her.

Winding the long, thick strand of bluish gray pearls about them in loving enchainment, Daniel gathered her closer and shifted her onto his hard lean body. Tamara knew by his thighs, hard under hers, that he wanted her, that his desire was at its greatest point.

"Oh, love, how you match me!"

Then they said no more. Eyes shut, Daniel was in ecstasy as she rode atop him while his large hands held her slim hips, tighter and ever tighter. He pulled her down sharply at the moment of heightened bliss. It came to them both, washing through their bodies as they were lost in rushing waves of ecstasy. She bent over him, still joined as he caressed her back, her hips, her buttocks.

After resting they came together again before the night had turned to pearly dawn. He came close, pressed teasingly into her, then withdrew, waited, kissing first her breasts, and then sliding down, nipping at her waist and thighs while the pearls rolled over her nipples, down over her belly. His hands rolled with them, smoothing her satin skin, and she felt the taut muscular frame of him, felt his manhood.

Again heat and excitement built up in her, and she moved restlessly, shifting beneath him. Her thighs had opened wide under his hand, and he lay between them, bracing himself on his elbows while he kissed her and rubbed his long body over hers. He kissed the pink pearl of her womanhood. And when his in-

267

timate parts touched hers, she began to shiver, pant, reach out. Slowly, her fingertips digging into his back, she lowered her hands down to his hips, teasing him.

She purred. "Daniel . . . such a big man."

"All yours . . . all."

"Uhmm, I know."

Then he crouched over her and came down with his hard maleness. His face, aglow with passion, was taut, intent. He was a man in love, lusting for his woman.

She glanced down to where their bodies almost joined. He hovered above her for one moment, one golden drop in love's eternity, touched her with it, bathed her, and then he slowly brought them together. But not all the way.

"Oh, Daniel . . . oh, please . . . do it now . . . do it . . . now!"

He entered to full hilt, deep, deeper, moving faster and faster. Now it was exploding in her, high and golden light, like expanding fireworks. She curled to him, loving the powerful sensation, wishing it could go on and on forever and ever. . . . He moved on her, powerfully, lustily, manfully, and she was whirled higher and higher into ecstasy. She felt him finishing, spilling, filling her, causing her to do a tailspin, then fly up again. She exploded softly again, again, and then again, clutching his back, pushing her slim hips up to his to get more and more. . . .

She sank down into fluffy clouds and he followed her, kissing her passionately all over while he remained in her. Their bodies rolled over and over, she half-fainting while he held her limply, straining.

With a final jerk, he finished his movements and sighed as if he'd died and gone to heaven.

She gazed on his face tenderly as they lay side by side. It had been so good. Every time it became better, for each learned what the other wanted. He rolled his head to look at her, long and lingeringly—to remember, to cherish, to hold close. And he would remember, as would she, this night before he left her.

The night he had returned to her the fine gold chain from which a beautiful cross dangled.

Friendship is composed of a single soul inhabiting two bodies.

—Aristotle

Chapter Nineteen

1856

"In enemy country, wisdom is caution. Night is a friend; darkness blinds bullets; horses cannot ride over rocks; bullets cannot see through thick brush."

After Cat-Face had spoken he jumped up onto the bank of the river—a feat requiring such strength and agility it almost took young Daniel's breath away. He stood still, looking at his new friend, a full-blooded Indian, who was as tall as himself.

Cat-Face, he with the dark gold eyes with green flecks swimming in them—eyes like a panther's—had been aptly named by the Cheyenne-Sioux.

He is happy because he is an Indian, thought Daniel. An Indian is not faced with distressing alternatives or troubled by thoughts that rage day and night at the back of his mind. Cat-Face belongs to the People, I belong to no one!

In Dakota, Cat-Face said to his friend Daniel: "I thank you for saving my life. You are sure enough a hawk-dreamer. You are my friend."

Daniel wanted to know, "What is this, hawk-dreamer?"

"You are white, and you saw with blind eyes. Do not shake your head. Listen: When I dreamed of the Hawks or the Thunderbirds, I knew. A brave man dreams of these just before a battle. My Thunderbird-dream came the night before last. Sure enough, yesterday came word that there was war among the Blackfeet. I took my arrows and started south, and directly I found you. I had fallen into a river in flood time . . . stupid, I know. I was being carried, but knew not where, by currents I could not control. Then I looked up to see your arms reaching out and the look upon your face. A hawk-dreamer. A Thunderbird-Man."

"Strange," was all Daniel could give as answer.

Cat-Face did not smile as he said, "Half-longhair."

"Me?" Daniel asked Cat-Face.

"You. That is right. Half-paleface. What does this name Tarrant stand for?"

"It is an old Welsh name meaning thunder."

"Good." Now Cat-Face smiled, but it did not reach his odd-colored eyes. "We will call you Tall Thunder."

The young half-breed nodded his dark head and repeated his new Indian name. Actually, all Cat had added was the word "Tall."

The full-blooded Indian brought out a big silver-bladed knife; this he handed to Thunder. "You will need this in Indian Country."

Thunder's sooty blue eyes shone with pleasure, for no one had ever gifted him with anything but food set on the table. The missionary people, on whose steps

272

he had been left, had been good to him, but he'd never known real family. And now he had struck out on his own.

"You will not be back in time for school," Cat-Face told Thunder, watching his new friend closely for a reaction to this reminder.

"The Agents won't travel to the Dakotas to find me, nor will they at God's Garden . . . they are too old now to go far," Tall Thunder said. "If I stay away for two years, I will be a grown man when I return to Minnesota. I am weary of school anyway. I can read and write and figure money. No trader or Frenchman can cheat me. Why should I let them shut me up in a school for half of every day when I can learn much more being out here with you?" He ended with a wide-shouldered shrug.

"Minnesota is nice too," said Cat-Face. "I have a feeling, a good feeling about Minnesota, and I will go there again soon. Perhaps I will return with you when the time comes."

Cat-Face sensed that his fate, his destiny, seemed to be there. In Minnesota, where the sun reflected upon the moon . . . the moon upon his heart. There where bright stars reached down and almost touched the mirror of still water, the northern lights played back and forth in shades of green and rose, and calling loons accentuated the silence of the night. I will go there when I have heard the wild wind sing, he thought.

Soon Tall Thunder and Cat-Face were running side by side, both wearing leggings and mocassins

273

ornamented with ribbons, feathers, and beads, while their long braided hair was adorned with a number of ribbons and quills, and their faces were painted a variety of colors, giving them both frightful appearances. In their hands they carried bow and arrows.

Running together, kicking stones and shooting arrows at them, yipping like young coyotes, the past seemed far behind them . . . as was the village!

They cried aloud at the excellence of their bows and bragged upon each other's marksmanship, declaring no two grown men in the Thunderbird hills could shoot as well.

"Come!" cried Cat-Face. "I will take you to meet *Eshtahumba.*"

"Who is he?"

"Sleepy Eyes, she is my cousin. She is older than us by five years. I know you have a secret fire, and she will know too."

Thunder complained, "I will be too tired to meet her."

"Somehow I doubt that."

Now, little more than fifteen years later, they were two grown men, Cat-Face and Tall Thunder, meeting at the appointed place in the woods, where ancient pines grew so close together their branches created murmuring shelters and the floor of the forest was fragrant with dropped pine needles. Like a pale floating ghost, a great horned owl passed through the trees.

"So, you have returned," Cat-Face said with an

infectious smile, "from wherever it was you disappeared for so long. Your young woman has gone away. Did you not know?"

"My young woman?" Daniel thought for a moment. "Ah, you must surely mean Tammi . . . Tamara."

"Little Oak."

"Yes." Daniel chuckled. "She is my wife now. We were married in Minneapolis."

The lean dark face lit up, making Cat-Face seem to be the boyish warrior whose life had been spared years ago when these two had first met in the Suland. "So that is where you have been, making a family for yourself."

"Well, not the whole time. In fact, I have spent most of these years of absence from the woods locked behind bars."

"Prison. That is bad."

"You don't know the half of it, Cat-Face."

"So, you look angry, my friend. Come, let us go into the clearing where I have made my camp. We will share a meal of venison stew and corn pones. I have brewed coffee. Very civilized. I even have a new frying pan."

Daniel's mouth twitched in a grin as he followed the silent Cat-Face out into the clearing where smoke curled upward in blue spirals from a cookfire. "You still make all your own meals, I see. No young squaw has caught your eye yet?"

"Not many," was all Cat-Face casually offered. He hunkered down to ladle out two bowlfuls of the savory-looking stew. He handed one to Daniel, saying, "You will like this. I even got hold of some fresh vegetables to add to the pot."

"This smells good." Daniel looked at his friend, adding, "Better taste good too, or else I will make tracks back to my woman who cooks food as delicious as she herself looks."

"You must eat often," Cat-Face joked and indulged in one of his rare smiles.

"You bet."

"Tammi Andersen."

"Tamara Tarrant. Mrs. Thunder, no less."

"Ah, she is skilled in cooking too."

"Of course, in that too." He stared at Cat-Face for a long moment then shook his head. "I believe you've been too long without a woman, my friend."

"Not very." Cat-Face paused, his spoon held in midair. "I remember her, lovely and gentle as a fawn." He looked nostalgic; this was a rare one too. Before he went on, he looked up at the pure white light of the fall moon. "Has Tamara got you tied to her apron strings now?"

"You might say that, but it's a place I love to be. She has picked up my straying soul and set me free."

"So, you are finally a man in love," Cat-Face acknowledged, his voice drily laconic. "You must have a little one by now?"

"Oh, yes. Little Bow is two years old." Daniel grinned happily. "Tamara and I, we just got married several moons back."

"Hmm." Cat-Face set down his half-eaten bowl of stew, brushed crumbs from his doeskin leggings. "Let me hear the story of how this came to be." He crossed his legs, Indian-fashion. "I would like to know."

"You are lonely," Daniel declared. "I can tell."

"How?" asked the dark-visaged Indian with the slanty cat eyes. He then lowered his green-gold gaze.

"You are willing to listen to my account of how we came to be together again, Tamara and myself. It is like a love story, you know."

"The age-worn story." Cat-Face leaned closer. "There are troubled clouds in your eyes, my friend. Though we are near in age and I am not a toothless old shaman, I can see you have gathering shadows in your life. I would like to see if I can be of help to you and your woman in finding a happy ending to your tale."

"Oh, believe me, Cat-Face," Daniel said to the lonely Indian, "you will be."

Jenny and Harold Olsky had just left the boarding-house after dropping Kristel off there. They promised to return after doing some shopping in Minneapolis and before heading back to St. Cloud. But this time they would be leaving Kristel to stay with Tamara, since her husband was away. Jenny had been shocked to hear that one of her youngest friends had gotten herself wed—and to none other than her husband's friend and business partner, Daniel Tarrant. Harold had deposited a considerable amount of money in the bank—the profits from a business venture in which he and Daniel were involved. It had paid well, very well.

"Kristel, let me look at you!" Tamara exclaimed. "Why, I declare you grow taller and more lovely each time you come to visit. You do not look sixteen, but more like a young woman in her early twenties."

"You are right, Tamara, and I am seventeen now."

"Oh, Lord, I missed your birthday." Tamara reached out to pull Kristel into her arms. Danny wanted to get in there, too, and peered up from where he stood between their legs. "Kristel! You have lost weight. My, you are almost too skinny now. Well, I will fatten you up a little with what we're having for supper."

"My favorite." Kristel licked her pink lips. "Roast chicken and mashed potatoes. With plenty of gravy." She laughed, tossing her long blond hair. "I can almost taste it."

"Oh, pie!" Danny piped up.

Kristel shook her head, and Tamara noticed the flattering new hairstyle. "Pie? Oh, we're having pie. What kind of pie, Danny?"

"Pu . . . punkin!"

"Very appropriate for November. Oh heavens, tomorrow is Thanksgiving." Kristel looked at Tamara who had a guilty expression on her face. "You forgot." She grinned, her lovely mouth lifting at the corners. "Well, you had the right idea, Tammi-Mama, pumpkin pie and . . . Wait a minute, I think we'll have to go out and shoot a turkey. Chicken will never do!" She recalled something then.

"Tur-key," Danny tried out the word, wondering what it meant.

All of a sudden Kristel looked as if she might faint. "You married Daniel Tarrant?"

"That has just sunk in, Kristel? Didn't you hear Jenny and I talking about the wedding, a small one, at St. Anthony Falls?"

"You married Daniel, scar and all?"

Tossing the potholder onto the cupboard, Tamara sat down with a thud on the nearest chair. "Oh my God . . . I have forgotten to tell you the most important part of all. It has been so complicated, Kristel, will you promise not to repeat what I am about to tell you?" Her hands smoothed her skirt.

"Cross my heart and hope to die!" Scooping up Daniel, Kristel pulled a chair close to Tamara's. "I just might die of curiosity before the telling, though. Hurry up! I know there is something strange about Daniel. . . ."

"Ohh," Tamara moaned. "That is only the beginning of it, Kristel dear."

Later, much later, as Kristel lay down for the night in the room down the hall, she found she was unable to sleep. Tamara had told her everything, down to the possibility that the dangerous twin might return to the boardinghouse, if he was not truly dead.

Kristel flipped over onto her back, closing her eyes. The sheet was cool against her hot skin. Cat-Face. The Indian who had saved her before she could burn to death in her brother Ole's house. He had carried her out of the smoke-filled interior, and even now she remembered how frightened she had been of him. The unusual eyes had burned into hers, twin flames reflecting the fires consuming the old house. She had seen something in those odd-shaped eyes and never wanted to look into them again. But she had; curiosity had overcome her nervousness.

Kristel stretched out on her stomach, and found some relief for a few moments. Her head began to toss back and forth on the pillow, and she could find no comfortable place to rest her head. She felt so hot. Was it something she had eaten for supper? Had she eaten too much? No. She'd barely finished her first helping of roast chicken and mashed potatoes, green peas, and had had *no* pumpkin pie. Tamara had been surprised that she had not taken dessert.

Why, oh why, did the long-forgotten memory of Cat-Face keep haunting her this night? She had thought he was erased from her mind and, she might as well admit it, her heart.

Heart? Kristel sat up straight in bed. That haughty Indian had never been in her heart. He was much too frightening to look at, much less think herself infatuated with!

He is a man, Kristel told herself, a man used to much older women, squaws and such. Listen to me. What am I thinking? There could never be anything between us, and when he comes he *will not* even give you a second look, Kristel Larson!

There! She punched her pillow down. That was settled!

Ah! could you look into my heart,
And watch your image there!
—Mrs. Osgood,
Poetical Quotations

Chapter Twenty

There was a hint of autumn crispness to the evening as Jenny and Harold Olsky and their little daughter Kathleen said their goodbyes to Tamara and Kristel. They had shared Thanksgiving dinner, Harold having saved the day by bringing a huge turkey will all the trimmings, which they all but devoured. Tamara had made the pies, for which she was famous, and even bread pudding and gingerbread cookies. The old folks were already abed upstairs, happy and well fed.

"Oh, I am so full I could burst!" Kristel groaned, finding a place on the sofa in the living room. "This mess is a place?" she joked as Tamara joined her after putting Danny to bed. He had been so full of food and play, he had fallen asleep right off.

"Thank God Danny is in bed," Tamara said with a sigh, kicking off her high-button shoes.

"He is a handful," Kristel answered, resting her head on the back of the sofa.

Tamara tossed her apron onto a nearby chair. "I

think if I had to go another step I would fall flat on my face. You know, it is so good to relax and"—she bent down—"remove one's shoes and massage the toes a little. Ah . . . that feels so much better. Please, don't turn the light on in here, Kristel."

"Don't worry. I couldn't move if I wanted to."

Through the window moonlight spilled across the carpet, but did not quite reach the two weary females. Kristel's voice was very soft as she spoke, the golden mist of her hair framing a face delicate as a cameo.

"I cannot count the stars or touch them, but in the magic of the night I feel their calm and glory."

"Oh, my . . ." Tamara stirred a little, tired as she was. "Kristel, that is beautiful. You sound like a poet." She pressed her head back again. "Let me hear more. I love the sound of your voice; it's soothing. Is that your own poetry?"

"Yes."

"I would like you to continue," Tamara said in a sleep-filled voice, thinking of Daniel, wondering where he was, if he was well fed this night and dreaming of her.

"All right." Kristel took a deep breath, then went on, hugging her knees to her chest. "The moon changes from a faint crescent of reflected light to full . . . and back again. Unseen, water rises from the midnight blue lakes, the rivers and the leaves of growing things, and returns to the earth as rain . . . snow . . . hail . . . and mist, as the great symphony of life goes on . . . to create what is to be . . . whether or not you sense the beauty of it depends upon your heart . . . and mine. . . ."

*   *   *

"Trees are always trees," Cat-Face went on in Dakota, staring up at the stars as if he'd heard a voice from afar. "With roots that go deep into the earth . . . trunks and limbs held high. By the feel of the bark, the spread of the boughs, the sweep of the twigs, each has a nature all its own. The winds that touch each shoot, the sun, the rains, the high, autumn-dry grass, the hills that are so green, the snow, and each tree, all are rare spirits, beautiful and free. For although all things are created by the Great Spirit, each is like no other. A bird calls; this is his world. Crisp and fresh. A clean white earth, the freedom of the winds."

"I feel," Kristel said to a sleeping Tamara, "as if my destiny is very near. As if someone were . . ."

"Hmm?"

Kristel knew that Tamara was half-asleep. "Let's go up to bed, Tamara. It's been a long day."

"Yes." Tamara stirred and came awake enough to go upstairs.

"Come on, it is time to sleep and dream of sugarplums," Kristel urged.

Together they went upstairs and then to bed. But Kristel could not sleep. She tossed and turned, then sat up to stare out the window . . . at the dim figure silhouetted in the moonlight!

Kristel's sharp scream was cut off as the lithe figure in two lightning-quick strides stepped to the bed to clamp a hand across her mouth. His dark eyes narrowed.

He was motionless as a rock.

"Hush, little one," Cat-Face warned, his high, slanted cheekbones gleaming bronze in the moonlight stealing in. He stared down at her as she squirmed and tried to speak. "You will wake every soul in this house. Do you wish to frighten the others?" He saw her eyes grow big and angrily defiant. "You are brave. I am sorry for frightening you."

Frightening! Kristel wondered if he realized how petrified she was. And who was this man, now seated on her bed! He certainly made her feel shaky all over . . . and he had her dangling on the fringe of some newly awakened emotion. She was cautious and intrigued, however. His hands were amazingly strong, dexterous, warm and, yes, exciting!

Her eyes locked with his in the moonlight as her muted voice emerged through his fingers. "How . . . dare you! Who are you? Where did you c-come from? And how did you get into my b-bedroom? Wh-why?"

"Be still," Cat-Face hissed, his eyes snaring her blue, pleading ones. "Someone is in the house." His other hand was at the back of her head, and he could feel the silky envelope of her golden hair.

"Don't I know it!" Kristel muttered against his hand. *"You!* That's who is in this house—*you!* What do you want?"

His compelling eyes were still locked with hers. "I mean there is someone else in the house," he said into her ear, his breath warm against her flaming cheek. "Not only me. Now, I will take my hand from your mouth." He shook his dark head, his voice soft and deadly cold. "Don't scream."

She took a deep breath once he had taken his hard hand from her face. Her tousled hair spread about her shoulders, she looked up at him, fearing for her life. "What do you mean, there is someone else in the house? There are two of you then?" Kristel asked with a groan, looking around the bedroom that was shrouded in shadow except for the encroaching moonlight.

It must be midnight, she thought.

"What are you men . . . robbers?" she asked the phantom of the night.

"Not me." Cat-Face slid silently off the bed, realizing he could have kissed her before she had sensed what he was about. "The others might be." He placed a long brown finger across his lips, saying, "Shhhh."

"You are not serious, are you? Th-there is someone robbing us? But . . . where did you come from?" Kristel stared hard at the ash gray face in front of her.

"I was following—tracking—the other two who came here." Cat-Face was listening at the door now, having left her alone on the bed. "You stay here. I am going out into the hall." He caught her staring at the open window and saw that she was shivering. "I will close the window first."

"Oh," Kristel said flippantly, "that would be ever so generous of you. Just who are you, mister?"

Understandably she was afraid, so Cat-Face answered, "No 'mister,' Kristel."

She gasped. He *knew* her name. How was this possible, when he did not seem the least familiar to her?

"Cat-Face."

"What?" Kristel gaped, but he had already gone out, silent as a ghost, closing the door softly behind him.

Before Kristel could gather her wits about her and go to waken Tamara— *No*. She could not go out into that hallway.

Sweet, so sweet, what were these new feelings? Kristel wondered, but she did not dwell upon it.

Cat-Face, he was here! He would not harm her, no, he could not. He had saved her life once, several years ago, and she could remember even now the feel of his strong arms as he had carried her away from the burning house. She had not seen much of him after that, for he was so silent and, catlike, always seemed to go off to be alone. He had never been in the company of others, neither men nor women, that she knew of, but was seen coming or going by himself. That is, when one *did* see him.

Though afraid of Cat-Face, Kristel had always been intrigued by him and she had often wished she could be with him more often. He was Daniel's friend, that was all she knew about him.

The door opened and closed so quickly that Kristel gave a frightened little shriek, short and very abrupt. Wave after wave of heat engulfed her.

"You scream like a scared little mouse. Short. Quick. Sweet." Cat-Face did not smile. He was angry that the two intruders had gotten away; he had spotted the silent ratlike figures scurrying down the misty street in the autumn moonlight.

"Well," Kristel began, catching her breath, "you would too if you'd been taken by surprise."

286

She stared at him; he stared at her. And she blushed, suddenly aware that she was half-dressed!

"Go back to bed, Miss Mousey."

She did not see his half-smile as he turned away, one instant here, the next over there, looking out the window.

"How dare you"—Kristel squared her shoulders in bravado, flung back her long blond hair—"call me a mouse." She smiled a sly little smile then. "So. If I am a mouse and you are a cat . . . are you going to catch me someday?"

Cat-Face halted suddenly before going out the door. He hadn't thought she would be so quick with a comeback. In fact, he had not taken the time to think before he'd called her that. Clenching his teeth so hard that his jaws ached, Cat-Face moved away from the window.

"You are also a naughty girl, Kristel. Shame, to think such a thing. A man might get ideas." He shrugged laconically. "Then again, you are just a little girl, and a man such as I does not have evil thoughts about a female child. But those other men might have. You should be careful who you speak to."

"I . . ." Kristel sputtered as he went out of the room, closed the door. "Shame on you, Cat-Face . . . I am *not* a child." She snuffled against her arm. "Tamara says I am like a grown woman now and . . . and I am seventeen already. What makes you think you are such an old man?" she asked the closed door. "Why, I think you are the same age as Daniel. *Huh!* You are but ten years older than me, that is all."

Kristel punched her pillow, pretending it was Cat-

Face. "Little girl! Child! I'll show you! I think it is you who are afraid of me." Her complaints ended in little gasps, and she blushed in the dark at remembering the warmth that had passed between them.

All of a sudden Kristel felt hungry. *Hungry?* How could she be hungry when she had eaten that feast? It did not make sense, but she crept cautiously down the stairs to see if there was some leftover pie . . . and cookies. Too bad there was not some turkey too.

Cat-Face was a silent wraith as he guarded the moon-silvered house, keeping to the shadows, his long blade stuck into the leggings beneath his black trousers. He also had a pistol, stuck into his belt. A knife is more silent, he thought. More silent and swift and deadly.

He stood for long minutes, listening intently. Ah, someone moves about in the house. They are safe, he thought, I am here.

The women, the child, and the old folks were secure now. Under the moon the cautious Indian guarded them while they slept on through the night. Occasionally he dozed against the side of the house, never feeling the chill of the crisp November winds circling and buffeting the walls.

She is only a youth, Cat-Face told himself. Do not bother to think about her, she is too young for you. You could never give her anything *but* heartache, Indian.

His heart wrenched beneath his buckskin shirt. *So wide-eyed and innocent is she. So brave. Too young for you, Indian.*

"Be still, heart." Cat-Face groaned, wondering what illness troubled him. It must have been the jerked venison he'd eaten earlier. It sat like a heavy log in the gut sometimes. Like now. It could not be the heart.

Kristel. Blond. Lovely. Child of the moon.

In the stillness is music. The trees talk, if one will listen as one walks softly in the woods. Smoke rises in the autumn, and the smell makes you think of childhood, of good things to eat, of coming home to a warm house, a warm embrace.... He had never known a warm embrace; he only could imagine what it would feel like to know that family awaited him. Oh, families had waited for him, but not like the one he imagined: of a woman ... kind and true ... all this soul of mine desires to keep it dreaming ... dreams ... love ... long-ago hopes returning over and over again ... in the moonlit night....

"No. No. This can never come to pass—she is not for you, Indian. She is white. Too young. Too good, pure. Never, never Kristel," he declared aloud.

Like a gray shadow lurking in the light,
He ventures forth along the edge of night. . . .
                              —Tekahionwake
                              The Wolf

Chapter Twenty-One

Now was the time for their congress.

Sunrise burst with glorious color upon the Dakota horizon. The sky, so blindingly beautiful, was a moving sea of mauve clouds upon a soft blue and lavender vastness. Then the sun itself shimmered yellow-gold behind the black silhouettes of winter-bare thrusting branches, erasing the pastels from the sky, replacing them with the hot rays of morning light. The scene was silent, peaceful, as if the earth were reborn.

But the landscape was a study in black and white, neutral gray, for the summer colors were gone now that the winter chill was just making itself felt.

Daniel and his stepfather had recognized each other right away, as soon as their eyes had made contact in the cold, blue and gold morning light falling on them and on the village in the near distance.

Wolf Pass's wrinkled brow and lined cheeks had smoothed out when he recognized his deceased wife Lady Slipper in this young man. "You are welcome here, Lady Slipper's son"—Wolf Pass continued with the slow grin—"my son also. Not of blood certainly, but of heart."

Daniel answered in Dakota. "I am happy to be here, husband of my mother Lady Slipper."

The iron gray eyebrows rose as the older Indian got to his feet. The two men entered Wolf Pass's tepee after Daniel's horse had been seen to, and they sat sharing the meal of the morning together while a pair of curious but silently humble Indian maids watched eagerly from the corners of dark eyes, examining Tall Thunder slantwise.

When the plenteous meal had been consumed by the two hungry men, and the bowls and utensils had been cleared away, Wolf Pass called for his long-handled pipe, which he smoked in fragrant silence for a time before handing it to Daniel, who tried not to cough or choke; it had been a long while since he'd had a smoke with Cat-Face. The Dakota name for the pipe was tchandahoopah.

Wolf Pass finally put the long pipe made of Minnesota clay aside. He sat enveloped in the smoky blue quiet for several moments before he spoke again, resting his strong wrinkled hands upon his knees. His eyes lifted and fell, again and again, as if he were looking up to someone who gazed down on them from a lofty height.

"You and I both know why you are here. We both know of Strong Eagle and his deception. His greed. His jealousy. His heart filled with bitterness and hate. Now I will tell you who you are, your mother's name, and what happened that day I sent her from my village"—his voice dropped an octave—"and from my heart."

Daniel was very quiet as Wolf Pass recited the story of how Lady Slipper had lain with a French trapper; at first it had been rape and then she had fallen in love with Gallagher Burke. They both had had blue eyes, as did Daniel's twin brother, and had been striking to look at.

Wolf Pass appeared saddened as he said he'd never been good to look at. "I have always looked as I do now," he said. "Old and tired. But I am very strong of arm and leg, of heart and mind."

Reaching over, Daniel touched the bronzed hand that was, indeed, wrinkled, though Wolf Pass could not be much past the age of fifty years. His eyes were younger-looking, that was true, but sad lights moved in them.

"You are the only father I know of," Tall Thunder said to the old chief, "on this earth."

"I am happy to hear you say this." Wolf Pass sighed as if he were a hundred years old. He went on in Dakota. "I knew you would come. You are a good son, a good father. Gallagher is dead, frozen in the woods many moons back, early in the Moon of the Snowblind. He trapped for the pelts of the beautiful creatures in the woods. By springtime, he had many carts loaded with the product of that winter's business in furs."

Daniel inclined his dark head. "What kind of furs—or skins?"

"Beaver. Kit fox skins, mink, lynx, wolverine, wolf, elk, and sometimes buffalo, but the buffalo has become rare on the Earth."

Daniel whistled. "He *was* in the business."

"Nice father you had, Tall Thunder, to kill so many living creatures. Gallagher worked for the American Fur Company. It is the custom of those engaged in the trade to set aside large portions of their goods for the Indians each year. . . ." He let it hang.

"Did Gallagher Burke do this?" Daniel felt strange, letting the name of his father roll off his tongue. A Frenchman!

"No. Many times Indians took his goods by force. I have heard him accuse the tribe of owing large debts to the fur company, to himself, to the stores in frontier towns. The game had begun to fade away so many Indians were unable to pay their debts, those acquired too freely, because of an old habit of the British and French traders to trust them. Ho! Their governments encourage this, you see."

"Yes, I do begin to see."

Daniel thought: This old man lives in the past, for the traders did this prior to the Civil War. He has been away from the Indian nation too long to know the present affairs of Indian and trader.

"Tell about yourself, Wolf Pass."

The older man shrugged. "I have lived well, in happiness and in sorrow. There is not much more to tell. I will tell you of the Grandfather . . . the Great Spirit if you would like. That will tell you much if you listen well."

The younger man felt the urge to frown, but did not do so. "I am listening . . . Father." Daniel leaned back on the old fur robe that had not been replaced with a newer, softer one in many a year. "Tell me."

Wolf Pass smiled, revealing teeth still intact,

happier now than he'd been in a long, long time. With such a son as this, one could be proud in his old age, even though Tall Thunder was not of his own loins.

"I see you wear the headband of your youth."

"Yes," Daniel replied, glad he'd held on to it for all these years. But how does Wolf Pass know this? he wondered.

"I know, that is all. Remember, son, the key word is 'dreams,'" the older man stated.

Daniel nodded, suddenly realizing the mysteriousness of this man. "Please, tell me whatever you wish me to know. Anything about my mother and all other matters of import, if you can. Tell me of your Great Spirit. I have not heard that one spoken of in many years."

"Oh, you have. You just do not realize this," Wolf Pass said with a wise grin. "The Great Spirit"—he moved his arm in a wide arc as if washing an imaginary sky—"He has always been. And before Him there was no one. Everything on our Good Earth has been made by Him. Nations all over the Universe has He made, the four quarters of the Earth has He finished. All creatures that live has He created."

Wolf Pass looked at Tall Thunder and knew his wife's son was understanding his words at last. He went on.

"We must walk the road to the day of Quiet, then it will be *Hetchetu aloh*, finished, on the Earth." He paused for a moment, then handed the young man a piece of jerked venison and they chewed together in companionable silence before Wolf Pass went on.

"Sometimes dreams are wiser than being awake. You can speak now, Thunder, my son. Have you heard the ghost voice of your mother? Your father?"

"Ghost voice?" The darkly lashed soot-blue eyes clouded for a moment and then cleared. Daniel realized what it was Wolf Pass wanted to hear. He went on in the Dakota language, his voice deep and filled with emotion.

"It was in the spring I first remember hearing the voices, before I played with bows and arrows or rode on the back of a horse. I was playing alone when I heard strange echoes, like someone calling me. A woman's voice . . . but there was no one there. This happened several times, and always it made me so afraid I would run home to my . . . people. Not Indian people, of course."

"No, not the true People. White men." Then Wolf Pass smiled, realizing his blunder: Thunder was white too. "Tell me more, son, I am listening."

"Often the voices would return when I was out by myself. Like someone calling." How sad he had been, so alone in the world. "What they wanted me to do, I did not have any idea."

"To see them."

"What?"

"Have you seen them, those who belong to the voices?"

Daniel shook his head, bewildered. What a question to ask! "No. Never," he answered. He wondered if the old warrior had smoked too much on the pipe; he himself felt a little lightheaded and strange. Floating, sort of. "What was in that pipe?" he said, feeling stupid for having asked.

Wolf Pass smiled. "The sacred pipe, filled with the

bark of the red willow. More than any man can understand, the pipe is holy."

Wondering about the validity of that statement, Daniel again asked about his mother. "Lady Slipper, this was her name?"

"*Sha.* When I met Lady Slipper she was wearing a fine white buckskin dress. Her hair was very long and very black. She was young and very beautiful." Wolf Pass grinned happily. "Want to smoke more pipe?"

The younger man stirred restively, wishing only to get this over with so he could return to Tamara and Danny. "Ah . . . I think what I've had is sufficient."

"Good. I do not like to become too high on smoke either." Thoughtfully the older man said, "Lady Slipper should never have gone with Gallagher."

"Oh." Daniel coughed. "I see. My mother was very beautiful, I understand. I have heard you speak of my father. I think I am getting the picture."

His father had not been an admirable man, at least not to the Indians. But his mother had fallen in love with this Gallagher and then Wolf Pass had sent them away . . . if Tamara's dreams were anything to go by.

What else should I know? Daniel wondered before the older man spoke.

"They became sick with the fever," Wolf Pass supplied, as if he'd read Thunder's mind. "Lady Slipper did not recover. Knowing she would not, she gave her children, the twins, into safekeeping, but not together; she parted them for some reason. Gallagher disappeared, then reappeared, to hunt the many furry children of the woods. It was believed that his mind was no longer sound."

"So . . ." Daniel sighed. "We can forgive him that then if he was not all there after the fever. What about Strong Eagle? What happened to my twin?"

"I do not know. He must have had the wild blood that was in his father. Not of the fever. Of the heart. Gallagher wanted all. Even Lady Slipper."

Just as Strong Eagle wants Tamara, Daniel thought, but kept it to himself.

"Beware of your twin, Daniel Tarrant, Tall Thunder."

"This I know. Do you think he will try to harm my woman Tamara; my son Danny, Little Bow?"

"If he is alive . . . and I believe Strong Eagle is. Now, you must listen to what my shaman has told me. It is about the cave. Of much importance."

Distantly Daniel heard children playing, a dog barking, a horse passing nearby. He licked his lips before he spoke. "The . . . cave?"

Wolf Pass nodded like a wise old man. "You will have to hurry before the winter snows come to the land."

"I believe I realize that now." Suddenly Daniel was worried. "Tell me about this strange cave?"

"It has long been the dwelling of kind spirits." In Dakota, he continued, "This dwelling is near the Laughing Waters. It is of great deepness and has foodstuff and treasure stored there."

Daniel leaned forward and asked in Dakota, "And how does one get into it?"

"The entrance is narrow, and the bottom of it is all in dirt and sand." He watched as Thunder nodded in eagerness to hear more, then went on, feeling Thunder's excitement increase. "There is another opening. Through this, one may enter from outside."

"Sounds like a house," Thunder commented. "And?"

"There are riches in this cave. A strange cave I had never seen before the shaman's dream revealed it. The darkness of it prevents all attempts to acquire knowledge of it. You can only get into it if you go down a narrow, steep passage that lies near another passage up. I believe the riches in this place are stolen from others. I believe Strong Eagle has something to do with these belongings of others." Wolf Pass shrugged.

Smoke spiraled up from the center of the tepee, and Daniel stared at it for a time. "It is here you believe something will happen?"

"*Sha,* yes. You must hurry as I said, before the winter winds blow and the snow blinds your eyes."

"Yes, I will go now." Daniel gathered up his things, the sack of food the Indian maids had hastily gathered, then looked back at the man he knew he would be seeing again when he brought Tamara and Danny back to visit. "I feel very close to you, Wolf Pass, and I only wish that you were my real father."

"Believe as if it were already so, my son. All things go right if you do this. Believe your woman and son are safe, and they will be. Believe that nothing will come against you, and it will not. Most of all, believe in the Great Spirit, he is the Grandfather of us all."

"Ah . . . Yes, I believe, Wolf Pass. Now, I must get my horse and set out before, as you say, the winter winds blow." Once outside the tepee flap, he shivered. "It is already cold." He took his horse as a young Indian lad handed over the reins, and he mounted, looking down at the beloved old man.

There was wisdom in Wolf Pass's eyes. "Your love will keep you warm and safe, my son. Remember that, and nothing will go wrong. Return in the spring, for I would like to see this grandson of mine . . . and your wife. She is Little Oak, I know."

"Yes. We will return."

"Good. Go with the Great Spirit. He will guide and keep you. When beauty fills the heart, it blesses every man."

Daniel looked down at the old, wise man. "I believe that now. Your God and my God. Be happy and healthy, Wolf Pass."

"I will. As long as I know you return to me. In the spring."

"I promise."

With that, Daniel kicked his horse, pulling his furlined coat about him, and was gone, while the older man watched, tears sparkling in his eyes. But those eyes were filled not with sadness but love. He had seen his wife Lady Slipper's son. The good one. *He leaves with peace between us.*

What is to happen to the other one? Wolf Pass wondered as he made his way back to his warm tepee. Waving one last time as he turned, he was happy to see that Tall Thunder had paused on the hill to lift a hand in a farewell gesture.

Then he was gone, heading in the direction from which he had come, a mere silhouette against the naked birches and pines poking dark fingers into the overcast sky.

* * *

That night, camped beneath the cold stars, Daniel—Tall Thunder—dreamed of his woman, wishing she were with him to keep him warm. Dreams have significance, Wolf Pass had said. He hadn't felt so alive in months, even in his dreams. She appeared to him as he slept, dressed in white satin, the moon behind her in the window. She was turning before a full-length mirror, her features pure, angelic. Her flaxen hair had been parted in the middle, pulled back in a sleek style becoming to her. She shimmered, like expensive jewels. She was everything to him.

In the next stage of his dream, he made love to her outside, snow swirling about them like frail silver cobwebs. As his hand came up to caress her, she begged him to let her catch her breath. She loved him. He knew it. This was his dream come true. When the dream vanished, he saw only that her eyes were shining like two great stars. . . .

Springwater green eyes.

He sat up with a start, instantly awake. Shaking his head, he again thought: Eyes? How could it be that he had seen eyes for real?

He was out here in the woods alone. . . . Wasn't he?

Just then the owner of the green eyes, a huge gray wolf, bounded happily out from a stand of pines, wagging his thick fluffy tail in playful greeting. He yapped like a puppy when he spied his long-lost master, and approached with head hung down in humble appeal.

"My . . . God," Daniel said, swallowing the fear that had lodged in his throat. "Gray Wolf." Fear changed to happiness and tears stood hard in his eyes. "Here, boy. Come here, fella. Haven't seen you for years. Gave you up for dead. . . . But no, you waited for me to return to these woods."

Gray Wolf, happy to see his master again, whined and pressed his wet nose against Daniel's hand as he sat down beside the blanket, his tail thumping joyfully, his powerful jaws gone lax after his senses confirmed this human was the one he'd missed for so long. His lupine face, as always when he was in the company of likable humans, gave the impression of a repressed grin.

"You're far from home, Wolf." Daniel patted the huge head that lolled back against his chest, the springwater eyes blinking trustingly up at him. "Guess you've been just roaming the woods wondering when I would return to the cabin, huh? Well, boy, we will be coming here to stay in the spring. You remember Tamara, Tammi." The wolf whined, sounding lonesome already. "She will be coming back, too, Wolf. And Danny, you'll love to play with . . ."

Just then the yap of a puppy was heard, a moment before Gray Wolf's offspring came leaping from the pines in search of papa. As he neared the man, the pup sniffed, then growled soft and low in his throat. Gray Wolf came to his feet, knocking the bad-mannered pup over with a swipe of his huge paw. The pup rolled into the human and growl-yipped when a warm hand tried caressing his fur.

"Don't know me yet, pup, but you will."

With that, yawning tiredly Daniel lay back down to stretch out beside the embers of his campfire. "You'll get to know my boy Danny, too. We will . . . come back."

Gray Wolf and his pup, the only two of their kind in this vicinity—at least Daniel hoped there was not a large female about—lay down together on the other side of the glowing embers to watch the human relax, and heard the not-so-unpleasant sighing sound. Closing his eyes, Daniel had a disturbing thought. Perhaps the two wolves were running with a pack. Then he told himself that Gray Wolf would never let any harm come to him. In fact, if only his friend had been near the day he'd been ambushed, he'd never have been taken away from Tamara; Gray Wolf never would have allowed that to happen.

Deeply and peacefully Daniel slept, confident that he was safe.

That night he dreamed about the cave. Only it was not a cave, it was the cellar beneath the boarding-house!

In his dream he tried to run, to reach Tamara and Danny, but his steps faltered and he wallowed in helplessness, in fear. . . . The cave . . . the cellar . . . He had to reach Tamara! Had to . . . had to. . . .

Delays have dangerous ends.
—William Shakespeare

Chapter Twenty-Two

Tamara was gazing up at the faint morning stars, wishful, dreaming of Daniel, of darkly lashed, soot blue eyes; the deep chord in his voice; the lazy, loose-hipped way he walked—the unrushed swagger of a confident man, a stride that said he knew exactly where he was going and how to get there.

Daniel . . . Wishing he were beside her, his arm around her waist pulling her close against his side, her head resting upon the secure padding of his shoulder. So wonderful. She sighed. *Oh, Daniel, return to me before the first snowflakes fall.*

One by one the stars were extinguished, and the golden hue upon the horizon foretold the coming of day. Arabesques of pale twilight fled the room, gray shadows being chased by the wan radiance of the late November sun. Tamara felt a shiver of prescience, quickly cast it aside as she walked away from the window to get ready for work, but lines of worry soon creased her brow once again.

She pulled a brush through her long blond hair,

which she then wound up into a topknot. When that was done and she had laid a creamy white petticoat and kelly green woolen dress on the end of the bed, she swiftly tiptoed into the water closet, then hurried across the back hall to traipse up and down the back stairs, fetching heavy buckets of hot water to fill the copper tub. She wanted to bathe before Danny awoke.

When she was just filling the seventh and eighth pails, a bronze hand reached out, making her jump. Her hand went to her throat before she remembered the Indian and his unanticipated cat-soft footsteps.

"I will carry those for you," Cat-Face told her in a soft masculine voice. "You should carry such heavy pails up that flight of stairs only one at a time."

Tamara stared into his oddly illuminated eyes, green and gold, with soft black pupils. Why did he always let his sentences hang like that, sounding so mysterious? If she had thought him unusual several years ago, that was even more true now. He seemed to belong in a different time and place.

"Cat-Face, I should have gotten used to your presence by now, you have been here for over a week. It is just that . . ." She shook her head; her eyes were large. There was that feeling again, that flicker of intuition. What did it mean? This feeling of prescience must have something to do with the Indian because she had experienced it since his arrival.

"I know, Tamara." He had finally begun to call her that, as she'd insisted he do, instead of Mrs. Tarrant all the time. "You got used to Tall Thunder living with you, and a strange man hanging around is making you jumpy. Unlike the old grandfathers who dwell here, I move quickly and quietly."

Tamara almost gaped at Cat-Face. She had never heard the usually silent man talk as much as he had in the last several days. It was almost as if a peculiar nervousness had overtaken him.

"You're very helpful, Cat-Face."

"I like to think so," he said.

She hid a smile then. That Kristel had been up to her old tricks was evident, sneaking up on Cat-Face—not the other way around—and startling him. As if the younger woman were repaying him in kind. Tamara had seen Cat-Face's eyes turn dark, as if he would very much enjoy taking a knife to Kristel's beautiful scalp!

The Indian seemed to read her thoughts because they both smiled at the same instant when Kristel's sleep-husked voice sounded in the hall. Now she was entering the kitchen, flinging loose strands of hair back with a toss of her pert head.

"Do you need some help with your baa . . . ?"

Kristel instantly halted, clutching the front of her pink robe where it gaped open, displaying a goodly amount of her newly matured form despite the white linen nightgown. She looked young and innocently lovely.

Her eyes snagged with the Indian's and she knew a shivery wonder as his eyes flame licked her face and body. He is not handsome, she thought, but not ugly either.

"Baa?" Cat-Face said, brushing past her with the water, a pail in each hand. "Are you a lamb?" He grinned as he went up the winding back stairs.

"Kristel," Tamara said with a smile. "Why the woebegone expression?"

Kristel pouted and then called up the stairwell to Cat-Face, "It's what you should have: a bath!" Returning to the kitchen, she told Tamara, "He needs his head dunked real good, that one."

Tamara smiled as she cracked eggs into the cast-iron skillet. "Have you gone out to the carriage house to see to the horses?" She did not turn to let Kristel catch her smiling as she put the question to the young woman.

"I thought that was Cat's job now that he seems to have come along and taken things over."

Tamara's eyebrows lifted. "Cat?"

Kristel blushed. "Yes. Cat. When you say Cat-Face, it sounds like his first name is Cat, his last name Face. Or as if he's a cat that lost his body, and owns only a face. Stupid."

Silly girl, she chided herself. Stop dwelling on his body, since that will get you nowhere. He will never want you as a woman, maybe just a plaything but possibly not even that. "I think he's afraid of women," she said under her breath.

Louder, she added, "Stupid name."

"I like it just fine."

Kristel jumped when the quiet Indian entered the kitchen from the hall. "Next time I'll make you jump in surprise, wait and see," she threatened.

"You already have, Miss Kristel Larson. It is embarrassing to say you are the first."

Kristel blinked. "First?" A creeping red flush came to her plump cheeks. "First"—she swallowed hard—"to *what*?"

308

"To come up on me and make me jump. No one has surprised me before. Not man. Not animal. You are the first."

Kristel smoothed her hands over apricot-colored skirt-folds. "Oh."

He looked at her with a strange half-smile. "What did you think I meant by the word." Tigerish eyes held hers.

Kristel did not answer that one, she only lifted her hair high off her neck as if she'd suddenly grown quite hot. "You have not even been surprised in the woods while alone?"

"Not even."

Lightning fast and reluctantly, Cat glanced away from her young, upthrusting breasts. *Be careful, Indian. Keep a hardened heart around this little maid. Pretend to be made of stone. Only the older Indian women for you. The ones who know what to do. You will only hurt this little one. She is not for you. Hear this: She is not for you.*

Cat-Face had never guessed the young blonde would be this full of surprises when he saw her again. He knew his presence had shaken her a bit. When he was gone, he would be wise to forget about her completely, he told himself.

Before Kristel could ready another question to fire at Cat-Face, the Indian was moving out of the kitchen with his plate heaped with eggs, bacon, and toast—four slices light on the butter—in one hand, and a coffee cup, steam rising from it in the other.

"Thanks for the breakfast, Tamara. Your bath is ready. Nice and hot. Better hurry."

When he had sauntered outside to sit on the porch

to eat his breakfast, Kristel muttered to herself, "Your bath is ready. Nice. Hot. Ugh, me Indian. *You paleface!*" The words exploded from her, giving Tamara a glimpse of her true emotional state.

Planting her hands on her gently rounded hips, Kristel trailed Tamara out into the hall. "Did you ever hear such clipped, precise speech? I mean, you would think by now his sentences would flow together, being around whites as much as he has. Why does he seem to pause after each word for a fraction of a second? Do all red-blooded Indians talk like . . . that . . . all . . . their . . . lives? Sheesh!"

Tamara shrugged, a towel slung over her shoulder. Her slipper paused on the first step. Kristel is growing fast, she thought poignantly, remembering that only a few years ago the girl had had thoughts only of dolls and hot biscuits. Now it seemed the Indian had turned her heart toward romance. She only hoped Cat-Face would see the situation for what it was: a mere infatuation with a virile man.

"Well?" Kristel persisted. "What's wrong with him?"

"I do not know, Kristel. Why don't you go ask him yourself?"

"Tamara, but . . ."

"I have to get to work. It's getting late. You have to feed horses and wake Danny, chatterbox."

"Ha-ha. Very funny."

Upstairs in the hallway, Tamara paused at the top of the stairs just as KeeKing Man was emerging from the nursery. "Danny's up," he said.

"I know, and thank you, Joshua. Your breakfast is ready and your clean laundry is folded on the chair by the kitchen door. I did it for you earlier."

He blushed at the mention of his laundry, since there were a few unmentionables in the pile. "Thanks, Tamara. We all depend on you to keep things running smoothly."

"Thank you Joshua."

"When I go down I will tell Krissy that Danny's up." He paused, tugging the loose tie of his baggy robe. "By the way, when's Daniel coming back? That Injun hanging around all the time gives me the willies. Does he have to be poking about day and night? I stuck my head around the corner yesterday, and there were those strange eyes lookin' right at me. Just about had to make another trip to the water closet."

"I'm afraid Cat-Face will be around for a while, Joshua. Daniel appointed the man to guard us."

"Yup." Joshua blew air through his lips. "Carries a wicked lookin' blade, that one does. Bet that Injun could carve a figure eight in a man's face before you blinked twice. Maybe once'd be all it took; then his victim'd be mincemeat."

Tamara shivered. "I hope he will not have to do any such carving, Joshua. Now, go down and have your breakfast before it gets cold as a millstone."

Lifting her shoulders to steel herself for the remainder of the day, Tamara had just entered the water closet when Joshua called down in an ear-splitting voice:

"Kristel! Danny's up!"

Oh Lord, keep me strong, Tamara sent up the silent prayer as she shook her head, closing the door quickly to let out as little steamy warmth as possible.

Her chin tucked low, she stared at the filled tub for only a second.

Disrobing in a hurry now, she stepped into the tub and sank down in it gratefully, the water closing over her shoulders. She smiled as memories of Daniel flitted across her mind. Imagining his lips upon hers, she felt her limbs turn to jelly beneath the warm water, and tears sprang to her eyes.

Resting her head on the tub's rim, she spoke softly. "Come home soon, Daniel. We need you—oh God how we need you. Most of all, I need you because I am suddenly afraid something will go wrong. Come back, Daniel, and make it all right again."

James Strong Eagle, alias Jay Creek, entered the hotel by the cook's entrance and slipped along the hall in a stealthful search for "Pamela Clayton." He wrapped his meaty arm about her waist and pulled her out of the room she'd been cleaning, then across the hall and into the chambermaid's supply closet.

Tamara, just coming along the corridor, had to blink twice at what she saw. Or had she really seen Pamela Clayton being dragged into that closet. What did the man want? Was he up to no good? Should she wait? Get help? Or just go and see for herself what mischief the man could be up to.

Cautiously Tamara walked to the supply closet, looking along the hall before bending down to listen at the keyhole. There did not seem to be anything untoward going on, and then she heard the unrhythmic sound of a man's low voice, the hushed-speaking answer of the woman.

"You have to do it, Pink Cloud. I mean it. It is time we made Daniel Tarrant guilty of some more crimes. He will be sent back to prison; this is where I want him to be. My plan will not succeed if you do not help."

Tamara felt her throat go dry. Pink Cloud? Her heart started to hammer. Who was this man that sounded familiar but she could not place?

"No, James, I will not set it up for you to rob that rich cattleman, then blame it on this Daniel Tarrant, a man I do not even know."

"I told you, the cattleman always comes out of the tavern plenty drunk. He goes home from there with money from the bank in his pockets. We need the money, our supply is getting low."

"You need the money; I have enough. I like my job here at Nicollet House, and I have many friends who think it is nice to have an Indian maid at their hotel." *Besides, you have become too fat, Strong Eagle!* She wanted to yell this at him and tell him to get lost.

But he surprised her by becoming familiar. "No, James. Not here. Not now! My boss, or one of my friends, might come!"

"You have it turned around, Miss Clayton. I am the one who is going to do that. More than once."

Feeling herself go numb all over, Tamara backed away from the door, then whirled as she broke out into a run. At this hour of the day, when most employees were having their lunch, or were resting, the halls were all but deserted. Only once in a great while during this time would a guest appear.

Her heart pounding, Tamara whipped her apron off and tossed it into a nearby cart—no doubt

Pamela's . . . Pink Cloud's. My God! They were conspiring to pin something on Daniel again. How was she to get word to him? Where could he be? She would never be able to find him if he was camped in the northern woods.

Outside the cold wind tore at the folds of Tamara's coat as she hurried to the carriage house to get her horse and buggy. She moved swiftly; this was urgent. But who was there to help?

Cat-Face! He would know what to do!

Tamara's fist flew up to her mouth. James Strong Eagle was back! What were they going to do to protect themselves now? Cat-Face was only one . . . there was no telling how many cohorts Strong Eagle had.

James's heart thudded painfully as, from the fifth story window, he watched Tamara run to fetch her horse and buggy. In the cold November wind, her soft blond hair blew in long silken tendrils against her shoulders and back, having escaped the neat and ladylike topknot she always secured at the start of a day.

He would get her back, he thought fiercely. His plans were going to succeed. But he had to hurry.

"Miss Clayton." He turned to face the vacant room Pink Cloud had been cleaning earlier that day. "Are you ready?"

A barely audible yes came across the room. "Then we will go. I have my men to meet. They will kidnap Tamara and the boy. It is better you do not know

314

anything else, *Miss Clayton.*"

Pink Cloud passed by the window, momentarily brushing the curtains aside, and she saw Tamara, the beautiful chambermaid, going down the street in her buggy. Tamara was in a hurry. Pink Cloud wondered why the woman had left work all of a sudden with no word to anyone. Had she caught sight of James going into the closet?

The breed turned to look at Strong Eagle. If only he had not become so fat she might still consider him as a lover, but the way he was, he repulsed her even when he touched her cheek.

"Hurry, Pink Cloud," James insisted angrily. "Get your things together."

"I will not need much and I—"

James interrupted sharply, "Put on the wig I have brought you."

Pink Cloud put the blond wig on and grimaced at seeing her reflection. How ugly she looked in yellow hair! Her coloring was much too dark, her eyes too black. She was afraid everyone would see through her disguise, especially the man she was supposed to set up so that James and his companions could rob him.

Pink Cloud turned to Strong Eagle. "I am ready, but I do not like this," she complained.

James shook his head. "Ugh. You look very strange as a yellowhair, Pink Cloud."

After grabbing her heavy shawl, she followed him out the door, moving quickly along the hall to the back stairs. And you look very ugly with your fat body, Strong Eagle, she thought, but kept it to herself as she was pulled along behind him, almost tripping

315

as they flew down the stairs and out the back door.

James frowned. "You are very clumsy," he snorted.

The acrid contempt in his tone scalded Pink Cloud. Hot anger darkened her cheeks.

Someone was going to die before this was over, and Pink Cloud hoped she wasn't the one.

> What! Canst thou say all this and never blush?
> —William Shakespeare

Chapter Twenty-Three

Kristel was busy with the preparations for supper. Danny played in a corner of the kitchen while Cat-Face quietly sipped coffee; he loved the white man's brew, everyone in the house had discovered. As he leaned against the door jamb, he watched the young woman move about the kitchen, efficient and quick as a squaw; the sunlight patchily illuminated her. He eyed her shapeliness when her back was turned and found himself growing warm. Too warm.

Rich aromas filled the kitchen area. Creamy rich potato soup laced with chives was to be served from the huge beanpot sitting in the middle of the table. The heavy beanpot would keep the soup piping hot for an hour or more while the boarders and the members of the household took turns eating. A plump cut of pork was roasting in the oven, crackling, its succulent juices wafting in the air.

There was a quickening in Cat-Face's blood. Suddenly he had found his days full of projects, like stacking firewood by the back door where the women could easily get to it, and keeping the woodshed filled with kindling. He was in an almost festive mood.

"Oh, I need a fruit sauce for the roast, Cat. Would you go down to the cellar and fetch one for me?" Kristel asked, not bothering to turn toward him. She knew he'd been ogling her from behind, and it made her feel warm and tingly.

Cat-Face stirred. "I will *get* it for you," he said. He watched her turn and look at him with a puzzled frown. "I am not a dog. I do not *fetch*."

She grinned mischievously. "Right. You are a cat."

"Wait for me! Wait Caffiz," Danny yelled. "Wanna go too!"

"What?" Cat-Face smiled at the running child who could not pronounce his name correctly. "Where does Little Bow wish to go?"

The Indian lifted the energetic child onto his shoulders and Danny giggled gleefully at looking down from such a lofty height.

"Oh!" Kristel stepped closer. "Be careful he doesn't fall."

"I would not drop the boy," Cat-Face told her, bothered by her sweet proximity all of a sudden.

I am too close to him, she thought. His voice was mesmerizing, and his breath caressed her face. But her nearness was devastating his senses, so he stepped around the table in order to put a safe barrier between them. Still, his body throbbed from need, wanting her.

This cannot be, he told himself.

Kristel stood quietly by, watching man and boy,

318

but mostly the man, as her fingers gripped the edge of the work table. Why did he always keep a distance from her? What was he afraid of? Touching her accidentally?

"I will get the sauce," he said, putting Danny down. He stood very still then, watching her.

The masculine tone of his voice reached her ears, like velvet thunder reverberating through her nerve endings. Oh, if only he would . . .

"Cat," she murmured, not voicing the thought, I love you. She did. Oh yes, she did. She knew it now, with all her heart. There could never be another man for her, ever.

Cat-Face still had not moved to go to the cellar for the fruit sauce. "Kristel," his tongue caressed her name, not meaning to. "You must not . . ." He tried again. "I do not wish to hurt you."

"Cat," she said, swallowing her fear of embarrassment. "You want to hold me, kiss me. Why don't you just do it?" Her eyes begged him. "I can't . . . sleep, Cat. If I do, I dream of you."

The much-troubled Indian took a few more steps toward the door. He moistened his lips with his tongue. "No, Kristel, do not say these things. I will not do as you ask."

Temperamentally, she cried, "You don't want to!"

Shaking his head, Cat-Face said, "You do not know what you ask of me, little one. We are not good for each other. You must know this."

"Tell me! You don't want to, am I right?"

"Kristel"—he heaved a deep sigh—"We are from different worlds. I have been with many women. I would only hurt you."

319

"You don't want to be with me!"

"Kristel, Kristel, lovely little snow maiden. You are too young for me. You must be silent in this and let it pass."

"It won't!"

Cat-Face did not move a muscle now. "You make this Indian want to do bad things to you. You do not know about these matters between woman and man. You are a maid untouched."

Kristel made a whimpering sound, a mixture of frustration and wanting. "How would you know?"

"A man who has had many women can tell these things." As painful as it was, he wanted to make her not want him. "So many women, Kristel. You and I would not join well. You could not please me, little one," he lied. "I am too old for you. My women are good. They know what to do."

Kristel shook her head, and pain, showed in her pale blue eyes. "You are *so* cruel."

He shrugged. "Maybe."

"Go away, Cat." Kristel turned back to the stove. "Just go away. Don't ever look at me again. You believe yourself too good for me. Go back to all your Indian women who know how to please you. Maybe you even have some white women, as well." She forced back tears. "Old man."

"Kristel . . . you do not know what you are saying."

"Stick it in your ear!"

Cat-Face clicked his tongue. "Such a child. You need to grow up, baby girl."

Kristel stirred the potato stew so vigorously that hot liquid sloshed over and burned her hand. "Ouch!

I'll show you some day, Mr. Ladies' Man. Sheik!"

"You need your mouth washed out with soap. Lye soap."

"Get out!"

Ordinarily in such a situation Cat-Face would have laughed, but this time he was serious. Too serious. He did not wish to become involved with a child-woman, tempting as she was.

"I'll get the fruit sauce."

"Stick *that* in your ear, too!"

Just then the back door flew open and banged loudly against the kitchen wall. Kristel and the tall Indian stared long and hard at Tamara. She looked as if she'd seen a ghost, one that had chased her all the way home!

As Tamara swayed, Cat-Face rushed forward to catch her, to break her fall. He swooped her into his arms and carried her to the sofa in the living room. Trailing close behind, Danny whined, upset to see his mother so distressed.

Kristel rushed to bend over Tamara. Cat-Face remained close beside her. Their hands brushed when they both tried to make Tamara comfortable. Then their eyes clashed, caught, and held, and they both swayed close as sexual desire rocked them.

Kristel swallowed hard, looking away from Cat-Face. "What happened?" she asked Tamara. She knew her voice shook, but there was no help for it. "Tell us!"

Again Kristel looked at Cat-Face, seeing his stern and formidable expression. In this tension-laced moment, her gaze fell to his buckskin leggings, and for a startling moment she wondered how he would look with his body bare from the waist up. She wondered, too, if he wore any underdrawers, and she blushed. But not for long.

A moan escaped Tamara's lips. "He's back." She shifted as a cold shiver rippled through her.

Pivoting on his heel, Cat-Face reached for a bright and colorful afghan, pulling it up beneath Tamara's chin, smoothing it along her frame. "Who's back?" he asked, soothing her with his quiet voice, his skin very dark in the dimness of the twilight living room.

Her teeth chattered. "James Strong Eagle!"

Kristel and Cat-Face could only look at each other and stare.

Dusk shadowed the land blue-violet.

The succulent roast was crisply done by the time the tension had eased. Kristel, Cat-Face, and Tamara ate sparingly of what remained after the three aged and hungry boarders had attacked the fare. The Indian and the two young women were just not very hungry. Not that night.

Cat-Face went back outside to stand guard over the house. All were in his safekeeping so he had to remain vigilant and cautious. He stalked the shadows, keeping close to the carriage house, watching the grounds for any slight movement or stealthy shadow.

The Indian knew what he would do should James Strong Eagle and his outlaw friends show up, for he was a seasoned warrior who could draw and wield his weapons as swiftly as he sheathed them.

Tamara and Danny had fallen into exhausted slumber on the big bed, but Kristel could not do the same; she was too frustrated to relax. The day had been filled with tremendous tension, and she had no idea of how to release it. But she felt if she could not rid herself of it she would go mad.

For days it had been thus for Cat-Face. Amazingly, however, on this night he fell asleep just inside the door to the carriage house, having had little rest in the days and nights since he'd arrived at the boardinghouse. But he was an Indian, a Sioux warrior, and slept with one eye open, so to speak. He would be alerted by any small noise or movement in the area, be instantly awake should the need arise.

It was dark in the house, and Kristel walked down the creaking stairs to the kitchen. Her eyes, adjusted to the dim light of the filtering moon, scoured the area; then slowly, by that wan illumination creeping in the window, she began putting things in order as best she could.

She did not want to leave a mess for Tamara in the morning. Tamara was upset enough as it was. So was everyone, it seemed, even Cat-Face. She had never seen him look so weary and careworn. She decided he probably hadn't slept much lately. Neither had she.

Kristel only wished that Daniel would come home soon.

She paused at the kitchen work table, looking toward the window and wondering how Cat-Face could stand the cold November night. He is an Indian and used to all kinds of weather, she reminded herself. She only wished he could get used to her.

Nightly, he crept into her restless dreams, and she

323

kept remembering things she should not. Cat-Face's skin was really too dark for her taste, she'd tried telling herself. And his eyes were a strange yellow-green, his hair too black.

He is not the kind of man I am usually taken with. Still, there was a virile handsomeness about him. She sensed the passion and the power slumbering beneath his passive facade.

"Oh . . . he is nothing but a savage! What do I need with a savage?" Kristel shrugged and vowed he would never come near her or touch her again.

She sighed. And sighed again.

After cleaning the kitchen and putting everything in its proper place, Kristel went back upstairs and lay down on her bed fully clothed. The moon and stars were cold comfort for her on this night, and she again wondered how Cat-Face could stand the chill, since she was shivering with a blanket over her.

Her heart was so heavy that it was actually aching. Her head rolled on the pillow. Did Cat-Face ache to hold her? No. How could he? She punched the pillow. He had all the women he could handle.

Kristel looked out at the stars winking in the ebony night sky. Cold stars. Cold night. She shivered, listening to the wind rattle the windows as if demanding entrance to the house.

"Cat-Face," Kristel murmured. "What a name. What an Indian. What a man. What is he really like inside?

"With all my heart," she vowed, "I love him."

She breathed out the words, swishing tears away with the back of her hand.

Quickly making up her mind, she then bounded

from the bed and walked along the hall, taking up the lamp she had lighted, and made her way up the creaking stairs to the attic. She looked behind her, shivering as she noted the spirals of light following her up the narrow flight of stairs. With each step she took the treads creaked more ominously . . . as if the house were protesting her wanton misbehavior in the dark of night.

She needed clothing that would keep her warm and safe, some dark baggy men's trousers, a jacket, and a slouch hat in case there were prowlers in the area. To cloak her identity. She found those things, put them on, then crept out to the carriage house to help Cat-Face guard against any unwanted "guests." Kristel could almost see herself as a heroine, beauteous and lionhearted, imbued with unflinching valor; and she would have clapped her hands in joy if the long sleeves had allowed her more freedom of movement. After so much boredom and housework, this was going to be some adventure!

She only hoped Cat-Face would be glad to see her.

In many ways does the full heart reveal
The presence of the love it would conceal.
—Samuel Taylor Coleridge

Chapter Twenty-Four

The moon sailed on a sea of midnight blue. Dark clouds scudded across the brilliant disc in the starry, cold, Minnesota sky, and crisp, biting air already foretold a frigid winter that would encase the land in a mantle of pure white, powdery snow. In the distance tomcats hissed and howled as they stalked one another in the cold night.

Dressed in men's clothing—too large for her— Kristel crept up behind the carriage house, keeping in the moon-shade, the night surrounding her and cold blue shadows spooking her. She was about ready to jump out of her skin, but was so intent on her midnight mission to help Cat stand guard on this ice-cold night, she did not sense a presence right behind her. . . .

He moved quietly out from the deepest shadow.

With Kristel unprepared, the attack came hard and fast. Like lightning striking. She would have screamed had she been able to, but her face was instantly covered by the dark hand attached to the long muscular arm that had suddenly snaked up over her chest. It held her and positioned her stiffly against a rock-hard body.

Frozen by terror and having difficulty breathing, Kristel could only protest in muted whimpers. A hard chest drove into her back, and she thought her spine would be crushed if she was held long in the viselike grip the stranger had on her.

Afraid now, Kristel began to struggle, turning, twisting, writhing against the muscular hold on her, and it was all to no avail. She thought of calling for Cat or Tamara—anyone who could hear her! But thinking it and being able to do it were different things altogether.

"Be still!" Cat commanded the "young man" he held in a merciless grip. "You are young, I can tell. I will not kill you if you tell me who sent you and if there are others." No sound. "Maybe I will kill you then." He breathed hotly into her ear.

"Ca—" She struggled to cry out the name of the man whose voice she recognized. But her effort was crushed and garbled by the strong hand that clamped ruthlessly over her tender mouth and oh-so-cold nose. *I can't breathe, Cat!*

The lad squirmed and kicked and wrenched his body so violently that Cat had no alternative but to push him to the cold earth. He stilled his captive's frantic struggles with the lean weight of his hard muscular body, pressed the baggy-trousered youth to the ground. "Who sent you?" he hissed in a stern voice filled with ominous warning. His eyes, now the color of the moon-swept river, were endless depths of iciness.

"I . . ." *Pant, pant, pant.*

Cat's knee lifted and came to rest in the crotch of Kristel's baggy trousers. Her eyes widened at the flood of warmth that swept through her. As the knee pressed harder, a powerful jolt of desire shot up through her untried body. The knee stayed where it was, but Cat's hand moved roughly to the lad's chest when he became aware that a vital part of the lad was below his pressing knee.

The Indian went as cold as the night. His eyes were steely, cold discs in his lean, hard face.

"Sweet Spirit!" Cat sprang angrily from the inert form he had thought was nothing but a timid boy. He jerked the dainty quivering mass to its feet.

Kristel's heart jumped into her throat. She knew she was in trouble, big trouble, when a lean hand shot out to knock the slouch hat from her head. Cat stood still as he watched golden hair tumble down around her shoulders and crest the tips of her . . . her . . .

"Breasts!"

Cat sucked in a deep breath to quiet his rage. "I thought you a silly child at times, but this night you are a stupid girl!" He lashed into her while she stood blinking at him. His gritted teeth made his jaw appear even leaner, harder, and more hostile.

Kristel gasped. Her heart raced, and she swallowed over and over. She wished the moon would come down and spirit her away to the heavenly realm!

"Do you know I could have broken your back with one snap? I might have used my knife." He swiftly brought that weapon before her eyes.

She winced. "I wanted t-to . . ." Kristel could not

go on.

Cat, one hand on a lean hip, leaned over her, hissing, "Be still!" He wanted to shake her, take her slim neck between his fingers or slap, spank, shake her—do anything to frighten the daylights out of her. *"Child!"* he cried, his eyes deep as midnight ice.

She stared at the hard, gleaming blade held before her and swallowed twice before finding her voice, then croaked like a frog that has been banished from its comfortable lily pad.

Kristel gulped and said, "I . . . I'm sorry, C-Cat. I just . . . wanted t-to help. Why are you s-so angry? I didn't do anything b-bad."

He glared at her. "Not bad?" Reaching out, he tugged angrily at her wrist, then dropped her arm as if it were a hot iron.

She stared into his face, noting the finely chiseled mouth, the Indian-straight bridge of his nose, his high cheekbones, his taut and bronzed flesh. Never had she seen him look this angry!

She sniffed aloud. "N-no, not bad."

"What are you doing in the clothes of a man?"

"It's my disguise." Again she sniffed and snuffled. "Don't you like it? I was going to come out here and help you—"

"Why should you hide yourself in this clothing of a young man?" Cat shook his head. "Such a waste. I do not understand you, Kristel. You never make much sense. You are hot one day; cold the next. You frown. You smile. You laugh. You cuss."

"I do *not* cuss!"

"I have heard you, do not lie to me."

Kristel flipped her hair at him, defiant, haughty. "I

330

am moody, and this is normal, after all. What do you expect? I am not an *old* person like you."

"You do not stay frightened very long." Cat moved closer. "I think I must teach you a lesson you will never forget."

Kristel's eyes sparkled and her heart beat accelerated. "What is this lesson?" Her pink tongue moved over her lips to moisten them, and she tried to look seductive.

Then, before Cat could pull his gaze from one prowling feline chasing another, howling, hissing, Kristel jerked and spun about; she ran for the door of the carriage house and, once inside, hurriedly found a place to hide. Way in the back by the horses. She wanted him to kiss her. Yes!

It was now or never. Kristel swallowed the lump in her throat. This was going to be the hardest trial of her life . . . and if she succeeded she would never be the same again. Not in the morning. Not ever.

Yet, it was what she wanted. She swallowed hard. Wasn't it?

"So, you are trying to hide from me," Cat said, his sharp eyes on her shadowed face, which she kept out of the moonlight. She flushed, a pink tint rising in her cheeks, though he couldn't see it in the shadowy interior of the carriage house. "I love you, Cat," she whispered, her breath soft in the night. "I have loved you from the first moment I saw you."

Cat went quiet and still all over. He finally spoke after he'd been in deep thought for several moments.

"That was years ago."

"Yes," she dared respond. "Cat." She said his name again, using the shortened version. "I didn't know it then, but I know it now."

"You are a silly girl, Kristel. You must go inside before Tamara awakens and finds you gone. She will be worried, you know this. She has had a hard time of it lately. You must not try her patience at this time."

"You are right." Kristel's eyes flickered. "But I think she will not awaken for a long time."

He lounged against a stall in which a horse nickered softly. "What if she does? Then what?" He bided his time. "Daniel might come home this night . . . then what will you say?"

She rose as gracefully as she could in the baggy attire, accepting his hand up. "Daniel is far away," she said in a whisper, looking at the nickering horse whose liquid eyes reflected the moonlight stealing in. "I love horses, don't you?" She breathed in the fecund smells that assailed her nostrils.

"Don't change the subject, Kristel. I said that you must go inside. Do not be more of a child than you already are."

"I am not a child!" Kristel protested. She had a sudden urge to reach out and touch his face, to feel its raw silk beneath her palm. But he was angry, she knew, and she feared his response to such an action. He might never speak to her again, or he might leave; and she wouldn't like it if Cat went away before Daniel returned home.

Cat reached out for her hand, then thought better of it and dropped his to his side. "Come. I will walk to the house with you."

"No! I want to stay here with you, Cat!"

Cat-Face groaned, wanting her to stay with him more than anything. "You will get cold, Kristel. It is not warm enough in here." He could have *warmed* her.

"It is!"

"I know what you are asking. But you cannot, Kristel." Her little body was virgin, she had known only youthful kisses, not lovers, he told himself. He could feel the longing shuddering through her and knew her innocence with his mind and with his body.

Cat felt a strange fiery sensation inside him. It was like none he had ever felt before. This time his mind must not stand aside and watch with cool amusement as when a practiced woman welcomed him, for Kristel was not such a woman. She was a virgin. He did not want to hurt her. She was too pure, too good, too . . . He could not continue this train of thought. He already felt much more than he should for a white woman. A girl. Stupid! He'd known only Indian women . . . but . . .

Kristel continued to stand in the shadows of the carriage house, mesmerized by the green-gold cat eyes that had narrowed into slits. Cat. He was a cat, just like his name. She imagined she could reach out and brush with her fingertips a narrow velvety nose, long whiskers, claws. She found herself dwelling on unmaidenly thoughts. . . .

He would capture his prey, but not this night.

Belatedly, Cat realized it was almost dawn, that they'd been gazing at each other through the silvery light spreading through the rough-hewn window of the carriage house. How sweet she was, how baby-soft the skin he had touched. He wanted her completely, but not then.

"We will go now. I will take you to the house."

"Yes," Kristel said with a reluctant nod, "I know you will."

As he walked her to the house, she told herself, You want him, silly, so why don't you throw yourself at him? He has made you feel things you've never felt before. But why be stupid, as he has called you. Just wait it out.

"Good night, Cat." She disappeared into the house.

"Good night, Kristel." He disappeared into the gray dawn.

The cold was crisp and biting, but it did not cool Cat's desire.

Tamara was ethereal in her loveliness. She wore a crisp white dress with a huge, dipping embroidered collar of French linen and lace threads. The pearls wound about her throat were strong and fine, a symbol of purity, just like this woman who inspired righteousness, honor, and truth. Tamara. Her eyes were neither green nor gray, but a soft blending of the two colors. Tammi . . . Tammi . . . a beautiful bride with a radiant countenance.

She seems so real, Daniel told himself, aware that he was dreaming in the bed he had taken to get out of the crisp, windy, Minnesota night. The northern stars were high overhead, their diamondlike light winding across the sky and around the cold, bright moon, winking through the silver-etched clouds floating past. Daniel was warm inside the boarding-house, aware that he was dreaming but unable to awaken, nor did he wish to now that Tamara was walking in his dream and about to come into his arms.

"You belong to me now. Come, come," he heard himself whisper, the sound like the sweetest movement of the wind.

He stood in the hall of a house, the walls draped with heavy shadows that seemed to crowd in on the spot where he was. Tight and quick, his breathing was almost labored. A familiar hunger gnawed at him, mounting in his loins, his muscles corded taut by the wrenching strain of the most acutely sensitive form of desire in existence.

"Come to me, Tammi, come. . . ." He heard the voice as if it were outside his body, yet he had sleep-knowledge that his mind had framed the words, his lips had moved in silent command.

In the night, there was the click of a knob, and Daniel gloried in a flush of quickened blood: his veins, his brain, his manhood, all heated by the liquid fire that rushed through them. He shivered like a rutting stag; panted like the Wolf. . . .

Tamara peered into the shadows, as she descended the dark, shadowy stairs saying, "Who is there?" The uncertain light from the moon and her hesitancy combined to make things seem hazy. She was in a dream! But this dream was different. She seemed to have lived this moment before. . . . Was she truly awake? Or had she done this very same thing before?

If this really is a dream, Tamara thought, why not see where it leads?

She halted on the fifth stair down from the top, but clouds obscured the moon at that moment, so the way was very dark. Then the words, from long ago, came to her: *"Ah-ha, Little Oak . . . come to me, my love."*

Daniel! Yes, it was he. And she was not afraid of him this time. She fled downward, and gasped, for at the precise moment the clouds passed the emerging moon's luminous face, she saw . . . *him!*

Daniel saw her plainly, her ashen hair spilling loose like platinum velvet, more intimate and alluring when flowing freely. Eyes that sought his and every familiar detail of his countenance matched his in emotion, as when they had first made love.

"You called me?" Her voice was stronger this time, not as tremulous as in the past . . . when they had been awake and younger.

He only nodded, but he moved closer through the fine, drifting purple mist that had entered his dream, and he was suddenly able to discern her thoughts.

From the back door of the house yellow moonbeams spilled into the hall, silver motes rising in them like a haunting mist from their bare feet to touch their bewildered . . . No! Their faces were now radiant, happy. They were evidently in love and very aware of each other as human beings.

The new, mature wonder of their mutual need filled them, overflowed with sweet liquid fire that ran from one to the other. Will I wake up soon? Tamara wondered. Hypnotically, she reached toward him and he spoke.

"I want you," he said, his hands reaching for her.

She frowned at his words and, for a moment, wondered if she really could trust him not to hurt her again. They seemed to have been tossed back in time, and she was afraid he would be unfaithful to her as he had back then. Yet, she wanted him to want her for herself, not just to sate his lust.

Plagued by confusion, Tamara closed her eyes, thinking that Daniel would vanish as he had so many times before. But when she opened them, he was still there.

"I mean it, Tamara, I want you. You. It is you I want, Tammi, only you. I commit my life to you, place my heart in your care."

He pulled her closer to him. "Come and love me. Do not be afraid this time."

Tamara looked about, saw the boardinghouse in the background, and smiled happily. "Yes, Daniel, I understand this time. You want me for who I really am. This time you love me."

"Oh yes, my beloved. This time is forever. Kiss me, Tamara," he said softly. "Kiss me, Tamara, like you did on our wedding night. Remember?"

Tamara's throat felt dry. "We are married?" she asked. Then, "When?" Once again a picture swept across the one in the background and they were standing beside tumbling, sunlit falls, then beside a strong-flowing river. There they lay down to touch, embrace, kiss. . . .

She remembered the delightful touching of their mouths from once before . . . no, more than once . . . they had made love on several occasions.

"I love you, Tamara."

He loves me. Tamara was speechless and confused.

He was going too fast, saying too much, she told herself as she met his loving gaze. *Daniel loves me?*

"I love you, Tamara, I belong to you. Just as you belong to me. I will not lose you again, not now that I have found you."

"Oh, Daniel, I do remember. *Daniel!*" Tamara's heart stood still. He was vanishing! His leaving struck a pain in her heart.

"No, Daniel . . . Daniel! Not again. Don't leave me, Daniel." She was panting, very fast, very hard. "I believe you, I belong to you, and you belong to me. . . . *Daniel . . . come back to me!*"

She was reaching out to him, but he was disappearing fast.

"*Tamaraaaa! Nooooo-ooo! Come back. . . .*"

"*Daniellll! Take my hand. . . . Please, don't go!*"

She was tossed from a swirling world of shadows onto her bed, landing hard on her back, her fall was broken by the soft mattress. Then she instantly realized she hadn't fallen at all, she had jerked about so violently she had imagined a hard landing.

The tears, they were real. Crystal drops of pain and disappointment rolled down her cheeks. *I am alone, so alone. Why did you leave me again, Daniel? I have nothing to remember you by. Why did you go?*

Something moved beside her on the bed, something real, yes, something alive. Tamara shook the dream from her brain and looked down . . . where two large, dark, liquid eyes were staring up at her. In wonderful trust.

Danny said quickly, "Mama?" He reached out to touch her face, feeling the moisture. "Why're you cryin', Mama? I'm not cryin'. Feel 'n' see." Taking

338

her hand, he led it to his soft, velvety cheeks.

"Yes, darling, I can tell you are not crying."

Hugging him close to her breast, Tamara kissed Danny's cheek and brushed his hair away from his face. It was dark brown now, for it had lightened since his birth, and Tamara and Daniel both thought he would have light brown hair when he had grown up.

"Why're you, Mama?" Danny persisted.

"Well . . . I miss your father, that's all. I had a dream about him and want him to come home and be with us."

"Me too!"

Tamara laughed softly. "Not so loud, darling, you'll waken the others."

"Uh-uh."

"No?" Curious, she looked into his face. "Why will you not awaken the others?"

Danny giggled, squirming beside his mother's warm body. "Krissy's 'wake. Saw 'er come in, say g'night."

"When?" Tamara wondered what Kristel had been doing up, for she had seen her go into her bedroom when she and Danny had gone to lie down. "It must have been a long time ago?"

Danny shook his head. "No-ooo." He giggled again. "Krissy's got Daddy's clothes on . . . looks fun-ee!"

Now Tamara sat all the way up. "Kristel has *what* on?"

She did not wait for Danny to repeat himself but went to look for herself and found Kristel lying across her bed, fully dressed in male clothing that was much

339

too large for her. Long blond hair spilled over her bent arm, the elbow pointing to the slouch hat perched precariously upon the edge of the bed as if she'd been too tired to remove it and the clothes she was wearing.

Tamara pressed a finger to her lower lip. What could this be all about? After looking Kristel over to make sure she was unharmed, she slipped out of the room, then started to step back inside to cover the girl with a blanket. Upon doing so, she looked down and saw evidence of the carriage house: horse-pucky.

What had Kristel been doing out there with Cat-Face? But the Indian would not have done anything . . . would he?

Now Tamara looked a bit worried. She reentered the bedroom and went to stand over Kristel, who was lying peacefully on the bed, smiling and then frowning as if she were dreaming. When she looked as if she were about to cry, Tamara caught her murmured words:

"Cat . . . why don't you want me? Why didn't you . . . kiss me?"

Satisfied with that, Tamara backed away from the bed, then turned to leave the room, deciding to let Kristel sleep before questioning her as to why she'd been wearing men's clothing.

Danny was just padding out into the hall. She shushed him with a finger across her lips, then took him up in her arms, adjusting his white cotton nightshirt while she carried him downstairs so she could begin breakfast. But today, though it was Monday, she was not going to show at work.

Placing Danny in his high chair, Tamara set

about gathering eggs, bacon, bread, butter, and coffee while she made up a plan. There was a steely look of determination on her face. As soon as Cat came in for his breakfast, she was going to tell him he must go for Daniel, inform him of his twin's deceit, and warn him to watch out for those who intended to set him up and get him sent back to prison!

While she made breakfast, fragments of her dream returned to Tamara. She had been in it with Daniel, at the Olsky house where they had made love in the upstairs bedroom. She shivered to think of the dream's meaning. In it, Daniel had reached out for her and then he had vanished, as he had so many other times. She stared at the steaming coffeepot. Like a vapor, Daniel had risen and quivered before her for a moment, clouding her vision before vanishing.

Tamara prayed fervently for his safe return. Soon. He had to come home soon! It was a matter of life and death. . . . She just knew it.

"Tamara."

With a hand over her breast, Tamara turned to see Cat standing there. Her smile was tremulous. "I should have gotten used to your noiseless approach by now."

"You have said this before. But on this day you have reason to feel you are on a cliff edge. I understand. No harm will come to you or the child." There was a humorous slant to his mouth now. "Kristel will be safe also."

"By the way," Tamara began, setting a plate of food before him, "Kristel is asleep on her bed . . . but she is dressed very strangely. I, ah, wonder if you have any idea why she is wearing the clothing of a male person."

Cat's cat-eyes twinkled merrily. "Of course."

Danny wrinkled his button nose. "Krissy's fun-ee!"

"Yes, Danny—Little Bow—Kristel is that," the Indian wholeheartedly agreed. He glanced up at Tamara before stabbing the yellow bits of scrambled egg, his fork paused in midair. "Kristel was dressed for guard duty." That was all he said before putting the eggs away.

Tamara was puzzled; then it dawned on her. "She has always been adventurous, Kristel has. One time, long ago, that adventuresome spirit got her lost in the woods and we did not find her for many months."

The dark head nodded. "I remember," Cat said, then sipped his hot, black coffee and licked his curving lips.

Tamara's puzzlement continued. "You do?" she asked.

"Yes. I remember that and a whole lot more."

"Kristel is special to you, I am beginning to think."

Cat decided honesty was best, as always. "She touches my heart like no woman, young or old, ever has."

Tamara looked into eyes that used to seem so lost and stern. Lately they looked as if he'd "come home." "She has a place in your heart then; I am correct, am I not?"

"She is too young."

"Too young?" Tamara wondered what he was trying to convey to her. "For what? Making babies?"

Blushing suddenly, she was hardly able to believe she'd asked that question.

Acknowledging her query for what it truly was, Cat answered, "I have not touched Kristel, not her body. We might have met and touched with our minds, but not our—" He suddenly stopped, realizing he'd been about to repeat himself.

Annoyed with the provocative direction his thoughts were taking, Cat abruptly silenced them and, with an uncharacteristic frown, said out of the blue, "The long white cold will be here soon." He handled the knife in the sheath upon his bent leg.

"Yes, Cat." Tamara employed Kristel's shortened version of his name. "That is what I would like to talk about now—that and more." Her eyes widened as he withdrew a pistol . . . for her use.

"I will find him," Cat supplied before she continued.

Tamara nodded. It was what Cat wanted also, she knew.

Those who play with Cats must expect to be scratched.
—Miquel de Cervantes

Chapter Twenty-Five

A pale moon westered as the two—a man and a woman—slipped from the shadowy cover. The starry beauty of the cold night was lost on them. Pamela—Pink Cloud—had no stomach for James Strong Eagle's ruthless plan, though she could see his ebony-blue eyes smoldering with excitement over the theft he'd plotted. She wanted to hurl curses at him, but she didn't know any since the Indian tribe she'd lived with had never cursed or used the Great Spirit's name in vain. Actually, she hated to hear foul words come from any man's or woman's lips, but at that very moment she heard them coming from the noisy tavern. She grimaced and cringed at what she was about to do.

"Are you ready, Pamela?" James's voice came to her through the night, silky and threatening. If she did not do as he commanded, he would carry out his threats. Everything about James is different, Pamela thought, even the new timbre of his voice.

"You have prepared me all week, Strong Eagle,"

Pamela remarked. "I cannot be anything but ready for this terrible thing I must do."

"Yes," James hissed, holding the knife close to her throat. "You are afraid of what I will do to you some night if you do not obey my commands."

"I am!" she agreed with a nod, the quick lift of her shoulders causing her blond wig's springy yellow curls to bounce across her tan throat. "Where are the others?" she asked, meaning Raymond Horse and the foul-tempered Rufus.

James stared at her for a long, hard moment before answering. "They have other business to take care of." *Like kidnapping Tamara and the child.* "Now, go inside and take care of *our* business. Be sure to mention the name of Daniel Tarrant—he is your partner in crime. You do not say that, you only say he is waiting up the street for you to bring Taylor to him, to discuss some business."

"I know what to say, James. I am not stupid."

"I will not say what you are or are not." He went on. "After I hit Taylor over the head and we rob him—no, we will not kill him; I promised I would not—then we will leave him near the tavern so someone will come along and revive him. He will awaken with the name Daniel Tarrant on his lips."

James's breath wafted her way and again Pink Cloud's stomach constricted, making her feel nauseous. James had overindulged at supper while she'd eaten nothing, and now he had buffalo breath. *Ugh.* Pamela shuddered, wishing she could escape his presence.

Bravely Pamela snickered. "You eat too much,

James. Soon you will blow up like a balloon." She grimaced as he moved closer to her, his overhanging belly preceding him. She giggled, mostly to relieve her own tension. "You will need another stomach pretty soon to contain all the food you put into your gut."

"Gut? What kind of word is that for an Indian woman to use?"

"I am only part Indian, like you."

"You talk too much, woman. Someday that will get you into much trouble."

"You still sound like an Indian, James. You will never fit into the white world as I have done."

"Go now!" James ordered, his harsh voice slicing through the night. "Taylor Handley has just gone into the tavern. See that he drinks up quickly and follows you out that door!" The wicked blade of the knife flashed up once. "Or else!"

"Pamela Clayton" sashayed into the tavern, rolling her dark eyes in search of an admirer. She did not get much admiring from James, nor did she want any from that man now. If only he was like he used to be, handsome, finely muscled, lean-cheeked . . . and without such an ugly belly! she thought.

She inhaled deeply, and almost coughed due to all the smoke in the room. A blue haze hung over the tables, and she had to squint to find the man she was looking for. Forcing herself to be outwardly strong, she moved farther into the room.

Though many pairs of eyes were upon her, she went directly to the table of the cattleman James had earlier described to her. His name was John Taylor

347

Handley, but most of his friends and acquaintances called him Taylor, *and better not forget!* she had been told.

He was not bad looking, this man Taylor, and under different circumstances she would have made a play for him; but Pamela Clayton was a much more decent woman now—and she meant to return to her job at Nicollet House when all this was over. Tears sprang to her eyes as she thought of all the brutishness she'd endured from men. She was Pamela now, and she did not have to take such treatment any longer—not after this night!

James is stupid, Pamela thought with sudden insight, if he thinks I'm going to use the name I go under at the hotel. He had some motive for instructing her to go by that name, but she would not—"No, sir!" as Dorothea would say—get herself thrown into jail. Her job at the hotel was much too important to her—as was her neck!

As she walked to the cattleman's table, she decided to use the name Peggy, since lots of fair-haired women seemed to have that name. Seeing that Taylor was alone, she sat down next to him, slowly began to talk.

"My name is Peggy," she disclosed in a quiet voice. "What is yours, mister?"

The bright blue, intelligent eyes that looked upon Pamela were full of questions. "You from around here, Peggy? How is it that I've never seen you in here before?"

"I've been here," Pamela said with a pretty smile, "when you were not in here drinking, mister."

Taylor caught the word "drinking" at once. "That's almost impossible, Peggy, since I patronize his tavern all the time"—he chuckled softly, to relieve the tension he felt in her—"when I'm in Minneapolis, that is, and that's a lot. I have a ranch a little south of here." He did not add that he had a lovely wife and four children eagerly awaiting his return.

Swallowing hard, Pamela watched him drink and noticed that Mr. Handley was not getting drunk as James had said he would. Then his plate of food—a huge portion—arrived, and Pamela stared at it as if the plump woman had placed "buffalo pies" before him.

"You hungry, Peggy?" the cattleman asked. "If you're of a need, I'll buy you dinner . . . or a drink. Just one," he added, not wishing to get her or himself inebriated. He was a good and faithful man, but sometimes he got lonely while in town away from his family.

"I do not wish to drink, Mr. Handley." Pamela's courage was fast dwindling. Truth was, she wanted to run for the door and never look back at this nice man!

"Well then, what's your business, Peggy?" He forked a bite of juicy roast pork oozing gravy into his mouth, watching her eyes closely, trying not to show his growing suspicion.

"I . . ." She gulped, then went on. "I have a friend who wishes to meet you. . . . He is"—she swallowed even harder—"waiting up the street in the : . . boardinghouse."

"Who's your friend, if I might ask?" Taylor asked,

not slurring his words as James had told her he soon would.

The plump woman was back, setting down an extra plate of rolls and butter; then she returned to her other customers. Pamela dragged her eyes away from the woman and looked at the curiously smiling man. All of a sudden she blurted out, "He is Daniel Tarrant . . . and he is not my lover at this time. He is only my friend who wants to do business with you."

John Taylor Handley wiped the moisture from his brow and returned the handkerchief to his vest pocket. "Daniel . . . I know him, little lady. He banks where I do, and he just purchased the Smith boardinghouse here a few months back."

Feeling lightheaded and tense, Pamela squirmed in her chair, trying not to look the man in the eye. All of a sudden she had run out of words. What now? The things she'd already said had sounded very stupid. Did he believe her? Would he follow her out that door? She almost hoped he would not. She liked this man . . . and she wanted suddenly to run!

"How is it that Daniel is staying with you, little lady, when he just got married to Tamara Andersen?" He smiled, adding, "Name's Mrs. Tarrant now. They have a lovely boy named Danny. He couldn't have himself a dark-eyed little gal, not when he's holed up with a beautiful wife like Tamara?"

"I—"

Taylor gripped her wrist firmly but not painfully when she slowly began to rise from the table, her dark eyes wide as saucers. "Say, little lady, what is your game?"

"I . . . must go. Someone is waiting for me."

The cattleman let go of her arm. "Sorry if I gave you a fright, but you should be careful about who you associate with. Just a minute," he halted her in his deep voice when she would have walked to the door. "Does Daniel Tarrant want to see me or not?"

Pamela looked over her shoulder. She was tired of James's deceit and games. All she wanted to do was return to the hotel and go to sleep. Everything she had said and done this night seemed so stupid. She looked down at the cattleman's dinner. When had she eaten last? She was hungry and tired, not up to any more foolishness.

"I do not know Daniel Tarrant, mister."

An inebriated storekeeper at a nearby table—he also had become acquainted with Mr. Tarrant—stood up and said, with a boisterousness brought on by the amount of liquor he'd swallowed, "Hey you, is he Daniel Tarrant or not? Just what is your friend's name?"

"I do not know," Pamela said, feeling her knees shaking and her palms sweating. "I guess I do not know Daniel Tarrant, then."

While she had been seated at Taylor's table, she had not noticed the note the cattleman had slipped to the plump waitress, nor the eye contact the two had had. At the moment, keeping to the shadows in the smoky tavern, Tamara stood listening to Pamela's exchange with the two men. She felt faint, wondering if Daniel was again being unfaithful to her. He couldn't be! she told herself, feeling sick inside. *No!* This had something to do with James Strong

351

Eagle, she just knew it. But why had Daniel not re turned to her by now? And why was Pamela Clayto wearing a wig?

As soon as Taylor caught sight of Tamara Tarran standing in the shadows, he let his gaze fall back t his meal, not wanting this dark-eyed, blond-haire woman to see the person he had sent for. Actually he had hoped Daniel himself would show up, no the man's wife. He groaned inwardly, wonderin, what the lovely lady must be thinking. He should no have sent that note. But what else could he hav done?

"Likely story!" spat the unruly storekeeper. "Ge out of here, trash. Go and peddle your ware somewhere else!" Catching sight of Tamara Tarran just then, Mr. Wally's gaze dropped to his plate an he felt embarrassed to have spoken so.

When the sorry-looking blonde with the dark eye removed herself from the tavern, Tamara walke directly over to Mr. Handley's table. "May I have word with you, sir?" she asked in a straight voic despite her inner trembling.

"Of course." The cattleman stood to pull out chair for the graceful lady, then waited until she wa seated before he resumed his seat. "How may I be o service to you, ma'am?"

Tamara's shoulders lifted and fell slowly, once beneath her dark green cloak. "I would like to know everything that woman said to you. If you do no mind."

Following a sip of water, which he needed badly Taylor nodded and asked if she'd had her dinner, t which she replied she had. He then proceeded t reveal the conversation he'd had with "Peggy."

Nodding to acknowledge all he'd told her, Tamara leaned closer so the drunken man would not overhear: "'Peggy' is no Peggy, sir, she is Pamela Clayton. She was wearing a blond wig, you see, for she really has dark hair and is part Indian."

"Of course," said Taylor. "I knew there was something familiar about her. I know of this woman you speak of, this Miss Clayton, who works at the Nicollet Hotel . . . or House. She was new there when I checked in several months ago." The man leaned closer. "What do you think she is up to?"

"I am not certain, sir. But I might need to call on you for aid in this matter."

"As I said, ma'am, I am at your service." He smiled brightly. "I do so love helping damsels in distress . . . but where is your husband at this time?"

Tamara looked away then. "He is away on business. I . . . He should have returned by now. I just hope he has not been sent back to prison for the crimes Pamela Clayton's gentleman friend has committed."

Mr. Handley sat back, pushing his half-eaten food aside since he had long ago lost his appetite. "What a tangle. May I call you Tamara? I feel that my fat pocketbook, or my life for that matter, might have been at risk here. Perhaps you can tell me more, that is, if you are up to it?"

"Yes, I can stay for another half-hour, since my child is being looked after by my stepdaughter, Kristel. They should be safe until I get back home." She patted her reticule, indicating that she had a weapon tucked inside. "Kristel knows where to hide if anyone should come to the house demanding entrance. You see, the man we had guarding the place has gone in search of my husband, and Kristel is alone with Danny and the elderly boarders."

"Ah, lovely name Kristel. My own daughter's name is Kirsten. Now"—he leaned closer, pouring her a glass of water since she had declined any food—"how might I be of service? First, let me know the facts, Mrs. Tarrant."

"Tamara is fine, sir."

"Then you must call me Taylor."

"Thank you, Taylor. I do so need your help. . . ." She blushed and looked away, embarrassed at having to call upon a mere acquaintance for support and protection.

"It is not as if we are strangers, Tamara. I have met your husband at the bank a time or two in the past months, and we've even had lunch together."

Which Daniel? Tamara wondered. "The real Daniel, sir, or the fake?"

"Oh dear. This is much more serious than I'd first suspected. Still, I love unraveling puzzles."

"This is much more than a puzzle. It has become a dangerous situation, one in which I am afraid someone might face harm—or death—very soon."

"Have you contacted the authorities?"

"No. I am afraid my husband might be apprehended for theft again."

"Ah, so that is what the pretty little 'Peggy' was trying to set my pocketbook up for, eh?"

"I am afraid she was, sir . . . Taylor. You see, I recognized her at once through all the makeup and the wig. Actually Pamela is a nice person, I just believe she is being forced to participate in these crimes. I read the question on your face, and no, I do not believe they will be so stupid as to show up at the boardinghouse. Not after they have just failed with you, and especially not after employing the name of my husband." Tamara shook her head. "I do not understand why Daniel's name was brought into it. . . ."

"Little lady, I am worried about your family. Are you certain they are not in some danger?"

"As I said, I do not believe they are—not yet."

But Tamara was mistaken. . . .

Outside, Pamela sucked in several deep breaths of fresh, cold night air, to steady her shattered nerves. What must I do now? she asked herself, afraid of Strong Eagle's wrath. When he discovered she had failed him, then what? Where was he? He was supposed to have met her right behind the tavern, where he was to have struck Taylor over the head and robbed him.

Strong Eagle's plan has been for naught! she told herself.

James hissed from the dark shadows. "Where is Taylor?"

She whirled on him, angry that he had put her through such misery. "My name is Pamela now!" She ripped the wig from her head and tossed it into a nearby trash barrel, then raked her fingers through her long black hair. She began to walk away, pulling

355

her woolen shawl about her shoulders. "I wish to return to my room."

"Where is he?" James's heated demand caught up with her before he yanked her back. He looked down at her, and a vision of Tamara's face supplanted Pamela's painted countenance.

"Getting drunk. That's what he's supposed to do. Hah!" she exclaimed mockingly. "That one has more brains in his little finger than you do in your whole head! No wonder he is a wealthy cattleman. He has control of his life. He doesn't have to worry about where his next meal or drink is coming from as you do, James Strong Eagle! Bah!"

"Don't be smart, little Miss Clayton. Did you mess up my plan?" He kept wondering where Tamara was at this moment, what she was doing and what she would think of him when she saw his new image. She would not recognize him he decided, and for a moment he was sorry that he'd allowed himself to become so unattractive. "Well?"

"No," she lied, not liking the way he was eyeing her. He had murder in his dark eyes. "Daniel Tarrant's name was mentioned, but what good will it do? Taylor was not buying any of my story. Besides, I could not get him to come out of the tavern; he was meeting another woman."

Startled, she felt herself being hauled hard by the arm, back to the shadows from whence they had come. James stood in deep thought, then spoke.

"Another way, then."

"What did you say?"

"Nothing. We will go to the boardinghouse now."

A fall of black hair trembled about her shoulders as she shook her head, saying, "Not as Pamela!"

"Yes, Pamela is coming if I must kick her all the way!"

She shuddered, wondering at James's lack of feeling. Truly he must have no heart, she thought, for he cares nothing for those around him.

Yanking her arm hard he pulled her along, keeping away from the entrance just in case someone came forth and recognized him. Not likely, since he was as fat as a stuffed hog . . . But that would change. When the day came that Tamara would be his, then he would be handsome and thin again . . . like Daniel Tarrant, Tall Thunder. Easy as pie.

James Strong Eagle had perished in the steamboat accident, so he was no more. James Creek would pick up where he left off, lose weight, and call himself Mr. Tarrant again! . . .

And if Daniel showed up, he'd prepared himself for that eventuality also. Just in case the sheriff, who must now be reading the note he'd received, did not believe it was worth his while to apprehend the man who might have slain Ole Larson several years back. Thinking that the concocted message would at least buy him some time with Tamara, James set off with Pamela in tow and made for the boardinghouse.

After putting Danny to bed, Kristel curled up on the sofa and tried to read the romantic novel she'd purchased just the week before. After managing a few paragraphs, she set it down on the table beside her.

Toying with the embroidered edge of a doily, she became lost in thought, her mind dwelling on the last hour she'd spent with Cat before he had gone in search of Daniel. . . .

She had been wearing a simple dress, a dusty blue shirtwaist, the same one she had on now, in fact. Tamara had bundled Danny up and taken him out for some afternoon air, and from the window Kristel had seen that her head often turned in the direction from which Daniel would arrive. Tamara had had eyes only for Danny and the vacant street down which no strikingly handsome man walked. Her hair was loose, and it blew across her face, rising in long golden banners above the creamy knitted hat she had been wearing. She watched and waited, patiently keeping an eye on Danny as he ran about the leaf-strewn yard where bare branches creaked in poignant melody in the cool, crisp wind.

Tears crept into Kristel's blue eyes, so forlorn was the sight of Tamara waiting for her love to return, her happily playing child unaware of his mother's intense longing. Kristel's heart went out to her friend, and she swallowed hard.

"Kristel is sad."

At the sound of Cat's voice Kristel slowly turned about, knowing that soon he, too, would be leaving, and then she would stand and forlornly wait for his return. Cat's face showed strain as he moved closer, always maintaining a safe distance between them.

"You are wrong, Cat. I am not sad." She drew in a deep breath. "You will be back; I just know you will."

That said, Kristel rose onto the tips of her toes and gently pressed her soft lips to Cat's leathery face. He drew back to stare at her tear-stained cheeks, thus breaking the contact that made him crave more of her.

His deep voice was rough with emotion. "I'll find Daniel, but I will not return to this house. It is much too dangerous."

Kristel was hurt. "Too dangerous for you . . . or for me?" she asked in a shaky voice she could not control.

Cat's heart missed a beat as he stared down into eyes that put to shame the sky blue waters of Minnesota's lakes. "For you, Kristel. You are too young, and you have no idea of how it is between a woman and a man."

She glared back at him defiantly. "I am not a fainthearted virgin, Mr. Cat-Face. I only want to share my life with you. And one day, mark my words, you will come to love me as much as I love you." *But first you will have to want me as much as I want you.*

Cat was not indifferent to her. If she believed that, she would have nothing. But she wanted more than the physical thing between them . . . she wanted his heart. Maybe one day she could make him fall in love with her. She knew he found her physically attractive. He most likely found many Indian women attractive too, but she would not share the man she loved with others. He would have to be all hers. He would have to know she was woman enough for him. And she knew she was.

He was looking down at her, steadily, but there

was no expression on his impassive, Indian face. Still, for an instant something gleamed in his eyes. She was suddenly aware of the way his fringed buckskin jacket emphasized his broad shoulders and narrow hips, the way his breeches clung to his powerful thighs, and her eyes skittered to and then from the closure below his pounded Dakota-gold belt buckle.

But he had caught their movement. "Keep your eyes where they belong, Kristel, otherwise you will drown. Trouble will come your way if you become loose with your gazes."

Bravely she moved closer. "The only trouble I want is from you, Cat." She looked him over, and her pink tongue flicked across her lower lip, making her seem womanly and provocative.

"You must not look at me like that," Cat-Face commanded abruptly, realizing that no woman had ever made him feel such desire.

With a catch in her voice, Kristel said, "Why?"

Cat's jaw clenched, but the concern in her pale countenance tempered his reply. "You know why." His voice was soft and low.

Kristel stepped up to him and pressed her palm flat against his chest, just inside his jacket. She felt love swell within her, love that by leaps and bounds was leading her to a new maturity, love that was molding her into a woman who desired to please one certain man. She had to win him, otherwise she would die or wither into an old maid.

"You will soon grow too old to have babies, Cat, and you will not be able to enjoy them while you are still young—well, somewhat young." Bravely Kristel stood her ground. "I want to have a baby—your baby." She reached for and took his hand, guiding it to her breast.

"Sweet Spirit!" Cat cried, leaping back as if she'd scalded him. "I have not even tasted your lips, yet you embolden yourself to bring my touch where it should not go. Your flesh is not for my pleasure, Kristel. You must feel shame to throw yourself upon an Indian who does not even know desire for you. You are white. I am an Indian, a full-blood. You think because Daniel has taken Tamara to wife that we will fit well together also." Looking at her hard, he said, "You are wrong, Kristel, and you waste your time on one who does not want you."

Kristel's eyes grew larger by the minute, and she swallowed hard to keep from sounding strained. "No, Cat, it is you who are wrong. I'll never stop loving you or waiting for you, and don't think it is beyond your ability to truly love—that is hogwash!" Whirling about, she cried over her shoulder as she fled toward the stairs, "I mean it, you arrogant savage, I love you, though God knows, you have made me wonder why!"

After Kristel had made her exit, Cat turned slowly, knowing he was not alone, for he had sensed Tamara's presence the moment she had come to stand in the opening leading to the kitchen. She watched him walk toward her, then brush past and head straight for the back door. He did not look back

361

or pause as she said, "I do believe Kristel means every word."

Tamara stooped to free the quiet, weary child from his outer clothing. "She has grown quickly into a woman any man would be proud to take as his wife . . . that is"—she looked kindly at Cat's back—"if he loves her."

Quietly, almost inaudibly, Cat said over his shoulder, "I have never taken any woman seriously, and I am too old to start now." Before closing the door, his eyes flicked over the child whose blood was one-quarter Indian, aware that the age of Danny's father matched his own. "I will find Daniel, for I know the path he travels there and back. You will see him any day now."

"Thank you, Cat. I am grateful."

After the door closed, Tamara stared at it for a moment, holding her half-asleep child in her arms, his chubby legs wrapped about her waist, his face resting on her shoulder, his dark eyes blinking wearily. She paused before mounting the stairs.

"Cat, you will return, surely," she said.

Several hours later the summons sent by John Taylor Handley had arrived, requesting that Daniel Tarrant come immediately to the tavern. Going upstairs to find Kristel, Tamara had spoken hastily to the teary girl telling her she would return shortly, she had some business to take care of. Hearing the wind howling outside, Tamara had dressed warmly and had made her way to the tavern.

*   *   *

James and Pink Cloud never got inside the boardinghouse, not in the usual way, but he made a discovery as he walked the barren halls of the old, boarded-up, dark Spanger house across the way. He had been thorough in his search and had found just what he needed.

> The little *Revenge* ran on sheer into the heart of the foe.
> —Alfred, Lord Tennyson

Chapter Twenty-Six

The hall clock struck ten.

Moving wearily into the living room, Kristel stood before the bookcase, searching for the novel she had placed in it earlier . . . or had she left it on a table? Deciding she did not feel much like reading something deliciously romantic—that would remind her of Cat—or sitting still and remembering him, she reentered the kitchen to look for a snack, and spied a juicy red apple. But she wasn't really hungry. Kristel frowned. She held the apple, recalling the beautiful sunset that evening. It had been so fiery, so vibrant, just like she felt inside when Cat was near. All fire and sunlight, kindled and aglow.

Ten o'clock. Tamara should have returned, and Kristel was beginning to worry. Tamara had stated that she had some business to see to, and that posed an even greater worry for Kristel: what sort of business would Tamara be conducting at this time of evening?

Rolling the apple in her suddenly moist palm,

Kristel smiled at remembering her words to Cat: *I am not a fainthearted virgin, Mr. Cat-Face.* She giggled softly. What a thing to say! Lord, she had been reading too many romantic novels, and now . . . now she wanted the real thing! But it had to be forever. Not a casual dalliance. She'd picked up that word from English novels. Dalliance . . . such a funny-sounding word when you thought about it.

Hearing a noise outside, Kristel went to the back door to investigate, hoping that Tamara had returned since she would like to discuss Cat with her, ask her what she should do. If Tamara were to tell her she was wasting her time pining away for a man who easily found his pleasures elsewhere . . . with many women . . . But no, Tamara would have no idea of what Cat's private life was like.

"Who is there?" Kristel asked as she stood at the back door, listening intently for Tamara's familiar step. "Tamara?" She flung open the door and found herself facing two strange men with shaggy hair and murderous-looking eyes!

Raymond Horse and Rufus stared at the lovely young woman who stood before them, stricken with surprise.

"That's her," Rufus said to Raymond and, nudging the man in the ribs, he hissed, "Let's get her!"

Kristel blinked again. *Let's get her!* What did he mean?

"Rufus, I do not think this—" Raymond broke off when Rufus lunged forward to haul the young woman through the doorway, clamping one hand across her face so she could not cry out.

But Kristel heard a hoarse cry, and it was coming from somewhere deep inside her.

"Let's go!" Rufus cried. "We got what we came for. There might be someone else in the house. Come on, Raymond. Don't stand there looking stupid. Grab that coat for her, and let's get the hell outta here!"

Her heart pounding, Kristel tried to kick the man who held her, but was thwarted by the lean, hard leg pressed against her limbs. Still, her arms flailed wildly, to no avail.

"Be still, girl!" the stranger hissed into her ear, wrapping the large coat about her quaking frame as if she were a sack of potatoes. Hefting her over his shoulder, he began to jog across the cold, moonlit yard, then melted into the frigid ice-blue shadows of night.

Paying close attention to the nuances in their speech, Kristel thought to herself: These are no ordinary men. They are out for blood—or money. Or both. But who can be paying them? Other questions flew at Kristel like the winter snowflakes which—she shivered—would soon be falling if the damp chill in the air was any indication.

Rufus felt the young woman named Tamara quiver and tightened his grip on her thighs.

Oh, Cat . . . Pain seared Kristel's soul. What had she gotten herself into? She had been so ignorant, not thinking twice before answering the door.

Where are you, Cat? . . . A snowflake descended . . .

Twilight blue colored the sky as shadows deepened

around the boardinghouse. Tamara, with Danny playing at her feet, sat with furrowed brow as she listened for Kristel's step at the back door. But no step came, nor had Taylor Handley and the peace officer returned after they had gone out to look for Kristel.

While Danny raced his toy buggy under a high-backed chair, Tamara watched with unseeing eyes, imagining Kristel lying frozen somewhere, her blue eyes never . . . Tamara could not complete the terrible picture summoned up in her mind's eye.

On her way home from the tavern the night before, she had momentarily delighted in the snowflakes falling around her, making her world a beautiful fairyland of whiteness and purity. By the time she had reached home, there had been an inch of the powdery white snow on the ground, so fast had it come down.

As soon as she had entered the boardinghouse, Tamara had felt an eerie emptiness, a foreboding. But she found a light glowing in the kitchen, and extra logs had been added to the fireplaces in the main rooms. Danny was snuggled fast asleep, in his bed, the old folks were snoring in their rooms. . . . But where was Kristel?

Swallowing her fear, Tamara had searched the house. Then, grabbing a coat, she had gone out to the carriage house. The horse was munching on his quota of hay, his sore leg having been rubbed down with linament . . . but Kristel was not about.

Returning to the house, Tamara had just been hanging her coat back on the peg when she'd noticed that the blue-gray coat was missing. And the shawl—where was that?

368

Kristel had gone out. But where? It wasn't like her to leave Danny unattended, since the elderly men slept soundly and would not awaken if he called out.

Now Tamara sat, worrying about Kristel. This had happened before; Kristel had vanished without leaving a clue. That other time she had been taken to an Indian village when she had been discovered lost in the woods. But there were no Indians living close by . . . Tamara shot up from her chair. Cat would not have kidnapped her. No. Impossible.

It had to have been James Strong Eagle's doing. For some strange reason she had felt him near the night before, as if he had been lurking in the shadows surveying her every move. He would have come forward then, she now believed, had not Taylor Handley arrived shortly after she had returned home.

Taylor had informed her that he had come to the boardinghouse because he'd had a crazy notion that all was not right with her. It had not turned out to be so crazy after all. When she had answered the door to find Taylor standing there, snowflakes dusting his hat and the shoulders of his coat, she had felt that eerie presence again. Looking into ice-blue shadows, she had sensed darker shadows in them, melting, then fleeing down the street, keeping to unlighted patches of darkness.

The concerned man had spent the night in My Emily's old office, then had gone for the peace officer at first light. She heard them returning and went to answer the door, trembling with dread and anticipation. The looks on their faces answered her unspoken question.

After the peace officer had left, saying he and his

men would keep looking, Taylor pressed a palm against Tamara's shoulder, showing her how terribly sorry he was. It was time for him to return home—his wife had been ill—but he would return the very next week and look in on her, he promised.

"You have done so much, Mr. Handley. I did not expect all the help and the comfort you've given, and I realize your family awaits your return. I thank you, and I will pray that your wife recovers from her illness."

Saddened by this lady's troubles because he found her sweet and kind, Taylor smiled and promised to return.

Several hours later Tamara lingered in the kitchen. She had fed Danny and the older folks, and now they had all lain down for a nap. She sorely needed this time alone, but it was Saturday and she had much to do. Without Cat's help, she had to bring in the wood, care for the horse, clean the house. Without Kristel, without Daniel, she had done most of the work by herself before. She remembered when My Emily was there to take on half the chores.

Tamara missed My Emily, especially with Christmas drawing near. Struggling with her loneliness, she swung a heavy shawl about her shoulders and went out to rub linament on the horse's sore limb, see to his feeding. She was just making her way back to the house in the blue of twilight, when she looked up and saw him standing there.

No, not standing. Almost falling over. Blood soaked the bandage around his forehead. His pantleg was torn.

Daniel had been hurt—badly.

Running and slipping across the icy patches, Tamara was hardly aware of the tears stinging her face in the cold.

He was home! Though he was hurt, he was home and she could take care of him.

Daniel turned and, looking dazed, cried out in a hoarse croak, "Tamara . . . Damn it, I'm sorry I went and got myself hurt. I was rushing to get home from St. Cloud, pushing the horse. He slipped and fell . . . rolled on me. . . . I got a ride to Minneapolis from a . . . a . . ." Just then he reeled dizzily.

"Don't talk, Daniel. Let me help you."

Rushing to his side, Tamara placed a muscular but quaking arm across her shoulders and helped him into the house. Before closing the door against the chill, she scanned the street and yard, and her heart sank. Daniel was home, safe; but Kristel had not yet returned. *Oh please,* Tamara silently cried, let her come home too.

It was snowing, and Tamara had not seen the shadowy figure watching from across the way.

The snow was drifting as Cat-Face trudged back to the horse, patting the pinto's black-and-white patched coat. While residing at the boardinghouse, he had kept Apache in a livery stable on the outskirts of Minneapolis, under the care of a half-breed who worked there.

He was about to go into the forest when he spied the blue spiral of smoke curling about the roof of the tumbledown house. Houses were few and far between along the prairie, and the boxlike structure was a welcome sight. Furthermore, something drew him to this old house. Perhaps Daniel is there, he thought.

Leading the weary pinto with all the trail gear strapped on him, Cat walked from the pine-scented woods to the ramshackle dwelling. Any way you looked at it, the house still seemed warm, inviting. And maybe there was some good food within, instead of beans and jerky.

"We can get into the house from here."

"I know. But, James, how will I get the child without being seen?"

"You will do it. There are two doors leading to the nursery."

"He is really a handsome boy?"

"You will see."

In the winter wild . . .
—John Milton

Chapter Twenty-Seven

Irregular puddles, the result of heavy sleet, wore a thin covering of ice, and the rising sun struck pink and gold rays from the frozen, pellucid teardrops clinging to the underside of naked twigs. Sunrise turned the eastern sky to an apricot hue under the low-hanging clouds that foretold more sleet or snow to come.

The long morning and afternoon dragged on. Numb to the bone, Kristel felt as if she had turned into a block of ice, except for her stomach, which seemed to float inside her like air, empty, growling, hurting. She had never been so hungry, nor had she ever subsisted on only dried meat and unpalatable fruits and brackish water.

Drawing the overlarge coat around her more securely, Kristel trudged behind one of her abductors, the other trailing along just in back of her. They had procured a heavy shawl for her, and she wore this over her head. As she was about to drop from exhaustion, the man called Rufus rushed to her and placed her atop the weary packhorse, where she swayed, listless and fatigued.

She looked down at them, knowing by the gentle expression on the face of the uglier one—Raymond—that she would come to no harm. What they wanted her for, she could not say for a certainty. They had given no indication of where they were going or why. I'll have to wait to find out, she thought, staring at the cold white sun that glared upon this frozen land that resembled an arctic tundra. She felt like a living icicle.

They had stopped at two houses along the way, both century-old dwellings owned by suspicious, shadowy folk, each time staying only for the night. Usually they slept in old shacks and lit low fires that would not be seen by other travelers. The strange men, who spoke with a drawl, did not try to take advantage of her as she'd first feared they might. She had spoken to them a little, but something she had said must have made an impression on them. They liked her and didn't really wish to hurt her. In fact, they seemed of two minds, and she dared hope that the pair would drop their hostile scheme and would allow her to return. But not by herself. She knew she'd never make it back to Minneapolis alone!

Believing she slept, the two men seated before the tiny fire glowing in the dilapidated one-room cabin discussed her openly but in undertones. Since Kristel was already bewildered by the melancholy tone in their voices, she listened closely to what they had to say.

"She is not the one," a male voice warned.

"She has the pale hair, the light-colored eyes. It is

er," the other man argued.

Kristel could not tell their voices apart when they were speaking in hushed tones.

"We will bring her to Wadena's, as *he* has ordered."

"Tah!" one of them spat out. "We don't always have to do what he says. I think we should take her back to where we got her. I don't like the pretty gal's sadness."

There was a chuckle. "Now it is you who feels sorry for her. Damn it all, what will we do?"

"I don't know. I'm tired and hungry and half-frozen, and I don't want to hurt that little one. Something's wrong. She's not old enough. The blonde we were supposed to take would be more womanly . . . you know what I mean."

Stung by those words, yet wondering whether to feel insulted or not, Kristel snuggled into her blanket, wishing to hear no more. She wanted only to sleep, since tomorrow she would again be worn to the bone and frozen. *A child, was she!* She would show them all, even . . . Oh, Cat was the only one she cared about—and of course Tamara, Danny. . . . *Oh go to sleep, Kristel.*

"Look!" cried Wadena. "They come!"

Unblinking, Cat looked at the slovenly woman with hair and countenance as filthy as the house she lived in. He shook his head, causing his raven hair to fall to one side as he loaded his rifle. Eyeing the woman again, he decided she must be frightened of him and didn't even realize she had called out when she had seen the men approaching.

Three of them. Two tall, one small.

Pulling the woman named Wadena over to a corner, Cat shoved her none too gently onto the floor and pressed her down. He gritted his teeth when he felt the moisture on his chin. That was the fourth time she had spit at him, but this time she had not gotten him in the eye.

"What is with you, woman?" Cat was not even looking at her or expecting an answer; through the window he was watching the three travelers approach the house, one plodding along as if the weight of the world rested on those slim shoulders.

"You lousy half-breed!" Wadena snarled.

"What does that make you then? You were not born on the edge of the blanket too?" Cat drawled.

Wiping the back of a large hand across her mouth and shoving a greasy strand of hair out of her eyes, Wadena snapped, "But you are Cheyenne, half-breed. I am Sioux," she said, pounding her hefty chest.

"No difference. I am Cheyenne-Sioux."

"Much difference, Wolf Man."

"That is not my name."

Wadena saw him in a new light. Her voice softened. "What is?"

"Never mind." Cat shifted his position, keeping a keen eye on those approaching. "Now shut up. If you do not, I will turn this barrel on you, woman, and stick it in your big mouth." He almost regretted those harsh words, then recalled the stream of abuse she had directed at him ever since they'd had the bad luck to strike up an acquaintance.

As Cat crouched in the shadows beside the frost-jeweled window, he remembered the conversation he'd had with Wadena when he had first arrived, taking her by surprise. She had made a mistake. A bad mistake. Flapping like a flag in a March wind, her mouth had not come to a halt until he'd politely told her to shut it. Luckily he'd gotten all the information he needed by then, and now he was prepared to greet the threesome with a smiling countenance.

Hearing snow crunch outside the door, Wadena popped up like a jack-in-the-box, but that was a mistake. Using the barrel of his rifle, Cat struck out for her shoulder, but caught her at the corner of the eye when she ducked. She yelped, and Cat grimaced, knowing the cry must have alerted the men beyond the door. One was awfully small, a boy perhaps.

Smiling, Cat held his rifle at the ready.

Kristel could not wait to get inside and warm up. She hadn't a care as to what the men had planned for her, not at that moment. All she could think of was warmth, food, and rest. Fear she could deal with later, after she had regained some of her strength. Maybe she could even escape. At least she could hope. Kristel thought of her favorite heroine. Catherina was "not crushed with despair or wrung out with hopelessness."

Before kicking open the door, Raymond called out, "Wadena! We're back!"

A corner of Cat's mouth curled. *Stupid mistake.*

Rufus groaned and clutched his stomach, which

had been loudly complaining of hunger for days on end. "Oh . . . that cannot be beans I smell cooking." His nostrils twitched at registering another odor, an even more welcome one.

The man was right. Cat could smell beans, and some variety of meat. And was that biscuits or bread cooking? Or—he sniffed—ready to burn? He could not allow that to happen, not to biscuits, not when he was this starved for something besides trail food!

As soon as the third man had filed into the room and pulled the door closed against the bone-piercing chill, Cat leaped from the shadows, his black hair streaked with wild blue lights, his rifle slanted across a lean hip. The man who was just reaching into his jacket was halted by a fierce command. "Leave it." Moving closer as that man's shifty eyes went to his companion in crime, Cat continued, "If you like living, leave it there."

"Yeah, do like he says, Raymond; leave it there." Rufus's eyes were shifty, as if he harbored a secret.

"No," Cat said, appearing to change his mind. "Put it on the table. . . . Move real slow!" he said abruptly when the man with the long, ugly face reached inside his coat too fast. "That's good." Grasping the pistol, Cat said, "I will take this. You won't be needing it."

Screaming like a banshee, Wadena rushed Cat and took hold of his long black hair. Kristel squealed, and her high-pitched voice caused the Indian woman to halt her attack and stare as the heavy shawl slipped from her head. Wadena glared at Rufus, plopping her hands onto her generously padded hips.

"So, ugly man, you have found yourself pretty

paleface?" she snorted. "This is what you bring home while Wadena cooks and cleans house and washes your filthy clothes?"

"You knew our plan, Wadena," Rufus whined, wishing he had never gotten involved in this foolish plot. "To bring Tamara, this paleface, here so that ..." His glance slid over to the lean, mean Indian, a full-blood by the wild look of him. A Cheyenne-Sioux, maybe.

Cat snorted. "You have made a mistake. This woman is not Tamara. She is— Never mind who she is. Just know you have been very stupid."

Smiling as if the world had suddenly become a glorious place, Kristel rushed to Cat's side, and he wound an arm about her waist. Looking up into his dark Indian eyes, Kristel glowed. She vowed she would get this man to love her if it took an entire lifetime. Worshipfully staring at Cat, she said, "You found me. How did you know?"

With a lopsided grin, Cat responded, "I kind of fell into it. You never seem to be far from me of late, woman."

He'd called her woman again! Kristel's spirits soared. She even smiled at the greasy-faced, scowling Wadena. The older woman's face lit up then, as her dark, pig's eyes went back and forth between the couple, and she beamed back at the youthful paleface.

"Biscuits burning!" someone yelled.

"Aiiiee!" Wadena cried, taking up a cloth and racing toward the oven. Opening it wide, she gave a sigh of relief, and brought out a huge pan of golden biscuits, then a giant loaf of grainy Indian bread.

"Ha, only one biscuit burned." Shyly she smiled at Rufus, and he returned the overture. "Made better beans, Ruf. Got vegetables from a faraway neighbor who stopped here to warm up, and he even gave us a big juicy ham he had on his sleigh. Cleaverson . . . he was bringing his sick son to doctor in St. Cloud."

"Oh, how nice of him," Kristel said, her smile revealing pearly teeth.

All smiled. All were starved. All were suddenly happy.

"We eat now," Wadena declared, grinning at Rufus and Raymond, then the other two. "What is your names?" she asked, in her bad English. "I like folks in love, like you are." Her nod took in Kristel and Cat.

Kristel, peeling off her warm clothes, piped up. "I am Kristel. This is Cat-Face."

Raymond snorted, then strode up to stand behind a chair. "I'm Horse-Face, and this here's our woman."

Rufus glared at Raymond as he said, "*Our* woman? Since when?"

"Well"—Raymond shrugged—"we share."

Looking up at Cat, Kristel said, "That is where we are so very different. I will never share my man, and I will never *be* shared by two men."

Smiling into Kristel's beautiful face, Cat picked up a biscuit, looked at it while rolling the delicious morsel between his long fingers, then at her again. He had been fighting his own instincts, but now he muttered, "First you have to get your man, Kristel." Taking a bite of the fluffy round, he continued to watch her closely.

Eyeing the biscuit, Kristel smiled to herself, cherishing a secret. "I'll get him," she murmured confidently. "I know the way."

Wadena caught the pale girl's eye and their exchange said much that was completely lost on the three men sitting down to the delicious feast, Cat resting his rifle between his muscular legs. Watching the young woman's eyes rest on their junction, Wadena brandished her wooden spoon.

"Wadena will never tell," she hummed, picking up her knife to slice off more thick slices of succulent pink ham and crusty golden bread. When the fry-bread was done, she placed that on the table, along with a huge jar of blackberry jam.

All through the remainder of the meal, Cat's eyes kept shifting between the men. Coolly aware of each movement they made, he knew he would not be spending the night under this roof. No, he was going to make certain he and Kristel were far away come nightfall. He trusted no one, no matter how friendly a body seemed.

Looking at Wadena while she busily served them, humming under her breath, Cat thought that life had weighed heavily on her. Right now she seemed trustworthy enough, but later, should he doze off, he might find a knife at his throat.

Dismissing his companions' motives, Cat turned his mind to more pleasant thoughts while all silently shared the meal. Then, all of a sudden, in order to gain the initiative, Cat asked, "Where is Daniel?" The other men seemed dumbstruck. "Have you seen him?"

After swallowing noisily, Raymond shrugged.

"We know of no one by this name."

Rufus, however, had had his fill of James Strong Eagle's plan. "Daniel, yes. This would be Tall Thunder. I have heard of him . . . through James Strong Eagle. That one would like to see Daniel dead if I'm not mistaken. Even as we speak, he's going after his wife, snooping around that boardinghouse and once he finds out we took the wrong female, he's going to do some kidnapping himself."

"Sorry, missy." Raymond turned to Kristel. "I didn't want to take you from that house. You are a nice little lady, and we did not wish to harm you. We made a mistake."

"Sorry?" Cat muttered under his breath, caressing the barrel of the rifle still standing between his legs. He surveyed the man through critically slanted eyes.

Kristel's slim brows came together in a frown as she watched the rhythmic movements of his hands, the play of long, dark fingers. After a minute she glanced up and, a silent question in her blue eyes, touched him on the sleeve. His eyes glittering with suppressed emotion, Cat said, "Yes. We will go soon."

Wadena looked disappointed. "Go so soon?"

Cat hesitated only a second before he gave a curt nod of his dark head, blue-black hair swinging against his throat.

Wadena's large hands made a short sweep. "You can sleep on the floor, with blankets."

It was suddenly quiet in the room, the tension so thick you could cut it with a knife. Kristel waited. She held her breath.

"No," Cat said smoothly, his eyes alert to any

sudden movements. "We must go. I have to catch up with Daniel"—his glance took in the two men—"before Strong Eagle does."

"I hear Daniel Tarrant can take care of himself," Rufus put in, his eyes adoringly resting on the pale-haired young woman he likened to an angel.

Chewing a morsel of fry-bread, Cat regarded Rufus thoughtfully. He distrusted the man's appearance of lazy calm and friendliness, knowing silent men like himself could change instantly and become dangerous if crossed.

Now, shrewdly, Cat did not ask questions or answer them. Instead, he listened while a part of his mind raced ahead to the evening he would spend alone with Kristel in the shack he had spotted some miles away.

She was noticeably silent, smiling but saying very little. Often she felt Cat's hard gaze on her, and her heart shook as she thought of the hours ahead when they would be alone.

Her nerves tingling, Kristel was only too aware that Cat was taking her away from there.

This very night . . .

Unwarmed by any sunset light,
The gray day darkened into night,
A night made hoary with the swarm
And whirl-dance of the blinding storm.
—John Greenleaf Whittier

Chapter Twenty-Eight

Gaslights glowed as the doctor came and went. Daniel was resting more easily now that he had been given something to relieve the pain. But he still groaned aloud when he moved the wrong part of his body. One side of his rib cage was a huge mass of purplish bruises, and he thought he had never felt so sore, not since he had been roughed up by the thugs who'd knocked him around several years back when they'd set him up for prison. Half-breeds he'd never seen before, and then only in glimpses through swollen eyes. Thanks to James Strong Eagle.

Rolling his head on the pillow, Daniel scanned the bedroom for Tamara. The lady's boudoir chair, covered in lavender material and crowned with a white lace antimacassar, stood unoccupied. She was nowhere in sight. He smiled lazily as his eyes traversed the room. Everything in it had been touched by her feminine hand. It was airy. Lovely. Just like Tamara.

His gaze fell on filmy night dresses. Hers. She had

changed since they'd become man and wife. Become more feminine.

Captured in a wash of gaslight were a feminine array of satin lingerie bags, gilt-edged boxes, a trumpet-bearing angel, the fine tracery of lace, sachets that evoked the scent of garden-fresh bouquets. A periwinkle blue, floral print dress peeped out from the pale oak wardrobe, and he glimpsed other gowns: cherry red and indigo blue, deep lavender, and rose.

Over there—his head turned painfully on the pillow—was Tamara's English pine box in which she cached letters from My Emily, tenderly tied with a violet ribbon. On the dressing table sat a cut-crystal and silver spray bottle, also a dresser set. The lacy embroidered skirt was pink and lavender, the soft pastels repeated on the upholstered bench where just yesterday she had sat while dressing her hair into a charming French roll. Her expression had been wistful and sad, for she had wondered where Kristel could be.

He remembered the days they'd spent together before he'd left for the Suland. The close of a summer's afternoon, lazy walks beside the river, joining hands and kissing . . . He smiled. If those flowers had had voices, they definitely would have been laughing . . . or giggling.

Now, suddenly, excitingly, a soft feminine fragrance wafted to him, a delicate tangerine scent blended with basil and coriander. Then she was there, standing beside the bed. Tamara. He smiled and happily greeted her.

They were alone, this man and wife who had had

no proper reunion after having been parted for so many long lonely days.

"Come here, woman," Daniel commanded huskily, propping himself, albeit painfully, against the lacy eyelet-edged pillows piled against the head of the brass bed.

The lace panels draped at the corners were framing Tamara. She had just seen the doctor to the door. Now deep blue eyes watched her as she neared Daniel, her palms pressed into the folds of her skirts. When she had gingerly seated herself on the bed's edge, Daniel growled hungrily and drew her into his arms.

"Daniel . . . you . . . we'll hurt you."

"Woman, I'm not dead in the saddle yet. It just might be a little loving would fully revive the tiger in me . . . *arghh!*"

Her hands slid up to rest lightly upon his shoulders. "You are not thinking of . . . I mean, you are in pain . . . we can't . . . not yet. You have to get better. Your leg . . . your ribs . . ."

"Hell with my leg!" Grabbing both her arms, he slid them around his neck. "Give me a real kiss, love, not one of those stuffy Victorian pecks you've insisted on while I've been recovering. Don't be afraid you will hurt me."

"But I will. I heard you groan just moments ago. You were in pain. You are not yet fully recovered, Mr. Tarrant. And, Daniel, we must talk." She pressed her cheek against his bruised and bandaged chest.

"Is that why we won't be making love yet? This must be something very serious." He ran a palm over her silken hair, down her back, let it rest on a buttock.

"Sure it can't wait?"

Her head rose, and eyes of sage green delved into his. "My mind and heart would not be in it, Daniel. There are too many things we must discuss. For one, remember last night after the lawman left, when we talked about Kristel's disappearance?" She waited for his nod. "You know Cat went searching for you . . . and there are new footprints in the snow. The officers have been checking them out. Danny has a cold. My Emily wrote to say she is coming for Christmas, and . . . Oh, Daniel, where is Kristel? I am so worried!"

He placed a hand on each of her cheeks, rubbing one thumb over her quavering lips. "Whoa, angel heart. You really are in a state. I'm sorry, love . . . I didn't realize. I awoke feeling much better after taking the painkillers doc gave me. All I could think of is how much I . . . want you. Forgive me. I have been selfish."

"And I want you, Daniel," she cried, her palm softly resting upon his bandaged chest. "The doctor says you have a few bruised ribs. The horse must have rolled over you after he slipped on the ice." She bent to kiss his chest, her eyes then lifting to his adoring ones, making him feel like warmed honey butter.

"Changing the subject awful fast, aren't you, love?" He crushed her to his chest and tried not to groan from the pain of that move. "Yes, the horse came hard along my whole length. Worst part was, I had to shoot him . . . put him out of his misery."

Tamara shuddered all over, recalling another time he had had to put away a horse. FireScar, Daniel's beloved stallion, had broken a leg. She would never forget how strong and intelligent and beautiful that horse had been. Daniel had cherished and cared for every one of his animals. He'd even called a laying hen by name. Had it been Daisy? The name escaped her. Well, the past is best left alone, she decided. For now, anyway.

"I am not sure you heard me talking to you last night, Daniel, after you had the painkillers administered." She sat primly on the bed, like a nervous Nellie, though she was not one, not by a longshot. Daniel had realized that long ago. This was new, this nervousness. "I spoke to you of James Strong Eagle, Pamela Clayton, Taylor Handley, the officers . . . and Kristel."

She looked to the window and wished Kristel were back home. But wishing did not make it so, nor did it provide any answers to the questions plaguing her.

Damning the medicine, Daniel said sleepily, "I remember some. I'm not worried about James so much, sweetheart, since you have pistols and rifles in the house. Did you load them and put them out of Danny's reach?"

"Yes." Tamara fiddled with her skirts. "And there is one atop the dresser in here. Oh, Daniel, please do not go to sleep . . . please. I need to talk some more. I . . . I feel all is not right today. Something is wrong. I just know it."

"You . . . I am not going to, love." He blinked his eyes. "Just have to rest my eyes a little . . . that's all. You shake me if . . . if I start to fall asleep . . . all right? And . . . don't worry."

"Daniel . . . ohhhh . . ." She clutched his hand in a tight grip. "You said something about a cave last

389

night. Can you please tell me more? I have to know exactly what you were talking about."

"I . . ."

"Daniel!" She pressed his hand to her cheek. "This is very important."

"C-Cave . . . oh, that. . . . It's just in the . . . cellar, sweet. . . . Wolf Pass had a shaman d-dream for him. . . . Cave . . . I dreamed . . . about . . . it too."

Shaking her head, Tamara gasped as his hand went lax. "No, Daniel, I do not understand. What about the cellar? A cave? It does not make sense. There is no cave . . . not that I know of. That is unheard of in a cellar where My Emily's old things are getting musty along with the fruits and vegetables we've put up. Daniel?"

As soft snoring filled the bedroom, Tamara slowly rose from the bed. Her eyes wandered to the window. It was snowing hard now, the thick flakes falling lazily, the trees brittle-silent sentinels. As Tamara stood watching the storm, a light wind arose to whip snow against the window, and the steel-cast twilight evoked a sense of panic in her.

Whirling, as if in a dream, Tamara wrung her hands. She itched to take the gun from the dresser. Cave? Cellar? Wolf Pass and a shaman's dream?

The rifle—it was loaded. Danny was asleep. The well-fed boarders were dozing in the parlor.

Gaslight danced against the sage color of her eyes. Her shoulders rose and fell. Then settled. It was a mere gesture, but it was the outward expression of her decision.

Reaching up, she took the long-barreled rifle from its perch. Smiling wryly, she backed to the door, ondling the weapon, making a nest for it against her waist. The snoring reached her ears. If they had made ove as he'd lustily suggested, he would be snoring hythmically in her arms at that very moment.

Tamara took the glass doorknob in hand, turned t, and slipped out, blowing the snoring Daniel a iss. Then her knees became jelly. Her palms weated. Her heart beat soundly against her cream-ace bodice.

She meant to find out what this "cave" Daniel had nentioned had to do with the cellar. Odd . . . She ould not begin to imagine what the connection was.

The wooden rocker squeaked to a halt in the parlor, suddenly, like a train run out of steam.

"Hey, Joshua!"

"Yeah?"

The KeeKing Man smacked his lips and stirred ightly in the platform rocker. "Careful you don't tip hat rocker, Henry, and fall on your ass like you did nce before."

Henry chuckled. "I don't sit on my face, Josh, like ou do."

"You woke me . . . so what's up?" Joshua peered over at Henry. "You look like your suspenders were ust snapped."

Aldwin came around just then, peering over his spectacles. He pushed them back up his long Roman nose. "Supper's ready, you say?"

"Not supper, dummy, we already ate hours ago. Suspenders, I said, suspenders."

"Well . . ." Aldwin looked up crossly. "What

about them?"

Henry's mouth stood agape, then snapped shut. "You must've been havin' a bad dream."

"Shhh! Both of you!" Joshua ordered crossly. "Someone's at the door."

Henry snorted. "That's what I was trying to tell you before, dummy."

"Naw." Aldwin shook his head, "That's just a loose shutter banging around in the wind."

"What shutter?" Joshua slowly rose to his feet, his limbs creaking. "We ain't got no shutters on this house. Someone's knocking, I tell you."

"Just like I said." Henry nodded haughtily to Aldwin. "Ain't no loose damn shutter. It's a body knocking like he's gonna tear down the place."

"It's in the cellar. I can tell. Listen."

"I'll go see," said Joshua, shaking his head as if annoyed by it all. He'd wanted to nap. "Damn snow," he grumbled.

"Where's Tamara?"

"Must be taking a nap with Daniel. Can't hear."

"Heh. Maybe they're . . . uh, you know . . ."

"They can't make that much noise. Can they?"

"This time of day?" Joshua plodded from the parlor.

"Day? Just look at those windows! This snowstorm turned afternoon into night. Get on over here, Henry, and turn up the gaslight!"

"Aldwin?"

"What, Henry?"

Henry gulped. "How could there be someone at the door in this storm?"

"Well,"—Henry used simple logic—"wasn't so

392

ad a few hours ago. Whoever it is, they must've set out before the snow began to fly like bats outta Hades!"

"Yeah." Aldwin giggled nervously. "Little white bats, round and furry and meltin' when they lights on your tongue."

"Aldwin, one way to save face is to keep your trap shut." Pause. A shrug. "You're tetched in the head, damn tootin'."

"And you're a character right out of the newspapers!" He stuck out his tongue and wiggled his big ears. "The funny papers!"

Upstairs Daniel tried to awaken, but the pounding in his head kept him submerged in his dream no matter how hard he struggled. In the dream he was asking Tamara if she had remembered to bolt the outside door to the cellar, telling her a storm was heading their way . . . and possibly more than just a storm. He struggled to get up, to help her . . . he couldn't.

Then he fell into a deep dreamless sleep induced by the strong painkiller he'd been given.

"Oh, you gave me such a fright!" Tamara placed one hand over her pumping heart, the other held the gun. In the shadowy corner pantry, she had just had a start. "Joshua . . . it's you."

"Yeah. Me. You all right?" The old man's query brought a swift little nod. "You sure don't look good, little woman." Joshua stuffed his hands in his baggy trouser pockets. "Well, I think me and the other fellas are gonna go upstairs, play a few hands of cards in Henry's room, and then turn in."

"Good."

Joshua paused. "You sure you're gonna be all right?"

"Oh, yes." Tamara wanted to do this alone. She had to make certain nothing was amiss, that no one lurked in the dark cavernous rooms of the cellar. And she wanted to check out why Daniel had linked it with the "cave."

The previous owner of the boardinghouse had built more than one root cellar, adding storerooms now damp and dingy that contained nothing except spiders and waterbugs, a few root vegetables, a few barrels, and some broken-down furniture long since cast aside.

"G'night then." Joshua yawned, stealing a glance at Tamara before he spoke again. "Didn't know I was so tuckered out. We'll play a few rounds, then turn in."

Tamara called softly, "Danny is asleep. Don't wake him when you go up."

Again Joshua peered at her oddly. "We never do, sweetheart. We're always quiet as little lambs." *What did I forget to do?*

"Of course you are." Tamara almost wrung her hands together, so great was her eagerness to get down into the dark, dank caverns below the house. Still, she had never felt such trepidation about going to the cellar. She looked up at the window. Suddenly it had grown very dark outside. The snow was falling rapidly.

Joshua could be heard taking his "lambs" up the stairs, and all at once Tamara felt quite alone . . . and rather shaky. In fact, she had not felt this alone since that day in the woods when Daniel had not been there and she had had to face life alone.

She seemed to have come full circle.

Kristel had disappeared. Daniel had returned . . . but something was not right at all.

As she walked over to check the back door, Tamara had a feeling that she'd find it unlocked, and chills of apprehension tickled her legs and arms. She breathed a sigh of relief at finding it securely bolted.

Turning, she stood looking at the door to the cellar, her back to the one leading outside. Her imagination overstimulated, she conjured up all sorts of nightmarish creatures that might lurk beyond the cellar door. She told herself she was rushing, half-blind and headlong, into something hostile—*There is something down there; I just know it!*—but she was determined to see what lay below. And that settled it. Still, her knees shook just a little, while her heart galloped at full speed.

Retrieving the rifle, she took it up, resting the barrel on one arm. It was loaded. Ready. And so was she. She gulped and shivered. Oh, nonsense, twaddle, My Emily would have said, There's nothing down there but spiders and old junk!

Be brave, dear. Remember: "Gentle knights were borne to fight, and war ennobles all who engage in it without cowardice or fear."

> Whatever you do, do with all your might.
> —Aesop

Chapter Twenty-Nine

The heady scent of burning pine logs floated around them as Cat drew closer to those pink, parted lips, such a sweet enticement. The moment hung suspended like a crystalline drop about to fall, and Cat thought: She invites me to taste her lips. So young, so young. What should I do?

He suddenly touched her silken hair. He wanted her, ached for her.

Kristel shivered as Cat tipped her head back to taste of her honeyed innocence. Her lips were so sweet, so pure that Cat was swept into a bliss he had never before known. And she was caught in his knowledge of woman. Their breaths mingled, and they kissed. She felt the heat of this man. He knew the joy of discovering a treasure, an angel to be cherished.

"It's cold in here, Cat," Kristel murmured against his ear. "Warm me. Please warm me real good."

"Oh, little one, your lips taste of honey. But I must not warm you too much."

"Why not? I want you to, Cat. I am not afraid."

He rose from the blanket spread on the floor near the crude hearth and added more logs to the fire. While doing so, he kept his back to Kristel, afraid that if he looked at her for too long he would take her to him. Her shy yet bold kisses had shattered his resolve not to touch her. Though he had only kissed her, there was an overwhelming heat in his groin.

Seated before the hearth, Kristel gingerly touched her lips with her fingertips, lightly as if she could still feel Cat's lips on them. How had it happened? All they had done was sit down on the blankets he'd spread after he had built up the fire. Before that, they had hurried to the shack, Cat gathering pine logs on the way. Now those were drying out, and the ones they'd found inside the shack were already burning.

"Come here, Cat . . . it's cold. The air is coming through the cracks in the walls, and I can't seem to shake the chill. Will you warm me?" She cocked her head in such a delightfully feminine way that Cat was lost; he nodded and went to her.

At once, his arms went around her, drawing her against his chest, and they were like newborns in a world of sensual delight. He inhaled her feminine scent, and she breathed in his manly musk. As they became more stimulated, Cat discovered he wanted more than a physical union with Kristel—he wanted her heart, her trust, her love.

When had this happened? Cat wondered. All of a sudden he never wanted to be parted from Kristel, and he now believed their love was predestined, a fire in their hearts already ablaze.

On one of Kristel's cheeks was a bright streak of

color, and the firelight made her hair sparkle, set her eyes alight. As she gazed at the reddish-orange flames licking at the hearth, an incredible longing tore at her heart, a craving.

Cat's manly face, a bronze study, was bedazzling her. Desire began to burn in her young blood, ignited by the kisses they'd shared.

That desire was growing into passion. Stormy, swelling, towering. Cat sensed it, and he drew her face closer, his lean fingers raising her chin as if he were handling a priceless work of art. His eyes dove into hers with a never-to-be-forgotten look of wonder in them, and she, desperately curious, was just a little afraid now of what was happening.

Those kisses had not been abstract. Each could feel the sexual tension in the other. This was quite different from merely dreaming about being with Cat. She *was* with him . . . and serious things were happening between them.

Running a dark finger along her jawline, Cat said softly, "What does Kristel think now? Are you afraid of what is happening?" He gave her a penetrating look.

She swallowed hard. "Yes. Just a little, Cat. I . . . Will you kiss me again so that I won't be afraid anymore?" Raptly, she stared up at him and watched his mouth lift at the corners until it was funnel shaped.

He blew softly on her lips, causing them to part automatically. A chuckle followed, when he saw how serious she was. "We do not have to kiss again, Kristel. We do not have to do anything but sit here warming each other from the chill stealing in."

She licked her lips, then looked into his deeply mysterious cat eyes. "What is it like, Cat . . . to make love? Does it hurt a woman the first time?"

His bronze features darkened even more, into a manly flush. "If a man and a woman have feelings for each other, then it is very good between them." As he watched, she dropped her eyes before his steady gaze. He said nothing about the question she had muttered low, about it being painful.

"Have you had an awful lot of women, Cat?" She dared to peek up at him now.

"Many."

"Man of a few words again." Kristel sniffed against his man-smelling shirt. She cleared her throat, pretending not to be affected by his nearness, or his words, or the fact that he was taking all this so lightly while she was being torn up inside by conflicting emotions.

"What are we going to do now?" she asked in a quavery voice, trying to sound strong but failing to do so.

"Lie down. Go to sleep."

Again Kristel swallowed hard. Lie down? Together? Oh . . . my!

Shifting and turning, Cat put a hand on her shoulder and pulled her down with him, and she slid beneath the blanket with her back to him while he tucked the covering around them. Then, he pulled the blanket up over their heads, making a snug cocoon for them. So close now you couldn't get a spoon between.

Several minutes passed before Cat broke the silence. "Warm?"

400

Kristel wriggled her backside. "Uhmm-hmmm. Very nice."

Cat sucked his breath in through his teeth. "Kristel . . . do not move like that."

She spoke over her shoulder, asking, "Why not? I'm just trying to snuggle back and get comfortable."

"If you push back any more we will soon be more than comfortable. I will want—" Cat clamped his mouth shut.

"What will you want, Cat?" Kristel moved again, tempting him, though not fully aware of what she was getting herself into.

"To make love to you. What else?"

Glancing at him over her shoulder, she said playfully, "When will you make love to me?"

Nibbling her earlobe, Cat spoke against her hair. "When we are man and wife."

A loud screech rent the air as Kristel popped up, breaking their lovely cocoon apart and throwing herself on Cat, kissing his face, his lips, even the tip of his nose. All of a sudden she became still.

"I knew you would fall in love with me." She clapped her hands together. "I just knew it! Oh! I'm so happy. And . . . and I'll make you happy too, just wait and see. I'll clean your place and cook your food, make love to you every day. . . ." Something crossed her mind. "Cat, where do you live . . . in a tepee?"

He cupped her animated face. "Hold still, girl. We are not going to live anywhere for a long time. I am talking about a few years from now. Not next week or next month. You are getting too far ahead of yourself. Slow down. I mention man and wife and

401

you go crazy."

She pouted. "Oh." She blinked and looked aside. Then she shrugged. "I would live in a tepee if that's what you want. How about what I want, Cat? What if I want to get married when we get back?"

"Too soon." He waved a hand in the air. "Kristel, you are too young to marry. We must plan. There is much to do. Much to talk about. I like to be around my people, the Indians. I cannot give up my old way of life. Would you like a husband to hunt all the time? I might want to live in a tepee. Would you like that?"

Kristel just cocked her bright head. "Do you really live in a tepee?"

"No."

She shrugged. "Where then? In a house? A shack?"

"Mostly outdoors, when the weather is nice. Otherwise I live with friends. Or . . ."

"Or?" Her eyes were alight with curiosity.

"Or other women."

She could not take that in; she didn't want to. "Then, you are saying you do not have your own home?"

"Not really. I live where it is best to live at the time." He lifted up her chin when it came to rest on her chest, in dejection. "Kristel, look at me. Ah. Yes. You do not look so happy about becoming my wife now. Things have changed very fast. You would not think much of living with one of my women, would you?"

Falling against him, Kristel pounded him hard on the chest. "You are mean! You are making fun of me. You do not want to marry me—not at all. You are trying to make me hate the way you live! Well"—she stuck her nose in the air—"I don't care what you do. You think I give a fig about what you do with all those women?" She shoved hard, almost knocking him off balance. "You can go to blazes—with each and every one of them—you loathsome Lothario! Gigolo!"

"Kristel!"

Cat reached for the flailing fists striking out harmlessly—until she got in one crisp uppercut to his chin. Then her hair got tangled in a beaded section of fringe on his shirt, and she cried out, thinking he was yanking at the yellow tresses that flowed across her forehead and eye.

"Let me go! Ouch! You're hurting me, Cat!"

"Hold still, Kristel!"

"No! Let me go, you brute! I hate you—hate you! Stop it. That hurts. Ohhh, it's coming out!"

She reached for and held the hands that were tearing her hair out. What she did not realize was that Cat was fighting to free the strands caught in the beaded fringe, but her violent turnings and twistings had worsened her situation, tangling beads and hair until they seemed a single twist of rope.

Tears of pain and frustration ran down her cheeks. "Oh . . . don't hurt me anymore. Cat . . . pleeease!"

"Kristel, Kristel, calm down. It will not hurt anymore if you do what I tell you. I'll try to get it out. It's all in knots."

When Kristel would not cease her struggles, Cat took out his knife. Seeing the blade, she exclaimed, "Oh, you hate me so much now, you are going to scalp me!"

403

"Kristel." He swung one arm around her throat to get her to stay still. "I am going to—"

"No!"

Holding onto the hank of hair, Kristel slipped from his loose embrace and painfully flipped about, which brought her back up against his chest. Cat stumbled and fell, Kristel landing on top of him and his blade clattering to the wide-boarded floor and slipping through a big crack.

"Oh!" Now Kristel was staring at the tangle of hairs and beaded fringe. Her eyes flew upward to encounter the hot look in Cat's. "I'm caught . . . on your shirt. I'm sorry. Oh dear, I didn't realize."

"I am happy you have at last discovered this."

"You could have taken your shirt off," she said as he untangled the mess. His leg had slid between hers, and as Kristel felt the hard length of it, she began to breathe harder. Cat's breathing had also quickened.

"I tried to," he said as he shifted himself a little and found the soft impression his body had been seeking for so long. *Ahhhh.*

He was lost.

She was lost.

Their eyes met, and he rolled over onto her, his fingers resting lightly beneath the plump swell of a breast. Kristel's breath caught. At the same moment his lips touched hers, his hand rose to cup that gentle swell. Kristel arched, bringing the hardened crest into his hand, and he pressed the nipple as his tongue sought entry to her mouth.

Kristel's lips parted, and when Cat's tongue thrust between them, her chest seemed to expand as she blossomed all the way to her inner core. Withdrawing his tongue, Cat said huskily, "A man could stand on top of these mountain peaks." Then he entered her mouth again, his tongue finding hers and mating with it. Finally he drew away again. "I am not happy about hurting you, Kristel. I saw your pain when your hair—"

Before he could finish, Kristel placed a finger over his lips and shushed him. "But it will be such nice discomfort, Cat. I can take a little pain."

Sucking at her earlobe, he mumbled against it, "I will not give it all to you at once, little one."

"How can you do that and . . . and still feel good?"

Cat struggled with his breathing. "I know a way you can remain a maid and still get pleasure out of it."

"How, Cat? How?"

"How. . . . You sound like an Indian, woman." While he spoke, he slowly slipped her skirts up her thighs. "I will show you."

Breathless, so breathless. As if she had been running hard. Then he touched her and she arched, her blue eyes widening. She had never known how good . . . *Oh!*

Before she was thoroughly lubricated, Cat came to his senses. He was lower than horse dung. He was trespassing. Kristel was not his to take. She was young, had not known a man before. He would pleasure her this way, with his touch, and then make her go to sleep. . . .

Are there little glowing eyes, or is it only my imagination?

On the last creaking step down to the cellar Tamara paused and looked around, peering into th dark. Leaning the rifle against the wall, she lit th lantern with shaking fingers. Then, taking a dee breath to steady herself, she scanned the rows o canned goods—jars of pickles, applesauce, jams and jellies, orange marmalade, crab apple conserve apple and peach butter—and then the burlap bag holding garden vegetables stacked in the corners The carrots had been replanted in the earthen floor where they would remain cool and eatable fo months to come.

She shivered, for it was much cooler down here and the chill gnawed at her clear to the bone. She had never been down in the cellar after dark, not ever to fetch a sweet midnight treat; My Emily was the one who had brought up anything absent from the upstairs pantry or cupboard.

Oh, Emily, I miss you. "I wish you w-were here Then I would not be frightened. You always made me feel special, Em." She kept talking and kept looking about, because this was a thing she knew she must do. To see what the shaman's dream had meant.

Walking with lantern in one hand, rifle in the other, she stepped down and began to search the other cubicles. They were stuffy and close, much more so than the root cellar. She came to three more steps down. Her voice shook. "Em . . . what do you suppose I shall find? M-maybe a few spiders—recluse spiders. You know how I detest them . . . they are so ugly . . . creepy . . . with their huge bulging eyes . . Lord, this does not sound like— Oh!"

Just then the wind set up a ruckus. Mournfully

owling and shrieking, it battered at the upstairs
indows, making it sound as if all hell had broken
oose. It was suddenly colder, too.

Setting the lantern on an old broken-down chest of
rawers, Tamara held the rifle in front of her and
ept walking . . . until she stood in the last room,
hich was a step up.

It was here she came face to face with . . . *snow!*

"Oh!" she squealed, feeling her heart leap into her
hroat as a blast of the white stuff struck her and she
ad to blink to clear its cold moisture from her eyes.

Moving on, she followed the footprints in the
now . . . and then she saw the stash. Stacks of money
nd jewels . . . "My Emily, is this yours? No. It
ould not be!"

My Emily had never stolen a thing in her life and
urely this loot had been recently secreted here,
udging by the footprints. And she'd never seen it
efore. Then again, she had never ventured this far
nto the cavelike cellar.

"But where did it all come from, and who brought
t here?" Her words carried on the chill air.

"It is mine. All mine. And yours, if you want it."

"Oh!" Tamara stood back and gasped. Who? . . .
Scared out of her wits, Tamara looked from the
eavyset man to the hidden cache. She was still
olding the rifle but her grip on it had gone lax.
'Who . . . are you?" she got out.

James Strong Eagle stepped into the lantern's
iffused glow. His voice became determined, but was
oft and low. "I am . . . a friend." *Good. She does not
ecognize me. Who would?* "My name is James
Creek."

407

Tamara's apprehension did not increase. She wa
determined not to lose her self-control. She woul
not whimper. She would not cry out.

"If you are a friend, then why have you stolen int
the house by the cellar door?" She now saw i
standing open and letting in the terrible biting cold
the swirling snow. No wonder the wind and the chil
had seemed so near! Why hadn't he closed the door

At once he went to pull both panels shut
Somewhat gallantly, Tamara thought. Deciding thi
man was strange, she vowed to be on guard.

When he returned, Tamara was pointing th
barrel of the rifle at him. "You would not want to kil
me. . . ." He let the words hang, hoping he coul
stall for time.

"Try me." Tamara said, mostly to catch him of
guard. She didn't want to kill anyone if it could b
avoided. But when it came to defending her chil
who was asleep, though ailing with a winter cold
she would. She would also do it for her wounde
husband, and for the old folks who could not defen
themselves. She most certainly would.

She trained the rifle on the stranger.

"Who are you?" she asked. "Do not tell me '
friend' again. I don't believe that story for on
moment."

He chuckled. "I have brought many treasures
You'll like them. Just come and look."

"No." Tamara stood firm, not believing the dar
stranger. "You are a thief, and I can't abide folks wh
steal. It is a sin to covet or take what belongs t
another."

He waved his hands. "These are all my own

Would I lie to a woman as fair as you?" For now. To get what he wanted. And then he was going to leave some evidence that would make Daniel pay once again for "crimes" James had committed.

She held her weapon firmly, her eyebrows peaking like the legs of a cricket ready to spring. "You would." Now her eyes narrowed. "I believe you are a thief. I want you to walk up those stairs, and then I am going to call the authorities. So get moving. Now!"

"Please." He went down on his knees. "Do not shoot me, I beg you."

"Stand up! Again, who are you?" Tamara hefted the rifle butt against a lean hip. "The truth this time, mister."

He was getting angry. "Damn!" He employed the white's swearword and rose to stand straight and tall. "If you don't believe me, then I will have to prove something else to you."

"Go ahead. I'm waiting."

"You can come out now," he called into the ghostly shadows. Something shifted, then loganberry-wine bottles rattled.

Tamara watched as a woman, visibly shivering from the cold, stepped out from behind the stacks of bottles. *"You!"* she exclaimed.

"Right." James Strong Eagle had a possessive gleam in his eyes.

"Oh, yes," said Pink Cloud, alias Pamela Clayton. She protectively held the bundle in her arms, the swaddled child sleeping soundly. "And this is my angel. No one will take him away from me. He looks like you when . . ." Her eyes swept from James to the woman whose mouth was forming a perfect O just like the bore of the rifle pointed at her.

"Hush," warned Strong Eagle.

The sleeping child sniffled in his sleep, and Tamara knew that could only be one very special child. Danny. She tossed the rifle aside, and James grabbed it.

"Oh . . . Danny!"

"Hey, Dan . . . wake up!" Joshua, having padded into the room from the nursery, shook Daniel's shoulder with a splayed hand. "The kid's gone. C'mon, wake up. I said the kid's gone and Tamara's not back yet. I think she went out. Don't hear her downstairs. Dan! Wake up, Dan!"

Daniel's dark head rolled on the pillow. *What was this? Tamara out? Where would she go? Is she leaving me? But I haven't done anything wrong. Danny . . . Is Joshua saying that Danny is gone, too? They must be together, downstairs. Danny has a cold. . . .*

Joshua persisted. "Dan . . . I tell you that Danny is gone from his bed. Tamara didn't come up to get him, so that means someone took him from his bed before she went down to the root cellar. I heard some noises then. Now I think they came from the cellar."

Joshua frowned. The cellar. Why had Tamara looked so strange, almost frightened when she stood by the cellar door? "Dan, I think Tamara went down into the cellar. But it don't make sense, 'cause she never goes down there, told me it's too spooky after it gets dark outside."

Half-conscious, Daniel muttered lackadaisically, "The cellar . . . the cave. Uhhh, Josh, get cold water . . . pour it on my face . . . bring pants to me. . . . Hurry . . . you gotta *hurry*. . . . Get the water, Josh . . . matter o' life 'n' death. . . . Come on, old -fella. . . ."

Joshua wasted no time mulling the commands over, but whirled and was back lickety-split, water sloshing from the basin he carried. Shaking his head and pursing his lips, he looked down at Daniel, feeling sorry for him, then *splashed* the chilly water on his face.

Shocked from semiconsciousness, by the vivifying water, Daniel coughed and blinked, coming to awareness. He looked up at the worried older man. "Joshua. It wasn't a dream then. You really are here talking to me." He coughed again, sending droplets of water flying as he gave his head a good shake. "Where are my pants?" he demanded as he rose from the mattress. Dizzy, he almost lost his balance while Joshua rushed about the room like a wind-up toy.

"Ah, here they are . . . I got 'em!" Returning to the bed as quickly as his age would allow, Joshua handed the trousers over. "Here!"

Daniel sat back down on the edge of the bed and reached for his pants, then shook his head, trying to clear it. "Are you sure Danny is not in his bed?" he asked. His tongue felt fuzzy.

"Nope. I mean yup, I'm sure he's not there. You think he could have slipped out by himself?"

"I will have a look as soon as I get my bearings."

When Daniel stood, grasping the bedpost, Joshua chuckled at the sight he made with lace bedhangings resting atop his head and flowing onto his shoulders

"Yeah," Joshua said. "And get your drawers on." The old man looked down and then up, blinking hard. "Better do that for sure. Must've been some dream you were having, you randy buck. That's some lollypop you've got there."

Joshua's remark did not register on Daniel for his mind was on his wife and child. He had to find them. All was not right with Tamara. He could almost feel her distress. That was waking him up, like another dash of cold water in the face.

"When did you last see Tamara?" he asked the old man.

"She was down in the kitchen, acting mighty peculiar if you ask me. Like she was hiding something."

"Tamara would not hide anything from us. She's always open and honest."

"That's what I mean. Something strange is afoot." Joshua licked his lips. "I always thought the house is haunted. Used to be some real odd folks living here before My Emily bought it."

Hurriedly, Daniel questioned Joshua. "Odd in what way?" He did up the four-button fly on his trousers, then sat to pull on his boots. His eyes lifting to where the rifle had been, he stood, grabbing the bedpost again to steady himself. "Tell me, Josh, quickly."

"Had a tunnel built down in the cellar a few years after the house was completed. It leads . . ." He scratched his head. "Now let me see, I believe My Emily said it leads to—"

"Never mind that now."

While Joshua watched in astonishment, Daniel grabbed a shirt, threw it on, then walked to the door as if he were stepping on eggs. Before entering the hall, Daniel shook his head and ran his hands through his tousled mass of dark hair, raking it back. He then tied it in a ponytail, with a strip of pink rag, and began making his way to the stairway, softly cursing the ribs that were hurting him so badly.

"Well, get going, young man," Joshua called. "Find out where your wife and child are. Hell— excuse me—they could be halfway through that tunnel by now, or in the one that leads to"— Daniel was looking back at him, watching, waiting—"that old house what's boarded up. Used to belong to the Spangers . . . all dead and buried now, they are. Think that lover boy Jervis had a thing going with the Spanger woman way back then . . . name was Lavinia or something. Hey, where'd you go? Never mind. Just hope you remembered to take a weapon along. Hey, come to think of it," Joshua continued while scratching his head, "thought I saw a light in that old house the other night. Could it be?"

The elderly man plodded down the stairs, intending to search for a snack and hoping he'd come across Tamara and Danny and Daniel, all sweet and cozy in the kitchen. Just like it should be. But something was wrong, definitely amiss, and Joshua prayed it wouldn't be long before big Dan had it all cleared up.

"I'll just get myself a little somethin' to eat." Joshua rummaged in the cupboards, then jumped back when he saw the bore of a pistol staring back at

413

him. "What's this doin' here?"

Lifting it down, he discovered that the piece w
loaded.

He caressed the black rod and polished it on th
end of his purple robe. "Loaded, eh? Well, Betsy, i
just you and me now."

He turned, his eyes going to the cellar door th
stood open. He walked toward it, humming soft
as he stuck the weapon in his robe's deep pocket.

A harmless necessary cat.
—William Shakespeare

Chapter Thirty

Cat let out his breath, unaware that he had been olding it in for several moments while Kristel owly opened her eyes to the dawning of a new day. he wind had died, the snow had stopped coming own, and the morning was bright and cheerful. deed, there was a crisp reborn feeling to the day.

Kristel sniffed the air. "Is that coffee I smell?"

"Of course."

Rising onto her elbows, she stared into the ompelling eyes of Cat who was hunkered before her, steaming cup of that dark liquid held in his bronze ands.

Kristel looked around the old house that was no ore than an abandoned shed, having once been sed for storage. Bricks had tumbled from the lonely ttle fireplace. "How did you make it?"

"That's my secret."

She took the cup from him and smiled into his es. "Smells good. I never thought a cup of coffee ould mean so much." She grinned. "Did you make breakfast, m'lord?"

"Lord?" Cat shook his dark head. He point[s]
upward. "There is only one Lord, Kristel. It is sil[ly]
that people call those English dandies m'lord." [He]
spoke in a deep voice, proclaiming his masculi[ne]
contempt for the fops of "merry old England."

"Well then, m'warrior, did you make breakfast[?]"

"Of course."

She waited as he pulled out the usual jerk[ed]
beef . . . only this jerky was a bit tastier than that [of]
the two outlaws. "Mmmm, what is in here? This [is]
very good."

"Crushed berries and a little bit of fat mixed wi[th]
venison."

"Delicious. Did you bring down the deer and je[rk]
it yourself?" She giggled.

"Yes."

She stopped chewing as he straightened to his fu[ll]
height and moved about the room like a cag[ed]
leopard. Any way you look at it, Kristel thought, [he]
certainly lives up to his name . . . always movin[g]
like a cat on the prowl.

Cat walked about the small confines, still fru[s]
trated from having spent the night wrapped in t[he]
blankets with Kristel. He had slowly and ma[d]
deningly pleasured her, and he could tell by the sil[ly]
little smile on her lovely face that she thought it t[he]
best time ever. Most likely it was the *only* time she[d]
ever been under the blankets with a man. Truth wa[s]
she'd never had anything to do with sex, blankets [or]
not.

She is the most sensual virgin ever created, C[at]
thought. He could not get out of his mind the wa[y]

416

she had arched against his hand, never realizing more delicious sensations were to come. . . . But would he be the one to finally possess her? To have her, he should—he would—make her his wife. Daniel had married Tamara. But Daniel was not all Indian as he was. Cat wondered if he could learn to live as Kristel desired. He could, couldn't he? Many an Indian man had given up his savage ways to live with a white woman . . . and been happy . . . and had beautiful children.

With a deep sigh, Cat came to a heart-searching decision. Turning to Kristel, he said, "We must go now."

"But"—she waved a hand—"how'll we get through all that snow?"

"It is melting already. Listen, you can hear Apache in the next room pawing because he is eager to get going."

Apache? Kristel's brow furrowed in puzzlement. Of course, Cat's horse. He had put the stallion in the covered lean-to beside the abandoned shack. Now she could hear the horse, too, pawing and snorting, as if saying it was time to move on. Could horses be so smart as to have a sixth sense, like some women did? Kristel wondered.

"We have to find Daniel," Cat said. "He is most likely close to home by now, or there already."

Kristel suddenly felt guilty. "Yes, and Tamara must be worried sick." She handed the coffee cup to Cat as she stood, and he drained the last drops from it before sticking it in a basin of melted snow, washing it out, and placing it in a saddlebag. "I hope everything is all right back at the boardinghouse.

417

Maybe James Strong Eagle—"

Cat held up his hand. "Do not say it, woman."

She felt like dancing and whirling about the old shack. *Woman*. He had called her woman again.

While she was adjusting the clothes she had slept in, Cat came up behind her and wrapped an arm about her slim waist, nuzzling her neck and sucking her earlobe. "Cat!" She turned into his arms. "You do like me, don't you?" Her heart was singing a jubilant chorus.

"No."

"No?"

Her heart sank as she stared down at the beaded shirt she had gotten her hair caught on. He didn't love her . . . then why was he holding her so . . close?

"No," he said. "I love you."

"Oh, cat! When are we going to get married?"

"As soon as we settle some differences, girl."

"No. Woman."

He looked at her, frankly dubious. "All right, Woman. You are woman. I am man. We got that settled. Now, let's go. Otherwise I am going to settle you back down on that blanket and have my way with you!"

Oh . . . Oh. Kristel's head spun dreamily. *Have my way with you*, just like in the Catherina novels. And she, like Catherina the blushing, pale-eyed virgin, could hardly wait to be deflowered by this man, the only man in her heart.

"Thank you, Cat."

Kristel rose on tiptoe to kiss Cat all over his face, even his eyelids. He unwound her arms and held hem before their quavering bodies. "What is Kristel hanking Cat for?"

"Uhhmm." She smiled romantically. "Kristel is hanking Cat for not dishonoring her."

She did know there was more to come. "You are very wise for one so young."

"Now where have I heard that before. That must be a timeworn phrase. Have you been reading books on the side, Cat?"

"I do know how to read some."

Kristel's gentle laugh rippled through the air. "Oh my God!" She broke away from him, holding her stomach, half laughing half crying.

Cat's eyes roamed over her bent figure, and his eyes narrowed. "You find my ability to read so funny?" He shook his head. "Well, I cannot find the humor in this." He folded his arms, Indian fashion, to show her he was a bit annoyed by her reaction.

She recovered from her laughter enough to turn and face him squarely, but still her mouth quirked at the corners as she tried to explain the reason for her fit of the giggles. "I . . . oh, this is so hard to say . . . I must ask you: what will my last name become when we marry?" Kristel began to grin broadly again. "Will it be Kristel Face? Mrs. Face, how do you do? And how is Mr. Face. Oh Lord, can't you just imagine that?"

"No."

She twiddled her fingers at seeing his stern countenance. "Well, I think it's funny. Ohhh . . ." She was laughing again. "And how are all the other little Faces?"

"Enough."

"What?" Kristel dried her eyes, blinking up at him. She pouted. "If you can't see the humor in life, Cat, then maybe we should not get married after all."

"Let us compromise."

A smile lit her lovely face. "Good. I like to hear you say that." A suspicious twinkle shone in her eyes. "How will we compromise?"

"I shall change my name."

"Yes. To what?"

"Favian."

"Ohhh," said Kristel, a dreamy expression stole onto her features as she went into his open arms. "That is so sweet of you, Cat." She gazed up into yellow-green eyes full of adoration. "What does it mean?"

"It is Latin. Favian means 'a man of understanding.'"

"You are so wonderful," Kristel cried happily. She let him kiss her, and delighted in the tongue-washing he gave her this time, even making some lusty movements with her own in his mouth. Their flesh melding together, they sipped and sucked. "I love to kiss this way," she declared, coming up for air. "It is so exciting. Must be like making love in miniature, huh?"

Cat cleared his throat. "Yes. You will learn about that in time, Kristel. I will teach you everything. Now, if we do not get out of here, I'll begin teaching you right away."

"You know what?" She waited for his nod before going on. "You are speaking in longer sentences all the time. Maybe there is some hope for you, Indian."

"And you are learning how to kiss. Maybe there is

420

ome hope for you, paleface."

Opening the door of the abandoned shack, they let the crisp morning light, and their gazes onfirmed that there really was some hope for a uture together.

Only because Cat was a man of understanding . . .

I would rather have one barleycorn than all the jewels in the world.

—Aesop
The Cock and the Jewel

Chapter Thirty-One

"Oh . . ." Tamara whirled on the man. "Now I ~~r~~ealize who you are . . . James Strong Eagle. You ~~h~~ave put on much weight, I see." She eyed the ~~w~~eapon she had foolishly cast aside and then made a ~~lu~~nge for it. But James swept it out of her reach.

"Uh-uh, Tamara." He held the weapon like a ~~w~~arrior going into battle, bore up, butt down. ~~C~~lasping the barrel, he jerked it outward, indicating ~~th~~at she must lead the way into the tunnel.

The lantern cast eerie spirals into the cavernous ~~w~~ay as Pink Cloud picked it up, James's eyes having ~~si~~lently ordered her to do so. Again, Tamara stared at ~~th~~e half-moon scar on his chin.

Tamara felt her skin crawl as she entered the ~~n~~arrow passage. She had been living in the boarding-~~h~~ouse all these years without knowing there was a ~~tu~~nnel underneath it. Where did it lead? And to what ~~so~~rdid end would this dangerous game come? She ~~w~~as certain James's purposes were not honorable. ~~S~~he watched him heft the heavy boxes and stack them

423

near the entrance to the tunnel, in his greed and haste carelessly dropping one and scattering some pilfered money. She paid the obese man no mind but swept on past him as he stuffed the cash into his coat pockets, his face filled with amusement and interest as she approached Pink Cloud and the child.

"Please, Miss Clayton," Tamara beseeched, coming up beside the woman who struggled to hold onto Danny and the lantern at the same time, "let me take my child. I am so worried about him. He has been ill; he has a cold. Please, let me take him."

Pink Cloud crushed the boy to her breast. "No! He is mine! You cannot take him away. I have always wanted a boy-child. I almost took one of my sister's for my own." She looked at Strong Eagle and hissed under her breath, "Once he was as handsome as this child, but look at him now; he is fat and ugly." She did not even think to ask who had sired this child that resembled the man James had once been. "Sometimes I do not believe that he is Strong Eagle; he told me once he was James's cousin. I begin to wonder now." She hugged Danny closer.

"Please, Pamela. That child is mine. I am his mother."

"I am not Pamela! I am Pink Cloud, and I am going to take this child home, to my people. He will be a proud warrior one day."

"You don't seem to understand, Pamela . . . mean Pink Cloud." Tamara held out her empty arms in the hope they would be filled with her child. "Danny will be heartbroken if you do not give him to me, his mother. He will awaken and be afraid when he does not see me holding him but a stranger. You must be able to see this, Pink Cloud, for one day you will be a mother yourself."

"No!" she spat out. "I am barren. I cannot have children, and do not think I have not tried. Many times I have lain with men to get with child. Nothing comes of it. So now, I have my own son." She nuzzled Danny's throat, and Tamara winced.

Tears in her eyes, Tamara touched the woman's arm. "Pam . . . Pink Cloud, this is a very evil thing you are doing, and you will be sorry if you don't give Danny to his rightful mother."

James came up behind them and, with the bore of the rifle, poked Tamara in the ribs to get her going. He thought her entreaties unusually pitiful. What he could not understand, being so ignoble and corrupt, was a mother's deep love for her child.

"Let her have him," James ordered, herding them further into the tunnel. "We will have offspring of our own, Tamara." He could not tell her that he planned to do away with Pink Cloud once he had used her to accomplish his evil plan. They would take Danny with them when they went away, riding in the wagon he had earlier concealed. It would be loaded with the money and jewels he had stolen. "Come now, move. We do not have much time. We have to get to the abandoned house and then transfer my cache to that place. We will leave the child here, bundled up and in a warm place, and work together."

"You are crazy if you think I will aid you in your crime!" Tamara said. When he gave her another painful jab in the ribs, she added, "You two will not get away with this!"

425

"Shut up," James ordered harshly.

"Yes, *shut up*," Pink Cloud echoed.

A mist rolled along the underground passageway dispersing and gathering again, like smoke, veiling the walls in moisture. The woefully dim light from the lantern barely penetrated the darkness ahead of them, and the way was spongy and slippery, as if moss grew on the dirt-and-sand floor. Tamara wondered what purpose the tunnel had served years ago and who had crept along it. How had it remained hidden all these years? She felt like someone who had awakened from a troubling dream only to discover that reality was worse than the dream itself.

Tamara's heart dropped each time the half-breed girl roughly hoisted Danny up when he began to slip from her grasp, then he was jostled on her hip. The boy began to whine at awakening to see his mother's worried expression and to find a strange woman carrying him. Tamara sent him weak little smiles and kisses brushed off her fingertips. Danny continued to whine, his wide dark eyes blinking in bewilderment. When the dark woman carrying him cooed at him, he smacked her face and yanked her nose, but this only served to make Pink Cloud smile more widely and to bounce Danny on her hip.

When Danny began to cry in earnest, Tamara said, "Please, Pink Cloud, let me take him. I will quiet him and then give him back. Just let me hold him so he is not so afraid."

"No! You will not hold him or care for him."

As they reached the end of the tunnel, there was a hollow sound, as if one had stepped onto the walkway of a covered bridge. Suddenly a revolving platform swung slowly into a large room. Pink Cloud deposited the child onto the dusty floor of the abandoned, boarded-up house, and James followed them into the old place. With a shudder, Tamara looked back into the pitch dark. Then she turned to the room they were standing in. A bedroom. Dropping plaster was scattered everywhere in it as if a messy ghost-child had been playing there.

Tamara read the words scrawled on the walls. THE SPANGERS AIN'T HERE NO MORE. ENTER AT YER OWN RISK. THEY'S GHOSTS' IS HERE THO. She licked her dry lips and shuddered for the hundredth time in the last hour. Ghosts, in her own neighborhood . . . No, there are no such things, she told herself. Nothing could be as evil as the man in whose company I am now.

"There, boy." Pink Cloud had only allowed Danny to come to his feet before whisking him up again. She had set him down to adjust her clothing, straighten the twisted waistband of her skirt.

"No—no!" Danny yelled into her face, smacking both her cheeks hard as he could. Twisting in her arms, the boy reached for his mother, but was yanked back hard against Pink Cloud's chest. "Go away!" he shouted into the strange woman's face. "Want Mama, not you! Danny get down—now!" he cried, squirming and twisting and kicking. "Bad wady, want Mama!"

"Shut that boy up," James ordered, his eyes blue-black marbles in his fleshy face. "Otherwise I will have to . . ." He lifted the butt of the rifle, meaning to aim it at the boy's head.

Tamara flew at Strong Eagle, tearing at his shoulder, kicking his shins, screaming in his face. "Don't you dare! Don't touch that child if you know what's good for you!"

Strong Eagle became angered. Gritting his teeth, he backhanded Tamara in the mouth, and his face twisted into an ugly scowl. "Tamara cares more for the child than for Strong Eagle?"

Her hair flew outward as Tamara was knocked to the floor, blood trickling from the side of her mouth. She fought back tears, aware that her lip was beginning to puff up. When James towered over her, she cried, "You are crazy, you really are. Someone must have dropped you on your head when you were a child." Tamara gasped, struck by the realization of the terrible things she had said. "I feel sorry for you, James Strong Eagle. If only you would release Danny and me, God might forgive you for the sin you have committed."

"Mom!" Danny hollered, kicking and bruising Pink Cloud as she struggled to hold him still.

"God?" James sneered, ignoring the child's outburst. "I do not believe in your silly Bible . . . only in the religion of my forefathers, the People, the Indians. And sometimes I do not even believe in the Great Spirit." Suddenly there was a soft whooshing sound . . . and then a click.

"Well"—the strong voice came from behind James—"you'd better start believing in something, James Strong Eagle, and you'd better say your prayers because this might be your last chance to make amends."

Daniel . . . oh, Daniel! Tamara cried, splinters

digging into her hands as she struggled to rise from the floor. "You have come, my darling," she said aloud, but softly.

He stood there, a battered veteran of the winter wild, wearing blue pants, boots, and no shirt, only a jacket from which a soiled bandage peeped out. Pink Cloud gasped and set Danny down. Mouth sagging, eyes blinking, she stared at Daniel.

"James," was all she could utter. She looked from Strong Eagle to the tall, handsome man. "You have come back." She sneered at Strong Eagle. "Who are you? Why have you told me that you are James when you are not? Ah. You are a fake, or you are really James's cousin." Her dark eyes narrowed. "You are a liar, an evil man!"

Tamara and Daniel exchanged confused looks, and Daniel could not help but frown at the man who had given his beloved wife so much trouble.

So this was Strong Eagle, his twin.

James turned to stare into the face that used to be his own, when he was handsome and thin and strong. He puffed out his chest, he was still strong and capable of much violence.

The rifle butt came up to James's shoulder, the bore pointing directly at Daniel's head. "I remember you." James snickered. "I feel everything you feel." His eyes darted to Tamara and she flinched at his words. "I know pain when you do . . . I desire what you desire." A strange smile lurked at the corners of his mouth. "Yes. We are identical twins. I feel what you feel, but it is not the same with you."

Tamara stood there, shocked.

Pink Cloud gasped. She could not believe that the

man who had entered the room minutes ago was no
James Strong Eagle. He had not told them hi
name . . . maybe he was James. Yes, the other was th
impostor. He had to be. Everything would work out
and she would have her child. Of course!

Just then Joshua came spinning into the dusty
room, tossing out his arms to balance himself agains
the fall he was sure he would take. He stuffed a hand
in his baggy robe's pocket and then stood still
wanting to know what was happening before he
made any foolish moves. He set down the lantern
he'd been carrying, having followed the murmur
of voices and found the platform partly ajar.

Danny screeched happily. "KeeKing Man!" The
child now thought the dangerous situation had
turned into a party. He toddled over to Joshua
smacking his lips and clapping his hands approv
ingly. "Good!" he cried, walking right past James
big as you please, and sending the tall, heavyset man
a frown of disapproval. "Monner!" he shouted
Monster!

"Danny, get behind Joshua and stay there,'
Daniel said as gently as possible, sending the
boy a smile and a nod.

"Da-dee!" Danny called, pushing out his lower lip
in giraffe fashion as he looked over his shoulder a
Pink Cloud, shaking his fist at her. Dragging his
blanket, he suddenly stopped to peer worriedly and
wonderingly at all the adults standing around and
gawking at each other. He then dusted his hands on
his pajamas and went into a fit of coughing, turning
red in the face, shaking his head. When his nose
began to run, Tamara could only stare at him and

wish she had a handkerchief with which to wipe it.

James still held the rifle. Tamara could make no move without endangering the lives of those she loved.

"Come here, boy," Joshua said, sidling closer to Daniel and bumping him with the gun at his hip. Daniel's eyes contacted Joshua's, and there was a question in them. "Yup," was all Joshua said, then, "Sure is."

James looked suspiciously at the old man. "What is?" he asked, his eyes narrowing.

"Uh," Joshua began, then his eyes were drawn to the boarded-up windows. "Still snowing outside."

"How can you see this?" James snapped, momentarily off guard while he looked toward the window through which moonlight sifted in, aware only that the night was cold and windy.

In that moment, Joshua slipped the weapon to Daniel. Taking up the child's hand, he then stepped back into the shadows and watched Daniel palm the gun against his lean hip.

The cold air had revived Daniel. His thinking clear now, he swiftly brought the gun out, pointing it directly at James's head. "Now it's you and I. Who's to die first?"

James blinked and his hand quivered slightly.

Daniel took charge. "Joshua, get the boy out of here."

Joshua picked up Danny, grasped a lantern, and stepped onto the platform and out of the room before Strong Eagle could speak. Trying to compose himself, James Strong Eagle finally said in a shaky voice. "Let us not do anything foolish."

Drawing back the hammer on the revolver, Daniel said, "I'm only going to tell you once . . . put the rifle down."

James thought for only a second, then lowered the rifle to the floor. Now Daniel moved to his twin, kicking the rifle aside with his foot and ordering Tamara and Pink Cloud to leave the room.

Pink Cloud, her mouth still hanging open, followed Tamara. They got on the revolving platform and disappeared into the tunnel.

Now Daniel glared at James.

"We have a long overdue score to settle." He looked down at the moneybags on the floor. "First, let's see what you've got stashed here—I know there's plenty in the root cellar because I saw it. Pick the money up off the floor." When James hesitated Daniel barked, "Now!"

As James bent to retrieve the cash, Daniel took a moment to wince at a sudden pain along his rib cage. Just then, James lunged forward and knocked the gun from his hand. Both men landed on the floor, James atop Daniel, who suddenly felt incredible pain.

"You will never leave this room alive," James hissed. At that same moment the gun that had ricocheted off a wall struck the floor and went off, the bullet lodging in another cracked wall and sending plaster dust flying.

Anger overcame Daniel's pain, and he lashed out, striking James solidly on the side of the head and knocking him onto his side. Both men labored to their feet, squaring off in the center of the dust-filled room.

With the speed of lightning striking, Daniel hit James again and sent him staggering against the wall, loosing more plaster that pelted James about his head and shoulders. But these chunks of plaster were like mere gnats and flies lighting on him in comparison to the heavy blows Daniel had been dealing out.

From the other side of the door, Joshua and Tamara heard the commotion, not knowing whether to stay or to return. Tamara, at hearing the shot, turned to Joshua while a still-dazed Pink Cloud only frowned. Ever since she had gotten a look at Daniel, nothing seemed to register in her mind; she moved about like a puppet on strings. Tamara was grateful for this, at least.

"Take Danny upstairs, Joshua, and go get some help," she said.

Unquestioningly Joshua took up a lantern and led the child away while Tamara stepped onto the platform, Pink Cloud trailing behind as if she had lost her senses. The platform revolved into the room and suddenly spun even harder, stopping with a thud, Tamara stared into emptiness. Where have they gone? she wondered, her heart beating loudly. Into another room perhaps?

She and Pink Cloud stepped out into the room.

"They are gone!" Pink Cloud cried, alarmed.

At that moment they heard a commotion and Tamara realized what had happened. James and Daniel had landed against the wall, and had been spun out into the tunnel while Pink Cloud and Tamara had been whirled into the room. They had all hit the revolving platform at the same time,

433

switching places.

Spinning around, Tamara came face to face with Pink Cloud. She shoved her toward the wall, and they spun, whirling back into the tunnel. Once again in the underground passageway, they found the two brothers locked in bloody combat, each fighting to escape the other and at the same time fighting to even the score.

Pink Cloud screamed at seeing the bloodied face of James Strong Eagle. Puffed and swollen, it seemed even more heavy featured. As the men fell to the floor, wrestling, James with his great weight fell on Daniel, and Daniel was pinned by a forearm across his throat.

He struck out, but his strength was waning. Though the punch landed in James's face, it did not seem to affect him. James pressed down upon Daniel's throat even harder, and Daniel found himself gasping for air. Then the weight seemed to have been lifted from him.

Staggering to his feet, Daniel saw a stranger, revolver in his hand, holding James against the wall. The stranger spoke. "There'll be no more fighting. I'm in charge now."

Tamara went to the side of the stranger, touching his arm, and Daniel became confused. "What the hell!" he muttered low.

The stranger ordered everyone upstairs, as in holding the gun on them all.

In the kitchen of the boardinghouse, with James seated on the floor, the stranger turned to Daniel and then to Tamara. "Your friend met me at the door, Tamara, the old fellow with the squeaky shoes. He ad your son Danny by the hand."

Tamara cast a worried glance about the room.
Where is Joshua now?" She gently gripped the
man's arm as she looked into his kindly eyes; Daniel
winced, but not from pain this time. Why was his
wife gazing so affectionately at this stranger. And
why did he think he had seen the man before?

Taylor said, "He took the boy upstairs."

Tamara sighed softly, the tension draining from
her at knowing that Danny and Joshua were safe.
Her husband was bruised and bloodied, but he was
alive and not seriously injured.

"Taylor," Tamara said, turning to the man who'd
saved her husband from death at James's hand, "I
wish to thank you for arriving when your help was
most needed." She smiled. "You are a friend; I can
truly say that now with my whole heart."

Daniel shook his head, shifting on the hard chair
he'd dropped into. "Friend?" Daniel looked up at
Tamara, reaching for her lily-soft hand. "He is your
friend? When did this come about?"

"Oh, Daniel. John Taylor Handley lives in
southern Minnesota. I met him at the tavern—"

Daniel's hand came up to halt her right there.
"Whoa. What do you mean, you met him at the
tavern?"

"He sent for me . . . I . . ." Tamara flushed clear to
the toes of her high-buttoned shoes.

Daniel eyed her narrowly. "He sent for you, did
he? Friends, are you?"

Tamara whisked her tongue across her lips, to
moisten them. "I . . . can . . . explain. Really, I can."

Clearing his throat, Taylor drew Daniel's attention. "Let me explain, Mr. Tarrant."

"Please do."

Daniel listened closely, and when Taylor ha
finished telling how he'd first met Tamara, and how
Pamela Clayton had been trying to set him up, the
younger man relaxed. He realized his wife had been
a true heroine trying to save him from disaster. She
had even, by her mere presence in the tavern, saved
John Taylor Handley from being robbed and pos
sibly murdered.

"Shitfire." Joshua ambled into the kitchen just
then. "What a tangle!" He smiled at Tamara
"Danny's back in bed, tucked nice 'n cozy under his
covers."

"Oh, Joshua!" Tamara flew across the room to
throw her arms around the old man and kiss him on
his blushing cheek. "You are wonderful and"—
tears misted her eyes—"you are a hero, do you know
that?"

"Pshaw, not really." He gently set Tamara aside
and directed a finger at Daniel. "There's your hero
He got the gun and—"

"—lost it," Daniel interjected.

"Lost it?" Joshua shook his head. "That is bad."
Then his face brightened. "But you sure gave this
fella here"—he pointed at James's hanging head—
"one hell of a fight." He turned to Taylor, saying
"Who's he?"

With a gentle laugh, Tamara said, "You let him in
the door, Joshua. He is John Taylor Handley."

Just then there came a loud knocking, and while
everyone stared dazedly, not making a move to
answer the loud summons, the knocking became a

ttering. *"Open up!* In the name of the law! Right
ow, or else we'll shoot this door down!"

Daniel rose and brushed past Taylor to answer the
oor. "All right, all right." He yanked the door wide,
tting in a blast of cold air. "Come in, you might as
ell join the party."

Wonder of wonders, Mrs. Williamson swept in
ast the lawmen, who followed, one of them closing
e door behind them. The pious woman came to a
dden halt, then gasped as she saw the wounded
an slumped in the corner of the room. She turned
ack to one of the officers. "I told you there was
mething going on in this house." She snickered.
Why, with all the comings and goings, I just knew
is little lady was up to something." She directed a
eer toward the blonde whose hand was held tightly
Daniel. "Look how sweet they want everyone to
lieve they are, while God knows what is going on
re. I'll just bet they are not even wed. Lord, this
ight be a brothel for all their neighbors are aware."

"Ma'am," Taylor cut her off. "You don't know
hat you're talking about, so I suggest you keep
ur mouth closed."

"Well, I *never!*"

"No," Daniel said, while the woman peered at him
ver her shoulder. "You haven't."

"I tell you, this is *not* a respectable boarding-
ouse," Mrs. Williamson said to the peace officers.

"Please," the man in charge said, stepping further
to the room, "let me be the judge of that. Now, will
meone tell me just what has been going on here.
hese two men look as if they've been in a war. One
them is already bandaged, so that tells me he's

437

been in a fight before all this occurred. The lawma[n] sighed as if it was all too much. "Speak up, please[.]"

"Sit down," Daniel said, offering the man a cha[ir.]

"I'll stand."

Daniel shrugged. "Your choice, but you'll [be] sitting down before I've finished."

"Yup," Joshua put in. "You sure will. Especial[ly] when you hear about all the loot that's stashed in t[he] cellar."

"There, you see!" Laurine Williamson screeche[d.] "A brothel, with stolen goods and God knows what[."]

"Please, shut up," the bewildered lawman ordere[d.] "If you can't do that, then remove yourself from t[he] premises."

"Right," Joshua echoed. "Keep your yapp[er] shut." He was going to add bitch, but thought bett[er] of it.

The other lawmen moved further into the room[,] one squatted to check James over for serious wound[s.] "This one's been beaten pretty bad," he informe[d] the others standing by with serious expressions o[n] their hardened faces. "Who did it?" he asked look[ing] around the room, his eyes coming to rest on t[he] tall, bandaged man.

Daniel sucked in his breath, then released it. "I di[d.] He's my twin brother."

"Yeah," said the lawman in charge. "He doesn['t] look much like your twin now. What were you tryin[g] to do, kill him?"

Mrs. Williamson gasped. "Twin? You mea[n] there's two of them?" She peered over the officer['s] shoulder at the man in the corner, but Daniel blocke[d] her sharp gaze with his tall frame. "Murder too." Sh[e]

438

ded one more crime to the list of those committed the boardinghouse. "They're all going to burn in ll, mark my words."

"Oh shut up." Joshua shot the words across the om, and they struck the woman like a slap in e face. She thinned her mouth out primly and uared her bony shoulders.

"Now, start at the beginning. Who is going to do e honors?"

"I will," said Tamara as she stepped into the circle staring men. She lit another wall sconce, then took leep breath and began her story. Starting with the st moment she set eyes on James Strong Eagle, she vered the piece in the paper about the steamboat aster, Daniel's return from the prison where mes had sent him, and ended by describing the ins' battle in the underground passageway, ylor's arrival, and the breaking up of the fight. She gan to tell them of Pink Cloud's part in the goings-

Her eyes searching the room, a panicky Tamara ked, "Where is Pink Cloud?" Before the question ded, she was rushing from the room, heading for e stairs.

"Tamara!" Daniel called. "Where are you going?"

"What?" Joshua looked confused and a little off lance. "Where's that crazy Indian girl?"

"Snooping, I suppose," Daniel breathed out, his ts held tightly at his sides.

Just then James began to laugh—an ugly sound nich rose in volume until he was roaring hysteri- lly, rolling from side to side. The lawmen thought m temporarily crazed, but he suddenly stopped

439

laughing and announced, "I am not James Stron
Eagle. He perished in the steamboat disaster."

"Oh yeah?" one lawman said. "Tell me anoth
one, but first let me tell you something, Mr. Stron
Eagle. You are wanted for the murder of one O
Larson."

"I did not kill him!" James pointed at Danie
"There is the one who did away with Ole Larson. H
is your man." James's eyes darkened.

"Well," the lawman explained, "two men ha
testified to your guilt, Mr. Eagle. One by the name
Rufus. The other, Raymond Horse. No matter, we'
got enough on you to put you away for the rest
your natural life."

"Traitors!" James howled.

The lawmen looked at Daniel as he departed th
kitchen just as the fair-haired one had, to check o
the whereabouts of one named Pink Cloud.

"I'll just come along with you," one of the pea
officers said, following the tall dark man with th
bandaged chest, who was wearing only a jacket an
a wrinkled pair of pants.

"No need," Daniel halted at the foot of the stair
turning to glare at the lawman who was so clo
behind him he'd almost bumped into him. "I can se
what my wife is up to by myself, if you don't mind.

The man backed up, not liking the dark smo
dering look in the tall man's eyes. "Sure, go rig
ahead. I just thought you might—"

Daniel poked him in the chest. "Don't think. Ju
return to the kitchen and get rid of that shrew i
there, then wipe up the puddles of melted snow you
men left on the floor. After that you can remove th
man in the corner and take the loot from the cella

440

here's some more in the old Spanger house across
e way."

"Who's this Pink Cloud?"

"That's for me to know"—Daniel grinned into the
an's face—"and for you to find out. Later."

Daniel arrived at the open bedroom door just in
me to find Tamara pinning Pink Cloud to the floor
nd straddling the straining, screaming woman,
hile Danny stood back clapping his hands together
ith glee.

"Mom's got 'er, Dah, lookit!"

"I see, Danny." Daniel leaned against the door
mb. "As usual, she has got things under control."

The moon spilled silvery light onto the bedroom
oor, across the bedside table with the Bible on it—
e one saved from the fire and placed there with
loving hand—across the lace-canopied bed, and
nto the lovely face of Tamara herself.

Daniel's heart reached out to her. When her eyes
uched on his, sending him a look of tender love,
e said, "Our lady, our heroine."

Still straddling Pink Cloud, Tamara smiled at her
andsome husband. "My hero."

"Yup," Danny said.

"Say"—Daniel peeled himself away from the
oor—"how did you get out of bed, young man?"

"Oh-oh." Danny spun about and hightailed it
ack into his room, where he climbed into bed with
e agility of a monkey scaling a banana tree. Daniel
aught up and nuzzled him, and Danny squealed in
elight.

"You are a very lucky and happy woman," Pink
loud said after Tamara had let her get up. She
oked at Tamara warily. "I have no fight with you.

441

You are the winner."

The moon was fading, and the pale shades of dawn were stealing into the room, as Daniel entered it with Danny in his arms. Tamara looked up at them, love in her sage green eyes.

"I have emerged the winner . . . I truly have. And am not boasting; I'm speaking from the heart."

Just then a lawman came into the room and took Pink Cloud by the arm, nodding to Tamara and Daniel. Pink Cloud turned one last time to the little family circle gathered in the wintry twilight.

She shrugged. "I am sorry."

"Don't be; you've paid," Tamara said. "Just go and never look back." To herself she said, Or you will be like Lot's wife who became a pillar of salt.

When Pink Cloud was gone, having been taken along with James Strong Eagle, to the city jail to await a trial, the small family stood in a loving circle.

With her chin resting on Daniel's shoulder, Tamara sighed. "I just pray the dream I had the other night comes true—that Cat has found Kristel and they will return in time for Christmas, because it won't be the same without them. My Emily is coming. Taylor and his wife are coming."

Wearily Danny rubbed his fist across his eyes. "Time for bed," Daniel said, carrying the boy to his crib, then closing the door softly.

As he headed to his own bed a welcome sight met his eyes. Tamara was already tucked in, her bare shoulders peeping out, silvery blond hair spread all about her in a beautiful cloud.

"Come here, husband."

"What?" His grin was full of mischief. "I am

442

ounded. You are exhausted."

"Just wash your hands and face, then come to
d . . . darling."

Rushing as fast as he could, Daniel washed up and
imbed into bed, in his haste forgetting to undress.

"I'll do that for you," Tamara offered. Flinging
ck the covers, she removed his clothing, then
vingly ran her hands across his male body.
Oh . . . what are you doing?" he asked in a strangely
igh voice when she dipped out of sight.

"I am making love to my husband. He is wounded.
e needs help. We are going to . . . well, you will
e. . . ."

Twilight was bathing the boardinghouse in
ades of violet, lavender, and deep purple. At any
oment velvet darkness would shroud their bed-
om.

After she had driven him to the point of despera-
on, Tamara brought her magnificent form up and
ver his body, straddling him and then giving,
iving all she had. There was so much to experience,
e knew they would never become tired of explor-
g new possibilities together. "Look at me," he
rged, and she obliged. As she continued to pleasure
im, he murmured, "I love you . . . beautiful." He
new he had come home to stay. At last.

Mrs. Williamson stomped through the snow in her
rim high-topped boots, heading home, away from
e place that certainly was no respectable boarding-
ouse . . . if you asked her!

My heart is full and glad,
And all because . . . I know!
—Anna Lee Edwards McAlpin

Chapter Thirty-Two

It was Christmas. My Emily had come home for the
lidays, bringing her sister who was feeling fit as a
dle. John Taylor Handley had arrived with his
fe and children. The house was decorated with
stletoe and holly, the tree was a magnificent sight,
d there was plenty to eat. The old folks bore
timony to the goodness of the food. They ate their
l, then retired to the parlor, to sip punch, play
iet games with Danny and the guests, and tell
ories. The atmosphere was one of fun and frolic.
When they all began to sing Christmas carols
amara became melancholy. Wandering over to the
indow, she gazed out at the beautiful white snow
wly fallen on the streets of Minneapolis. The air
as hushed, seemingly in honor of the Savior's birth,
d the Star of David had shone that morning as
amara walked through the house, missing Kristel,
aying for her safe return. She just knew she would
e her beloved friend—soon. *Please God.* Tamara's

hand touched her brand-new sewing machine.

For Christmas, Daniel gave his son the fawn [he] had whittled, and Tamara exchanged gifts with [her] husband, his being a new shirt with his initi[als] embroidered on it and a carving knife with a leath[er] sheath—the one he'd been eyeing in the window [of the] store. Smaller gifts were exchanged by the guests a[nd] the boarders; some the Handleys' children h[ad] fashioned with their own hands, others the ol[d] folks had made. Even Danny had a picture [for] everyone, drawn with crayons. He'd filled th[e] creations with stick-people and funny-looking cr[ea]tures—and a lot of zigzagged lines.

The wind was laughing. Danny could hear it.

All joined him at the window to see what the b[oy] was so exicted about. One of Taylor's daughters[, a] girl named Kirsten, who was wearing an o[ld-] fashioned, plain blue dress with a stand-up lace c[ol]lar much like Tamara's own, took Danny's ha[nd.] "What do you see, Danny?"

"Hear't? The wind is waffing!"

Kirsten Handley giggled. "Waffing? Oh, y[ou] mean laughing." She herself laughed then. "Y[ou] are *sooo* cute."

"W . . . Laffing!"

And so it was, as Cat-Face had remembered, th[at] day . . . long ago . . . *I have heard the wild wind sin[g,] I have heard it light on angel's wings. I have seen t[he] moon's light kiss the Minnesota prairie and woo[ds.] Yes, the wind sings with all its heart and soul. It w[ill] lead to my life's glittering goal.*

Today it sang for all of them, and as moondu[st] spread across the new-fallen snow, My Emily's b[...]

y tomcat made tracks to the house. As Tamara
rned away from the window, trying to conceal the
oebegone look on her face, another pair of tracks
sscrossed the cat's—two pairs, belonging to humans,
ading to the house.

Then Tamara looked up at the Christmas angel
readings its wings at the top of the towering tree,
d she felt as if she were suddenly up there with it,
ght and free. As her eyes lowered they met her
usband's. They both sensed something.

The knock sounded. Then another, a lighter one
is time.

A girl's laugh, a familiar one.

"It has to be . . ." Tamara's shoulders went back.
She whirled toward the door, and her heart lifted as
e children began to sing: "Silent night, holy night,
l is calm, all is bright . . ."

And it was. It was the *brightest* Christmas ever!

If you would like to have Sonya Pelton's latest bo~~
plate or card please send a large self-address~~
stamped envelope to:

Sonya Pelton
c/o Zebra Books
475 Park Avenue South
NY, NY 10016